A

Cobras

**** Beginnings ****

Christopher Merlino

Sola Fide

Christopher Merlino

©2013 by Christopher Merlino

ISBN: 978-0-9912503-1-8

All rights reserved. No part of this publication may be reproduced, transmitted, or distributed in any form or by any means without written permission from the publisher.

Any Scripture references or quotations taken from the New American Standard Bible.

This book is a work of fiction. Names, characters, places, and incidents are either products of the author's imagination or used fictitiously. Any similarity to actual people, organizations, and/or events is purely coincidental.

Cover Image by MCM

Published by Sola Fide Publishing, P.O. Box 831 Mays Landing, NJ 08330
www.solafidepublishing.com

This book is available in both print and eBook formats.

Printed in the United States of America

To Charm

My Deepest Love

My Dearest Treasure

In Christ

ACKNOWLEDGMENTS

There is only one name on the cover of this book. The truth is that this book exists because of the work and support of many more individuals, without whom I would not be exaggerating by saying that it never would have been written. I have been blessed with a group of people in my life that offer support and encouragement not only in my writing but in my life in general, especially in my walk with Christ, which is the most important area in which to encourage another human being.

A Christian man ought never to begin his list of "Who to Thank" with anyone other than the God of all Creation. I certainly thank my God for the obvious, my life, my family and friends, and most of all, my salvation. But in this moment, as I consider the specific blessings he poured out on me as I wrote the pages of this book, I find myself profoundly grateful. Writing about how people struggle with their religious beliefs really made me think about how Christians ought to act in the world, especially toward non believers and those struggling with faith, but most especially, their fellow Christians. I am thankful for the inspiration, the peace and contentment I had as I wrote, and the joy I got out of doing something I love. All of these, along with every other good thing, comes from the grace and mercy of God. Thank You, God, for saving me!

Books do not get written alone, at least mine don't. In my Author's Note I will go into some detail on this, but for now suffice to say I owe a great deal of thanks to a few special people, without whom, I'd probably have little more than a handful of scenes and another pile of unfinished thoughts to add to hundreds of thousands of wasted words accumulated over two decades of adulthood.

Family is the most important thing after Christ in my life. I am blessed with a wonderful wife who not only puts up with my foolishness, but who loves me even when I'm unlovable, which is most of the time. She's the one who had to read the earliest drafts of scenes at midnight, when inspiration struck and I had to get the ideas down. She was the one who tried to talk me down off the ledge when I thought the whole project was falling apart. She was my editor and manager, but most of all, she was my rock and my comfort throughout the whole process. Charm, there is no way I could ever find the words to express my love for you, so I'll just say that I would be lost without you.

My daughters, Alexis (11), Cecilia (5 1/2), and Isabella (4), are a constant source of joy in my life. As I wrote this book, I took many breaks just to go find them and hold them, drawing energy from their love and joy. When Alexis realized that Daddy was writing a book, she was very excited. Her excitement overflowed in school and she told everyone that "when Daddy finishes his "bestseller", we're going to move into a big house..." No pressure.

Mom, Dad, Step Parents George and Vickkie, thank you for always being there whenever I needed you. You are all a blessing from God and your love is always appreciated. Thank you John and Tim, my brothers, both of whom I love dearly and take great pride in. They are both very talented in their fields and inspire me to elevate my efforts in the things about which I am passionate. Thank you both for your love and support.

There were only a few people who were directly involved with this project. They acted as editors, readers, sounding boards, or just encouraged me by listening when I wanted to talk about the project. Thanks to Kim Eaves and Katy Callahan for reading and critiquing. Kappy Huber, who read some of my earlier work and has encouraged me for years to write, was among the first I wanted to tell when I first began the book. There are few people in my life whose opinion I value above my own (*what arrogance!*). Kappy is one of those people. There are few people in my life who I really hope to impress with my writing. Kappy is one of those people. Kappy, thank you for your encouragement, not only recently, but in years past. Your opinion of my earlier work has never been forgotten and continues to inspire me.

Finally, I can state unequivocally that I would never have written this book had it not been for the encouragement of one person, my best friend, Duane Eaves. I go into greater detail in the Author's Note, but my gratitude for your encouragement and support throughout this project is inexpressible. Thank you.

AUTHOR'S NOTE

I'm always interested in what inspires the books I read. Often, the inspiration is obvious, but sometimes I am left wondering how the author came up with his ideas and what inspired his approach. For a guy approaching forty years of age, who hasn't ever finished writing a novel he'd begun, most people are surprised when I tell them what my first book is about. Though I work with high school kids in our church youth program, I don't teach high school and have little regular interaction with kids of that age. So what could possibly inspire a book focusing entirely on the everyday lives of a bunch of high school kids? Who needs *that* kind of drama in their life?

A Quiver of Cobras is the result of years of frustration at how Christians are portrayed in movies, television, books, etc. Christians are always the murdering psychopaths, self-righteous, holier than thou jerks, hypocrites, and friendless weirdos who are social pariahs. The liberal community's, and in particular, Hollywood's, hatred for Christianity comes out even when they are trying to be accurate. Shows involving Christian characters often portray them as well-intentioned, though judgmental and hypocritical. Their goal is often to show how Christians *ought* to behave, and what Christians *ought* to believe about society and the world around us. Of course, these "oughts" have nothing whatsoever to do with God or scripture, and basically serve the worldly viewpoint that we should all tolerate one another's depravity silently and without judgment. As a Christian who lives his life right alongside non Christians, who has non Christian friends and family, and who is able to peacefully coexist with non Christians, it is frustrating that our media is so denigrating to such a large number of people.

In recent years, there have been many television shows portraying Christians. The same thing always seems to happen. The Christian is judgmental or opinionated to the point of being an unreasonable jerk, and by the end of the season is doing the very thing he or she was judging earlier in the season. Ultimately, the whole point of the character is to demonstrate that Christians are no better than anyone else and we should keep our religion to ourselves.

So, with that frustration constantly in my mind whenever a new show comes out, I began to ask myself some simple questions: Could these stories be told without the bogus Christian character? Or, better yet, could they be told with a *realistic* Christian character in the story. Would the impact of a real Christian character destroy the plot of your average family drama or comedy on network TV? When I began to consider these questions, and others, I started to play out the various scenes in my head, considering what the Christian *should* have done or said in each situation. In my mind, nothing would have really changed. Nothing needed to. Christians live their lives alongside non Christians all over the world and sometimes they have an impact on events, while other times they don't. Some certainly fail in major ways and commit grievous sins, both publicly and in private. I'm not trying to imply otherwise. But to *never* portray a Christian character realistically is just silly and a transparent effort to ridicule and mock.

That is more or less where I left it for several months. It was just an idea. In fact, it was little more than a thought. And I had two other projects in the works that I wanted to write. One was a theological book about love and loving God, the other was an action novel about…well, you'll just have to wait for that one to come out. Both of these books were well under way and I was intending for one of them to be my first completed book. After twenty years of starting book projects and never finishing a single one, I was determined to write a complete book.

Then disaster struck in my financial life. I lost my job and in this economy had no real hope of finding anything that would support a family of five. I was frustrated and bitter, trying to trust that God was in control, trying to practice what I preached, that God is good even when things seem bad for us. But my financial troubles were real and they had been so for many years. I was barely surviving even with the job I'd had, and now even that was gone.

That was when my best friend, Duane, and I had lunch together and afterward, talking in my driveway, we discussed the possibility of working together on a project. He and I used to play in a rock and roll band together and we were always trying to find a way to work on something together. He asked me a simple question: "If you could do any job you wanted, what would it be?" The answer to that was fairly simple. I always knew that if I could find a way to make money writing, that would be my first choice.

It's the thing I'm most passionate about. Being an author is my dream job, especially since I could work from home and be with my girls all the time.

Duane was instantly on board. He asked what I wanted to write about. I described to him the action book (which I'm not going to tell you about, so stop asking), the theology book, and this spark of an idea about teenagers in high school. So, rather than choose one of the already started projects, both of which, I was really passionate about, he latched onto the idea about the teens. No matter how I rephrased the conversation, I couldn't get him to change his mind. Don't you hate people like that? They just won't take a hint, no matter how hard you're trying?

Thankfully, Duane stuck to his gut feeling about this vague idea of a group of high school football players and the girls in their lives. The working title for the book was Teens, which was brilliant…you know, because the story is about *teens*. See? Authors are *not* creative all the time. The first thing we did was to have a meeting. That is what he and I are best at, getting together and planning out a project. We never follow through, at least, we never had before, but we love the planning process. For our first meeting he had a whiteboard set up in his basement where he was listing all of our ideas and goals. He even took a picture of it with his phone so we wouldn't forget what we'd written. I had my laptop with a spreadsheet created where I listed anything I needed to remember for my writing.

I remember thinking at the time that this was going to be no different than any of our other projects. We'd create a plan, and we'd begin moving forward and before long, either he or I would flake out as usual and the whole thing would just dissolve and fade away. We had done this with music, with previous writing projects and everything else we had set out previously to do together. I remember thinking that Duane and I just possessed the same weaknesses. We could never succeed together because no one was there to pick up the slack in our weak areas. For me, the weight was heavy because I had to do the writing. Without me writing, and keeping to a schedule of some sort, he would have nothing to edit or critique. His job was to be a sounding board for ideas, and then to help me edit as I wrote. So I had to write.

I made a conscious decision as I began putting words down that this project had to be completed, even if it turned out to be a lousy book. I had to complete something. In truth, what I was hoping to accomplish with this project was a jump start to my other projects. I thought if I could just get some confidence that I could finish something, while at the same time getting rid all of my lousy ideas, then maybe I could take that momentum and carry it into something I was really excited about.

What happened to me is indescribable, but I'll try anyway. Rule one of writing is very simple: Write! Nothing gets written if the author doesn't write. I don't believe in writer's block, not because I never get stuck and not because I always have great ideas flowing, but because even if I get stuck and all my ideas are garbage, I still keep writing. The great thing about writing a book is that you can always go back and rewrite a scene. So I committed myself to writing no matter what I thought of it at the time. This resulted in exactly what you'd expect. I had some good stuff, but mostly junk. But through it all, the story began to take shape. The scenes all needed work and mostly to be rewritten, but the story was there. It was beginning to emerge.

Now at this point, it's important to understand that I had a plan for this story. I had the beginning and I knew where the book had to end. I had several things that the characters needed to do or say in order for the story I had in mind to work. There was a very specific layout in terms of how I wanted these characters to interact. I had a plan and I had every intention of sticking to it.

I haven't had the opportunity to talk to other writers all that much, particularly about character development, so I'm not sure if their processes are similar or if I am borderline insane. But what happened to me as I wrote these scenes was that one by one, the characters became very real to me. I didn't realize it was happening until I was halfway through a scene and noticed that things weren't going the way I had intended. As I reread the scene over and over again, I couldn't help but feel great about the writing. It was, in my opinion, the best stuff I'd ever written. The only problem was that the characters had gone in a completely different direction than what I had intended. Now that's not such a big deal, except that it was at this point I got mad at them. I actually got angry at the characters that I had written as though they had taken over my story!

The thing was they *had* taken it over. And it was the best thing that had ever happened to me as an author. The characters were so real to me, so vivid in my mind, that they pretty much wrote the story for me. For anyone thinking of or trying to write a novel, find a way to get yourself to this point. If your characters are real to you, they can be real to others. I can tell you everything about these characters. They are not just figments of my imagination anymore. Write a story that's real to you. That's the story of how A Quiver of Cobras came to be.

Through it all, I was praying constantly, asking God for direction and inspiration. Now I'm not one to claim that God inspired me or led me to write what I wrote. What I will suggest is that God gave me a peace about my work that I'd never had before. He gave me a confidence in my writing that I'd never had before. But most importantly, he placed people in my life who were there to support me and encourage me through the whole process. I mentioned my family in the Acknowledgments section. My wife was a great sounding board and also helped me in the editing process. She was a critical reader and helped me work through many sticking points. She was my strength when I did get frustrated and anxious.

God also placed my best friend, Duane, in my life. We began this project together, and just four months later, we completed it together. And through it all, he never failed to encourage me. Every scene I sent him to read, he loved. He was constantly telling me that I had a great story and that I was a great writer. To me, that kind of uncritical critique had never been helpful. I always wanted the raw truth. Tell me what you *really* think. But as I got to the midway point of the book and felt like I had a full head of steam, I began to really appreciate it. I never thought about how lonely it was to write a book. In the past my work was always done in solitude, total concentration. And I never completed a single thing. Duane's encouragement was critical and I'm convinced that this book would never have been finished had he not been involved the entire time. There are no words to express my gratitude.

The thing I learned through writing this book is that the most important resource I can have at my disposal, next to my relationship with my Creator, is a really good friend. My advice to aspiring authors is to make sure you have a person in your life that will read whatever you send them and encourage you whenever they can.

This is my first novel and at times it may ramble, but I wouldn't change a word of it.

Preface

Kendall Township.

Someone once said that it was the biggest small town they'd ever seen. You could live there all your life and never really know anyone. It might even be true...theoretically. There is no evidence of anyone having accomplished this feat. Indeed, there is no evidence of anyone ever having attempted it. The guy who said that did not live in Kendall Township or anywhere near it. He had been passing through, and noticed the decidedly small town feel, though he knew that it was an unusually large municipality in terms of square miles. He had noticed that wherever he went, people seemed to know one another. He had noticed that even though they sometimes clearly did *not* know one another, they still seemed to share a connection. It was a connection they did not appear to share with *him* though, so he figured it only existed between residents of the Township. He was right...in a manner of speaking.

What this man had failed to notice during his brief stay in Kendall Township was the fact that there was indeed a bond between the people of the local community. But it wasn't a psychic connection, as he had supposed. It wasn't a supernatural phenomenon that created this small town effect. It was something far more tangible, far more real. If you asked a Kendall resident what it was that connected everyone, they might give you a one word answer: Venom. Understandably, most people would look strangely at a person who answered in such a way. In fact, they might even back up several feet. It is a strange answer to a straightforward question. But if you were in Kendall Township on a Friday night in Autumn, you would require no further explanation.

It was on Friday nights, under the bright lights of the Cobra's Nest at Kendall High School, that the Kendall High Cobras played their games. It was high school football that transformed this large Township into the small town it really was. And you didn't have to be at the field to hear the chants coming from the home stands: VE-NOM! VE-NOM!

What our visitor had not noticed about all those who "knew" one another was their attire. They'd all been dressed in black, from head to toe; or they might have been wearing a Kendall Cobra T-shirt or jacket. The women might have been carrying little black and silver handbags with the word "VENOM" embroidered on it in silver. Many of the younger girls braided black and silver cords into their hair. On Fridays, the entire town turned black and silver. That's how you knew you were in Kendall.

Fanatical was one word used to describe it. Psychotic was the word many citizens in the surrounding cities chose to use. It was something not often seen in this part of the country. You could find towns like this in the south or the Midwest maybe, but Kendall was an anomaly in New Jersey. The Kendall High School varsity football players were special in this town. They were celebrities in their community. Their every move was watched, their entire lives lived in public, their every decision judged as to how it impacted the program. Their relationships were followed, especially the starters. Their girlfriends were treated like queens and princesses. They were royalty…for a little while.

This story is *not* about football, though it would be impossible to tell a Kendall High School story that didn't have *something* to do with football. Rather, this is a story about the people who play the game and those in their lives. It is about love, hate, success, failure, passion, but most of all, it is a story about confusion. Simply put, this story is about high school.

Welcome to Kendall High…

Chapter 1

Lindsey glanced out the window for the tenth time.
When would he get here? This is torture!
For the past week she had been all smiles as this day approached. With each passing moment, August 1st was getting closer and Kevin would finally be home, and she would be back in his arms. They had finished the eighth grade two months ago, together, as a steady couple. They had spent many nights making out over the weeks preceding and Lindsey was smitten and in love. But then Kevin had to leave for two months to go to Japan. They wouldn't see one another until August. This began the worst summer break in Lindsey's life. She endured eight weeks of watching everyone in the entire world run around and have fun with their boyfriends and girlfriends while she was all alone.

She didn't have many friends, or any for that matter. In fact, despite her stunning looks, Lindsey Overton was not all that popular. While the rest of the girls her age were doing everything they could think of to accentuate their bodies, Lindsey dressed to cover hers. She wasn't embarrassed. She just didn't want the attention. Too often when boys approached her, Lindsey's quick mind and sharp wit put them off. At this age, boys tended to think that she was mean, even scary. She was okay with that. At least she didn't have to put up with their stupid jokes.

But not Kevin. No, Kevin wasn't afraid, or even the slightest bit intimidated. After three days of trying to talk to her in the halls, where she generally made a sarcastic remark and fled to class or the bathroom, he finally sat down at her table at lunch and began talking to her as if they had been friends for years. At first she was amused, and was preparing to make yet another wisecrack before pulling out a book and reading it in front of him, but then she lifted her eyes to meet his, and all of a sudden felt a change. *Wow*, she thought, *His eyes are amazing!* Kevin had green eyes, but not the usual hazel color we're used to. Kevin's eyes were a deep, but really bright, green, kind of like the green she had seen in old bottles. It took only a second and she was hypnotized. She could not take her eyes off his. At some point, she'd snapped out of it and realized that he was asking her a question. He was interested in her; really interested. He asked her questions and listened as she gave her mumbled answers. They spent that entire lunch period talking and Lindsey gradually loosened up enough to look up at Kevin as they spoke. And then the unthinkable happened. As the warning bell sounded for next period, they rose and collected their book bags, and Kevin took her hand and led her out of the cafeteria, just like all the rest of the couples. Being the most popular boy in the school, this action by Kevin drew every eye as they made their way to Lindsey's algebra class. At the door, Kevin faced her, lifted her hand to his mouth and lightly kissed it.

"Thanks for spending your lunch period with me, Miss Overton," he said in an exaggerated formal tone. "Shall we meet here in say, 40 minutes?"

She couldn't help it. She rarely smiled in public, but now her face beamed. This was too much!

Kevin grinned. "Aha!" he exclaimed. "There it is. I knew you had one in there somewhere."

"What are you talking about?"

"A smile, of course. I knew you were able to smile. Just wanted to see it."

He turned to go to class. "I'll see you right after class."

It all began there. He met her right after class like he said and they spent every moment after that together.

...that is, of course, until he left for stupid Japan. *Who does that?* she wondered. Who flees the country after starting a relationship? Thank God for Skype. At least she got to talk to him once in a while, though it wasn't the same. No matter what she did to the color settings on her monitor, she couldn't get his eyes to look right. They were always too dark, hidden in the shadows because of the angle of light when he looked at his screen. She had thought of asking him to move a light so that she could better see his gorgeous eyes, but he might think that a bit too weird. She definitely didn't want to make things weird. No, better to wait it out and then spend as much time as possible staring into his eyes when he got back...*which should have been five minutes ago! Arrrrggh!* She grabbed for her cell phone. One more text couldn't hurt, could it?

"No!"

A hand snatched the phone away just as she reached for it. It was her sister, Tracey. She stood there, frowning at Lindsey and shaking her head disapprovingly.

"What the..? Give it back!"

Tracey raised her eyebrows and shook her head once again.

"I don't think so, Lindz. You're gonna make this guy think you're a stalker."

"He's not going to think I'm stalking him. He's going to realize that I'm worried about him and he should let me know he's okay."

Tracey smirked, "Yeah, right. That's not how guys think, Lindz."

"And you would know how guys think? How many boyfriends have you had, Trace?"

That was mean. Lindsey knew it right away. Tracey's face fell slightly. It wasn't that she wasn't used to it. It wasn't even that she wasn't expecting it. Four or five years ago, when the boys began looking differently at the girls in her class, she realized that she wasn't getting much attention from them. She didn't really understand it at the time and was afraid to ask anyone about it. However, it didn't take her long to realize that it had everything to do with the way she looked. While not terribly overweight, she *was* a bit heavy. But worse than that, she was tall for her age, standing three or four inches taller than the tallest boys in her class. At that age, it can be an awkward thing for a girl to be taller than boys. But that wasn't even the worst of it. She had bright red hair as well. So she was this super-tall hulky beast with glowing red hair at an age where you definitely don't want to stand out in a freakish way. To make matters worse, Tracey suffered from a condition that made her skin somewhat splotchy in patches, so she looked even weirder. It didn't help that she was also terribly shy. She wasn't picked on all that much, just ignored. She actually knew kids who got picked on all the time and often found herself envying their situation because at least people paid attention to them.

By the end of her eighth grade year, the boys and girls in her class were all dating and the high school social scene loomed. By this time Tracey had gotten over some of her shyness and was in her fifth year of dance and gymnastics classes. She had loved these classes until the moment she realized she wasn't pleasant to look at. Then she wanted nothing more than to quit. Her mother would have none of it. In this family, you were not allowed to quit something in the middle of the year. Now, Tracey was thankful that she had been made to continue the dance season, because over the course of the year, it was only dance and gymnastics that took her mind off her social discomfort. She worked harder and harder at it, and spent all of her spare time dancing and practicing her gymnastic techniques. She was even invited to join the competition dance team. It meant that even in the summer, when the rest of the dancers were off, she would continue to train and dance with the best dancers in the school. It was dance that got her through Jr. High and freshman year.

As she began her training over the summer heading into her sophomore year of high school, Tracey noticed for the first time that something had changed. Actually, a lot had changed. First of all, as she stood in front of the huge mirrors in the dance studio, she saw that her body did not look quite how she remembered it. The person she saw in the mirror was a stranger to her. She recalled a tall, heavy, splotchy kid. She had somehow stopped paying attention to her looks and focused completely on her dance technique. How long had it been since she had really looked at herself in the mirror? She was slim and lithe, her muscles toned and firm. She had no discernible fat. Her red hair had grown in past her shoulders and now fell midway down her back. It was a bit shaggy and in need of a trim, but it was really quite beautiful. What was amazing more than anything else was her skin was perfect. The splotchiness was gone. She vaguely recalled a nutritionist telling her that exercise and a healthy diet often was all that was needed to correct some of our bodies' problems. As the rest of the dance team began to filter into the studio she also realized that the boys were all taller and bigger than she was. Somehow, without her noticing, they had all grown past her. Even the girls had begun to catch up to Tracey. She was still rather tall and her build was still more broad, but she looked more or less like everyone else.

With new found confidence in her appearance and talent, Tracey was prepared to make the most of her high school experience, though she hadn't the first clue how to begin. She was a bit envious of Lindsey's relationship with Kevin. Lindsey's looks came so easily to her. Tracey was always amazed at how Lindsey so nonchalantly discarded those boys, and even girls, who attempted to strike up conversations with her. It was one thing, at age fourteen, not to care about having boyfriends, but no friends at all? While Tracey had always craved attention, Lindsey had it in spades and couldn't care less. Until Kevin came along. Tracey had seen the change instantly. Lindsey came home one day with stars in her eyes. She'd tried to hide it behind her usual cynicism and sarcasm, but you can't keep that up for long. Lindsey was never a smiler. She would rather hide any joy or pleasure behind a facade of indifference, but Kevin caused that facade to crumble. He didn't change her personality, but Lindsey was unable to keep her feelings completely hidden. It was actually nice to see, and Tracey felt protective of that. As the older sister, she felt it was her responsibility to keep Lindsey from screwing it up if possible.

"I might not have experience with boys, but that doesn't mean I'm stupid. If you don't stop crowding him, he might push you away. Just find a way to kill time and wait for him to get here."

"Fine." Lindsey fell back onto the sofa and closed her eyes. *When was he going to get here?*

And then, suddenly, he *was* there. She glimpsed him walking up the driveway. Though she couldn't see his face through the stupid gigantic weeping willow tree, she knew instantly that it was him. He had a way of moving. It was a silent steady glide, similar to the way some of the better dancers at onStage moved, only Kevin was far more effortless. There was a power about his gait that made him stand out to Lindsey. Though she wasn't a very outgoing type, she noticed everything about people. She was a watcher, a studier.

She couldn't contain her excitement and jumped off the couch, running to the downstairs powder room to check her appearance. Tracey couldn't help but smile. She wished she had thought to record this on her cell phone. *No way Lindsey will ever admit to this later.*

"Get the door, Trace." Lindsey called out from the powder room.

Trace? So, now we're buddy, buddy? "He's *your* boyfriend."

"Seriously? You're gonna play that card on me *now*?"

The doorbell rang. "Ughhh! Come on, Tracey!"

Tracey chuckled, getting up and heading for the door. "Calm down. Your face gets really red when you're stressed."

"Really?" Lindsey peered more closely at her image in the mirror. "No I'm not. Just get the door. I don't want him to think I was sitting here waiting for him."

"But you *were* sitting here waiting for him. You know, lies like this have a way of coming back and biting you."

"Shut up and get the door. Then disappear."

Tracey opened the door, peeked out, and actually had to catch herself. She had forgotten about those green eyes. "Hi Kevin," she managed, opening the door all the way. "Come on in."

"How are you, Tracey?" He walked in, holding a big bouquet of roses. Tracey looked at them in amusement.

"I'm okay. Nice flowers. They for Lindsey?"

Kevin grinned. "Yep. Think she'll like em?"

Tracey nodded ultra solemnly. "Oooh yes. Lindsey is all about roses. I see you have red ones, pink ones, white ones, yellow ones, and even lavender ones."

Kevin snickered. This was a running joke. Lindsey hated romantic overtures. He loved to do the most ridiculously stereotypical dating things just to aggravate Lindsey. He brought her chocolates and flowers, stuffed animals and cutesy figurines. He took her on a chariot ride just before going off to Japan. He'd actually liked doing that and thought she did too. One time he even rented a limousine and had the driver take them all over the area while Kevin pointed out every single moment he and Lindsey had shared together, every restaurant they had gone to, every mall they had shopped in, even the local WaWa, where they usually bought meatball subs on the way home to watch a movie. She was an easy mark because she was very clear about not being interested in that sort of thing. Giving Kevin that kind of information was like telling a kid where the cookies were and then telling him not to eat any.

Tracey grinned knowingly. "You know her so well."

"I like to think so."

"By the way," Tracey said a little too loudly. "She's been sitting here all day waiting for you and getting pissed that you didn't return her texts."

"*Tracey!*" Lindsey was coming down the hall. "I will hurt you."

"Hey, Lindz," Kevin grinned from behind three dozen brightly colored roses.

Lindsey didn't smile. She should never have mentioned her abhorrence of typical dating type stuff. He was never going to stop. Who cared about flowers anyway?

"You think you're pretty funny, don't you?" she said. Kevin was now unable to keep from laughing. "Well, you're really pretty stupid. You know that, right?"

"Yeah, I know," Kevin handed the roses to Tracey. "Could you take these before she pitches a fit?"

Tracey took the bouquet. "Sure. I'll just go ahead and put them in water. I know just where to put them so Lindsey can see them when she gets home."

Lindsey turned to her sister who was walking down the hall toward the kitchen. "Stay out of my room."

"These will look so pretty on your dresser…"

"Tracey."

"…but you'll have to make sure to open the curtains and let in some sunlight so they last longer."

"Tracey! I will *cut* you! I'll cut that…" She turned to Kevin. "What's that ligament right behind your knee?"

"The posterior cruciate…"

"Your posterior cruciate ligament! I'll cut it right in half! You hear me, Tracey?"

Kevin grabbed both of her hands and pulled her close, wrapping his arms around her and bringing his lips to hers. They kissed for several moments, Lindsey barely able to stand because she was so relieved to be in his arms again. She couldn't explain why she was feeling relief, but she was. She let him hold her up, and laid her head on his shoulder.

"I really missed you," she said softly. "Don't ever go away again."

Kevin held her closely and stroked her hair, softly. "I'm here for a little while, I think."

"This is a perfect time for a ham and Swiss cheese sandwich. Are you hungry?"

Kevin thought for a minute. "Hmm. I could eat. Spicy brown mustard?"

Lindsey made a face. "Uhh…yeah? Is there another kind?"

Kevin replied, "Sure there is. What about yellow mustard?"

"That's not mustard."

"It says mustard on the label."

"So what? Labels don't tell the whole story. Yellow mustard is mustard *paste*. It's not genuine mustard."

"Paste? Really? It still tastes pretty good."

"I didn't say it tasted bad, just that it is not mustard. And it is not acceptable on a sandwich. Mustard paste is for soft pretzels."

"That's it? Just soft pretzels? Actually I like spicy brown mustard on soft pretzels."

She led him down the hall toward the kitchen. "That's because you're an idiot."

They sat together on an outdoor style couch on the back deck, he with his feet up on the table, and she reclined with her legs across him. His head was tilted all the way back, looking straight up except his eyes were closed. He gently stroked her legs and feet. This was the type of thing Lindsey had missed all summer. Kevin, though he was a football player who was known for violent hits and hard play, who was expected to bring that toughness to his high school football career, was actually very gentle when it came to Lindsey. She knew he liked her. She knew that he liked to touch her. She also knew that he was very conscious about where he put his hands. When they kissed, his hands never slid too far down her back. They never strayed too far up her leg. She would often sit on his lap, watching TV, cuddled against his chest or sprawled across him like he was a mattress. Kevin would wrap his arms around her, but would keep them firmly in place around her stomach, never moving up or down, never causing her any discomfort. Somehow, that made it feel even more intimate for Lindsey.

It really was a comforting thing to her. While the rest of the girls had to deal with boyfriends that couldn't keep their hands off them, Lindsey felt completely at ease whenever Kevin touched her. He had once told her that being raised by a single mom made him particularly sensitive to things that hurt women. He was referring to things like cheating, harsh criticism, and violence, but he seemed to have an instinct for making a girl feel safe and secure. She also knew that he had a softness instilled in him that he reserved for those females he cared for. She had seen that gentleness in how he interacted with his mother, and had felt it herself in times like these. Sex was a topic that was constantly in the faces of everyone in school. Boys talked about it crudely, like they knew all about it, and often made poorly thought-out advances on the girls in class. She was even pretty sure that one or two of the girls had actually gone through with the act during last school year. The pressure was immense on the girls in her class, and going into high school would probably not reduce it any. Part of her relief was the knowledge that Kevin would be by her side through it all. She would not feel any pressure from him…she hoped.

"Are you glad to be back?" she asked, her eyes closed in the bright sunlight.

He was half dozing off. "Sure," he mumbled. "I missed this."

Lindsey smiled. "Me too. Are you ready for football?"

"Can't wait." She could hear the smile in his voice. When he had spoken of football before, it always seemed so far away. They had met well after last year's championship season. Now, it was here, looming like a giant shadow over the whole town. Kevin all of a sudden had a certain urgency in his voice. He was excited. Lindsey had never seen him play. She had only heard the stories. They were hard to imagine based solely upon her personal experiences with this kind and gentle, if not completely ridiculously romantic guy, who had these green eyes you just couldn't stop thinking about. But with just two words, *Can't wait*, she began to get a feel for it.

"Really? Why not? What's so special about a game that this whole town goes completely out of its mind?"

He never even opened his eyes, but the slight smile on his face hinted at his reaction. "It's the greatest game ever created. It's the ultimate team game."

"It's still just a game."

"Yeah, it's just a game."

"So, why the hysteria over winning and losing? We're not talking about life and death here."

Kevin finally opened his green eyes and looked at her quizzically. "It's because football is much more serious than life and death." He leaned back and closed his eyes again. Lindsey stared at him for several seconds, looking for the smile to crack or any other sign that he was joking. It never came.

He spoke again after several moments of silence. "You'll see in a few weeks, Lindz."

"I guess."

He smiled, his eyes still closed. "You know, you have to wear my jersey to the games."

"What? You're kidding, right?"

"Nope. The girlfriends all wear their boyfriend's alternate jersey at the games."

"Alternate jersey?"

"If we play at our field, I'll have my black jersey, so you'll wear the white one. For away games, it's reversed. You've seen the girls wearing the football jerseys to school on game day."

Lindsey was well aware of the tradition. She had always thought it was kind of silly, girls wearing the boys' jerseys, and she was definitely not excited about it. Those things were huge, meant to be worn by big guys with even bigger pads on. The girls who wore them all looked like they'd put on judges robes tucked into their jeans. Plus, she hated to stand out. If people saw her with Kevin's number on, they would surely want to talk to her about him. There was no questioning his popularity. He was already a hero of sorts in this town. His name was being bandied about as a potential superstar in the making. Everyone connected with football and anyone who paid any attention at all knew who Kevin Sinclaire was. That meant before long, they would probably know who *she* was as well.

"Do I *have* to wear it?"

"Yep. I think it's a city ordinance."

"Really? Like, I'll get a ticket if they catch me at home with a tank top on?"

"Well, you won't be at home. You'll be at the game."

"I have to go to the games too?"

"Absolutely. Girlfriends are not permitted to miss games. I'm pretty sure they take attendance."

"And I have to wear your stupid shirt while I'm there?"

"Yes. Actually, you have to wear it all day, everywhere you go."

"What if I go to the beach?"

"It's probably best if you go to the beach on Thursdays."

"I don't think this is going to work out between us…"

He had enough. He quickly grabbed both of her arms, and pulled her quickly up to him, wrapping his arms even more quickly around her back so that she was now sitting on his lap. She immediately shut up and kissed him, running her hand up through his short, dark hair, feeling it slide out of her grasp as she tried to grab it. They spent the next hour in this very spot, doing this very thing.

Chapter 2

    The first Monday in August is always a special day in Kendall Township. It's not a holiday. It's not a celebration. Everyone goes to work. Everything is open for business. Nothing appears different from any other day of any other week. It's not really even a day that impacts anyone in the township. That is, unless you want to play football for the Kendall Township Cobras. If you *do* choose to play football in Kendall, then the first Monday in August is the beginning of the two most grueling weeks of the year. It's always hot. The sun is always blazing down relentlessly. There's never a breeze. You get there by 7:00am or you don't come at all. You're there until 5:00pm. You run and run and run. Then you do up-downs, push-ups, sit-ups, six-inch drills, crab-walks up and down the length of the field, and every other torturous exercise the coaching staff can come up with. Then you run some more. And that's just the first two hours. Next come the hitting drills. Players line up and smash into each other over and over again. By lunchtime, most guys can barely move. Then the real work begins. Offense; Defense; Passing; Catching; Rushing; Tackling; Receiving; and God forbid you drop a pass, miss a block, or fumble the ball. You might *never* get to stop running. The coaches yell, curse, swear, scream, and drive the squad relentlessly. And all the while, the sweat pours out of every single player. Every muscle screams for

Beginnings

rest. And then you get to do it all over again tomorrow. That first week, many players simply quit. The first Monday in August is the start of Summer Camp. The players and coaches refer to that first week as Hell Week.

Kevin arrived ten minutes early and saw about a hundred guys already there. Being on time was Rule #1 in the Player's Handbook, which he was given in the previous spring when the Booster Committee came to him for the umpteenth time to make sure he still planned to attend Kendall and not some parochial school like Holy Trinity or St. Augustine's. Those schools generally recruited all the good players to their private academies, which tended to set those schools up for success and leaving the public schools to live with whichever players they could muster together. This was why Holy Trinity hadn't been beaten in league play in over two seasons and had won last year's parochial state championship.

As he strode though the gate and onto the field, Kevin noticed the three men from the booster committee sitting in the bleacher seats, watching the boys intently. When they saw Kevin one of them waved. It was Leo Forsythe, the chairman of the committee. Leo was possibly the richest man in Kendall Township. He owned a chain of those self-storage places where people rented lockers. He had real estate all over the country. Jerry Hoffinger, the bald one, is a partner in Waldman, Hoffinger and Smote Law Firm, and the other guy, Kevin Murphy owns the Murphy Group, a large real estate ownership group, with a few other minor partners, mostly contractors who do the work to restore homes which they then resell for a profit. These three sat at the head of an unofficial committee, but their influence was felt all the way at the top of the local government. Money, like what these three men had, was not something politicians ignored. Kendall Township listens to these three men, and what these three men care most about is Kendall High School Football.

"Guess this is it." Kevin turned to see who was speaking, and nodded to Scott Webber, his quarterback for the past three years since he moved to the Township.

"Guess so."

"Awwwwwyeaaaahhhh!" came the shout from the blue Ford Pathfinder, just pulling up to the curb alongside Kevin and Scott. Neither of them needed to look to know it was Tony Yavastrenko, or "Yavo", as everyone except his mother called him. He jumped from the car before it came to a halt as his mother yelled at him in Russian to be careful. He smiled, waved, and blew her a kiss. His demeanor always bordered on the obnoxious, but he was one of those characters who seemed to always pull it off. He got away with saying things, especially to girls, that would normally get a guy slapped. Yet he always managed to avoid trouble. He had played football all his life, and was one of the few who could play with an intensity and ferocity to rival Kevin's. He had charisma and good looks. He was also crazy, but in a good way. His particular brand of lunacy was fun and often adorable to the girls, who were steadily becoming the major focus of his attention.

That lunacy translated a bit differently to the football field, where he and Kevin both were generally considered to be borderline psychotics by more than one frightened parent. It was a bad idea to be on Tony's bad side, and even worse to be on the bad side of one of his friends. He was loyal and unconditional in his friendship. He'd back up his friends in any situation, right or wrong. The saying "one guy lies and the other swears to it", came about precisely because of people like Antonin Yavastrenko. He was Kevin's best friend. Kevin would probably tell you that Tony was his only *real* friend.

Tony and Scott, along with Kevin, had been heavily recruited by Holy Trinity, the nearest parochial school, and last year's parochial state champions, but none of them really wanted to go there. You have to go to mass or something like that, and part of the curriculum included religious classes. No, thank you. Kevin had enough of that every weekend when he attended church with his mom and step-dad. Not that he minded all that much. He wasn't against religion, but he knew he wouldn't be able to handle catholic classes. Tony had summed it all up for both of them last spring.

"No way I'm going to any fruitcake Amazing Grace academy."

And with that, they had committed themselves to playing football for the silver and black; way cooler colors than the Crusade's sissy gold and blue, according to Tony.

He was in rare form for a Monday morning. "Who's ready to crack some skulls? Kendall football in the houuusssse! What do ya say, Six?"

He generally called football players by their numbers. Scott had worn the number 6 all through Pop Warner. Though Kevin wore number 27, Tony only rarely called him by it, opting instead for some variation of his name. Kevin never bothered to ask him why. He doubted Tony even knew.

Scott and Kevin both grinned. Tony was an old-school type football player who thought the game was basically about hurting the other guy. What he liked to do most was hit people. Between Kevin and Tony, last year's team was so intimidating on defense that there wasn't a receiver in the league that was really eager to take them on. Add to that, Scott's cannon of an arm and it was no wonder the boosters had agonized over keeping these players in the Township system. Tony didn't really pay them all that much attention. He thought they were idiots anyway and ignored them, mainly because he never intended to go to a private school, especially if Kevin stayed in Kendall. In fact, he had decided to play football at Kendall High School strictly because he thought it would expand his opportunities with certain girls he knew would be attending Kendall High. Now he was looking around with a frown.

"Hey, I thought the cheerleaders would be here too. Don't they have camp over the summer?"

Scott grinned. "Nope. Not for another week, Yav. Looks like you'll have to play just for the fun of it."

Tony winced. "Really?" He thought about it for a second then grinned widely. "Then I guess it's all about cracking some skulls! Right, Six?"

"That's right."

Tony wouldn't be disappointed for long. The girls would show up. The girls always showed up. They usually came in groups to watch the boys during Hell Week. They never showed up early because the players pretty much just ran and did exercises for the first half of the day. But after lunch, the practice fields were usually surrounded by spectators, many of whom were female high school students at Kendall High. One particular group of girls that never failed to show up was the Brette Girls. The Brette Girls is an unofficial booster club of sorts made up of only juniors and seniors. It is financed by the Booster Committee and originally intended to be the conduit between the committee and the players.

Originally, they were to be called the Cobrettes, a not-so original name Leo Forsythe came up with, but that name got voted out by the original group of girls in favor of dropping the C and the O in Cobrettes, and just calling themselves the Brette Girls, which, incidentally made for an obscure and accidental double entendre. Those who are old enough often mistake their name for *Breck* Girls, and wonder why these girls are named after a shampoo company that no longer exists. In any case, the Brette Girls were originally formed to help elevate the Kendall players and make them feel special. Each Brette Girl would be assigned a specific player for the season and her job was to provide a small snack or treat on game day for her player. It could be cookies or brownies, or whatever. Usually, the girls would just ask their player what he liked. They would do things like decorate the player's locker on game day, collect newspaper articles about the team and the player and send them to the parents of the player. Often, the Brette Girls would even create a giant scrapbook made up of all the materials they collected throughout the year and publish it for sale in the school store. It was about doing little things that would help to inspire the players and give them a sense of status.

It didn't take long for this group to become controversial. The Brette Girls would often escort the players as they came off the team bus at away games. They were expected to be available to be their dates at parties or school events if called upon. Even though the concept was perfectly innocent, this didn't sit well with many in the community. To them it felt as though the school was promoting a sexist mindset and these girls were being used as servants for the pleasure of the boys. Interestingly enough, as is often the case, these complaints never once arose from a parent of a Brette girl. But to be fair, the Brette girls soon achieved for themselves a reputation for being willing to cross the line of good taste and good sense in their "support" of their football team.

Of course, as with any rumor, there was some truth to what was being said about the Brette girls. It wasn't all of them, but it was enough that there was often an expectation from the football players that their Brette Girl would be available for more than just the cookies and locker decorations. The complaints often got loud, but the Brette Girls were not an official Kendall High School program. It was a volunteer club that met off school grounds and raised their own funds, so there was little to be done about it. Aside from that, everyone knows that football players get the girls, and often the girls are more willing to compromise themselves physically for the status of being with a football player. It didn't take an organized group for this phenomenon to occur, but the idea of forming a group for this purpose was distasteful to some. What many in the community failed to understand was that the Brette Girls didn't really care what anyone thought.

If the Brette Girls were seen as being a little bit dirty to some people in the community, they were all but worshiped by the rest of it. For one thing, it was an exclusive club. It was really run like an exclusive sorority. You didn't sign up. You had to be selected. Freshmen and sophomore girls at Kendall High often had no idea that they were being evaluated by the Brette Girls. They were evaluated for their looks, their personalities, and their spirit. A Brette Girl had to be a real fan of the Cobras. The group's existence revolved around the team. They were the closest thing Kendall Township had to a local sorority. They were essentially a sorority of the hottest girls in the school. They had their own clothes, logo, website, rules, *and* they were self sufficient. They supported all of their activities by raising their own money.

One thing they had started doing to raise money was designing Kendall Cobra apparel and accessories. It used to be a joke in Kendall that the school store sold the *official* stuff, but the Brette Girls had the *real* Cobra gear. Over the years, the Brette Girls began supplying the school store and now were the *only* supplier of Kendall Cobra items. They even had a booth at home games where they sold their merchandise.

When the Brette Girls showed up, you knew it. They always arrived in their Brette Girl shirts, jackets, even skirts and sun dresses for the warmer months. The boys of Kendall High could only gawk at them because they pretty much belonged to the football team. There was no record of a Brette Girl dating a non football player during football season.

*****

Week two of high school football camp marked the beginning of preseason camp for the various support squads. The cheerleaders, the drill team, and even the Brette Girls kicked into gear in preparation for game 1, which always happened the first Friday of the school year. In a region that was dominated by professional football and baseball, Kendall Township had found its hope in its local boys. In a region dominated by politically correct, big-city thinking, the Township had drifted to more of a small-town mentality. For such a huge area this was no mean feat. The diversity of race, financial status, religion, and culture in the area was vast. However, as summer was in full swing, and the upcoming school year loomed in the distance, the whole town began to shrink. After Hell Week on the football field, the whole town descended on the high school. In this school, if you weren't involved in the football season in some way, you were missing out on the social scene. The boys played on the team, worked the games in some way, or at least showed up every week to cheer the team on. The girls cheered, drilled, joined the Brette Girls, worked the refreshment stands, or showed up to root for the team. If you weren't involved with the Cobras in some way, you might as well be invisible at Kendall High.

    Tracey was invisible virtually everywhere she went. She had never been popular, but likewise had never really been on the receiving end of ridicule. She danced. She kept her head down and went about her business. She was polite and kind. She was friendly whenever people did speak to her, which was rare. She was never one to initiate a conversation, so most kids left her alone. She just danced. The other dancers were nice enough, even encouraging. Some of them even expressed their admiration for her skills and technique. But until very recently, she had never connected their words to her own feelings. Their compliments were received with grace and dignity, but it always ended there. The words never impacted her in such a way as to give her any additional confidence or to make her feel particularly good about herself. She just danced. She danced for herself mostly. She wasn't looking for compliments, though it was nice to get them. She wasn't particularly interested in the recitals, though it was nice to perform. The applause never impacted her. The response of others never really inspired her, mostly because she never connected their response to anything she did.

    Right around the time she had begun to notice the wonderful changes that had taken place in her body and appearance, Tracey had also begun to notice the attention that was being paid to her by others. It was like coming out of a fog. She was a self conscious individual who really didn't want attention. Her mind had somehow turned off that portion of her personality when she danced so that she was completely unaware of anything but dancing. Now, that switch was back on and she was terrified And that was when she met Kelly Presidian, Director of Cheer Leading for Kendall High School.

Kelly oversaw not only cheer leading, but also the drill squad. She had taken a position teaching modern dance at onStage during the spring session because she wanted to be there while her young girls learned to dance. She spotted a pretty red-head on her first day and saw her spectacular abilities immediately. She saw the raw talent underneath the exquisite grace and technique. She also saw that this young lady had no real social interaction with the other dancers in her classes. She wasn't mean or standoffish. She just kept to herself. She said "hello" and "goodbye" whenever someone initiated the exchange, and even managed to smile when someone paid her a compliment. But she was an outsider. Though she stood head and shoulders above even the best dancers in the school, she was not one of them. Tracey Overton was a true artist. She danced for the pure pleasure of it. Kelly could see the joy in her every expression as Tracey soared through technique after technique. But Kelly could also see what was hidden behind those expressions of joy. Tracey was hiding a deep pain. Dance pushed that pain down deep, but it could never wipe it away. Tracey was a tortured soul, and Kelly felt for her. She felt an immediate kinship with the shy Tracey. She knew that Tracey was on a path to greatness. Kelly could spot that sort of thing a mile away.

Tracey always arrived at least a half hour early for her classes and warmed up by herself. Kelly came in early one day and walked into the studio where Tracey was stretching.

"Hi, there," Kelly said brightly, in her Texas accent.

"Hello," Tracey replied, continuing to stretch.

Kelly came over to her and put out her hand. "Ah'm Miss Kelly. Ah've been teachin' modern dance for a couple a weeks now. Ah don't believe we've met."

Tracey stopped stretching and shook Kelly's hand shyly. "I'm Tracey."

Kelly smiled. "It's nice to meet you, Tracey. Ah've seen you dance a little bit. You're a wonderful dancer."

"Thank you." Tracey went back to stretching.

Kelly nodded silently. "Do you mind if I warm up with you a bit?"

"Sure." The reply was quick and noncommittal. Tracey was obviously someone who was used to minding her own business.

They stretched in silence together. Tracey then began running through her warm-up routine. She had worked out a series of steps that increased in difficulty as she ran through them. Kelly observed as she went through it with flawless execution. Tracey was truly an inspiring dancer.

"You know," Kelly said, after Tracey had completed her two minute routine. "I don't think Ah've ever seen someone with such raw talent as you on a dance floor."

Tracey continued warming up, running through some freestyle combinations. "I doubt that."

Kelly chuckled. "Course you do. But it's true. Ah've seen better dancers, let me be clear. But you have a talent that has nothing to do with what you been taught. You got the "It" and that means sky's the limit for you."

Tracey stopped in the middle of a combination, and faced Kelly for the first time.

"What does that mean?"

Kelly nodded. "I'm talkin bout the way your whole being comes out when you dance. Who you are is completely wide open when you hit this floor. You can't teach that kind of…vulnerability, I guess is the word. You can't teach it. You got to *have* it. That's the "It" I'm talkin bout."

Tracey shrugged. "I don't know about that. I just dance."

Kelly raised her eyebrows and nodded. "Exactly. It's not something you can control. You just *do* it. That is what makes you special."

Tracey almost burst out laughing. "Special? Sure. Okay." She went back to her combinations.

Kelly frowned. "You don't think you're special?"

Tracey continued dancing. "I suppose everybody's special in some way." She continued through a complicated series of leaps and spins before landing in a perfect finishing pose. "But I've never thought of myself as particularly special."

Kelly nodded. "That's a shame."

Tracey quickly added, "Look, I know why you're here. I'm the shy girl who has no friends. I just dance and I go home. I don't hang out with anyone and I don't have a boyfriend. People wonder what my problem is, why I'm so weird. I don't care about any of that."

Kelly sat down on the floor. "You don't care? How is that? Do you like things the way they are?"

Tracey spun a couple more times and then stopped. "Actually, I've never really thought about it like that. Do I like things like this?" She considered for a moment. "I guess I don't really *like* it. It just is. I just accept it and go from there."

"Why not change it?"

"Change it? Just like that?"

Kelly shrugged. "Change like that only can happen if you take a step. My guess is that you've shut yourself off from everyone else. Most kids will usually leave you alone if you really don't want to be bothered and you make that perfectly clear. I bet that if you took a step and tried to connect with them, they'd be happy to have you around."

Tracey doubted that. "I've always been the weird one. Bright red hair. Bright red cheeks. Did you know that I was almost a foot taller than the tallest boy back in the fifth grade?"

Kelly understood. "But, Tracey, you're what, fifteen? Have you looked at yourself in the mirror lately?"

Tracey glanced at herself in the wall-to-ceiling mirrors lining the studio. "I don't really pay much attention to be honest."

Kelly's mouth dropped open. "Well, sweetheart, you are missing out. You are drop dead gorgeous and the boys can't take their eyes off of you."

Tracey shook her head. "They're just watching me dance. I'm pretty good. All the instructors say so. I also teach some classes for the beginners and kids."

Kelly laughed out loud. She couldn't contain herself. "Oh, really? Honey, you couldn't be more wrong. Boys don't watch girls dance to see them dance. They watch girls dance because we wear tight outfits and they like watching pretty girls in tight outfits. End of story. The boys are not watching a dancer. They are watching *you* dance. They are watching *you*."

Tracey's face reddened slightly, but she shook her head again. "Look, Miss Kelly. Boys have never looked at me. I have always been strange to them. They don't think about me that way."

Kelly nodded. "Look, girl. I'm a little bit older'n you, and I can tell you a thing or two about boys." She paused. "I can also tell you a thing or two about *you*."

Tracey stared blankly. "About me? What can you possibly tell me about me?"

"I can tell you everything. I used to *be* you."

Tracey looked at Kelly skeptically. "You used to *be* me? You must be kidding."

Kelly shook her head. Taking the hair band out of her hair, she shook it out, letting it fall to her shoulders. "See anything familiar?"

Tracey shrugged. "You have red hair. So? That doesn't make you like me."

Kelly nodded. "True, but back in high school I weighed about a hundred seventy pounds. That wouldn't have been so bad, but I also had a streak of shyness that makes *you* look like an extrovert. I couldn't even talk when my teacher called on me. It was the most embarrassing time of my life. But then I started dancing. Sound familiar at all?"

Tracey was silent. She knew no one who understood.

Kelly saw it on her face. "Oh yeah. I understand. I *get* it. That isolation from the world gave me plenty of time to work out and dance and excel. Then it kind of just became easier to ignore all of them, the people who ignored me. Before long, I was at the top of my dance class. But I still had no friends because I had no idea how to interact with people. I figured they didn't want me, so I withdrew. Know anyone like that?"

Tracey nodded silently, her heart in her throat, unable to speak. Kelly stood up and came over to her. She took Tracey's hand and held it. After a moment, Tracey lost her composure somewhat and began crying. Kelly took her in her arms and held her until Tracey's sobbing stopped.

"Feel any better?"

Tracey nodded. "A little."

Kelly looked in her eyes. "You are not alone, sweetie. You can talk to me and I will always understand."

Tracey nodded again. "I will. I promise."

Chapter 3

Hell Week is about shocking their bodies. It is about jump starting the conditioning process. For most of the players trying out, it is pure torture because they most likely hadn't spent much time over the summer preparing for the upcoming season. Those who chose to continue on after the first day or two would likely end up playing on the JV or Freshman squad. The ones who came into camp ready and in shape, had a shot at earning a coveted spot on the varsity team. That is the show. That is where everyone wants to be. It is the varsity players who get the prettiest girls. It is the varsity players who receive special treatment in school and even in the local community. It is the varsity players who are celebrities in the Township of Kendall.

Prior to the summer break, Kevin and Tony had committed themselves to being in the best possible shape when they walked onto the field for Hell Week. Tony spent his summer running and working out, doing push-ups sit-ups by the hundreds, and lifting weights. Kevin went to Japan. His trip was not a sightseeing adventure. It was no vacation. Kevin had been a martial arts student from the time he was five. His Teacher, Sensei Cenzo Tanaka was so proud of his young student that he got permission from Kevin's mother to take him to Japan for the summer to train with *his* old sensei. The intensity of the training had been like nothing Kevin could have ever imagined, but he poured everything he had into every moment and came home faster and stronger than he'd ever dreamed. His mental state was also different. Any fear that might have resided in him previously was gone. Most of the players on the field were typical high school athletes. Kevin Sinclaire was more like a trained killer. It didn't take the coaching staff very long to see that they had something special on their hands.

Following that first grueling week, the players were split up into their initial teams: Varsity, Junior Varsity (JV), and Freshmen. The varsity got to take the best players and the JV and Freshmen were left with the remaining groups. At that point, freshmen were on the freshmen team and the rest of the players were on JV. Kevin, Tony, Scott, and a couple other freshmen got selected to practice with the varsity. This was the first step toward getting a position on the final varsity roster.

"Have a good practice."

Kevin nodded and hopped from the car. His mother was used to this silent intensity. Kevin always got this way before practices. Games were another level entirely. She often wondered how he managed this change so consistently. Karen used to blow it off as though he were faking it so that people would think he was scary and intense. But now she realized that it is far more than that. Something changed inside him every time he prepared himself for football. She wasn't sure it was healthy, but he was so good at the game. He really only had three things that he truly seemed to love: Martial Arts, Woodworking, and Football.

She knew that he had little or no interest in what was most important to *her*, which was God. But she prayed every day for him to come to faith. He was so smart, but his intellect, which had served him so well in school seemed to constantly get in the way of his faith. He had an anger inside of him. At least it seemed that way. He wasn't what you'd call a sullen teenager. Kevin was a bit introverted, to be sure, but he was not downcast and miserable all the time. In fact, more often than not, he was actually quite pleasant. But when it came to football, a switch seemed to flip on and whatever was deep down inside of him came out all at once. It truly scared her. She could barely watch sometimes.

Beginnings

*****

"Looks like you got 'Quan."

Kevin was in line, awaiting his turn in the latest tackling drill. The other players were counting the other line, determining who they would all be matched up against when their turn came up. They were referring to Anquan Griffin, the starting halfback. He was the kind of runner who liked to slam into people and get the hard yards. He had the size to do that. But he was also deceptively quick. Anquan Griffin was hard to stop and no one really wanted to have to try to bring him down one on one in these tackling drills. Kevin looked over and saw some shuffling going on. Number 88, Matt Kildare, a senior, and easily the best player on the team for the past two years, was switching places with Griffin. They were both grinning, gesturing, and looking over at Kevin, who quickly put his head down and stayed loose. He had embarrassed Matt earlier by outrunning him and now it looked as though this would be Matt's payback for the indignity. The difference now was that there were about a hundred girls standing around watching.

When his turn came up, he got into his three point stance and waited for the whistle. Then he sprang forward and met Kildare one step after he took the handoff. He got there so fast that Kildare never even saw him coming. The ball went flying backwards as Kevin put his helmet right on it. He wrapped both his arms around Kildare's upper thighs, driving his shoulder pad full force into his gut. Kildare's feet shot out from under him and he went down hard, Kevin slamming down on top of him, then rolling right to his feet and running to the back of the line. The players let out a series of cheers.

The girls watching turned to one another asking who number 27 was. The black and silver-clad Brette girls began taking closer notice. Matt Kildare was not just the starting receiver. He was more than the Kendall Cobra's top player. He was also the most popular boy at Kendall High. His reputation was such that when the girls came out to watch the Cobra's practicing, most of them were focused on him. Matt was known as Kendall's Golden Boy. It had even been written about in the papers all last year.

Coach Shultz was right in Kildare's face, grabbing him by the facemask. "Kildare, what in God's name are you doing? This is football! You can't take a hit? Good God, Son! If a freshman can take the ball away from you what good are you to me?"

Before Kildare could respond, Shultz pushed him toward the line. In front of so many people he knew, Matt couldn't have been more embarrassed. He silently jogged to the back, steaming mad and resolving to get Kevin on this next turn. He counted and then got into position to face Kevin again. When their turn came, Kildare was fired up and ready to lay it on Kevin. He quickly got into his stance. Kevin knew exactly what Kildare was going to do. In this drill the ball carrier was not allowed to spin, or jump out of the way. The drill was about getting hit and winning the one-on-one battle. Just by looking at Kildare's urgency, Kevin knew that he was coming in high, looking for a big hit to restore his bruised pride.

As they lined up, Kildare no longer had that big, arrogant grin on his face. He was all business. Kevin stared straight ahead. The crowd around the field sensed the tension between them. Something was about to happen. The whistle came and Kevin took the ball and accelerated. As Kildare approached, Kevin sped up and then Matt launched himself right at Kevin's chest.

Too soon, idiot. Kevin immediately lowered his shoulders, got beneath Kildare's pads, simply letting Kildare glide onto Kevin's back, then flipping over onto the ground as Kevin straightened and continued forward. Kildare hit the ground with a thud and an, "Ooomph!" Kevin flipped the ball to the coach and trotted to the back of the line as everyone around reacted to the play. Though he didn't really care, he could tell he was getting the attention of the young ladies around the field. They were shouting to him, but he didn't react to any of it.

Coach Shultz shook his head, watching Matt as he struggled to his feet. He was shaking his head in amusement. "You know, Kildare, this is just not your day."

*****

For a girl whose father was barely in the picture, and whose mother was so focused on her work, and whose sister was also a social disaster, Tracey had never had a person who could understand her. She had never felt as though anyone was truly interested in her and how she felt. Kelly Presidian listened to her and gave her advice whenever she asked for it. She was not judgmental and never made Tracey feel bad about herself. But she was also tough. She didn't allow Tracey to dwell on her failures. She was not going to sit by and allow Tracey to be alone. She was encouraging about having Tracey explore her social options at school.

Tracey finally settled on the drill squad. There were positions on the squad specifically designed for dancers. At least she would be able to participate without the potential for embarrassment that would surely accompany something new, like cheerleading. Can you imagine screaming and yelling in front of a few thousand strangers?

No, thank you. Dancing will do just fine for now.

And today was the day. Tracey was dressed in shorts and a tank top, hand-picked by Miss Kelly, who had broken the news to her about how these girls dressed only two days ago. Tracey generally dressed in baggy clothing. She was in this habit because she had always wanted to hide her heavy body. Miss Kelly squashed this attitude.

"First of all, Honey, you don't have any fat on you, so get off that. You don't need to show it all off, but there is no reason on God's green earth for you to hide from everyone."

They had gone to the beach together over the past several weeks, so her embarrassing pure white skin had at least gotten a little color. She had pulled her hair back tightly into a pony tail, and then twisted it up into a bun to keep it from bouncing around. It was still dancing. You kept your hair out of the way. She splashed some water on her face, wiped it dry, and then looked at her appearance in the mirror. She wondered if the football team practiced close to where the drill team would be today. She wasn't sure she could handle it if Matt Kildare was watching on her first day.

Oh God, this is a mistake. What if you fall on your face?

"Oh, my..." Tracey snapped out of her daydream. Lindsey was standing in the doorway, nodding, with a half smile on her face. "Very different."

Tracey turned to her. "Don't start with me today, okay? I'm nervous enough as it is."

Lindsey shook her head. "Not at all. I'm just interested. You're really going through with this, aren't you?"

Tracey took a deep breath. "Of course. I promised Miss Kelly I would try out, and I am going to try out." She took another deep breath. "Look, it's just dancing, right?"

Lindsey nodded solemnly. "Sure. It is what*ever* you make it."

Tracey frowned. "What?"

Lindsey replied, "Look. Just go for it. I think it's great that you're putting yourself out there. Good luck with it."

Tracey smiled. "Thanks, Lindz."

Lindsey smiled sweetly. "No problem." She headed off to her room. "Maybe Matt Kildare will be watching and fall in love today…"

Oh God.

When Tracey arrived at the school, she was surprised to see just how many people were already there. She had known that today was the day that many different squads, teams, and clubs would begin their training, but she was unprepared for the reality of how many students would actually be involved. It felt as though the whole school was there. And here she was with her bare legs and arms showing. This could get really embarrassing.

Okay, here you go. Deep breaths now. Try not to make a fool of yourself.

She made her way to the gym and signed her name under the drill squad sign-in sheet and listed "dance" as her skill. This was getting more and more real. Vaguely she wondered why she felt so nervous when she had been performing on stage for years now. For some reason this was just different. She felt sick.

Just hold it together. You're going to be dancing. It's no big deal.

"Tracey?" The shout came from behind her, snapping her out of her fog. She turned to see the smiling face of Brittany Morgan. Brittany was possibly the most perfect person ever. She was pretty. She was a straight A student. She never got into trouble. She was always smiling. The teachers all loved her from grade school right up to high school. She was involved in many different activities in school and out. Everybody knew her. Everybody loved her. Other than the good grades and staying out of trouble, Tracey had nothing in common with Brittany, but Brittany always greeted her like they were best friends. Tracey didn't think much of it because she knew Brittany greeted everyone like that. It was just how she was.

Tracey managed a tight smile. "Hi, Brittany."

Brittany was beaming. "I'm so glad you came out. Miss Kelly just told me that you had decided to try out for drill squad. I think you'll be awesome."

Tracey shrugged, looking around at the mass of students, her heart in her throat. "I don't know. I guess we'll see."

A little confidence maybe...just sayin...

Brittany leaned in close. "You know something? I get really nervous on the first day too. It's like I'm starting all over and have to relearn everything."

Tracey nodded. "For me, this really *is* the first day. I've never done anything like this before."

Brittany replied, "Sure, you have. I've seen you dance in plenty of recitals. You're great."

"But this is different."

"How's that?"

Tracey shrugged. "I was already dancing when they asked me to be in a recital. By the time anyone really saw me perform, I had been dancing the routines for weeks. I really don't think I can do this."

Brittany grabbed her by the shoulders. "You can't think like that."

Tracey pulled away. "Look, I'm not like you."

Brittany frowned. "Like what? How am I?"

Tracey leaned against the wall. "I'm not pretty. I'm not popular. No one likes me."

Brittany glanced around the room. "Is that what's bothering you? You think you're still invisible?"

Still? How does she know...

Brittany saw it in her eyes. "Yes, Tracey, I remember what you said back when you came to my church a few years back. You told Miss Linda that you were invisible and no one ever noticed you. Remember? You and I played checkers for nearly the whole time because you didn't want to play dodge ball with the others?"

Geez. Remember that? Tracey had completely forgotten that day. She actually remembered thinking that she had made a friend. But then for whatever reason, she had decided she didn't want to go back to Sunday School.

Brittany was snapping her fingers in front of Tracey's eyes. "The only problem now is that you won't *let* anyone talk to you." She pointed her thumb over her shoulder. "See those guys over there? They're in the marching band. See the guy in the grey T-shirt? He can't take his eyes off you." Tracey quickly began to deny it. "Nope. He's not looking at me," Brittany said. "He watched you walk in and has been staring at you ever since. And he's not the only one. Are you telling me that you never noticed *any* of the guys looking at you all last year?"

Tracey shook her head. "They weren't looking at me. Not like that."

"You're crazy," Brittany laughed. She grabbed Tracey's hand. "Come with me. We have a few minutes. I have an idea."

She practically dragged Tracey out of the gym and through the halls of the high school to a bathroom several sections away where no one else was. They went in and Brittany brought Tracey to the center of the room and faced her towards the mirror.

"Now, close your eyes."

Tracey closed her eyes, wondering what this was all about.

"Okay. Tell me one thing that you think boys like."

Like you would have any clue.

"I have no idea."

"About girls in general then. Come on. One thing that you *think* boys like. What do you *think*."

Tracey sighed. "I don't know. Big boobs."

Brittany giggled. "How did I know you were going to say that? But you're right. Something else. Keep your eyes closed."

Tracey shrugged. "Um. I guess they like girls with nice bodies."

Brittany nodded. "So girls that are maybe athletic, thin, with nice curves and skin?"

Tracey nodded. "Sure."

"Okay. Now open your eyes."

Brittany stood right next to Tracey so that they were side by side in the mirror.

"Now you tell me. Which one of us looks more like the description we just came up with?"

Tracey looked at the two girls in the mirror skeptically.

This is stupid. It's not that simple.

Brittany prompted her. "Well? You know the answer. You won't offend me. Tell me who the more desirable girl is based on the description we just agreed on?"

Tracey shook her head. "This is ridiculous."

"It's *not* ridiculous. You and I just agreed that boys like girls with nice trim athletic bodies and big boobs. I'm thin and I'm athletic enough, I guess, but I don't have big boobs. You, on the other hand, have an amazing body with much bigger boobs than me. Now, why is that so hard to accept?"

Tracey nearly lost it. "Because boys don't *like* me, okay? They like *you*. They like your blonde hair and big blue eyes."

Brittany was having none of it. "Look at yourself in the mirror. Look! What color did you say your eyes were?"

Tracey turned back to the mirror. "I know I have blue eyes too, but…"

"But what? Blonde hair? That's the big winning difference? Please. Some guys like blonde hair. Some don't. Trust me. Look at Vivian Parker. Red hair, just like you and she is captain of the cheerleaders *and* dating Mike Doyer, okay? QB1. Red hair, *brown* eyes, not even blue, and dating QB1. End of discussion. Look in the mirror. Now I want you to tell me one thing about the appearance of that girl in the mirror that you don't like."

Tracey looked closely. She hated her hair, but Brittany would just tell her how easy it would be to change it. She had always hated the redness of her cheeks, but that had gone away some time ago so she couldn't complain about her skin. She began to shift around to look at her features more closely. Brittany stepped back. Tracey's facial expressions changed as she seemed to go through each and every body part, looking for blemishes or ugliness. Her face softened somewhat as she did this. The girl in the mirror was not ugly. It really was just that simple. In fact, the girl in the mirror was actually kind of pretty, horrible red hair and all. Brittany placed a hand on her shoulder.

"Well? Do you see it?"

Tracey was near tears. She couldn't speak. She just nodded, unable to express what she was feeling.

Brittany smiled. "Trust me. You go out there and do your thing. Smile and hold your head up. The guys will fall all over themselves to get to you."

Tracey laughed through her tears.

Brittany continued as they left the bathroom and headed back down the hall. "So, is there anyone in particular we should be targeting?"

Tracey laughed again. "I wouldn't know where to begin."

Brittany laughed. "Well, what kind of guys do you like?"

"I have no idea."

Brittany stopped and made a face expressing disbelief. "Seriously? No idea? You expect me to believe that all this time you have absolutely no idea what kind of guy attracts you?"

"It's not that. It's just that it's embarrassing to talk about."

Brittany feigned offense. "It's embarrassing to talk about these things with your best friend?"

Best friend? You're best friends now?

Brittany saw the confusion in Tracey's eyes. "What? We're not friends?"

Tracey smiled. "We are. It's just...well...I've never really had friends."

Brittany looped her arm through Tracey's. "Well, you have one now. And I guarantee you you'll have more in a few weeks. And guys will be drooling all over your brand new school shoes. You might want to wear an older pair at first."

Chapter 4

After practice, Kevin was showered, and nearly dressed when Tony nudged him.

"Heads up. Eights is headin' this way."

Kevin glanced up and saw Kildare making his way toward them. Everyone in the locker room sensed a confrontation about to happen, and cleared away. Tony didn't move. Kevin didn't even look up as he finished tying his shoes. He pulled his bag out of the locker and filled it with his dirty uniform. Kildare yanked it from his hands and threw it down. Tony stood up. Kevin shook his head and waved him back.

Kildare put his finger in Kevin's face. "If you ever pull that crap on me again out there, I'll beat your little freshman butt in front of everyone."

Kevin looked at him quizzically. "What crap, running faster, or knocking you on your butt?"

Matt stepped closer. "You think you're funny? You're nothing but a little punk freshman. Watch your attitude or I'll have to knock some of your teeth out."

Kevin nodded thoughtfully. "Really?"

Kildare nodded. "Really."

Kevin closed his locker, making sure the lock was engaged.

Turning back to Kildare, he locked his green eyes on him and said, "Try it. You might not find it so easy."

Kildare took a step back, and then got right in Kevin's face, grabbing for his throat. It was over in less than three seconds. As Matt lunged forward, Kevin simply leaned back slightly, twisting his body out of the way and letting Kildare fly by, helped along by Kevin's left hand in the small of his back, propelling him forward even faster. He slammed face first into the lockers causing a nasty gash on his forehead. Blood immediately came pouring out. Kevin then grabbed him by both shoulders and threw him backwards to the ground. It was a toss-up between who was more stunned, Matt Kildare or the rest of the team, who thought Kevin had been on the way to getting his butt kicked.

For his part, Kevin calmly picked up his bag and put his dirty laundry back into it. Kildare was struggling to get back to his feet, determined to get back at Sinclaire. He shrugged off those who were trying to help him up, and lunged again at Kevin, who side stepped a couple of times, before finally deciding that enough was enough, rolling his eyes and tossing his bag aside.

"Uh oh." Tony saw the look in Kevin's eyes before anyone else and tried to get there in time. He also saw that this time Kevin had set his feet. Now when Kildare moved in with a punch toward Kevin's face, he did not side step. Kevin easily blocked the poorly thrown head shot and landed a vicious front snap kick to Kildare's mid-section, doubling Kildare over. He drew back his hand to deliver the fight-ending strike when Tony grabbed him from behind and stopped him.

"No, no, no, brother," he said softly. "This one's over." He pulled Kevin back as Kildare dropped to the floor, the wind knocked out of him. "Get your stuff."

Kevin went over to where he had thrown his bag and picked it up. When he passed the still out of breath and bleeding Kildare on the way out, he leaned over him. "Hey, Kildare, why don't you sit there and bleed a while before you taste some *real* pain."

Tony pulled him out of the locker room before anyone else decided to get in his face.

*****

Tracey burst through the door at home and quickly ran

upstairs to her room. She had already texted her mom not to pick her up from the school after practice because Brittany had invited her to sleep over and give her a ride in the morning. Mrs. Morgan drove her home to pick up some things. The plan was to swim in the Morgan's pool all day, have a barbecue, and talk about boys all night.

Just like real girlfriends!

She blew past Lindsey in the upstairs hall and ran into her room, leaving the door open and a shocked looking Lindsey standing in the hall. She quickly grabbed her onStage bag and threw in the clothes she would need for camp the next day. She then found a pajama top and bottom and some underwear and threw it all in the bag. Next she went into the bathroom and gathered her shampoo, conditioner, and body wash, as well as her toothbrush, and put it all into the bag. Lindsey watched her sister go back and begin ransacking her drawers, in search of something. She stood silently as the frantic search went on for a few moments.

"What are you looking for? Why are you packing clothes?" she finally asked.

Tracey continued searching. "My bathing suit. I need my bathing suit. I'm sleeping over Brittany's and we're going to swim in her pool."

Lindsey raised her eyebrows. "Brittanyyyyy....?"

Tracey looked up. "Morgan. Brittany Morgan. You know her."

Lindsey stared at her. "The church girl?"

"Yes. The church girl. Where's my bathing suit?"

"It's not like you ever use it."

"I need it now."

"Why are you sleeping over Brittany Morgan's house?"

"Because we're friends and she invited me. My bathing suit?"

"You're friends? You and Brittany?...from church."

Tracey shrugged. "What difference does it make? We talked earlier in the week and she asked me to sleep over tonight."

"There has to be more to the story than that. How are tryouts going?"

Tracey sighed. This could take all day. Lindsey didn't do well with change. Neither did she for that matter. "Tryouts are going fine. Brittany and I are friends now. She asked me to sleep over. I need my bathing suit so I can swim in her pool. Where is it?"

"Are you a Born-Again now?"

"What?"

"A Christian; A Born-Again; That's what Brittany Morgan is. Are you one too?"

Tracey couldn't resist. "Are you one too? No, I'm two, three."

"Very funny. Are you a Born-Again now?"

"What is *wrong* with you? I need my bathing suit. They're waiting for me."

"Who's waiting for you?"

"Are you kidding me? Brittany and her mom are waiting for me."

"Why are they waiting for you?"

Tracey was completely exasperated. "Because I'm sleeping over! They're waiting for me to get my things so we can go to their house and have dinner! WHERE IS MY BATHING SUIT?"

"Don't you think this is kind of weird?"

"What, Lindsey? What's weird?"

"Well, just that you wake up one morning and you have no friends, and no life, and all in one week you join the drill squad, make a brand new friend, and start having sleepovers? It's just a little weird, that's all."

"Why is it weird?"

"Why do you want to start hanging out with a bunch of Born-Agains all of a sudden?"

"*One* Christian! I'm hanging out with *one* Christian! And who cares anyway?"

"Trace?" The call came from downstairs. "You all right?"

Tracey ran to the top of the steps. "Up here, Brit. Come on up." To Lindsey she said, "Don't start."

"Trace? Brit? Oh, my God. You're *besties* aren't you?" Lindsey asked, following Tracey back into her room.

"Oh, my God! You're an idiot! Stop making fun of me. Have you seen my bathing suit or not?"

Brittany came to the door. "Everything okay?"

"Sorry," Tracey said. "I can't find my bathing suit."

"Oh, that's okay," Brittany replied. "You can just use…"

"So, why are you friends with my sister all of a sudden?" Lindsey interrupted.

Brittany was taken aback. "What?"

Lindsey pressed. "My sister leaves the other morning all normal and comes back with friends, having a sleepover, and swimming. Are you trying to make her a Born-Again?"

"Lindsey..."

"Am I tr...?" Brittany started.

"Because she's not interested in all that, you know. We don't believe in God."

Tracey was turning red. "Will you leave, please? No one cares what you believe."

Lindsey turned to Tracey. "Don't go joining up with any cults, okay?"

Brittany shook her head. "I don't belong to a cult, Lindsey."

"Sure you do. All religions are cults. Don't try to make my sister join."

"It's really not like that."

Lindsey pulled out her phone and held it up, facing Tracey. "Here; just look here for a minute."

Tracey looked at her. "What are you doing?"

Lindsey touched the screen and waited a second. "Got it." She showed Tracey the picture she took of her. "This is for the police when you disappear with the cult, so we can give them a recent picture of you."

"Are you being serious right now?"

Brittany shook her head. "Listen. We don't belong to a cult. Nothing is going to happen to Tracey at my house. You can come too if you like."

Tracey quickly added, "No, you can't. She's just being nice."

Lindsey shrugged. "No way I'm coming over there. Are you going to chant and light candles and things like that?"

Brittany started to reply but Tracey waved her off. "Don't bother. She's an idiot. Where's my bathing suit? I know you have it."

"Do you even know how to swim?"

"Have you seen it anywhere?"

"You know, a person can drown in less than six inches of water."

"I'm not going to drown. I'm a better swimmer than *you* are anyway."

"How would you know? You don't even have a bathing suit."

"I have one. I just can't find it because you hid it from me."

Lindsey smirked. "Yeah. That's right. I hid your bathing suit from you. I knew you'd come home today with your very first friend ever and that you'd be looking for your bathing suit so you could go on a cult sleepover pool party. So I hid your bathing suit. You caught me."

Brittany broke in. "Don't worry about it. You can just use one of mine."

Lindsey continued. "Like I care about your stupid bathing suit."

Tracey shrugged and looked at Brittany. "Fine. Let's get out of here before I kill her."

As they got to the bottom of the stairs, Lindsey dropped something down from the second floor onto the floor next to Tracey. It was her brown and pink bathing suit.

"Hey, Trace," she said sweetly. "Don't forget your bathing suit."

Tracey looked up at in silent frustration, ready to say something about immature little sisters, but Lindsey had already disappeared from sight.

*****

Word of the incident between Matt and Kevin somehow didn't make it out into the community, which was kind of unusual in this town. The players took their cues from the seniors, who didn't want their friend and teammate any more embarrassed than he already was. Plus, there was no telling what coach might do if he found out about the fight. It was best to keep this quiet. The only wildcard in the matter were the freshmen involved: Kevin Sinclaire, and Antonin Yavastrenko. As team captains, Mike Doyer and Anquan Griffin decided to be proactive. They drove over to Alder Ave. to see Kevin. They knocked on the door and met Kevin's mom, Karen.

"Can I help you boys?"

Mike Doyer responded, "Yes, Ma'am. Is Kevin home? We're from the football team and just need a few minutes, if he's available."

Karen Timmons pursed her lips. "Is this about whatever happened at camp today?"

Mike nodded. "Yes, Ma'am."

She studied them for a second. "If you're here to continue that nonsense, you can turn around and leave right now."

Mike shook his head. "Oh, no, no. We're not here to cause trouble. We just want to make sure that whatever this is, is over before camp tomorrow."

They were directed to a building about 20 yards back behind the garage. It was about 30' x 30' in size, with a 20' garage door opened in the front. They could see Kevin in the back of the room, leaning over something. His back was to them.

Mike banged on the side of the door frame.

"Hey, man. Can we talk to you for a minute?"

Kevin's head rose, though he still didn't turn around. "Sure. Come on in."

He stopped whatever it was he was doing and walked over to a refrigerator in the back corner and opened it, pulling out three water bottles and tossing one to each of them. He looked at them as they opened their bottles and took a drink.

"I really don't know why you're here. I didn't pick that fight. I haven't done anything to anyone. He's pissed because he thinks I showed him up in practice. You should go talk to your receiver."

Mike nodded. "Don't worry. He's my best friend. I'll get on him. That's my job. But I also need to be sure it's over. Tomorrow, Coach will know about this and I need to be able to tell him that it's handled. Otherwise, the whole team'll end up doing up-downs for an hour."

Kevin shook his head and shrugged. "As far as I'm concerned our account is settled."

Doyer nodded. "That's what I was hoping."

Kevin picked up his work again. "He comes at me again though..." He looked Mike right in the eye, his green eyes ablaze. Then he blinked and looked back down at the wood in his hands. "Just make sure he doesn't." He went back to work.

Mike and Anquan exchanged glances. Anquan raised his eyebrows and shook his head. They boys headed back to the car. "See you tomorrow, dude."

The next stop for the two team captains was the Kildare residence. This was going to be a different conversation. Mike had to let his best friend know that what happened today was his own fault and that he had to stop the nonsense immediately. This is what a captain had to do. He had to be able to lead, and that included leading his friends who are on the team. This meant talking to his best friend as the captain and not as a best friend. He hoped Matt would be in a receptive mood tonight. He glanced over at Anquan as they pulled to a stop in front of Kildare's house. Though they had both been there many times before, this was different. They got out and went up to the door, ringing the doorbell. Matt answered the door himself.

"Hey guys," he said. The gash on his forehead had stopped bleeding, but still looked pretty nasty. "Come on in."

Doyer and Griffin followed him into the den. Matt started before either Anquan or Mike could open their mouths.

"Look, don't even get in my face about Sinclaire. I don't want to hear it."

Mike shrugged. "No choice, dude. We have to protect the team. You guys can't be fighting in the locker room every time he knocks you on your butt."

Matt's eyes flashed in anger. "Nice, Mike. You're a real friend. Thanks for the backup, by the way."

"You expected me to help you beat up a *freshman*? You're lucky *his* friend stepped in when he did. Otherwise you'd be in the hospital right now."

"Yeah, right. That little punk got a lucky shot in, that's all."

Anquan shook his head. "Look, bro. I'm on yo side, but this team needs to think about winning ball games. Dis my last year in this school. Next year I'll be sitting on the bench hopin I get some reps on the practice squad somewhere. I don't wanna spend this year pulling you and that kid apart after every practice. 'Specially since it looks like you gonna be the one gettin whooped up on."

Matt turned toward Anquan and pointed at his face. "*Screw you*, Quan! You think you're some kind of tough guy? Why don't you take your best shot right now?"

Anquan got in his face and poked his finger in Matt's chest. "Boy, you ain want none a dis. Best watch yo mouth, fore someone knocks dem pretty white teeth out."

"Let's see you try," Matt spread his arms, challenging the all-star running back.

Mike Doyer quickly got between the two teammates. "Knock it off, you two."

Matt and Anquan stared each other down for a few seconds, before Matt finally shook his head and backed away, turning his eyes on Mike. "Oh, now it matters if we fight? Earlier you didn't seem to care. What's that all about?"

Mike shook his head. "Earlier it seemed like a little freshman hazing, but you picked the wrong guy and it got out of control. This is different. We're all best friends. You're making a jerk of yourself and we're all paying the price for it."

"Are you serious? You guys are still pissed you had to run a little extra?" After Kevin had beaten them in the two mile run, the coach had punished them by making them run the whole two miles over again. When Matt protested, they ended up running triple that.

"Man, you a piece o work, you know dat?" Anquan stepped to him again. Matt didn't back down, spreading his arms again, welcoming the challenge. Mike pushed both of them back apart.

"Matt, sit down. Quan, go sit in the car or something."

Anquan, stepped back, shaking his head, his dark eyes still leveled at Matt's. "Man, whatever." He left the room.

Mike turned to Matt, who shook his head and waved him away. "Don't even bother, dude. Not interested."

Mike stood there in disbelief. "Really? You're not interested in anything your best friend has to say?"

"Not right now."

"Well get ready anyway because you're gonna sit there and shut up and listen to what your *captain* says."

"You're really trying to pull that card on me right now? I'm a captain too."

"Yeah? Well I'm the *team* captain. This team is mine. And I'm telling you right now that this crap is over..."

When he came out, Anquan was sitting in the car, listing to his iPod. He had calmed down considerably and was now nodding his head to whatever rap song was playing. When Mike opened the driver's side door, though, he quickly pulled the ear buds out and looked at him expectantly.

Mike nodded. "That was not pretty, dude."

"He on board?"

"Yeah, pretty much, I think, no thanks to you."

Anquan raised his eye brows. "Why? What'd I do?"

"Are you serious? Why'd you have to go in there and pick a fight?"

Anquan shook his head. "Man, He got ta get over hisself."

Mike wasn't totally in disagreement. "Yeah? Well what about you? Huh? Matt's just worried about his position. He thinks he'll end up as the number two if Sinclaire is as good as everyone thinks."

"Well, then he got to deal wit it."

Chapter 5

It was the best time she'd had in a very long time. Tracey felt like a new person. She laughed and talked in ways she couldn't ever remember doing. There was something about being out of her routine and away from those who knew her so well that seemed to free her both mentally and emotionally. It was like someone hit a reset button and changed her personality. What a waste the past few years had been! She had no friends. She had no relationships beyond her family, and those were all disasters. Lindsey was okay some of the time, but between the two of them things could get very dark and depressing very fast. It was different with Brittany Morgan.

Tracey knew she was not even close to the bubbly personality that Brittany Morgan constantly brought. But Brittany's joy and cheerful nature brought out whatever joy and cheer Tracey had buried deep beneath the depression and self-loathing she had carried for so long. She knew she was the same person and that at some point she would have to deal with things, but for this one night, she was a normal teenage girl hanging out with her friend.

They didn't talk about anything in particular at first. When they got to Brittany's, they immediately changed into swimsuits and jumped into the pool. They splashed around, dove off the diving board, and even teamed up and dunked Brittany's little brother, Dillon, after he cannon-balled almost on top of them. After they ran him out of the pool and settled down, they just lay there, floating on rafts.

"So, this week was good, right?" Brittany's eye's were closed. She lay flat on her back.

Tracey was laying on her stomach, half on and half off her raft, floating with her legs dangling in the water. "Actually…it was a pretty good week, yeah." She giggled.

Brittany was nodding, her eyes still closed.

"I'm really glad you came out."

Tracey was quick to reply. "*I'm* really glad *you* were there."

Brittany opened her eyes and was about to reply when a shout came from the house.

"Girls!" Mrs. Morgan interrupted from the back deck. "Dinner will be on the table in ten minutes! Get washed up! You can shower after you eat!"

Brittany paddled over to the steps, Tracey in her wake. "Kay, Mom! We'll be right in!" Turning to Tracey, she said, "To be continued later."

Dinner was an unusual affair for Tracey. For one thing, the whole family was gathered at the table. At home, Ms. Overton cooked dinner, and she was actually a pretty decent cook, but they all ate more or less on their own. Sometimes they'd all sit together at the table, but they didn't make a point of it. A lot of the time, she and Lindsey would grab their plates and go up into their rooms and eat in front of the TV. In the Morgan house, Mr. Morgan prayed for the meal, even going so far as to thank God for Tracey's presence at their home. It felt a little weird, but Tracey just bowed her head, closed her eyes, and hoped she wouldn't be asked to pray in front of the whole family.

Mr. and Mrs. Morgan asked them about their day and how things went at camp. Brittany gave them the quick version. Tracey just smiled dumbly, hoping they wouldn't put her on the spot. No one did, and she gradually relaxed and felt more comfortable. Brittany did most of the talking and seemed to keep the attention away from the shy Tracey, who couldn't help wondering if she was doing it on purpose to shield her from questions. It was hard to tell because Brittany didn't seem to care about getting extra attention, but her personality was such that she talked a lot. It really didn't matter to Tracey because as long as *she* was not the center of attention, she was okay.

The Morgans did not ignore her though. Peter Morgan waited until his daughter ran out of things to say and turned to Tracey with a gentle smile.

"So, Tracey, how is your mother?"

Tracey was a little surprised to be asked about her mom. "Uh, she's okay."

He nodded. "And your sister? Lindsey was it?"

Tracey was a little surprised. How did he know her family? "Yes, Lindsey. She's okay too."

Mr. Morgan smiled. "It's not a trick. It's my job to remember people and their families."

Brittany broke in. "My dad's a pastor at Grace Gospel. If you walk through the doors, he knows your name."

"It's not quite like that," Peter laughed. "But it helps to let people know you remember them. Your family came a few years back, if I recall."

"It was four years ago, I think."

"That's about right. I never met your father though, I don't think."

Tracey shook her head. *Yeaaah, no. Not in church, right, Trace?* "No. You wouldn't have. He and my mom split right around that time and he isn't really around much."

Peter nodded with understanding. "I'm sorry to hear that. It's terrible when a marriage ends, especially for the kids."

Tracey responded, "It's really not a big deal. He wasn't much of a father even when they were together."

Good God, girl! Why are telling him all this?

Peter Morgan nodded again. "Some men struggle with giving up parts of their lives to put in the necessary time with their families. It's not right, but it is not uncommon either, unfortunately."

Tracey nodded. "That sounds like him. All he really ever cared about was his work. He's a professor up at Princeton."

Mr. Morgan raised his eyebrows. "Ah. So he's a smart guy, huh?"

"He's actually brilliant. He teaches physics and cosmology and always has some major project going on. We see him on holidays and whenever he comes to town. He's never totally here, even when we're with him."

"That's too bad. I'm going to pray that your father changes."

Tracey didn't know how to respond to that so she just nodded. Brittany grabbed her by the hand and pulled her up.

"Come on. Let's go."

Tracey got up while Brittany hugged her father. "Stop hogging my friend, Daddy."

"Sorry, Sweetie. Nice to see you again, Tracey. You're welcome here anytime."

"Thank you, sir. Thank you for dinner, Mrs. Morgan."

"It's my pleasure, Sweetheart. Have fun, girls."

Upstairs, Brittany shut the door to her room and they got into their pajamas. Brittany flipped on the TV and they sprawled out on her bed, watching in silence for a few minutes. Brittany could see that Tracey was lost in thought, but couldn't tell whether it was positive or negative. She just sat there, staring ahead, but obviously the wheels were turning in her mind.

"You okay?"

Tracey blinked and turned to face her. "Yeah. I'm fine. I just wasn't expecting to talk about my family. I wasn't ready for it."

"Sorry about that. Daddy can draw that kind of thing out of you."

"It's okay," said Tracey. "He's very kind. For some reason, I didn't mind talking to him."

Brittany smiled. "Yeah. Everybody talks to him. I just didn't want to you get depressed thinking about sad things."

"No. Not today. Today was too much fun for that."

Brittany smiled. "It *was* fun, wasn't it?"

Tracey replied, "I just want to tell you how much it meant to me that you helped me earlier. And then inviting me over...it was all really nice. So thank you."

Brittany hugged her. "It was my pleasure. Just so you know, I really do want to be friends with you."

Tracey shrugged. "I just don't know why. You have a million friends."

"Really? You think so?"

Tracey shrugged again. "Everybody seems to like you at school. Plus you must have friends at church after all these years."

Brittany shook her head. "I have *some* friends, sure. But I don't have all that many. Believe it or not, most people at school think I'm just a "church girl" who is sitting there judging them all the time. Hang around me long enough and you'll hear the little comments they make. They're not always being mean on purpose, but they know I'm different or something and they are not totally comfortable. Just like your sister, I guess."

Tracey winced. "Yeah. I'm really sorry about that. She's a creep."

Brittany laughed. "It's okay. Don't worry about it. I thought I was going to die when she took your picture though. That was really funny."

"If you say so."

"Come on. You have to be able to laugh at things, Trace. Don't be so serious."

"It's just embarrassing, that's all. Someone comes to our house who she knows is a Christian and she goes out of her way to insult them."

Brittany waved her hand. "Not a big deal, trust me. I get a lot worse at school. Sometimes the girls talk about their sex lives around me on purpose, just because they think it makes me uncomfortable, which I suppose it *does*, but they like to get really foul sometimes, like over the top foul, just to bother me."

Tracey shook her head. "Really? How pathetic."

"I know, right? The hard part is not responding. I have to sit there while they're saying all this stuff, pretend like I don't even notice how disgusting they all are, finish what I'm doing, and then walk out so I don't give them the satisfaction."

Tracey's mouth was open. "You're kidding me. I would never have guessed."

Brittany nodded. "Yep. So don't worry about what Lindsey said.

Tracey nodded. "I don't believe what she believes, by the way."

Brittany looked at her for a moment before responding. "You don't? Well, what *do* you believe?"

Yeah, what do you believe?

Tracey wished she hadn't said it. "Well...actually...I don't really know to tell you the truth. I'm just not like Lindsey. I don't think you're a part of a cult."

Brittany laughed, and got up off the bed. "I hope not! You came over." She went to the door. "I'm going to get us some snacks, kay?"

"Sure."

Brittany went downstairs and returned with two bottles of cold water, and a plate of cookies, cheese, and crackers as well.

"Mom made this plate for us. Help yourself."

"Thanks." Tracey took a couple of crackers and cheese squares.

"So," Brittany said, sipping her water. "We were talking about what you believed."

Tracey nodded. "Yeah, but I really don't think I believe *anything*."

Brittany cocked her head. "Really? How can that be? Everyone believes *something*."

"I guess, but I don't have any clue what it is I believe in."

"How about we start at the beginning? Do you believe that there is a god at all? *Any* god?"

Tracey shrugged. "I never really believed there was a god, I guess. My dad is an atheist, I know *that* because he told me once. My mom isn't necessarily an atheist. At least she doesn't seem to have a problem with people who believe in God. I think she just doesn't know one way or the other, like me."

Brittany nodded. "So, she's an agnostic."

"A what?"

"An agnostic. That's someone who doesn't know one way or the other."

"Well then, I guess we're both agnostics."

Brittany shook her head. "I don't think you're an agnostic."

"Why not?"

"Well, an agnostic is usually someone who has thought about it, searched for answers, but concludes that there isn't enough information to know one way or the other. You just said you never really thought about it."

"But I still have no idea."

Brittany sat on the floor, pulled her blonde hair back into a pony tail, and took a cookie off the plate. "Well, do you even care?"

Tracey didn't know how to answer that. The truth was, right now, she didn't think she cared all that much about whether God existed or not.

Go ahead. Tell her you don't care. See if you get invited over again...
"I...I just don't know."

Brittany smiled. "It's okay if you don't care, Trace. It won't offend me. You don't have to believe what I believe to be friends with me."

Really? Well now...

"Right now, I guess I don't really care. I never spent a whole lot of time thinking about it."

Brittany nodded. "Well, promise me this. That you'll think about it some and we'll talk about it some other time."

Tracey nodded. "Deal."

Brittany munched her cookie. "So, what do you want to talk about now?"

"Whatever. I don't care."

Brittany raised her eyebrows a couple times. "Boys?"

Tracey laughed. "Are you kidding?"

"No, I'm not kidding. You think I don't like boys?"

Uhhh. Actually...

"I don't know," Tracey sputtered. "I guess I just thought..."

"You thought that because I'm a Christian girl that I'm not interested in boys."

Something like that...

Tracey turned red. *Stupid much?* "When you put it like that it sounds silly, I guess."

Brittany grinned. "Let me tell you something, Trace. Christian girls like guys. Christian guys like girls. Christians date and *kiss* and even sometimes go too far and have sex. Believe it or not, Christians like sex as much as any non Christian."

Tracey nodded, unable to keep her cheeks from burning. *I'll bet they're red as a fire truck right now.* "I didn't meant to insult you."

"You didn't insult me at all. Now, who do you like?"

"I don't know."

Brittany made a face. "Are we going to go through this again? You don't know? You're telling me if you could snap your fingers and have any guy in the school ask you out, you don't know who you'd pick?"

Tracey shrugged. *Of course you know who you'd pick...* "Well," she said reluctantly. "If I could snap my fingers..."

"Yes. *Any* guy in the school." Brittany's big blue eyes were twinkling. She was really interested.

Tracey took a deep breath. "I guess I'd pick Matt Kildare?"

Brittany's mouth dropped open in surprise. "Matt Kildare? Really? I would never have guessed that! He's a football player!"

Tracey's face was burning now. She had never told this to anyone. "He's really..."

Brittany made a face. "He's really what? Matt Kildare is totally HOT is what he is! But he's a football *player*. Emphasis on the PLAYER part."

Who cares about all that? Just look at the guy! Tracey knew his reputation. "I know, but we're talking Fantasy Land here, aren't we?"

Brittany shrugged. "I don't know. I think you could totally pull it off, but that is one guy that thinks about nothing *other* than sex. Look at his girlfriend, Emily."

Tracey asked, "Is Emily his girlfriend?"

"They always deny it for whatever reason, probably because they both want to have sex with other people. But they are also always together. Who knows? That's the problem. Why would you want a guy who wants other girls?"

Tracey was getting back to her normal color. "You *have* seen the guy, right?"

Brittany nodded. "I know. I know. I just said he was totally hot. But I could never date him." She smiled slyly. "It doesn't mean I don't look."

Tracey's mouth opened in feigned shock. "Aha! You look at *my* guy?"

Brittany laughed. "I didn't know he was *your* guy until tonight. I promise I'll find another guy to gawk at."

Tracey flopped back onto the bed. "Don't bother. He's not my guy at all. That's like...the impossible wish that I torture myself with."

"You know something, there are plenty of guys in this school. Who else do you like?"

"Believe it or not, he's pretty much the only guy I ever looked at."

Brittany sat there, a doubtful look on her face. "Seriously? I don't buy it."

"My sister dates Kevin Sinclaire, do you know him?"

"Oh, my gosh! He's the hottest guy in the whole *world*! I've actually known him forever. *Lindsey* is going out with him?"

"Yeah. They started up last spring and he was just over the other day. He just got back from Japan."

"And you think your sister's boyfriend is cute?"

"No...I mean...well, yeah, he's obviously gorgeous, but he has a friend, Tony. They all call him Yavo, except my sister, who calls him Antonin because she's an idiot. But he is really funny and really smart, and he's super strong. You should see his muscles."

Brittany gave her a knowing look. "Ahhhh! So you like guys with muscles, huh?"

Tracey smiled shyly. "I guess so, yeah. I mean, not huge guys, like bodybuilders, but you know."

"Like football players?"

"Exactly."

"Blonde hair? Brown hair? Red hair? Any preferences?"

"Not really. Matt has blonde hair. Tony has really dark hair, brown or black. I guess I don't care all that much."

"I don't care either. I guess I like blonde slightly more, but it doesn't really matter to me either. Eyes?"

"Light eyes, definitely. Although...Kevin's eyes? Oh my god, I could stare at them for hours."

Brittany nodded vigorously. "You're exactly right about that. What color is that anyway?"

"Green? I don't know." Tracey shook her head. "I feel like I'm looking into one of those antique green bottles. They're not really light though. I don't know. Lindsey gets to stare at them as much as she wants. Do you believe that?"

Brittany laughed. "Lindsey's a really pretty girl. It's not that big a surprise."

Tracey rolled onto her stomach, her feet in the air behind her. "I guess. What about you? I thought you had a boyfriend last year."

Brittany made a face. "I'm technically not allowed to date until I'm sixteen, but I think they might trust me enough to let me date someone now if I really wanted to and asked their permission and all that."

"But didn't you date that guy from your church who goes to another school?"

Brittany wrinkled her brow. "You mean Tyler? Tyler Lazgrove. He's a really nice guy. We've been friends since we were babies. He's gone to our church his whole life too. He likes me, even tried to kiss me last year on New Year's Eve."

Tracey grinned. "What happened?"

"Disaster. I wasn't expecting it, so it was pretty unimpressive. He'd never kissed a girl before, so he was nervous, but it wasn't great. Mostly because I wasn't ready for kissing then."

"But you are now?"

Brittany took a deep breath. "I'm *sooo* ready now!"

Tracey laughed. "Wow! How do you know?"

Brittany shrugged. "I don't *know*. Last year I was nervous about school. I was nervous about guys. Tyler and I were sort of together, but neither of us really knew how to behave. This year I feel different. Less pressure, maybe? I've been through the wringer I guess you could say. I've dealt with all the things the guys say to you and all that. Now I kinda know what to expect and I just want to...I don't know. I just want tooooo…"

"Kiss!" Tracey shouted, laughing.

"Exactly," Brittany laughed. "With the right guy, obviously. I don't want to be pressured to have sex. I don't want to have some jerk groping me and I have to fight him off all night. I just want to have a boyfriend who will kiss me and hold me and spend time with me."

Tracey laid her head down, visualizing what that would be like. "Mmmmm. Me too."

Brittany came close and put her forehead against Tracey's. "Here's the deal. We both have to get boyfriends this year, kay?"

Yeah, Trace, kay? Well?

"I don't know if I'm ready for that."

"I'm kidding, Tracey," Brittany said blandly, sitting up. "We don't need boyfriends."

We don't? What the..?

"Then why are we talking…?"

"Because *they* are talking about *us*. About girls. That's pretty much what everybody does."

Chapter 6

For the rest of camp, the tensions were high between Matt and Kevin. The coaches had gotten wind of their fight and it did not go well for them. They each spent half the following day doing excruciating exercises before being allowed to rejoin the team. Matt spent the entire time staring daggers at Kevin, who simply used the exercise time as just a further opportunity to strengthen himself. When they were on opposite sides of the ball in drills and scrimmages, many of the players expected them to come to blows after every play, but they never did. What did happen was Matt's play suffered. He was dropping balls he would normally catch. He was caught out of position. The coaches were all over him and he was getting increasingly frustrated.

Kevin, on the other hand, was performing brilliantly. His speed and quickness was no match for even the experienced varsity players trying to cover him. He caught every ball that got near him and was very difficult to bring down. On defense, he was a fierce hitter and relentless in covering his territory. The coaches saw him as a potential starter for the varsity, which was high praise indeed for a freshman at Kendall High.

*****

The programs surrounding varsity football at Kendall High School were almost as intense as the football program itself. Being a member of any of the supporting programs gave you a status that was unusual for a kid. If the varsity players were royalty in Kendall Township, the supporting groups were the royal court. Many citizens of the surrounding local towns wondered how all of those kids could buy into such a bizarre scene. Why would an entire Township, so big, with such a diverse population, come together so completely around something so ultimately meaningless?

Brittany often wondered this herself. Having been born and raised in Kendall, she was used to the hype that the football season always brought, but over time it had grown into a full blown hysteria and she knew that it was only getting more and more out of control. Last year she had not made the varsity cheer squad. She had found herself strangely disappointed, not only that she hadn't been good enough to make the top squad, but she actually couldn't help but wonder what it was like to be one of the elites. This year, she was determined to make it.

She was warming up out on the field next to Keisha Mays, a new student to Kendall High this year. Keisha was a sophomore as well, and a phenomenal cheerleader. She was loud and happy, and loved to dance. She was also a well trained gymnast. As far as Brittany could tell, she would be a shoe-in for the varsity team. The two had met on day two of camp, when they were paired together for drills. They had gotten to talking and became fast friends. Brittany was actually hoping to introduce her to Tracey, but the drill team never seemed to be around the cheer squad.

"Hey, sister," a couple of cheerleaders called out as they strode past the stretching girls. They crossed themselves and giggled as they walked away.

"Hi, guys!" Brittany called out after them, smiling as they glanced back at her with strange looks on their faces. Then they laughed again and walked off.

Keisha was frowning. "Okay, that's about the tenth time I heard them call you 'sister'. Why do they call you that?"

Brittany shook her head and shrugged. "You know..."sister", like a nun?"

Keisha frowned. "I thought you were a Christian."

"I am," Brittany replied. "But if they're going to make fun of me, 'sister' seems like a harmless enough nickname. It could be a lot worse around here, believe me."

"And you just put up with it? You were even smiling."

Brittany grinned. "I smile at them and wave and all that because then I can pretend I'm friends with them. I say hi and bye to them. I laugh at their jokes, well, the ones that aren't raunchy. It makes them wonder what they're doing wrong because they think they're insulting me and I don't get it."

Keisha laughed, shaking her head. "Are you serious? Why bother?"

Brittany shrugged. "I don't know. It's better than fighting with them, I guess."

"If you say so."

Tracey had a newfound confidence, both in dancing and her drill team work. Sure, it was dancing, and not all that complicated dancing at that, but it was still fun. There was an energy surrounding the program that she could not put her finger on. She knew that the entire Township worshipped the football team, but she never dreamed that the energy would extend to the girls' programs as well. She really enjoyed the excitement that all the girls seemed to have. They were happy to be putting this time in, perfecting their routines, working on their technique, and generally having a great time with one another.

The coaches were very interested in her and seemed genuinely eager to get her working with the varsity squad. Before the first week was over, Tracey was basically on varsity and the lead dancer in all routines. She would lead the band out for each game. She didn't know exactly what that meant, but she was sure it would be terrifying. She tried not to be anxious about it. People were watching her and they wanted her to be a part of their program. That was what mattered. She was actually making friends. She was actually happy. Miss Kelly had stopped by several times to peek in and make sure Tracey was comfortable and loose. When she saw that the shy redhead was finally talking to the other girls and even working with them on the various techniques involved with some of the routines, she kept her distance. She didn't want to interfere. Tracey had to ultimately sink or swim on her own.

At home, her mother and sister were seeing a vastly different Tracey. They were used to a loving, caring Tracey, who was constantly alone, not quite depressed, but never too cheerful. Her happiness had always seemed to derive from how well her family was doing, but really never from her own experiences. Even her dancing seemed to come from an exterior source. Lindsey, who was never one to give heartfelt…anything, had even managed to sit her down and tell her how happy she was that Tracey seemed to be making positive changes. Though that could have been a dream. Everything seemed so surreal these days, it was possible that Lindsey had never made those comments. Her mother was always so busy that things often took more time to get noticed by her. However, one evening she appeared at Tracey's door and they had a long talk about what was going on in her life. The highly intellectual Abigail had actually come close to tears as Tracey expressed her recently acquired joy and happiness. All in all, Tracey was walking on clouds as week two came to a close.

"Hey, girl!" Tracey whirled around. She was walking toward the parking lot where her mother had parked and was waiting for her. Brittany came hurrying up to her. They hugged.

"You look great," Brittany said, looping her arm through Tracey's and walking with her.

"Thanks. What are you up to this weekend?"

"*We*…are hanging out tomorrow. Wanna sleep over?"

Tracey considered. "Why don't you sleep over *my* house? You haven't met my mother. I told her all about you. Plus Lindsey is dying to see you again."

Brittany wrinkled her forehead. "Really?"

Tracey stopped walking and turned to look at her, slightly amused. "No." She shook her head. "No, of course not. It's *Lindsey*. She only cares about Kevin Sinclaire."

Brittany laughed. "I don't know why I fell for that."

"So, you're coming over?"

"Of course. Chinese?"

"Yum."

Brittany showed up about fifteen minutes before Abby Overton arrived with a big bag from the Golden Buddha Chinese restaurant, which was generally considered the best Chinese restaurant in the world by the people of Kendall and anyone else who tried it. Tracey and Brittany sat at the kitchen table with Mrs. Overton. Even Lindsey chose to sit with them, a bemused look on her face. Dinner was usually not a family affair unless there was a problem requiring a family meeting.

The conversation remained light-hearted as Abby Overton asked the girls about everything that was going on. They told her about the programs they were involved in and how tough the past week's workouts were. Tracey actually enjoyed having this conversation. Her mother was seldom mentally available for idle chats even with her daughters. It wasn't that she had no interest. Her work just consumed her. She was always busy. But tonight Abby was just a regular mother, not all that much different from Mrs. Morgan.

"So, girls," she asked. "How does our football team look this year?"

"Very cute," Tracey said, giggling. Brittany laughed along with her.

Abby chuckled. "Anyone in particular?"

Tracey nudged her sister. "Number twenty-seven looks pretty good in *his* uniform."

Lindsey's face began to turn red. She was about to make a wisecrack, when her mother burst out laughing.

"It's okay, Sweetie. All the girls will be looking at the boys in those uniforms. Why do you think women watch football?"

Lindsey scrunched her face. "You only watch it because Rick watches it."

Rick Reading was Abby's boyfriend for the past two years.

"That's not true. I actually *like* the game. I like sports in general, though I was never any good at them. You girls are far more athletic than either your father or me. I don't know where you get your athleticism actually."

"Anyway," Tracey said. "We're going to the field tomorrow afternoon." She turned to Lindsey. "You're coming too. You're going to support your boyfriend."

"You just want to watch Matt Kildare."

Brittany put her hand over her mouth to hide the grin.

Tracey didn't miss a beat. She had known it was coming. "Yeah, so? One of these days, I might even talk to him."

Lindsey smiled sweetly. "Now *that* I would come to see."

*****

The first string offense was tearing apart the defense. It wasn't a totally fair fight since several first string defenders were playing offense, so they were beating up on a bunch of second string players. Nevertheless, the second string ought to have been at least competing. Right now, they looked like they were asleep.

Kevin and Tony stood on the sidelines with the rest of the second team. They were learning the offenses and defenses along with the rest of the new players. This time was supposed to give them a look at how the Cobras played, how the shifts were executed, where each man was to be positioned at every moment. They watched as the first team offense decimated the defense. Kevin and Tony were getting very impatient watching the slaughter.

Six more plays and six more big gains later and Coach Sommers, who was in charge of the defense, was ready to pull his hair out. "Yates and Taylor! Sit your butts down! Sinclaire, get in there! Yava...Yav...Whatever your name is, get in there!"

Kevin and Tony didn't need a second invitation. They snapped their helmets on tight and sprinted to the defensive huddle, ignoring the catcalls coming from the offense, who smelled blood with a couple of freshmen on the field. Ozzie Winfred, Middle Linebacker and defensive captain had a grin on his face.

"You ready, freshmen?" he said, he said in his harsh, captain's voice. Without waiting for a response, he called the defense and everyone got to their positions. As the offense came to the line, Kevin could see grins on their faces and knew immediately what the play was going to be. It was like new life had been injected into the defense. Kevin and Tony were all over the field, smashing into anyone that got in front of them. That got everyone excited and the defense began to push the offense around.

This didn't sit well with Matt Kildare, who had finally had enough of Kevin and these freshman punks. Who did they think they were? A Pop Warner championship was nothing. It was time to show them what Kendall High football was all about. On the next play, he shoved Kevin aside and took off down the field looking for a long pass from Mike Doyer. Just as the ball got there, Kevin ran up and knocked it away. They tried it again on the very next play, and this time Kevin intercepted the pass.

For the rest of the scrimmage, Matt found himself blanketed by Kevin Sinclaire. He could not get away from him. When he did manage to catch a ball, Kevin was there to pummel him to the ground. He had to admit, the kid hit like a sledgehammer. He was getting frustrated.

When the coach switched Matt to defense and Kevin to offense, Matt found out just how good Kevin really was. He was faked out several times, resulting in scores for the offense. When he played tighter, Kevin used his martial arts skills to break free and make even more plays. Every time Matt thought he had Kevin lined up for a big hit, Kevin made a slight move and left him grasping at air. Any time Kevin got past him, Matt was left behind. He couldn't keep up with the speed Kevin had at his disposal.

On one play, Kevin caught a short pass and was quickly grabbed by Matt, who tried to bring him down, but Kevin muscled forward, refusing to be taken down. Ultimately, the two of them went down to the ground together, Kevin landing on top of Matt, who didn't take kindly to it. He threw Kevin aside and then as Kevin stood up, Matt shoved him hard. Before Kevin could respond, the other players got between them and kept them apart.

*****

The drill team's routines were really getting tight now. Tracey was given some major solo routines that she even got to help choreograph, so she was very excited for Friday's game. Though the drill team would not be performing at the game since it would take place at the Holy Trinity field in Geffney, Tracey and her teammates, Melinda, Skylar, and Laney, would lead the team out of the locker room. They would be dressed in their sleek silver and black outfits and at the signal they would run out onto the field ahead of the Cobras, doing their flips, handsprings, and twirls as the players ran out behind them through the gauntlet of cheerleaders who would be shaking their pom-poms and cheering them on. This would be the closest she had even been to Matt Kildare and she was determined to look her very best and perform flawlessly in front of him.

Like he'd ever notice.

Lindsey was nervously counting the days until game time. Kevin had become scarce since his visit two Saturdays ago. He was fully preoccupied with football. She understood, sort of. She had not been with him the previous year, when he had played on that championship team everybody kept talking about, so she really had no idea how it worked during football season. Maybe she had been spoiled with all of the attention he had paid her last spring. Maybe you just had to deal with it during the football months and then make up for it during the off season. She didn't really know what to think, but she did know that watching Kevin practice on Saturday had changed something in her mind. She had always considered football to be a brutal, barbaric activity. But watching Kevin and the varsity squad, she began to see the beauty of the sport. At least, she saw how it *could* be beautiful. Kevin certainly played the game with a grace that seemed at the same time unique while right at home amongst the violence of it all. She could not wait to see him play under the lights in a real game.

She was a little nervous about wearing his jersey. Everyone would be sure to see *that*. She could already hear everyone in town talking about her boyfriend, how great he was going to be and all that. She wouldn't know what to say to someone who tried to talk to her about football *or* Kevin. But she couldn't break the tradition. Girlfriends wore their boyfriend's jerseys. That was the tradition in Kendall. Players who had no girlfriend would still offer their jerseys to females, often family members, friends, or perhaps girls they liked. This was actually a great way for the shy players to meet a girl. Tradition almost guaranteed that they would accept and it could really open up lines of communication. Having a black and silver jersey worked wonders for those who wore them. In any event, their Brette Girl would always be willing to wear it. At least that way you were guaranteed to have a very pretty girl wearing your number.

In Kendall Township, the Cobras actually sold jerseys out of their school store. You could buy any number you wanted and could even put your own name on it. Each year they probably sold two or three hundred black and silver jerseys. When a particularly good player came through the program, those sales always surged. The stands of Kendall Township games were always filled with black and silver jerseys.

Monday began the final week of practice before game one against the Trinity Crusade. The entire town was on edge, excited about the start of a new season, but nervous about the first game. Trinity was a monster team that hadn't been beaten in over two years. Kendall High was a school with a rich history, having won their share of championships, but it had been a long time since they had really competed with the best schools. Kevin Sinclaire was intent on changing that. He was focused on winning. The team had begun to feed off his intensity. They had begun to gel together as a unit.

Matt Kildare was a different story. He was probably the only player not positively impacted during this week. He was not making waves. He was not pushing the younger boys around. He was not yelling at them. In fact, he barely spoke at all. He played his position, ran his routes, and did his best, but he was not fully into it. He was seeing his team changed right before his eyes. He was seeing his opportunity for greatness slipping away and felt like there was nothing he could do about it. He was alternately angry, depressed, and apathetic. His mood swings caused him to lose sleep. He could not remember the last good night's sleep he'd had. As the week progressed, his insomnia got worse and worse. He'd even bought some of those over-the-counter sleeping pills that were supposed to help. They made him super tired, but he still could not find rest so he threw them away. As Friday's game approached, he began to wonder if he should just quit. That would surely remove the pressure, though the entire town would hate him, and his dad would probably disown him. No, he had to stick it out, at least for now.

Chapter 7

As excited as the Kendall community was to get the high school football season underway, they knew that their Cobras had a very tough matchup for game one. The Trinity Crusade won the state championship the previous season and were seeking to continue a two year unbeaten streak. They humiliated the Cobras the previous season and were expected to do the same again tonight. As the Kendall fans streamed into the stands on the visitors side of the field, the home fans taunted them with loud chants, reminding them what happened last season when these two teams met. The Kendall fans did their best to put up a brave front, but they knew what was coming. Everyone in the area who followed high school football had written this game off for the Cobras.

The Cobras were running through their pregame warm-ups when the Crusade filed out onto the field. They liked to try to intimidate their opponents even before the game started. Some of their guys walked right through the Cobra's as they were running their warm-up drills. Kevin, catching a ball right near one of them had no intention of being intimidated. He caught the ball and slammed into the unsuspecting Crusade player, knocking him several feet back and to the ground. For a second, no one could believe what had happened. The Crusade were known for this kind of rudeness, but they had never been called out on it. Now, they had a player taken out right in front of them. Kevin Sinclaire stood, staring defiantly at the Crusade team, his arms spread.

Several of the Crusade players came at Kevin, who stood his ground and began grappling with them. In the struggle, his helmet was knocked off so his head was exposed. He didn't back down at all. Within seconds, both teams were at it, pushing and shoving all over the field. The player Kevin had knocked down was Zach Higgins, star wide receiver for the Crusade, who was being scouted by most major colleges for a scholarship. He jumped up and came right at Kevin, shoving him. Kevin shoved right back. Coaches and refs quickly got in between them, trying to pull them apart, but the two were grasping one another's shirts and pads.

"You think you're tough?" Higgins said as he was pulled away. "I'm gonna break you in half, you little punk!"

"You go ahead and bring it."

"We'll finish this out on the field tonight!" Higgins screamed. "You're dead!"

"Keep it cool, kid," Coach Van Pelt said quietly, his arm around Kevin's shoulder's to keep him moving away from the Trinity line. "Let's not show them too much too soon, huh?"

"Yes, sir," Kevin replied, picking up his helmet and strapping it back on. He was calm on the outside, but inside he was seething. *Control,* he thought silently. *Reign it in, until it's time.* He took some deep breaths and got back into line with his team.

"You're crazy," said Scott. "Make sure your team is close by if you're gonna start something like that."

"Yeah," added Anquan. "Don't try to take em all on yourself. Maybe if we beat em up, we can keep the score close."

Kevin quietly said, "It's not going to be close."

"Ha!" Anquan laughed. "Das the spirit." Then he looked closer at Kevin. "Oh, you mean you think *we* gonna win this thing?"

"Absolutely."

Anquan shook his head. "Well, you got some guts, I'll give that to ya. But these guys are good…real good, so just play. Try not to piss em off too much."

Kevin smiled slightly and nodded.

From up in the stands, Lindsey and Abby Overton saw as Kevin stood toe to toe with what looked like the entire Holy Trinity football team. Lindsey was relieved to see the scene break up before a fight started, but wondered if a game that started out this way could possibly end well. Tensions were high on the Kendall side. Over on the Trinity side of the field, the fans were expecting another Crusade blowout and were really just hoping to see some good old fashioned fireworks by their boys.

Kevin moved into position in the middle of the field and deep. His job was to keep the play in front of him and not to allow a deep pass to get behind him. He watched the Trinity players closely as they came to the line. First the quarterback, then the receivers. He took a step or two back. It was definitely a pass, but probably not a deep one. Zach Higgins, their main deep threat was shifting to the slot position. Kevin made sure that there was plenty of field in front of him that the quarterback could see. When the quarterback looked across the line at him, he moved back even further. He knew where the play would go.

"*Huuuut!* HUT!"

The ball was snapped and Zach Higgins came off the line full speed, sending Tony racing back, but then Higgins cut to the inside, which was wide open. Landers saw that his man was open and set to throw. The ball came out fast and a little high, but Higgins reached up and snatched it out of the air. That was the last thing he remembered, because Kevin Sinclaire had the play figured and from the snap of the ball he was running full speed to where Higgins and the ball would meet. The collision was violent as Kevin hit *through* Higgins just under his outstretched right arm into his ribcage. The ball went flying incomplete as Higgins doubled over Kevin's shoulder and then snapped back toward the ground as Kevin continued through the tackle. It was a clean hit, but Kevin heard the sickening crunch of bones cracking and immediately began waving for the Trinity medical team to come out as soon as the play was over.

Lindsey could not believe the violence of the hit by her boyfriend. It frightened her how fast he had run into the other boy. Those around her were screaming their approval so it was obviously a good thing. Apparently this kid was the best player on the Trinity team. It looked as though Kevin had knocked him out of the game. Lindsey couldn't believe that Kevin walked away from the collision. Abby looked concerned about the other boy. The funny thing was that going to the game, they had discussed *Lindsey's* fears that *Kevin* would get hurt.

Zach Higgins finally came around. The medical staff were taking no chances. They called for a golf cart with a flat bed on the back and lifted Zach Higgins up and onto it. He was strapped to the stretcher, his head immobilized, which was standard procedure whenever loss of consciousness happened. The medical team wanted to be absolutely careful with head and neck injuries just in case. After the ambulance took Higgins away, the game resumed.

The Trinity offense never really got going. Their all-star team was taking a beating as the Kendall defense, led by the efforts of Kevin Sinclaire, got bolder and bolder. Sinclaire's style was having an impact and creating an identity of sorts. Holy Trinity managed to keep from turning the ball over for the rest of the first half, but near the end of the half, they got into trouble again. As usual, it centered around Kevin Sinclaire. It was third and two. The Trinity offense had not been successful throwing the ball at all, but their running game was helping them to move the ball a little. They needed this first down to give them a chance to get into scoring position. Kevin took off just as the ball was snapped, racing straight towards the line at full speed. He met the Trinity running back head to head at the line of scrimmage and stood the bigger boy up for a second before driving him straight backwards and into the ground. The ball flew from his hands and the Cobras recovered it.

The Kendall Cobras took a 28-0 lead into the locker room at halftime.

Lindsey had worn a sweatshirt over the #27 jersey Kevin had given her. It wasn't really breaking the tradition to have something over it, she had reasoned, although right now, for some reason, she was feeling the urge to take her sweatshirt off. Perhaps it was a tinge of pride that it was her boyfriend out there doing all the damage. She felt somewhat guilty that his number was not represented in the sea of black and silver as it ought to be. She quickly took the sweatshirt off. Her mother hid the amused look that crept onto her face as she observed her daughter's transformation.

Lindsey and Abby hurried down to the refreshment counter as the two teams hustled off the field and into the locker rooms, which were actually in the high school itself. As they stood in line, Lindsey noticed that she was getting a lot of attention all of a sudden, both from Kendall Township fans as well as the Holy Trinity faithful, who were milling about. There were whispers, fingers pointed, and looks thrown her way. The Kendall fans were learning all about #27 tonight, and if she was wearing the jersey, that meant something special to them. Abby and Lindsey were treated to their food and drinks by a stranger when they finally got up to the front of the line. The man must have been seventy years old, and he didn't even introduce himself. He just tipped his hat to Lindsey, gave Abby a polite smile, took his wife's arm, and walked away.

Tracey and Brittany saw the whole scene as they approached. Tracey had spent the entire first half hanging around where the cheerleaders were stationed, watching Brittany and her team cheer the Cobras on. She was excited to see Lindsey proudly displaying Kevin's number. The way he was playing, he deserved to have his number represented.

"Did that guy just buy your food?" Tracey asked.

"Can you believe that?" Abby asked.

"Believe me," Brittany said. "If Kevin is a star on this team, Lindsey will be treated like a princess all over Kendall. She'll never pay for anything."

Lindsey was shaking her head in disbelief. "I guess I could get used to that."

They all laughed. Tracey decided to spend the second half with her sister and mother, so they all walked back up to their seats.

"So, Lindz," Tracey asked. "What do you think of Kevin now?"

Lindsey shrugged. "I can't figure out whether to love all this or not. He's a scary guy to watch out there."

Beginnings

The first half had been a flurry of action. The second half was a study in control. Lindsey felt like she had been sucked into a different world. The Kendall fans had initially been as stunned as the Trinity fans. In the second half they went absolutely crazy. It had taken them a while to realize that this was for real. Number twenty-seven had galvanized them. He was all over the field, hitting opposing players on every play. It was like someone had released a psychotic demon and he was terrorizing the Trinity squad on both sides of the ball. Even his own teammates didn't know quite what to make of him. The defense began to play with a reckless abandon, flying around the field and swarming to the ball. They didn't give the Trinity Crusade any room at all to breathe.

In the end, Kevin had completely taken over the game. What the Kendall fans were taking away from this was that they had a new star in town. Kevin Sinclaire looked like the real deal. It had been a very long time since the Kendall defense had been scary. Their best teams over the past decade or so had always been more finesse than anything else. When Kendall had won their previous championships they had done so with speed and explosiveness. Now they seemed to have a guy who was a big time hitter, who wouldn't back down. But the most important factor he had brought to the game was his attitude. He had shown the Cobra team how to attack. By the end of game one, they were attacking relentlessly and mercilessly. By the end of the game the VENOM chants were in full throat.

As the Kendall Cobras filed into the locker room, there were shouts and hoots as they celebrated the victory over the state champs. For the seniors, this game meant a whole lot more than just a single victory. They had suffered three consecutive humiliating defeats previously at the hands of this team, including a 70-12 loss last year. These memories made this win all the sweeter. No one, including themselves had given the Cobras any chance at all to win this game. It had been checked off as a loss from the day the schedule came out. For the coaching staff, the victory meant at least for the next week, the town would worship them. Wins like this one would mean more money for the program and far more support from the township. The stands should be full for the home opener next week.

For his part, Kevin collapsed into a chair in front of his locker in the Trinity visitors' locker room. He had given everything he had on every play. Now he was exhausted, mentally and physically. His teammates slapped him on his back, his knees, and his head. On the field he was tireless. Now he could barely lift his arms to remove his gear. As he struggled out of his shoulder padding, Anquan Griffin came and sat down on the bench across from him.

"Man, you put on a show to-*day*!" He broke into his famous huge grin, holding his hand up in the air, waiting for Kevin. "Ain' none of us know you was this crazy."

Kevin put his hand out for Anquan to slap it. "I don't know about all that. I was just playing ball."

Anquan laughed loudly. "Yeah, you was. You see how scared they was though? Second half, they ain even wanna play no more. That was *you*! Ain' none of us thought we was gonna win. You the only one came out ready to play." He looked back over his shoulder. "Hey Mike! He say he was just playin ball! Ha, ha, ha!" He held up his hand and slapped Kevin's one more time, this time grasping it and shaking it, pulling Kevin in for a quick shoulder bump.

Mike Doyer came over and slapped Kevin on the back. "Unreal game, kid. I've never seen anything like that. You really do like to hit, don't you?"

Kevin shrugged. "Hard to play football unless you do, I guess."

Mike smirked. "You'd be surprised. You really seemed to zone out though. What happened out there?"

Kevin shrugged again. How could he even begin to explain it? "I don't know. It just kind of happens. Hard to explain."

Mike nodded. "Cool. I hope it happens every game cause I'm gonna be looking for you."

As the team exited the locker room and headed down the hall toward the side entrance of the school, where the bus was waiting to take them back to Kendall High School, they saw the crowded parking lot through the glass doors. Andrea Frollier came running up to Coach Shultz.

"Coach. They're out there waiting for you all."

Coach Shultz peered down the hall through the doors. "Who?"

Andrea shrugged. "I don't know. Everyone. I don't think anyone from Kendall has left yet."

Coach straightened up his tie and turned to his team. "Well then...straighten up everyone. Look sharp. Look like winners. Try to act like you've won a football game before."

The team filed through the glass doors in two lines, side by side. The Kendall crowd cheered for them and cameras clicked as reporters struggled to shout out their questions to the coach and team. Coach Shultz stopped to answer questions while the assistants guided the players through the crowd to the bus. They didn't want to have the players talking to the press just yet.

As they began filing onto the bus, Kevin caught sight of his mom and step-father in a heated conversation with a couple of men. He stopped in the middle of the bus, leaned on a seat, and peered out through the window. Anquan leaned with him.

"Who's that? Your mama?"

Kevin frowned. "Yeah, and her husband. But what's going on? Who's that guy?"

He was about to take his seat when one of the guys began to shout loudly enough to be heard by those outside the bus. Many in the crowd turned to see what was going on. Kevin stiffened when he saw the guy get in his mother's face and yell at her. From the comments in the crowd, Kevin realized that the bigger guy was Zach Higgins' father, Frank. Kevin had knocked Zach out of the game on one of the first plays and he had been sent to the hospital. Now his father had decided to pick a fight with Kevin's parents over it? Kevin felt Anquan's hand tighten on his shoulder.

"Chill, man."

Kevin pushed down his anger, and watched as his step father, Jeff, stepped in between the guy and his mother. The man was much bigger than Jeff, and began pushing and shoving him around, tripping him on the curb and sending him sprawling to the ground. In the pushing and shoving, Kevin saw his mother lose her balance and go tumbling to the ground as well. He completely lost it at that point. Shrugging off Anquan's hand, he scrambled off the bus, the other players jumping out of his way. The coaches tried to grab him, but he shoved their hands aside and strode purposefully toward the big guy who had knocked his mother to the ground. The crowd of people parted as he quickly moved through them. No one wanted to be the one who tried to stop him.

"Hey!" Kevin shouted. The guy turned toward him. Kevin sped up slightly. "Yeah, you! You knocked *her* down! Why don't you try knocking *me* down?"

When Higgins realized that it was Kevin heading toward him, he lost all control and even though some tried to hold him back, he came at Kevin, ready to beat him to a pulp for what he had done to his son.

"Come on, you little cheap-shot punk!"

Just as they came within range of one another Kevin leaped into the air and came down with his right foot and then his left foot into the chest of the bigger man, sending him hurtling backward onto the pavement. Kevin landed and rushed forward as Higgins bounced quickly to his feet. Higgins drew back his right arm to throw a punch, but never got the chance. Kevin reached forward and with his left hand grabbed Higgins' shoulder, keeping his elbow out, effectively blocking the punch before it was ever thrown, and using the shoulder as leverage, Kevin jumped up again, slightly, coming down with the heel of his hand in a hammer strike right on the bridge of Higgins' nose. He went down so fast that the first thing to hit was the back of his head, cracking on the pavement with a sickening sound. The force of the blow had nearly flipped him over, so his feet actually touched the ground over his head, folding his neck awkwardly before they snapped back to the pavement. Kevin allowed his momentum to carry him past Higgins, and then simply walked away without ever looking back. He knew it was over. As he approached the bus, there was silence as no one knew how to react. The whole thing had taken seconds to transpire. The coaches gingerly took Kevin and steered him toward a bench off to the side. Karen and Jeff Timmons rushed over to where Kevin was seated.

Calls to 9-1-1 went out as Higgins lay unconscious on the pavement. Team doctors scrambled to apply first aid to the bleeding areas. No one wanted to move him for fear of inflicting further damage. Sirens began wailing in the distance. There was actually a police squad car already on the premises, as there are for all high school football games, but the altercation had occurred on the opposite side of the parking lot, with almost no warning, so the officer never had a chance to intervene. He now did his best to push the crowd back away from Frank Higgins. The sirens grew louder as squad cars began rolling into the parking lot, followed closely by an ambulance. The EMTs quickly rushed to take care of Higgins, while the officers began sorting out what had happened.

Statements were given, contact information secured and within ninety minutes, the Kendall Township football team was on the road back to Kendall High School. Kevin stayed behind with his parents while the officers continued to compile statements from the crowd. TV crews had recordings of part of the incident, which gave the officers a pretty good idea of what had happened. Ultimately they decided to let Jeff and Karen take Kevin home rather than make a hasty arrest. They warned that the prosecutor's office might see things differently and to be prepared for many more questions over the upcoming days.

Chapter 8

They drove home in silence, with Kevin sitting in the backseat, his eyes smoldering as the events replayed in his mind. He hadn't really said a word since the incident. Jerry Hoffinger, of Waldman, Hoffinger, and Smote law firm happened to be a major contributor to the Kendall High School football program and was also on the program committee. He was present for the altercation and had quickly asserted himself as Kevin's representation. He told Kevin to remain quiet and talk to no one without him being present. He didn't have to worry about Kevin tonight because Kevin was in no mood to talk. He was even ignoring his phone, which had been vibrating in his back pack all the way home. He would have to call Lindsey later and talk about what had happened. He just didn't feel like doing it in front of his parents.

The ten mile drive seemed to take forever and he just wanted to get out of the car. The rush of violence was still coursing through his veins and he was having trouble sitting still in his seat. His mother kept glancing back at him, her eyes betraying her fear that things were amiss. She silently prayed all the way home that her son would be okay. She glanced over at her husband, who was also sitting there in his own little world. He didn't look any better than Kevin.

As they pulled into their driveway and came to a stop, Karen turned off the car and said quickly. "Dinner in a half hour. Please shower beforehand because we will need to have a discussion about this after we eat."

The hot spray of the shower stung his back as he rinsed the soap from his body. He let it run over his head and down over his body for several minutes before finally shutting it down and drying off. He looked at his phone. There were *twenty-two* missed calls! He had already texted Lindsey and Tony to let them know that he would get back to them later that night. Most of these calls were probably from friends on the team and possibly coaches. He tossed the phone onto his bed. He would deal with that later.

Dinner was just as quiet as the drive home, for which Kevin was grateful. He had a feeling his mother was upset with him, though for the life of him he couldn't figure out what he could have done wrong. You can't be mad at a guy for defending his mother, could you? After all, he had not used any foul language, which she despised. He had not picked the fight himself. He had not made any snide comments after the fact. He didn't gloat and brag. He didn't see as he had anything to be sorry for. He would just have to wait to see what she wanted to say.

Finally, as the meal was just about done, Karen Timmons brewed herself a cup of coffee and returned to the table. She took a sip and addressed Kevin.

"Sweetheart, I want you to know that I am thankful to have a son that would stand up for me and defend me against anyone or anything. I want to be clear that I am not upset that you stuck up for me. Do you understand that?"

Kevin nodded. "Sure."

She continued. "But I have to say that the violence you displayed was *not* something I am comfortable with. Not at all. You could have *killed* that man. Did you think of that before you charged out after him?"

"Not really, no." He said it so quickly and matter-of-factly that Karen was taken a little off guard.

She stared at him. "That's it? Not really, no? You think that clears things up for me?"

Kevin leaned back in his chair. "I don't know what needs to be cleared up, mom. Some guy decides to confront you and knocks you down. My reaction is to put the guy down as fast as possible.

That's what I train to do. My training doesn't include worrying about how badly the other guy is hurt. The damage done to the guy is not my primary concern. I wasn't trying to *kill* him. But I was definitely not willing to have him get up and flip out on us. He didn't give us a choice. That's all I'm saying."

"Kevin, there's a difference between restraining a guy from hurting your mother and cracking his skull on the pavement."

Kevin shrugged. "Sure there is. The difference is that a guy that size is a little tough to restrain. Just ask Jeff. He tried the nice guy approach, just like you're saying, and it didn't work. What's worse, it gave him the opportunity to *use* his size and strength. Did you see how much bigger he was than Jeff? There wasn't going to be any restraining him."

"So your way was the only way, is that what you're saying?"

"Of course not. But it was the way I had at my disposal after he knocked *both* of you down."

"Honey…"

Kevin stood up. "Look, mom. There's really no debate. A fight is a violent thing. The more violent guy usually is going to win. It's no different than football. It's no different than the world in general."

"The world in general, huh?"

"Yeah, mom. The world is generally controlled by people who are willing to use violence to achieve their goals. The only way to defeat them is to be more violent than they are."

*****

The Penner party was a Kendall football tradition. Archie Penner Senior began throwing this party the very first year his son Archie Junior made the Kendall High School football team back in 1986 and he threw it every year since, even after Junior graduated. Archie Senior loved high school football. He was originally from Midland, in the great state of Texas, where high school football was a way of life. He brought that mindset along with him to New Jersey and found that he was alone in his passion for the sport. That is, until he found himself at Kendall High School. He had spent many a Friday night watching Texas high school football and had come across some wild and manic fans. But the fans at Kendall High School were different. They approached high school football with an attitude bordering on insanity. He was instantly hooked. Within the next year, he had moved his family to Kendall Township and became a Kendall High School football booster.

One thing that Archie found out very quickly was that the Kendall fan base was organized. High School football fans generally are made up of the student body, the faculty, and the parents and family of the players on the team. In Kendall, the fan base included former students and faculty as well, along with just about everyone else in the community. The local social scene often revolved around Cobra football. Archie had a desire to take the existing booster committee to the next level and worked toward really building up a program. Ten years into his mission he found willing support from three former Kendall players: Jerry Hoffinger, Kevin Murphy, and Leo Forsythe, all of whom played on Kendall High championship teams. With Archie leading the way the original Booster Committee was formed. These men set out to ensure that the Kendall players remained in the Township to play for Kendall High School. They accomplished this by creating a variety of college scholarships for players who excelled on the field and in the classroom. They gave thousands of dollars to the football program, and even to the cheerleaders, providing them with top-notch outfits and training equipment, as well as things like choreographers and additional coaching positions. And, of course, they had encouraged and financed the start of the Brette Girls, probably their most successful venture, if they were willing to be honest about it.

One thing the boosters did was to begin a series of traditions for the football season. And tradition number one was the Penner party, which always took place right after the first game of the season, win or lose. The whole team was invited, along with their family. Cheerleaders, Drill Team, Brette Girls, and anyone associated with the football program had an open invitation. The mayor and other local politicians came, there were usually members of the local media present. All of this took place at the Penner estate, which was situated on a huge property right on the lake.

Matt Kildare had been to three of these parties, every single one of them following a season opening loss. Today was the first time the Kendall Township Cobras opened the season with a win in six years. The players all felt pressure on game day, especially the season opener. Expectations were always high, and the fallout from a loss always made for a rough, depressing week. Tonight was different though. This was a celebration, not only of the start of a new season, but of a season opening victory! And against Holy Trinity, no less! The state champs had been slaughtered on their home field. Kendall was in full celebration mode. Except for Matt Kildare.

For Matt, the victory was bittersweet. He really hated the Crusade, having gone through three consecutive humiliating losses over the past three years. This win should have been special, but he had performed so poorly. On top of that, the win was really due to Kevin Sinclaire's efforts. There was really no way of getting around that. Before today, Sinclaire's skills were little more than practice field heroics. Matt had been fairly certain that when faced with the monsters on the Holy Trinity defense, Kevin would surely crumble. But he hadn't. He stepped up his game to astronomical heights. He was so dominant that the other Cobra players began to believe that they too could play with the state champs. But Matt didn't respond in kind. He blew it. He dropped five passes. He couldn't get open. He got jammed repeatedly at the line. He got totally outplayed by the Trinity defender opposite him, while Kevin couldn't be stopped, slowed, or even distracted. And on defense Sinclaire had been even more dominant. By halftime, there wasn't a Trinity receiver who wanted the ball thrown his way. They ran slow routes, not even trying to get open. Their quarterback was left to scramble for his life. Even their running game was too scared to take on the speedy freshman. For God's sake, Sinclaire had knocked two of their biggest stars out of the game in the first half! Oh yeah, then he knocked out one of their fathers who had picked a fight with Kevin's mom. Matt actually respected that, but…Wow! It still took guts for a freshman to go after him like that. Matt wasn't sure he would have had the stones to do what Kevin had done.

All in all, though the team had won the game, Matt felt like he had lost his spot on the team. He was certainly the number two receiver now. Coach would make sure Kevin got plenty of passes thrown his way. Even Doyer, Matt's best friend, would certainly be looking for Sinclaire more and more. It wasn't going to be the senior season he had planned for himself. As he stood on the dock by the lake, he looked out across the water, which was peaceful and sparkling in the full moon. He raised the bottle in his hand to his lips and took a gulp..

"Are you serious? You're drinking?"

He glanced over his shoulder, then turned back toward the lake, putting the bottle on the railing.

She stepped onto the dock in her black suede high heels and her form-fitting black and silver dress. It wasn't exactly a formal gown, but she had certainly dressed up for the occasion. Her long dark hair shone in the moonlight. Emily Vasquez had a face, hair, and body that belonged on the cover of magazines. But tonight, Matt didn't care. She came up behind him and hugged him from behind, pressing her body to his. He quickly pulled away.

"Em, not right now."

She loosened her grip, but didn't let go. "Why? What's the matter?"

He grabbed her hands and physically separated them, stepping out of her grasp and turning to face her. "I'm not in the mood."

She smiled seductively. "I can think of a way to *get* you in the mood." She stepped close to him, placing her hands on his chest, and sliding them up around his neck. Matt, rolling his eyes, quickly grabbed them and removed them, taking another step back. He was leaning against the railing. Emily was not amused.

"What is your problem? You blow me off after the game. You don't return my calls or texts. Now I have to find my own ride here, and I spend a half hour looking for you and find you out here, alone, and drinking. What is this?"

Matt rolled his eyes and turned away.

"Are you drunk *already*?" She grabbed his arm and turned him back around, looking into his eyes. "You *are*! How ridiculous is this?"

Matt backed away, spreading his arms. "I'm not drunk, Emily, okay? Who cares anyway? All right? What is the difference? I looked like a big idiot tonight, while a little freshman punk becomes the big star. I played like a scared wimp. This was supposed to be *my* year. This was the year I was going to make it all happen. Now that's all gone. It's over." He turned to the railing and grabbed the bottle, then turned back to face Emily, again spreading his arms. "Anyway, since my life pretty much sucks right now, I figured I'd drink a little."

Emily nodded, more frustrated now than before. "That's great, Matt. Really great. One bad game and you quit on yourself? I thought you were a bigger man than that."

Matt turned away, tears beginning to well up in his eyes. Self pity, combined with booze makes for an ugly scene. Emily's heart melted. She knew she should just walk away, but they had been through too much together. Well, not really *together*. They had never really been *officially* together. That would imply some sort of commitment on their part. Neither of them were the sort to make commitments of that nature. But they had spent a lot of time together since last year, her freshman year at Kendall. They had a connection that was sort of special. She didn't want to leave him alone right now.

She reached out and touched his back gently. "I'm sorry. That was mean. Can we start this over?" She moved close to him and laid her head on his shoulder. He didn't resist this time, but when she began unbuttoning his shirt, he rolled his eyes and pushed her away firmly.

"Just leave me alone, Em. Okay? I don't want any attention right now."

Emily caught herself before she fell to the ground. "Really? You don't want attention? No problem. Why don't you jump in this lake, you big jerk?" She grabbed the bottle from his hand and drew back as if to throw it.

Matt lurched forward. "Don't even think about it."

"Why don't you try catching *this*," she replied, and tossed it right over his head and into the lake. Matt turned and watched it splash, go under, and then resurface, floating gently out towards the center of the lake.

She then put two fingers to her pursed lips. "Oops! Looks like another *missed* pass by Matt Kildare! Too bad Kevin *Sinclaire* wasn't here to pick up the slack."

Matt's eyes flashed. "You're a snotty little whore. I don't know why I ever started screwing around with you."

Emily didn't flinch. "Yeah? Well don't think too hard about it. It was no big deal. Sort of like the game you had tonight."

He nodded. "Just get away from me before I toss you in the lake along with the bottle."

She shrugged. "No problem. Have a nice life." And she turned away from him. She got about twenty yards away before the tears began to cloud her vision. Fortunately, there were trees blocking Matt's view at this point so he wouldn't get any satisfaction over this. She was glad she managed to hold up as well as she did.

Chapter 9

Kevin was in his shop, sitting on his large rolling bench, talking on his cell phone with Lindsey. He had already gotten back to Tony, who just wanted to make sure he was okay and tell him what a great game he'd had and that he was proud of him for dropping that scumbag who put his hands on Kevin's mother. Lindsey was genuinely concerned for his state of mind. She had been held back from running to him by her mother and Tracey just after the incident. They took her right home where she proceeded to have a nervous breakdown, worrying over how Kevin was doing and whether he had been arrested and was spending the night in jail.

He quickly calmed her down and told her everything that had happened including the conversation he'd just had with his mother.

"So," she was saying. "Is your mom still mad at you? Like, you're not grounded or anything like that are you?"

"I don't think so, Kevin replied. "I think she just worries that I'm going in the wrong direction. I can see her wanting to talk to me about religious things, but she knows I already know what she is going to say."

"Can you ever see yourself becoming religious?"

Kevin shrugged even though he was on the phone and she

couldn't see it. "I don't know. I suppose that if God wants me, He'll just come and get me. It doesn't really matter what we think right now. If God exists, I expect He has the power to change your thinking."

Just then, Jeff walked into the shop. Kevin glanced over and nodded. "Lindz, can I call you back in a little bit?...okay, cool...I'll call you soon...Bye."

Jeff came in and leaned on the workbench against the wall. He looked around the shop. He had to admit that this place was pretty impressive. The boys had done a great job on it.

"Listen," he began. "I just want to say that your mother isn't all that mad at you. You know that, right?"

Kevin shrugged. "To be honest, I don't know what to think."

"Well, she's just worried that you're heading down a dangerous path. This trip to Japan seems to have changed you a little bit."

Kevin grinned. "Really? How?"

"You seem more...I don't know how to say it. You're more sinister now."

"Sinister?" Kevin almost burst out laughing. "How am I more sinister? I don't even know what that means."

"You know exactly what sinister means."

"I know what the word means, yes. But how exactly am I sinister? Because of football?"

Jeff shrugged and shook his head. "I'm just telling you that you seem different and your mother is worried. Other than that, I don't know what to say. I thought what you did tonight was awesome. You stepped up and defended your family. I will stand behind that any day of the week, so we're on the same page there. But your mom sees a real spiritual problem with you."

Kevin nodded. "I see. It's a religious issue. I don't know what else I can do about that. I go to church every Sunday. I sit through Sunday School and then I sit through a sermon in the big church. I don't see myself as a bad son or a particularly bad person. I know there's more to it than that spiritually, but that's not my thing. It's *hers*...and yours. You can't make someone believe. All you can do is make them *behave* the way you want. And I behave, so what else is there?"

Jeff shook his head. "I guess nothing. Anyway, thanks for letting me interrupt your phone call, Kev. Have a good night."

Kevin stood there, in the center of his shop, shaking his head. His mother wanted so desperately for him to believe. He wished he could give her that gift, but he couldn't honestly do that. It seemed strange to him how so many Christians agonized over the salvation of people, all the while claiming to trust in God's divine plan, which was also perfect and un*change*able. He couldn't understand the apparent paradox within which so many Christians existed. If one believed in God and trusted His judgment, then why not pray and ask Him for what you want and then trust that His decision will be the right one? Why all the angst? Of course, Kevin wasn't a parent, so there's that, but it still seemed as though many Christians put themselves through an awful punishment over something they had no control over.

*****

Tracey was bored and uncomfortable. She had come with Brittany and her friend Dylan, but felt like a third wheel. The problem was that Dylan really liked Brittany, but Brittany thought that they had an understanding that they were just friends. Brittany really wasn't allowed to date just yet anyway, but her parents allowed Dylan to take her to the occasional party or dance because they knew he was a solid Christian young man whom they trusted. Tracey could see that Dylan was not happy with that arrangement and felt bad for him. She was kind enough to at least disappear so that he could have some time with Brittany alone. She found a group of cheerleaders and Brette girls, but it just wasn't her crowd. When some football players joined their group, Tracey felt really out of place. She just didn't know how to handle all the smack talk and innuendo involved in these kinds of situations. It wasn't that they treated her differently. They actually welcomed her into their fold. This shocked her most of all. It was as though no one realized that she was the ugly fat girl from Jr. High. She mostly just stood there with a dumb look on her face and tried to laugh when everyone else did, feeling like an idiot the whole time. She finally got tired of the cheerleader talk and eased away from the group after a short time. She wondered if she'd ever be able to get comfortable with these people.

She looked around for Brittany and Dylan, but they were nowhere to be seen. They probably went inside to look for the food. She wished Lindsey were there, but with all that had happened after the game, she was just planning on staying home and talking to Kevin on the phone. He was staying in as well. Everyone at the party was talking about him though. They were talking about what a fantastic game he'd had and what guts he'd had going after the guy who'd pushed his mother down. In a single night, Kevin Sinclaire had become the talk of Kendall. He was a hero and wasn't even here to accept the accolades.

Tracey found a path leading down towards the lake. She took her high heels off and began exploring the path. It seemed quieter this way, so Tracey wandered along the path until she came to a boathouse, and a dock. She stepped onto the dock and went to the railing, leaning over to peer straight down into the dark water. The full moon seemed to cut straight through to the bottom, though all Tracey could see was darkness.

"Don't jump."

The voice startled her, and she quickly swung around to see who was there.

Oh, my God! It's him! Her heart began racing uncontrollably. Her breathing became shallow. Matt Kildare was standing there, smiling, with a wine bottle in his hand. He had slipped away to find another bottle and then snuck right back, doing his level best to remain out of sight of everyone.

"You found my hiding spot."

What do I say? Tracey's thoughts came a mile a minute. *Say nothing! Just don't say a single thing!*

Matt frowned slightly. "Are you okay? You look kind of pale."

Tracey kept her mouth shut tightly. *What are you doing? The man is talking to you! Answer him, you moron!* "Uh, I'm uh, fine…okay…I mean, I'm okay." *You are such an idiot! Babble much?*

Matt didn't seem to notice. "Cool. Mind if I join you?" he asked, stepping up onto the dock.

Tracey was frozen in place. *Weeell? Do you mind, moron? It's only MATT KILDARE!* "Shh…uh…sure," she managed. *Oh, my God. What do I look like right now? Is my hair at least presentable?*

"Want some wine?"

"Uh…Umm, I've never had wine before." *Maybe you should just tell him you want to be alone. Any chance we could be social for one stupid minute, Trace?*

Matt turned to her, his eyebrows raised. "Hmm. Sooo, should

I find you a cup?" He walked down the dock toward the boathouse. "Hang tight. I think this is open." He yanked on the door. It opened and Matt went inside. "Mr. Penner leaves it open just in case some of us want to come down here and make out on his boat."

Tracey gulped. When she didn't respond he poked his head out the door. "That was a joke, by the way."

Tracey nodded. *OMG, you're such a buffoon!* She nervously tried to fluff her hair and straighten her dress out. *Thank God she had dressed up for this! Small wonders.*

Matt quickly reappeared with two Styrofoam cups and poured the two of them generous portions of wine. He handed her one. *I swear to God, if you drop it...* Tracey pushed aside the thought and did her best to steady her nerves. *Matt Kildare was talking to her!* She could not even find the words to describe it in her mind how surreal this was. Matt Kildare was the single hottest guy in the entire school, really the entire *world*, as far as Tracey was concerned. He walked the halls of Kendall High with a cool confidence, his blonde hair and blue eyes making him the quintessential all American. He was tall, muscular, athletic, and had the kind of smile that girls could not get enough of. He also had the reputation of being very loose with the ladies, but they didn't seem to care all that much, as long as he paid attention to them sometimes. Tracey had spent all last year staring at the guy longingly, knowing beyond a shadow of a doubt that she would *never* have a chance of ever being even noticed by a guy like that. Until *right now*. He was here, talking to her, about to share a drink with her. He didn't seem at all repulsed by her presence. In fact, if she didn't know any better, which she had to admit she really didn't, but he actually seemed to welcome her company. He raised his little cup and waited until she raised hers. Then they both took a sip.

He put out his hand. "I'm Matt, by the way."

She almost choked on her wine, but caught herself just in time. She was almost laughing now. "Really?" she said sardonically. *Oh no!* It just slipped out. It was a natural reaction. She immediately wished she could take it back. *You are so stupid, you know that? You're a nincompoop!*

But Matt chuckled. "Yeah. I guess everyone knows me...the great Matt Kildare." He rolled his eyes, shaking his head, almost sadly. He dumped his wine out. "I'm not a real big drinker. It just seemed like the thing to do."

Tracey didn't know what to do now. Her instincts were screaming for her stay put and don't do anything that might upset the evening. *This might be as good as it gets so make it last as long as possible.* But another part was curious. This ultra popular star athlete looked so forlorn and friendly that her compassionate side was beginning to win out. *Don't do it!* She couldn't resist.

Tentatively she asked, "Is something wrong?" *Oh, please don't tell me to go away!*

But he didn't react that way at all. In fact, he seemed eager to talk, to unload the burden that was weighing him down. He sat down on a bench built into the dock right alongside the boathouse. She sat beside him in the light of the full moon. Tracey listened as attentively as possible, trying not to stare too hard into those gorgeous deep blue eyes. Everything else faded away as Matt gave her the details of how his life had been turned inside out due to the arrival of the freshman super star, Kevin Sinclaire. Being upstaged at this point in his career could affect his college options, to say nothing of the status he had in the Township as the star wide receiver for the Kendall Cobras. To lose all that in your senior year made for a depressing start to the season.

Tracey didn't know what to say. She had never experienced popularity or any kind of public success, so she had no way to comprehend what Matt thought he was losing. How do you comfort someone you couldn't relate to or empathize with?

"Well," she began. "I have no idea what that all feels like. That's a different world to me, so really all I can say is I'm sorry."

He brought his eyes up to hers and smiled. "That is actually enough." He reached over and took her hand.

Oh my God! This is not happening! Is he really holding my hand? No way he's holding my hand right now! Keep cool. Please don't blow this!

Though her breathing was labored and her thoughts were once again beginning to scramble and race, Tracey kept an outward calm as much as possible and allowed Matt to take the lead. When he stroked her fingers with his, she responded in kind. When he reached out to touch her face, she closed her eyes and tried to keep calm as his fingers lightly brushed her cheek and then her lips. When he moved closer she thought she was going to have a heart attack, and it was all she could do to keep still.

Matt suddenly stopped, and pulled back slightly. *Noooo! No, no, no! Why is he stopping? It's because he realized who he was about to kiss, that's why.* He looked at her a little more closely. "You haven't done this much, have you?"

She sighed, her shoulders slumping slightly. "Is it that obvious?"

He smiled slightly. "Well, yeah, kind of. But it's okay," he added quickly as her posture slumped even more. He lifted her chin with his fingers. "Do you *want* to kiss me?"

Oh, God, YES! Please don't be kidding me right now!

Tracey nodded shyly. "Yes, but I don't really know how to do it right. I'm sorry. I feel so stupid right now."

Matt gently took her in his arms and held her head on his shoulder. "It's *not* stupid. Tell you what. How about this?" He pulled his head back to look at her face. "I'll start, and you just follow, okay? We'll go really slow."

She took a deep breath. "That actually sounds wonderful." *Oh, my God! Wonderful? It sounds wonderful? Can we try talking like we live in the twenty-first century? A little less Charles Dickens, please!*

He smiled at her. "You're petrified." He brought his hand to her face again, just barely touching her this time. "This is *supposed* to be fun. Just try to relax and let it happen. Don't worry about being good at it."

Tracey felt faint. She closed her eyes and did her best to keep from shaking. "Okay."

He continued lightly touching her cheek and hair. "Do you want to know a little secret?"

She nodded.

He grinned easily. "Even a bad kiss is still pretty good."

Matt abruptly stood up, pulling her gently to her feet. "I have an idea." He led her to the railing. "Do you want to get out of here?"

Is this a trick question? "With you?"

He laughed. "Yes, with me. I really want to kiss you, but...let's make it a real date. You look perfect. Let me take you out and I'll try to make it special for you."

I swear to God, if you pinch yourself and we wake up and this is all a dream...

"You're not drunk are you?" *Hello, wet blanket. We have a saboteur among us.*

Matt laughed. "I was starting to get there earlier, but someone threw my bottle in the lake."

"Oh." *Thank God. Any other thoughts on how we can blow this?* Tracey took another deep breath. "Lead the way."

"Okay. We're off. But first...*this* is how you do it." He took both her hands and pulled to him, placing them around his waist and bringing his hand up to lift her face slightly. He leaned into her and kissed her softly. It all happened so fast, Tracey had no idea what to do, so she just closed her eyes and allowed him to lead. It wasn't a quick kiss either. He kissed her deeply and passionately, caressing her shoulders and back as he did so. It was pure heaven and better than her wildest dreams. When he pulled away, and she opened her eyes, he was looking right into hers, his hand again gently touching her face. She was definitely dizzy, but in a good way. It took ten seconds for her head to clear.

He smiled. "You were perfect. Promise me we can do that a lot more tonight."

My God! You're gonna blow an aneurism and die right here in his arms, aren't you? Not a bad way to go actually...

She laughed, and they walked, arm in arm along the lake, heading for the driveway, where Matt had parked his car. No one saw them leave. They made a clean escape from the party and drove off together into the night.

Chapter 10

Oh, my God! What do I do now?

It was morning. The sunlight was glaring through the large picture windows. Tracey could barely keep her eyes open it was so bright. She lay there, trying to figure out what she was supposed to do in this situation. Matt was fast asleep, laying on his stomach, his right arm hanging off the side of the bed.

Do I wake him?

NO! You do NOT wake him! WhatEVER you do, DON'T wake him!

But what about...?

DO NOT...WAKE HIM!

Ugggh! Geez, he's so cute. Look at him!

Uh, huh. Isn't that how we got here?

Tracey's eyes widened. The reality of what had happened was on her without warning. She looked under the blanket.

Oh, my God!

She frantically scanned the room for her clothes. Her blue dress was fortunately laying on the floor right next to the bed. She carefully picked it up and slipped it over her head, doing her best to not disturb the still sleeping Matt. She slowly got out of the bed and smoothed out the dress, doing her level best to remain calm, though every muscle in her body screamed for her to run away.

Okay. What now?
Shoes?
She looked for her shoes. There was one midway between the bed and the door, and the other was just at the foot of the bed, right next to a couple of other pieces of clothing that belonged to her. She felt sickened by the scene.

Could this be anymore cliché?

She sank to her knees, sobbing softly as she gathered her undergarments. She didn't even know *why* she was crying. She just knew that something was not good about all of this. She stood up, trying to compose herself.

What else?

She checked both ears. Her earrings were still in place.

Pearls!

She nearly panicked, dropping her shoes and clothing as her hands both shot up to her neck. They were her grandmother's pearls, given to her while she had still been alive.

Oh, thank God!

They were securely around her neck.

Is that all you had on?
Why? Is that another cliché?
It was in a movie, I know it.

Tracey stooped down and picked up her things. She stood back up, took a deep breath, and tried to clear her mind. *Okay, what now?*

Get out as quickly and as quietly as you can.

She slipped out the door, leaving it slightly open so as not to wake him with the click of the door closing. She was on the second floor. She made her way down the hall to the steps.

Wait a minute! No one's home right? He did say no one was home, didn't he? Is anyone here? Who could be here?

Matt had been pretty clear last night that his parents had left town right after the game for a weekend in New York, so Tracey was confident that they would not be surprising her. Matt's only siblings, a brother and sister, were older and away in college. No worries there. She started down the steps, taking them as fast as she could move in her dress. At the bottom of the steps, the foyer opened up and she could see the large space to her right and left.

Man, this place is beautiful!

She reached for the front door handle, then hesitated. Something wasn't quite right.

What are you going to do, Princess, walk home? Do you even know where you are?

Her shoulders slumped in desperation. *Now what?*

Tracey was in a tough spot. She had no idea where the Kildares lived. She wasn't calling her mom. No way. She needed time before she could face her mother, not to mention Lindsey.

Oh, God…Lindsey. She'll see right through me.

She definitely didn't want to have to deal with her family until she had some time to process. But she needed to get out of this house and away from the potential humiliation if Matt were to wake up now, with her up, dressed, and downstairs trying to escape barefoot.

The heck with it. Just start walking.

Tracey sat down on the steps in the foyer and put her head in her hands. She really needed to cry her eyes out, but right now was not the time. She doubted she could cry anyway with her adrenaline pumping this quickly. What she needed to do was think. She took several deep breaths, trying to clear her mind.

BRITTANY!

She hopped to her feet, reaching for her purse…

Where's your purse, Trace?

She looked all around her. She couldn't remember if she had brought it in last night.

You know, if you leave your purse, he'll have to bring it back to you…

The thought flashed across her mind unsolicited. It wasn't a bad thought though, *if* she wanted Matt to come and talk to her. She didn't know if she wanted that or not. What if she hadn't been any good at sex? What if he never wanted to talk to her again? What would that make her?

Right now it really didn't matter. Her phone was in her purse and she needed to find it. She rolled her eyes and slowly crept back upstairs, leaving her shoes and things in a pile on the bottom step. At the door to Matt's room, she stopped and listened. She heard nothing and gently pushed the door slightly open, poking her head in to see if Matt was still asleep. He hadn't moved at all. She opened the door a little wider and slipped in as quietly as possible, keeping her eyes on Matt's sleeping body. The sheet covered him up to his waist, leaving his back completely exposed. Tracey couldn't help but stare. He was so beautiful. His muscles, though completely relaxed, were so well toned that she could see every striation clearly.

She was beginning to remember details from the previous night, how she had felt in his arms. She also remembered how scared she had been, how she had felt her body shaking uncontrollably at times. Matt had been nothing like how she had imagined. His reputation and his demeanor in school suggested that he would be self-centered and that he would use a girl selfishly. But he had not been that way at all. He was very gentle with her, always asking her if she was sure, giving her a multitude of opportunities to stop if she had wanted to. She remembered nervously telling him how much she wanted to be with him.

So why not wake him up and talk to him, or better yet, why not climb back into bed and let him *wake* you?

She immediately dismissed both thoughts. What if he rejected her? She assumed he would. Matt could have any girl he wanted. While things had progressed very quickly the previous night, even more quickly than she probably would have liked, she had not gone into any of it blind as to who or what Matt Kildare was. And that was the very reason she did not want to face him right now, in his room, the morning after…

She couldn't see the purse right away. It was not on the nightstand or the dresser. It was nowhere to be seen. She thought for a minute, then dropped to her knees, pressing her cheek close to the ground. She looked under the bed. There it was. She lay flat on the ground and reached under the bed, grabbing the small purse and quickly and quietly standing back up and retreating from the room. Matt never even stirred.

She hurried downstairs, feeling like she was living on borrowed time. At the bottom of the stairs, she pulled out her phone, took a deep breath and found Brittany's number. After several rings, Brittany's sleepy voice came on the line.

"Hello?"

"Brit…It's Tracey. I need you," she said in a hushed voice.

"Hey, Trace. What's up? I can barely hear you."

"I'm sorry I woke you. Please don't be mad at me."

"Mad at you? Why? What's wrong? What happened to you last night? I called and texted you a million times."

"Promise me, Brittany." Tracey went into the kitchen to get as far as possible from the steps so that Matt wouldn't hear.

"Promise what? Tracey, what's wrong?" She was wide awake now, her voice sounding much stronger. Tracey was imagining her friend sitting up in bed now, borderline freaking out.

Tracey's heart was beating so rapidly that she could barely think straight. This was worse than being in Matt's room looking for a purse. She hadn't really thought this conversation through. Brittany was going to flip out.

Yeah, you probably shouldn't call your Christian friend for help getting out of some guy's house after having sex with him...

She couldn't worry about that anymore. Brittany was already on the phone and worried.

"Listen, Brit, I need you to come get me. But not with your parents," she added quickly.

"What? Come get you where?"

Yeah, come get you where, Trace?

Tracey swallowed hard. "I...uh...I'm at...um. Look, I'm at Matt's house."

There was silence on the line. Tracey closed her eyes, imagining the look on Brittany's face. Actually, she couldn't imagine the look. Brittany was always happy and cheerful. If she had an angry face, Tracey couldn't remember seeing it.

"Brittany..."

"What did you just say?"

"Brittany, please..."

"You're at Matt *Kildare's* house right now?"

"Yes," Tracey breathed out.

"And you were there all night?"

"Yes."

"Tracey, you didn't...did you..?"

Tracey sighed. "Yes."

"Oh no."

"Brit..."

"Are you okay?"

Tracey was a little surprised. She had been expecting her friend to start yelling at her over the phone. "I'm fine. I just don't know what to do now. I'm here and he's asleep and I don't want to wake him up. I just want to get out of here. Can you come get me? Is there anyone you can call?"

"Okay, let me think. Who can I call?" After a few seconds she said, "Dylan...I'll get Dylan to come get me and we'll come get you."

Oh great...Dylan...from church. That's all we need.

Tracey nodded to herself. It was all she had right now. "Okay, fine. Do you think he'll come right away?"

"I'll call him now and call you right back."

"Okay. Thank you, Brit."

She switched her phone to vibrate only and waited several agonizing moments until it vibrated. It was Brittany.

"Hey."

"Okay. Dylan's on his way over here. We'll be there as soon as we can. Text me the address."

"Okay. Thank you so much, Brittany."

She pressed "End", then breathed a sigh of relief. Brittany had really come through, although Tracey imagined she was going to have to hear an earful from her once they got safely away from this. At this point, all of that was well worth it as long as Matt stayed asleep for just a little while longer. All she had to do was text Brittany the addre...*Oh, no...*

So, what was that address again, Trace?

How do you figure out the address of a place when you're inside it? It seemed silly, but as she looked around she really drew a blank, and tried not to panic. After all, she was *in* the house. There had to be something...

She looked throughout the first floor rooms and finally came across several magazines on a small hall table. The one on top had what she was looking for. She punched in the address and sent the text to Brittany, who responded quickly with a "thumbs-up" icon. Tracey gathered her things and quietly opened the front door, slipping out and closing it behind her. She walked down the long , winding driveway, thankful at least that Matt's room overlooked the back yard. He wouldn't be able to see her slinking away if he woke up.

Within ten minutes, a dark blue sedan pulled up, Brittany was in the passenger seat with the window rolled down. She smiled grimly at Tracey.

"Hop in." To Dylan, she said, "Take us to my house."

"You got it." Dylan drove in silence. He had obviously been instructed not to ask any questions or say anything at all.

Brittany turned around in her seat. "Are you okay?"

Tracey nodded sheepishly. "I'm fine. Thank you so much for coming to get me."

"Don't worry about it. We'll talk at my house. By the way, you remember Dylan."

"Hi, Dylan. You saved my life. Thank you so much."

"No problem."

*****

Saturday morning Kevin awoke to the constant ringing of the telephone. He had slept in far later than usual, having spent most of the late hours of the night talking to Lindsey, while texting back and forth with Tony on his tablet. He had finally drifted off to sleep around 2:30am, roughly two and a half hours before he usually got up and began his daily routine. When his eyes opened and he saw that it was past nine, he quickly got up and put on a pair of shorts and a tank top before heading downstairs to the kitchen where he saw his mother hanging up the telephone, shaking her head.

"What's up?" he asked.

"Reporters," she replied. "Everyone wants to talk to you about last night."

Kevin chuckled. "They have nothing better to write about?"

"I guess not." She opened the refrigerator door. "Eggs?"

Kevin looked at the clock. He was way behind, but couldn't go without breakfast.

"Sure. Over easy?"

Karen smiled. "You mean Dippy Eggs?"

It was a family joke. Ever since Kevin was a little boy his mom had been making him eggs over easy and cutting up his toast into strips so he could dip them in the yolk. He had always called them "Dippy Eggs". Karen, still constantly called them Dippy Eggs whenever he tried to call them eggs over easy. She was so consistent about it that even Tony had picked up on it and now tortured his own mother with the phrase "Dippy Eggs" and insisted that she cut his toast into strips just like Kevin's mom did for him.

Kevin grinned. "Yes, Mommy. Three Dippy Eggs please." He used his best little kid voice.

"Coming right up, my little punkin." Karen would always win at this game. Mothers simply had the upper hand when it came to embarrassing little nicknames for their children. Kids were really helpless and at the mercy of their mothers whenever their friends were around. Karen Timmons never set out to embarrass Kevin, but whenever he used to stray too close to the line of disrespect, as many kids do, showing off in front of their friends, she would only have to suggest that there was perhaps an amusing nickname she had for him and maybe she should let his friends know about it…It worked every time. But when they were alone, Kevin was only too happy to play along.

"Thank you, Mommy. Mommy, can I have some milk too, Mommy?" Kevin's tactic was simply to see how many times he could say the word "mommy" and maybe he could win by making her laugh first. It almost never worked. She just went about making breakfast with a contented look on her face. For all of his smarts and quick wits, Kevin could never get under her skin as he could with other people. He assumed it must have something to do with the fact that she had nothing whatsoever to prove to him. No matter how smart he was; no matter how strong he was; no matter if he became the wealthiest man ever; she would always be the one who gave him life. She was his mother. She would never be beneath her son. It simply didn't work that way. Mothers were special. To Kevin, mothers were to be revered, exalted above all others.

She placed his plate in front of him. This morning breakfast included several links of breakfast sausage which Kevin loved. She poured him a glass of milk and he dug in, dipping his toast into the yolks and sopping up the yellow liquid before cutting up the white part and downing that. He made quick work of the eggs and sausage and drank his milk. The whole scene took about five minutes. His phone vibrated. It was a text from Tony. He got up and headed for the door.

"I have to work out," he said. "Tony is here."

Karen held up a hand. "Kev, there are reporters all over the place today. Jeff said they were out there when he went to get the paper earlier and they were still there when he left for work a little while ago. Let's not talk to them, okay? Mr. Hoffinger told us to say nothing to anyone as long as there is the possibility of you getting arrested."

Kevin nodded. "Don't worry about me. I don't have any reason to talk to them."

Tony came flying up the driveway on his bike and skidded to a stop right in front of the back deck. He bounded up the steps and came to the sliding glass doors. Kevin slid it open for him.

"What's up, Yavs?"

"Nada." He pounded Kevin's fist. "Hi, Mrs. Timmons, do you know there are a bunch of clowns standing in front of your driveway?"

Karen smiled grimly. "I do, Tony. They've been there all morning."

He nodded, pursing his lips. "Want us to go out there and get rid of them?"

She held back a laugh. "I think it would be best if the two of you would go out back and work out for a while. Mr. Hoffinger is on his way over and he will handle the press for us. Please don't do anything to make trouble."

Tony nodded, and then nudged Kevin. "Have you been online at all?"

Kevin shook his head.

"Oh boy. You're gonna go nuts. Someone posted a video of the fight, I mean the whole thing, online. It's gone viral. I'm talkin over a million hits over night!"

"Are you serious?" Karen said.

"Yes, Ma'am," Tony replied, nodding. "People think Kev's a hero. That Higgins guy is getting skewered, judging by all the comments. I don't think you're in any trouble, Kev."

Karen was pulling up the video on her own tablet. "My gosh," she said. "Look at how big that guy is."

Tony looked over her shoulder. Kevin just stood there by the door.

"You don't want to see it, Kev?" he asked.

Kevin shrugged. "I already saw it firsthand. Come on, let's get to it."

The boys slipped out the back door and made their way back to the workout room behind Kevin's shop. Karen was left there, watching the frightening scene put on by her son from the night before. The video had indeed gone viral. Sure enough, the hit count was now well over one million.

Chapter 11

After Dylan dropped them safely at Brittany's house, the girls made their way up to Brittany's room where Tracey was given a change of clothes, towels, and then sent to take a shower. She was relieved for Brittany's gentle treatment of her in all of this. She had expected some sort of condemnation of her behavior and actually felt like she deserved it. But through it all, Brittany's focus was on caring for her friend.

As Tracey stood in the shower, letting the hot water run down her back, the previous night's events seemed to wash away with the soapy water. She felt revitalized at first, but as she dried off in the steamy room, reality came back, stifling her. She was glad that the steam had obscured her reflection in the mirror. For so long she had treated the mirror as her enemy. In the past few weeks, all of that had changed. Her reflection had become something she began to take pride in. She had begun to see herself as others saw her, pretty. She had begun to see her bright red hair, not as the boy repellant she had always assumed it was, especially when people called her Carrot Top as a kid, but as an attractive feature that made her particularly striking, especially with her soft blue eyes. The boys liked to call redheads, particularly the pretty ones, "Gingers". She liked that. Ginger was the beautiful movie star on the island. Tracey desperately wanted to be in the category of "Gingers" rather than the category of "Carrot Tops".

But right now, in the aftermath of a decision that she was no longer quite sure about, all of the self-loathing that had previously controlled her came flooding back all at once. It was amazing how quickly it came back, as though it had never really left. It must have always been there, lurking beneath the surface, just waiting to bubble back up. Tracey's new found confidence and pride in her appearance didn't replace her previous self image as she thought it had. Instead, it had simply been pushed aside, suppressed by the latest thing, the fad of self worth. Now, in one fell swoop, all of her progress was lost. She felt ugly again. She felt uncertain again. She felt alone again. She felt lost…again.

When she came back into Brittany's room, Tracey was near collapse. Her eyes were red and swollen from constantly being on the verge of crying. The muscles in her neck and jaw felt stiff and sore from trying not to cry. Her hair was a tangled mess. She had forgotten to brush it. She stood just inside the doorway of the room, staring down at the floor, feeling almost unwelcome in her friend's presence. Brittany came off the bed quickly, seeing her Tracey in pain, and embraced her, leading her over to sit on the edge of the bed as Tracey finally broke down, the weight of everything finally consuming her, crushing her spirit.

Brittany said nothing. She just stroked Tracey's hair, removing knots one at a time with her fingers as Tracey struggled to get her sobbing under control. She broke down several times over the next few minutes, the tears endlessly flowing, soaking a large part of the shoulder of Brittany's T-shirt. She didn't care about that. Her friend was in agony. She just wanted to be there, to somehow take her pain away. With tears in her eyes he began silently praying in her heart.

God, I have no words for her right now. I can't take away her pain. I need you to help me. She needs You to speak to her. I'll just screw it all up. Please do not let me say something foolish. Give me wisdom. Just help me, Lord. Please, help me!

Brittany kept her eyes shut in silent prayer for several agonizing moments. All of a sudden, she became aware of the sudden calm and quite in the room. She opened her eyes and realized that Tracey had curled up with her head in Brittany's lap, and had fallen asleep. Brittany hadn't even noticed. She pulled a pillow over and lay back on it, determined to stay with her friend and do whatever she needed her to do. If that meant spending an hour or two watching her sleep, then so be it. She would spend the time in prayer. She would pray that God would call Tracey to salvation and that Brittany would be an instrument in His hands to accomplish that very thing.

It didn't take hours. In fact it took less than one. Tracey's eyes opened nearly forty-five minutes after she had fallen asleep on Brittany's lap. She lifted her head to see Brittany's smiling face, her bright blue eyes twinkling as she stared down lovingly at Tracey.

"How do you feel?"

Tracey tried a smile, but it didn't feel right.

"Like an idiot." She pushed herself up and sat back on the edge of the bed, her legs dangling just above the carpet. She couldn't look her friend in the face right now. "I'm so sorry for all of this, Brit."

Brittany slid forward so that she was sitting right behind her friend, and put her head on Tracey's shoulder, wrapping her arms around her, hugging her tightly. "Sorry for what? You are my friend. I love you. I would have killed you if you *hadn't* called me."

Tracey's hands came up and squeezed Brittany's arms. "So you're not mad at me?"

"Of course not."

"Disappointed?"

Brittany chuckled. "Do you want me to be disappointed? Would it be easier if I started yelling at you, telling you what a slut you are?"

Tracey's hands fell to her lap. "I don't want you to be disappointed. That's worse than being mad. But I know you are, even if you don't admit it. Am I really a slut?"

"Seriously? You had sex *one* time, with *one* guy. That doesn't make you a slut."

"Yeah, but on the first date?"

Brittany sat back and pursed her lips.

"Well...it was lousy judgment, okay? *I* think it was the wrong decision. But I don't expect you to make the same decisions *I* would make. So I try not to judge everything other people do."

They sat in silence for several moments, Tracey's eyes never leaving the floor.

Brittany softly placed her hand on Tracey's shoulder. "Do you want to talk about it?"

Tracey frowned, wrinkling her brow. She turned to face Brittany, swinging her legs up onto the bed, then sitting cross-legged, her arms in her lap. "I just…I can't figure out how I'm supposed to feel here."

Brittany nodded. "This is going to sound stupid, but…"feel" about what exactly? Sex? Matt? What?"

"All of it. I'm confused for some reason."

Brittany nodded again. "That makes sense. It all happened kind of quickly, don't you think? Were you really ready for it?"

Tracey shook her head. "I don't know. It was just so perfect, you know? We met totally by chance down by the lake. He was so sweet and gentle. He was sad and depressed. We talked and…he kissed me."

Brittany nodded in understanding.

Tracey looked at her with a kind of desperation in her eyes. "It was just like you would want it to be, I swear. Everything seemed exactly like in a dream."

It was making Brittany sad to listen to this, but she remained attentive as Tracey told her story.

"He took me to the boardwalk, and we spent an hour or so there, just kissing and talking." Tracey's eyes were glazed over as she recalled how she had felt. She snapped out of it and looked at Brittany. "Have you ever wanted something so desperately?"

"I think I understand."

Tracey shook her head. "I don't think you do. You've always had a life. I've *never* had one. I have always stood off to the side and stared while the pretty girls all got the guys. Last night, for the first time, I was one of *them*. *I* was pretty. He wanted to be with *me*. Guess what? He had even blown off *Emily Vasquez* earlier. He didn't want to be with her last night. But he wanted to be with *me*. That *has* to count for something."

"Are you trying to convince me or you?"

Tracey teared up again. "I don't know. I just want you to understand."

"Tracey, please trust me. I *do* understand. Matt is a seductive guy."

"He didn't seduce me," Tracey said urgently. "It wasn't like that. Believe me, I've heard all the stories about how Matt Kildare can talk a girl into bed. He didn't talk me into bed."

Brittany frowned. "He didn't?"

"Of course not. Don't you understand what I'm trying to tell you? I *wanted* to be with him."

Brittany brought her hand up to her mouth. "Oh."

Tracey nodded. "Now you get it?"

Brittany nodded. "You wanted this to happen right from the start."

"Well, not exactly. I always dreamed of being with Matt, but last night was kind of the dream. I just sort of let the dream happen. He didn't have to trick me or get me drunk."

Brittany nodded. "So if I would have told you yesterday that you were going to sleep with Matt Kildare last night, you would have behaved the exact same way."

Tracey nodded sheepishly. "Probably. What does that make me?"

Brittany shook her head. "It doesn't make you anything. If you want my opinion, it was bad judgment, but you got what you said you wanted, so what can I say?"

"You aren't mad at me?"

"No. I'm not mad. *I* wouldn't have done it, but I can't expect your decisions to be the same as mine."

"What does that mean? That's the second time you said that. You *expect* me to make bad decisions?"

Brittany shook her head. "No. That's not what I mean. I'm a Christian. So hopefully my decisions will be based on my Christian beliefs, which happen to be very different than what the world believes, especially about things like sex and relationships. But how can I expect you, someone who doesn't even believe in God, to do what I would do?"

"So you just have lower expectations for non Christians."

"I don't know if they're *lower*, but definitely different."

"So you don't think I was wrong?"

Brittany shook her head. "I didn't say *that*. But I'm not here to judge you. I want to be your friend. If you're asking me about right and wrong, you're going to hear what the Bible has to say. All I'm saying is that if you don't even believe in God, how can I expect you to act in a way that would be pleasing to Him?"

Tracey shook her head. "I can't figure out why I feel this way. I thought I would be so happy to have finally had something I had dreamt about for so long. And the funny thing is, I *am* happy on the one hand, but on the other hand, I can't seem to enjoy it. Does that make sense at all?"

Brittany nodded. "Actually, it does. I think your problem is that what you did was just unnatural."

Tracey made a face. "Unnatural? Are you kidding? What's more natural than that?"

"I don't mean sex, exactly, but sex outside of marriage is not the way it is supposed to be in my opinion."

"What difference could *that* possibly make?"

"Well, think about how you're feeling. If you and Matt were married, would you have snuck out of his house in the morning? Would you really be sitting here wondering if sleeping with him was a good decision or not?"

Tracey frowned as the argument began to take shape in her head. "I guess not."

Brittany continued. "Forget about religion. What about disease? Do married couples have to worry about catching diseases from their spouse? Not really. Children? It's perfectly okay for a married couple to get pregnant, even if they didn't plan it. It's not okay if you're not married, especially if you're in high school."

Ugggh! Do we have to sit here and listen to this?

*****

Kevin and Tony stretched in relative silence for about twenty minutes. Tony was watching his friend closely. He had seen him fight before, though not with such decisiveness. Now, in the space of three weeks, he had seen a different kind of fighting from Kevin Sinclaire. He had always been able to fight. He had never backed down from one. People generally didn't want to tangle with him anymore. One look from those fierce green eyes was usually enough to back most people down. But now there was a frightening polish to his abilities.

He had always had perfect technique. His training had begun at the age of five, when Sensei had first met him. They had moved into the house next door in Albertson. It was a small house, but it was affordable. The landlord happened to be living next door. His name was Cenzo Tanaka. Every day, Kevin would watch him as he went through his routines in the backyard, which was a small slice of paradise, with a beautiful little plot of perfectly lush, green grass surrounded by amazing plants and flowers. Kevin would sit on his bike in his back yard and just watch as Mr. Tanaka moved. He was mesmerized by the way the man seemed to float above the ground, his movements so effortless and smooth. He began to imitate Mr. Tanaka. He would watch his every move and try to duplicate it. Within a couple of weeks, Kevin was doing the routines on his own, having memorized every step, every movement of the arms and hands, every position of the head. Mr. Tanaka watched him often through the window of his kitchen, impressed by the young boy's efforts and how well he was doing with no training whatsoever.

After several weeks, Mr. Tanaka called to Kevin to come over to his yard. Kevin didn't hesitate. He asked Kevin if he would like to join him and train together with him each day. Kevin eagerly said "yes". Karen Timmons, who was still trying to figure out how she could afford a babysitter for Kevin, had her prayers answered when Mr. Tanaka knocked on her door and offered to watch Kevin every day if he could have the honor of training him in martial arts. With Karen's amused permission, Kevin began his martial arts training in a system that Mr. Tanaka called "Aikido". It was a mostly defensive art, based on the same principles used by Japanese sword fighters. The idea was that every move you could make with a sword, you could do without one, just using your hands. Aikido mimicked sword fighting to a large extent, but was designed as a self defense art. Kevin responded to this training like a fish to water. He had the tall, lean body that enabled him to be very flexible. But his greatest asset, according to Mr. Tanaka, who insisted that Kevin call him Tanakasan, was his mind. Kevin's super fast mind was able to calculate things so quickly that Tanakasan was often amazed by Kevin's reflexes. They trained relentlessly each day, beginning as soon as his mother left for work and ending more or less when she came home. They took breaks for food and water, and Tanakasan offered breaks for Kevin to watch TV or play with toys, but Kevin was not a typical kid. He had little interest in toys. What he *wanted* to do all the time was train.

As Kevin's training progressed, Tanakasan introduced Kevin to the art of Kenjutso, Japanese sword fighting. It was in this system that Kevin's speed and reflexes would be on full display. After several weeks of basic techniques of strike and defense, Tanakasan and Kevin faced one another in the center of the lush grass. Karen Timmons was just getting home from work and looked through the window just in time to see her landlord prepared to attack Kevin with a big wooden pole. She rushed to the door and got to the back yard just as her five year old boy fended off what looked like a pretty violent flurry of strikes by the older and much stronger Tanakasan. She watched in stunned amazement as the two clashed again and again, with Kevin, his bright green eyes flashing in the sunlight, moving effortlessly from position to position, from defense to offense, from parry to counterstrike. After several moments of intense sword fighting, the two backed away from one another, bowed and laid their swords down. Kevin then ran around the fence and came to his mother, who could not find words to describe what she had just seen. Tanakasan merely nodded, bowed slightly to Karen, and went into his own house.

By the time Tony and Kevin met, Tanakasan had already taken Kevin from a five year old prodigy to a level rarely attained by a child so young. He had explained to Kevin much earlier that in this form of training he would not be given different color belts, like some of the other kids who took karate would get. As far as Tanakasan was concerned, you had either mastered the art or you had not. When Kevin was ten years old, Tanakasan presented him with a *hakama*, which is the skirt-like article of clothing worn by Japanese masters. He'd had a relative in Japan make it especially for Kevin. When he presented it to Kevin on his tenth birthday, his eyes filled with tears as he watched the young man accept it with such dignity and grace, seeming to fully understand what it signified. Kevin had taken a keen interest not only in the training but also in the culture from which these arts had come. Kevin had a surprise for Tanakasan that day as well. It had come from his study of Japanese culture. From that day on, Kevin never called him Tanakasan again. From that day forward, Cenzo Tanaka was always called "Sensei", which meant "Teacher".

Cenzo Tanaka had not demanded this title of respect from his young student because, to be quite honest, he hadn't expected the boy to continue for very long. American children often did not want to put in the time required to excel in these arts, choosing rather to pass tests to earn themselves belts of varying colors until they spent enough money and time in their class to be rewarded with a coveted black belt. His instruction to Kevin had always been to strive for mastery, and nothing less. There is no achievement except mastery. Therefore there is no reward for anything short of that pursuit. Kevin had never once complained about that principle. He never once asked how much farther he had to go. He just showed up every day and worked towards perfection. His sensei was so proud of his student that he sent letters every so often to his friends and family back home, documenting this astounding young American boy's progress under his tutelage. No one really believed him.

After 4 years of Tanaka's persistent letter writing, his own Sensei, Kansatsu Shiri, insisted that he bring his young prodigy to Japan to demonstrate his skills. They finally made the trip this past summer. For the first time in his life, Kevin was completely immersed in the world he so desired to be a part of. He soaked up every second of the experience like a sponge. From his first unpleasant moments of being teased as the *gaijin*, which is the slur used to refer to Americans by the Japanese, to his final moments with the Shiri clan, he did his level best to remember everything. He had proven himself to Sensei Shiri, who had bestowed on Kevin the title of "Sensei", and welcomed him into his family as a son. "From this day on," Kansatsu had said, "You will always have family in sunlight."

"But more importantly, you will also always have family in the night. One day, you will understand why this is so important."

With this cryptic thought in his head, and with the promise of returning, and possibly receiving his mark, the hand-tattooed dragon symbol of the Shiri clan, on his next visit, Kevin returned home, filled with an entirely new perspective to go along with his extraordinarily increased skills. Ten weeks had changed Kevin Sinclaire forever.

Tony now stood in ready position, Kevin facing him. Kevin had brought him to Sensei three years ago, when they had first met. He presented Tony and asked permission to teach him. Sensei had accepted Tony immediately, leaving Kevin to handle the training under his direct supervision. Tony progressed rapidly and was committed and persistent. Where Kevin was methodical and naturally gifted in the martial arts, Tony excelled through brute force and a determination to learn. Kevin was also a fine teacher, taking time to ensure that his student was learning everything properly and without rushing to the next step before he had perfected the one before. They were now at the point where Tony could go at Kevin full speed and they frequently had sparring matches. Kevin had spent the money on real bamboo flooring for his workout room. He kept the machines and weights all off to one side, leaving a large area for them to train.

They began with some basic attacks and throws to get them warmed up and used to the contact, then gradually moved into more advanced clash techniques, one of them ultimately throwing the other or executing a submission technique. Finally, they advanced into a full contact match which Tony knew he could not win but thoroughly enjoyed nonetheless because he was learning some pretty dangerous techniques from a pretty dangerous guy. After several high attacks where Kevin easily repelled him, twice sending him crashing to the floor, Tony decided to change things up.

He moved quickly into a forward stance, aiming another attack high at Kevin's left neck. It was a simple but fierce downward chop, that Kevin immediately set up to defend. But at the last second, Tony pulled his arm back in and, spinning to his left aimed a vicious backhand chop at a point just above Kevin's right hip bone. The feint took Kevin by surprise, but he quickly regrouped, simply stepping back with his right foot, taking the aim point away from Tony, who, with his back to Kevin, never saw what had happened. His chop sailed past Kevin's midsection and as his head whipped around into position, he saw the heel of Kevin's right hand aimed right at his chest. Fortunately, he was well trained and his defense was already there, a simple left hand swipe block, followed by an immediate flurry of punches as he did his best to penetrate Kevin's front defense. They clashed violently for several seconds, ending up in a grapple situation that could not be resolved. A stalemate! It was as much a victory as Tony could ever have hoped for. Kevin grinned as they released one another and bowed. Heading off to the side for a drink of water.

"Very nicely done," Kevin commented. "I thought I was gonna knock you on your butt when you tried that stupid spin move."

"That was a brilliant move," Tony replied. "I almost had you there."

Kevin laughed. "It *did* surprise me, I'll give you that. You're really getting creative with your technique."

"Well, I have the best teachers around."

"Awww. What a sweetie you are to say so."

Tony took a long drink.

"So what is going to happen with all this nonsense? You know they're trying to get you suspended."

Kevin shrugged. "I don't think the lawyers will let that happen. It all really depends on whether or not they try to prosecute me, though if the video online shows the whole thing, I can't see how they could justify it. Better chance of prosecuting the Higgins guy."

"Well the whole thing is on there, and I downloaded it just to be safe, in case they try to pull it down. At least now you'll have a high def copy to show everyone."

Kevin nodded, grinning. Tony always had his back. There wasn't a better friend in the world than Antonin Yavastrenko. Once he became your friend you had a guy who would go through hell with you without a complaint. If anyone wanted to get to Kevin, they would have to go through Tony first, and that included cops and parents and anyone else who decided to come after him. That was what made them such a great team on the field. They always knew that whatever the situation, one always had the others' back. They were never on their own.

*****

Lindsey was concerned. She had spent the entire night talking to Kevin, trying to probe how he felt about all the notoriety he was sure to receive when they returned to school on Monday. He was about to receive a hero's welcome, and this was just the beginning. If the Cobras continued to win, and if he continued to play as he had the night before, girls would be throwing themselves at him every day. They had only been in high school for three days and she already had seen the reaction the football players got from the girls. As a freshman, Kevin was not really known, particularly by the upperclassmen, and until Friday's pep rally, had mostly escaped notice.

But once he had been named as a starter on the varsity Cobras, everyone knew who he was. He was looked at differently by everyone for the rest of the afternoon. That really hadn't bothered Lindsey. In fact, she had barely noticed. It wasn't until Friday night that it struck Lindsey that she was dating a boy who about to become the most popular person in the Township. She was not prepared for that. As she considered the way the older girls acted towards the football team, the way they dressed, their obvious desire to be with them in more ways than friends, she began to think of all the ways she could lose Kevin.

Sex was not something Lindsey had ever been in a big hurry to do. Part of what made her relationship with Kevin so comfortable was that he had never pressured her in any way to do anything that was remotely uncomfortable. Once, before the previous school year had ended, when she knew Kevin would be leaving for most of the summer, she asked him if he wanted to have sex with her. It was during a period when all of the girls seemed to be talking about it. Lindsey, for a brief period, got the impression that they were all out there doing it. Thankfully, Kevin did not take advantage of that poorly thought out proposition.

But now, they were in high school, where the girls were older, more experienced, and willing to have a good time with the popular guys. In Kendall High, that meant football players, the princes of Kendall Township. Being the girlfriend of a Kendall Cobra was a special thing in and of itself. Those girls were pretty much worshipped by the rest of the girls, like they had done something special. Lindsey knew that the "something special" probably had more to do with sex than anything else.

She wondered if her countdown to sex with Kevin had already begun. She hated the thought of *having* to have sex in order to keep her boyfriend. It didn't seem right, but she knew that at some point she would probably have to make that decision. The question right now was when would the decision be forced on her? What would her answer be if the question came sooner rather than later? This is where having an older sister around would probably be useful, but Tracey was never home anymore. She was probably getting "saved" over at Brittany Morgan's house while Lindsey suffered with life decisions all by herself.

After several moments of consideration, Lindsey pushed aside the thoughts of sex with Kevin. After all, she had no control over when he would begin to demand it, or even whether or not he would demand it at all. He might not even care right now. He was focused on football, right? He didn't have time for girls, did he? She dismissed this line of thinking in favor of a more practical one. Instead of worrying about things she could not control, maybe it would be best to concern herself with something she *could* control. She hopped off the bed and opened her closet door. She began going through her entire wardrobe, pulling out all the items she would try on today. As she tried on several garments, she realized that she hadn't gotten a new dress in quite some time. Nothing in her closet really fit and worse, everything was outdated and no longer in fashion. She was in real trouble.

"Mom!" she called out, staring into the empty closet. She had pulled everything out.

"Mom!" she called again. She could hear the footsteps on the stairs. Her mother came to the door, and stopped short when she saw the mess.

"What's the matter?"

Lindsey turned to face her. "We need to go shopping right now."

"For what, dear?"

"I have no dresses, no skirts that fit, no blouses…nothing to wear to school!"

"I thought you didn't want…"

"Mom." Lindsey whined, and slumped her shoulders.

"I mean, you are the one who told me that you hated…"

"*Mom*," Lindsey said with a little more force.

"…and that you didn't care what anyone else thought. You could wear whatever you…"

Lindsey rolled her eyes. "*MOM!*"

Abby stopped speaking. She had a slight smile on her face.

Lindsey took her mother's hand and held it up to her face, batting her beautiful blue eyes like she had been doing since she was two. "You were right. I was wrong. I would like to go and purchase some pretty dresses and skirts to wear to school."

"Thank *God*. Put some shoes on." Abby started to leave the room. "Oh, don't forget to bring stockings or pantyhose. You're going to need shoes too and you can't try them on without something on your feet. In fact, just wear flip-flops or something. Good. You've got them. Girl, we're going to have fun today. I was beginning to think you might *never* dress like a girl again. I mean sweatpants are fine once in a while, but come on. You can wear nice things too. And don't slouch so much, sweetie. Stand up straight. We're going to get you all set up. The boys are going to go out of their minds. Wait til they see you…"

But Lindsey only cared about one boy. For him she was willing to suffer an afternoon's shopping with her mother, who considered herself a fashion princess. At least she wouldn't blink at spending the money. Clothes were her favorite thing outside of books. Lindsey prepared for an afternoon of being dragged from shop to shop, getting everything she was going to need.

As they drove, Abby Overton continued to express her joy at getting a chance to "shop for her beautiful daughter", something that both Lindsey *and* Tracey had deprived her of for the past couple of years for different reasons. Both girls had early developing bodies. Their curves had begun just a bit earlier than most of the other girls and had developed just a little bit quicker. For Tracey, this had meant very little as she didn't even seem to notice or care. Her self-image was a hopeless situation as far as Abby could tell. Nothing she said or did would convince her oldest girl that she was really very pretty, and not the ugly freak she considered herself to be. Lindsey, on the other hand, was acutely aware of her body, but reacted in a decidedly negative way toward it. She went to great lengths to deemphasize what was happening to her. She wore loose fitting clothing and basically "dressed down", which distressed her mother, who wanted her girls to be empowered by their beauty, by their femininity. Tracey was beginning to emerge, she had noticed, over the past few weeks, which was gratifying even if she'd had nothing to do with it. Now Lindsey wanted a change of wardrobe. Amazing what three days of high school could do. Of course, there was also the game the previous night…

"Lindsey," she said. "Why are we going shopping right now?"

Lindsey had been hoping to avoid any explanation. "I just need some new clothes."

"Dresses and skirts?"

"What's wrong with dresses and skirts?"

"There's nothing wrong…" She almost got caught in what she called a "Lindsey Loop", which was where Lindsey managed to avoid whatever it was you were trying to talk about and take you on an endless journey of inane questions which would make you sorry you had ever started talking to her. Most of the time, Lindsey managed to avoid conversations by using this technique. She was actually very good at dodging questions.

"I'm wondering what made you decide all of a sudden to go shopping for skirts and dresses, that's all."

"I just want to wear skirts and dresses. Is that a crime?"

"So you're not going to tell me what's on your mind?"

Lindsey sighed. "You're not going to let this go, are you?"

"Baby, we've got all day. You can hem and haw all you want, but in the end, your mother will get the whole story. Now spill. What are you thinking with all this?"

Lindsey knew the game was over. Basically, when her mother wanted to get information out of her, she always got it. She sighed deeply.

"Well," she began. "On Monday morning, Kevin is going to be the most popular guy in school. Every single girl at Kendall High School will be after him."

"I see. And you think you'll be able to keep him around if you dress nicer?"

"Actually, I'm not all that worried about Kevin. I guess he could break up with me and go out with someone else. I can't do anything about that, I don't think. But maybe I can show all the girls that they aren't good enough for him."

Abby laughed. "Wow. You know what? You're not all that far off. There are two reasons why girls your age dress up. Either they want to attract the guys or they want to upstage the other girls. Most of the time it's both."

Chapter 12

Kevin was dreading the next four hours. Sunday morning always meant church, but today, it also mean that he would have to answer stupid questions about the game and about his altercation with Frank Higgins, whose wife Sandy had been making a fool of herself all over the news calling for the arrest of "that mad dog" who attacked her husband. Kevin had actually laughed when he had heard about that. Tony called him late the previous night to inform him that he might have a new nickname come Monday morning because the "mad dog thing" was going viral in Kendall Township. There was a rumor that the Brette Girls might be staying up late over the weekend to design new "Mad Dog" T-shirts and banners. While it was kind of cool to hear that the community was rallying behind him, Kevin dreaded having to deal with certain people at his church who undoubtedly were going to feel the need to express their disappointment over his behavior.

On the way to church, Karen Timmons turned in her seat and addressed the situation directly.

"Kevin," she said. "I don't want you to lose your temper in church today, do you understand?"

"Yes."

"I mean it. No matter what anyone says to you, you are to remain respectful, especially to adults."

"It sounds like you are expecting *them* to be disrespectful to *me*."

"Maybe they will be, but you will be respectful to them no matter what."

"Okay. But I don't see why they get to express their opinion to me. Can't you tell them to leave me alone?"

"I'm just saying that you represent this family. You don't get to stand up and be my defender one day and then humiliate me the next."

And that was that. The Trump Card. Kevin would never intentionally embarrass his mother, and she knew it. So here she had made it plain that any disrespectful responses to the comments of people at the church would do just that. She didn't need to say another word about it. She turned back around in her seat and they drove the rest of the way in silence. Kevin was effectively muzzled this morning. She didn't often pull this card out, but when she did, Kevin's overly acute sense of chivalry toward his mother took over.

Kevin's relationship with his mother was a unique one. Karen had been a single mom since virtually the day Kevin had been born. Duncan Sinclaire, his father, had married her when they had first found out that Karen was pregnant, but he hadn't wasted any time finding other women to run around with while Karen dealt with her pregnancy more or less by herself. Once Kevin was born, Duncan settled down for a while, but by the time Kevin started school, it was obvious to Karen that he was never going to remain faithful. As a new Christian, she struggled with the Biblical concept of marital relationships. The Bible was clear about fidelity and that unfaithfulness in a spouse was just cause for divorce, but it was not something she took lightly. She felt that if there was any chance of saving her marriage, she had to try. Two more years went by, but Duncan Sinclaire was not going to change. When that fact settled in her mind, and she finally made the decision to put an end to the doomed relationship, Kevin had just turned seven.

When Karen finally threw her husband out of the house, her greatest fear was how Kevin would react to it and how he would handle not having his father around. She needn't have worried. Kevin handled that transition with little or no obvious ill effects. Unbeknownst to Karen, her son had grown to hate his father in a very quiet and passive way. He had seen how his mother was always left alone to care for him. Kevin was well aware of how she was often awake at late hours, crying and praying, asking God to somehow take the pain away. He knew instinctively that it was his father causing all this pain, even if he didn't know or understand why. Even though Duncan constantly did his level best to be the good guy to Kevin, buying him things, taking him out to ball games, movies, and all that, Kevin quietly nurtured a smoldering anger and resentment towards the man.

When Kevin was eight years old, his father was arrested for his third DWI. The previous two had just been routine traffic stops where Duncan had been pulled over for driving erratically. He had lost his license in both cases and had taken the required classes and paid the required fines in order to get his driving privileges restored, but this time he would not have that option. On this particular night, Duncan had crossed the yellow lines on Route 9 in Southern New Jersey and struck another car head on, nearly killing the passenger inside. He was arrested on the spot, charged with his third DWI and attempted vehicular manslaughter, which later got knocked down to criminal negligence in a plea deal which put Duncan Sinclaire behind bars for seven to ten years. Kevin never visited him a single time.

It was right around that time that Kevin's mind began flourishing in ways Karen would never have dreamed. He began reading books at lightning speed and recalling virtually everything he had just read. He was so bored in school that they suggested bumping him up to a grade level more appropriate to his abilities. Karen had resisted that, wanting Kevin to grow up with friends his own age and be as normal as possible, especially since his home life would be in turmoil for a while. He was a straight A student without ever really having to study. Homework usually took less than an hour, and that was only because he couldn't write as fast as he could think. His penmanship was incredibly sloppy because his hands were always playing catch up. He frequently had to rewrite his entire assignments just to make them legible.

By the time he turned ten, Karen could barely understand what he was talking about half the time. He was reading advanced math, science, and history books on his own time and soaking up the knowledge within them with a seemingly limitless capacity to retain it all. He even read and talked about the Bible, which was quite encouraging for a mother who constantly prayed for her son's salvation. He had deep thoughts and questions at a very young age which Karen felt ill-equipped to handle. She often left him with one of the pastors at church for hours on end as they discussed the various scriptural doctrines contained within the Bible. He even got one of the pastors, who happened to be very interested in ancient history, into a long debate about how the various pagan religions surrounding the ancient Israelites actually contributed to the overall style and substance of the Old Testament. It took Karen some time to realize that a mother doesn't have to keep up. Her job was to make sure he was being brought up in a scriptural way, and to teach him about Jesus. She didn't have to know or understand Einstein's Theory of Relativity to do that.

They spent over two years living at the house in Albertson, just the two of them. During that time, Karen had begun spending a great deal of time with Jeff Timmons, who seemed a nice enough guy, but Kevin had always secretly thought he was a bit of a blowhard. He was always talking about some great business idea or another. Even at a young age, Kevin didn't take Jeff all that seriously. But by the time he was ten, his mother and Jeff were engaged. It just happened. One day she came home and told Kevin that Jeff had proposed and she had said yes. Kevin just nodded. She hadn't discussed it with him, and wasn't asking his permission, so he didn't feel the need to express an opinion. Karen knew immediately that she had misjudged what Kevin's reaction would be, not that she would have changed anything. The child doesn't dictate what the parent does in *her* house. It had never been that way, but she realized that the two of them had always done things together. This decision had been made and dropped on him with no warning. Her attitude was that he had better get over it because he wasn't going to dictate things to her.

What she didn't realize was that while this was certainly the prerogative of a parent, there would be consequences to it. Had she read Newton's *Philosophiæ Naturalis Principia Mathematica*, as Kevin had, she might have remembered that Newton's Third Law of Motion specifically stated that every action would have a reaction. Thus, Kevin's relationship with Jeff began as an adversarial one. His mother had placed him in a position of authority over Kevin and he was quick to take advantage of it. He constantly called for Kevin to get him things. He would come in from work, plop himself down on the couch, turn on the T.V., and call for both

Kevin and Karen to essentially wait on him, going to the kitchen to get him snacks, drinks, etc. Karen didn't seem to mind, but Kevin grew to think of her husband as a colossal jerk, and a lazy one at that. As time passed, Kevin saw that while Jeff and Karen clearly loved one another, Jeff thought it was somehow her job to serve his every need. Kevin couldn't stand how Jeff treated his mom, but Karen never complained or even made a sour face. She just dutifully did whatever he said.

Kevin generally kept his mouth shut and didn't usually bother to get into confrontations with Jeff. There were certainly times when Kevin got into trouble and Jeff took the reins in the punishment department. Early on, Kevin actually laughed through a few spankings, much to the chagrin of Jeff, who considered himself to be quite frightening when he got upset. Kevin was clearly not intimidated by Jeff's tough guy approach to fatherhood, and it only caused Jeff to get even more incensed every time he tried to punish Kevin. Finally, Jeff realized that Kevin's toughness might come from his training with Sensei Tanaka. He demanded that Karen disallow the training to continue. She consented and when she explained it to Kevin, he turned his back and said nothing. He did not complain. He did not throw a temper tantrum. He did not cry. He never said a single word or gave any indication whatsoever that he was upset. It was impossible to get any satisfaction from his reactions because they never knew what he was thinking.

What he did do was to remain absolutely silent for almost four weeks. Whenever Karen or Jeff tried to speak to him, he just stared through them until they got so angry with him that Jeff began smacking him around and poking him in the chest. His face would get so red Kevin would have sworn he was going to blow a blood vessel. Kevin took all of Jeff's punishment silently, not even raising his hands to defend himself. In fact, he often held his head up, staring Jeff right in the eyes, silently daring him to take a real shot. Kevin's hatred grew with every little poke and prod. All this scared Karen because of how angry her husband would get, but a boy needed a man sometimes to handle him. Finally, Karen sat him down and pleaded with him to speak. Kevin broke his silence to make one single statement.

"This is *your* choice, mom. *You* brought that scumbag into *my* life, and I never said a word. Now I have to run around and serve him like I'm some kind of unpaid servant. I'm not his kid and he's not my dad. If you want to be a slave to that lazy bum, then that is *your* business, but *I* don't. Then you take away the one thing I really love in this world, and I don't even complain. And why did you do it? Because that guy can't stand that his spankings don't hurt. What do you want me to do? *Pretend* I like him? I'd *never* do that. I hate everything about this. The only things I can do are to shut up and wait until I can find a way out of it."

Karen sat stunned as her son's feelings poured out. She couldn't believe the profound hatred he was feeling. However, she wasn't one to bow to a child's demands, though Kevin hadn't demanded anything. She was not going to allow him to control her.

"You know, sometimes all it takes is an apology."

He stared at her blankly. "From *me*? Apology for what?"

She replied, "Well, for one thing the way you treat us."

"Which is..?"

"Which is disrespectfully."

"In what way exactly? Is it in the way I get called out of my room to fetch a bag of chips? Or is it how I get called into the house to go find his work boots, which are usually three feet away from him? Or is it how I don't cry or complain or even say a single word when I get pushed around or slapped around whenever the big tough jerk gets mad? How am *I* disrespectful?"

"You haven't said a word to us in weeks."

"That is because of what *you* did to *me*. That's not disrespect. It's nothing. If anything, it's dis*regard*. But this all started when *you* took my training away. And that was because the tough guy couldn't make me cry. And you *know* it."

"Well, it doesn't matter. You don't get to stay quiet and ignore us just because you're mad."

"I don't?"

"No. *I'm* in charge here."

"Okay. What should I say?"

"Don't get smart with me."

"I have nothing to say either to you or to that jerk. If you have something you would like me to say, then you'll have to tell me so I can say it."

"You're not going to win, Kevin."

"*Win*? Are you kidding? I lost a long time ago, when you married that jerk. There is no winning for me. There is only waiting. And that's what I'm going to do."

"You will talk to us and you'll do it respectfully, do you understand?"

Kevin shook his head. "I'm no longer a part of this conversation."

Karen threw up her hands in frustration. There was a great deal a parent could do when a child was misbehaving, and she and Jeff had really gone through them all. Kevin seemed perfectly willing to accept whatever punishment they meted out. At this point he was basically consigned to his room with no T.V., which he rarely watched anyway, no computer, which was a punishment of sorts, but he really was seldom online for the simple fun of it. He was usually researching something for the purposes of educating himself, so Karen knew that while the punishment kept him from doing something he liked to do, he was secretly laughing at them because by implementing such a punishment they were essentially keeping him from doing school work. All he was currently really allowed to do was to sit in his room and read, which is what he generally did anyway. Taking books away from him would affect him, no doubt, but can a parent really justify refusing their kid the tools to study?

To this day she could not figure out how she had let an eleven year old kid get the best of her. She could deal with his stubborn refusal to talk, because they would just continue the punishments they had implemented. He would not get his way by being an immature brat, but it had been several weeks. The problem was that Kevin felt empowered by his silence. Kevin knew as well as Karen that he could handle any *physical* punishment they could throw at him and unless they were willing to go over the line of abuse, he would never break. So all they had left was to take things from him. The problem with that was that he didn't care. They were taking away things that most parents have to force their kids to do. There was really only one thing left to take away. Kevin would have about two weeks to decide one way or the other on that.

One night, Karen and Jeff sat Kevin down and asked him to speak to them so they could have a discussion about the situation. Kevin agreed to participate.

Karen began by saying, "Kevin, this has got to stop. You have to know that we can't do what you demand just because you throw a temper tantrum or refuse to talk to us."

Kevin nodded. He had no expression on his face, but his eyes told his mother exactly what he thought of that statement.

She continued. "We have tried everything to deal with you and the only thing left is football. If this continues, you will not be playing football this year."

Jeff sat there with a half smirk on his face. He knew how much Kevin loved playing football. He knew this had to be the straw. Kevin looked him dead in the eye.

"Okay," he said and then fell silent again, staring blankly at them for a few moments before getting up and returning to his room.

And that was that. There was no further discussion. There was no further argument. Karen and Jeff sat there, staring after an eleven year old boy who was in complete control of his emotions. They couldn't tell if he was angry or sad, but he had made his choice. When Kevin failed to show up for August practices in a couple of weeks, every parent and coach would be asking why. When Kevin went to school, all the kids would know that it was his parents who were keeping him from playing. They in turn would tell their parents, and Jeff and Karen would look like major league jerks. Karen didn't really care about that, but Jeff sure did. He secretly loved that his step son was the best football player in the Township. He loved to be on the sidelines when Kevin was scoring touchdowns. All the parents slapped him on the back and he was often the center of attention. If Kevin did not play, all that would change. In Kendall Township, where football was a way of life, Jeff was not eager to see how people would react to *this* decision. After all, it affected *their* kids too.

Jeff had an idea. "We could send him to one of those boys camps where they teach him discipline and respect and all that."

Karen shook her head. "He'd actually volunteer for something like that. He hates it here, so getting away, even for boot camp would not be a punishment."

Jeff came to Kevin's room alone later that evening. He opened the door without knocking and came in and sat down on the chair from Kevin's desk. Kevin barely looked up from the book he was reading. Jeff could see it was called *"The Rise and Fall of the Roman Empire."* He shook his head slightly, thinking about the comics and sports magazines he had read when he was young.

"I want to talk to you, man to man," he said.

Kevin thought for a moment, then rolled his eyes slightly and set his book down, still opened, on the bed next to him. He looked silently at Jeff. The two sat there in silence for a moment before Jeff began.

"Listen, this isn't fair to your mother."

"Why not?"

"Do you think she deserves to be ignored by her son?"

"It's not a question of what she deserves. It's a question of action and reaction. She took away my training with Sensei. This is the reaction. It's not about what is deserved."

Jeff shook his head. "I'm the one responsible for taking away your training, not your mother."

Kevin shook his head. "It may have been your idea. In fact, I'm sure it was, but she made the final decision. You don't have that authority."

"I don't have that authority?" Jeff was getting annoyed again. Kevin could see it. He didn't care.

"No, you don't. You only have the authority my mother *allows* you to have."

"And you don't think she has given me authority over you?"

"I *know* she has. But she could take it away at any time. That's my point. You may have made the call, but she could have overruled you. She didn't, so it's on her."

"But it's not on me?"

Kevin shook his head. "It affects you, but it has nothing to do with you. I don't care about you. You're not my dad. You're just my mom's husband. I deal with you because I have to. As soon as I can get away from you, I will."

"You hate me that much?" If the look on Jeff's face hadn't been one of arrogant amusement, Kevin might have answered differently.

"Hate you?" Kevin shook his head, his green eyes softly staring back at Jeff. They almost seemed sympathetic. "No, Jeff, I don't hate you. You aren't worth hating. Hatred takes energy. I wouldn't spend any more energy on you than I had to."

Jeff's cocky grin vanished. Kevin had expected anger to erupt, but that didn't happen. He could see that his words had struck Jeff in a deeper place than that. He picked his book back up and leaned back against the headboard, reading. Jeff sat there, silently contemplating Kevin's revelation, not really knowing how to react. He knew that Karen would have blown the statement off, rolling her eyes and shaking her head at the melodrama of it all. Jeff would generally follow her lead in that since she knew Kevin much better than he did, but over the past few weeks he felt like he had grown to understand Kevin a little bit better. He wasn't so sure that Karen had the best handle on him. In her mind there were parents and there were children. The parents were in charge and the children did what they were told. Again, Jeff generally agreed with that. But the current situation had somehow gotten away from them. Maybe this particular child needed a different approach. He had a thought.

"Believe it or not, Kev, I'm sorry you feel that way. I actually hoped we would be friends. I know I'm not your dad, but you still need a man in your life. I hoped that could be me, but now I think you trust Mr. Tanaka more than me. I think maybe we made a mistake taking him away from you."

Kevin stopped reading and lowered his book. "You do?"

Jeff nodded thoughtfully. "I do." He nodded his head for several seconds, trying to formulate his plan. "So, here's what we're gonna do. We're going to start over, okay? You get to do your martial arts, football, whatever. You're not punished anymore, but..." He raised his finger pointedly. "We are going to have to be able to live together as a family, and we can't do that if you have no respect for either of us. So you're gonna have to keep your attitude in check too."

Kevin nodded. "That's fine. I can work on that."

Jeff stood up. "Good. Now I have to get your mom to agree to all this. But we're on the same page, right?" He stuck out his hand. Kevin set his book aside and stood up, shaking Jeff's hand.

"Right."

That crisis had changed things in the Timmons household. Kevin and Jeff would never be best buddies, but they had made a connection that night. They were beginning to understand one another. Karen and Kevin would talk often over the next few weeks and months about things, working through their problems. They grew incredibly close after the incident was put behind them.

Chapter 13

Tracey lay in her bed, thankful that Lindsey had distracted their mother the previous night with her new wardrobe choices. She needed time to process the events of the past two days. She needed to figure out how she felt about things and how she was going to proceed, particularly on Monday, when she would inevitably have to face Matt Kildare. She was struggling to get her feelings in order. She was confused as to how she felt about what had happened between them because there were so many questions about *him* and *his* feelings toward *her*. Life would be so much easier if he had asked her to be his girlfriend before all the physical stuff had happened.

Leaving his house the previous morning had seemed like the only acceptable option at the time, but now there was a deep feeling of regret setting in. Sure she had avoided any opportunity he would have had to treat her like some kind of skanky one-night-stand, but would he have really done that anyway? He hadn't seemed like that kind of guy the night before. In fact, even if he considered it to be a one-night-stand, he probably would have been okay with her the next morning. She wished she could call him and talk to him before school on Monday. Maybe things would be easier over the phone.

Like you'd ever pick up the phone and make THAT call…

Brittany's words kept ringing in her head. Not the religious stuff. She wasn't prepared to subject herself to any religious judgments right now, even if Brittany had claimed not to be making them in the first place. But religious people all had their opinions about things like sex. Tracey was more concerned right now about the practical things Brittany had mentioned. There was something to be said for the simplicity of a life lived without having to worry about sex outside of at least a committed relationship.

At least, Tracey thought, some of this confusion would disappear.

She was just beginning to sort through some things mentally when there came a knock at her door.

"Tracey?" It was Lindsey. *Bad timing, Lindz.* "Yes?"

The door cracked open. "You busy?" Lindsey asked, poking her head in the door.

Uhhhh!

"Not really," she said tentatively. "What's up?" Lindsey usually kept to herself. Either something was wrong or she was up to something.

Lindsey came in, shut the door behind her, and sat down on the bed, crossing her legs and facing Tracey. She looked concerned.

Tracey frowned. "What's the matter with you?"

"You haven't been around lately."

"I had the game, and then the party, then I was at Brittany's…busy weekend. Why?"

"Well I kind of needed some advice and then you weren't here and so I talked to mom about it and now I have all these new clothes and I don't know what to do."

Tracey shook her head. "Wow. Guess I missed a lot. Start from the beginning."

Lindsey took a breath and began, telling Tracey about her epiphany, she actually said 'epiphany', on Friday night at the game about Kevin's popularity and all the girls. She told Tracey about her idea of dressing in such a way as to make it more of a challenge for girls to try to steal him away.

"So you're basically trying to make sure he can't take his eyes off of *you*," Tracey said. "And that way, he can't be looking at other girls."

"Actually that's only a small part of it," Lindsey replied. "The bigger part is that these other girls will see that have to outdo me in order to get him."

"Out*do* you?"

"You know. They'll have to look better and all that."

Tracey took a deep breath. "And so what do you need me for?"

"Do you think I'm an idiot?"

"An idiot?"

"For going crazy over all this. Or do you think all this stuff won't happen?"

Tracey nodded. "Oh yeah. You can count on it happening. These girls will trample all over you to get to Kevin. He is target number one, I can tell you that right now. Every girl in the Township wants him, or soon will. So, no, you are not crazy."

"So you think this is a good idea?"

Tracey shrugged. "Why do you care what I think anyway?"

"Because you're my sister! And besides, I don't have any friends, so you're it."

Tracey smirked. "Oh, my God, this is so sweet!"

"What?"

"You're actually coming to your big sister for advice!"

"I didn't say that."

Tracey came over and threw her arms around her younger sister.

"Tracey, I didn't *say* that!"

"There, there, little one. Big sister is here for you."

"I'm leaving." Lindsey struggled to get away from Tracey's bear hug.

"Don't leave, Lindz. I'll tell you what I think."

Lindsey sat back down.

"I think if you go to school looking good and let everyone know that Kevin is taken, then it really is in *his* hands. If he decides to cheat, or break up with you for another girl, there is little you can do about it."

"So I'm basically stuck. I have to wait to see if he'd rather be with someone else."

Tracey nodded. "Sort of. But it's always that way, isn't it? Kevin just happens to have a lot of girls that will be after him. It actually is a great test for you. If he cheats or leaves you, then that's that, but if he stays with you and he's faithful through all that, then you know he's the real deal, right?"

Lindsey nodded slowly. "I guess." She stood up and headed to the door. "Thanks, Trace…"

Tracey closed her eyes in a moment of indecision, but then she took a fast deep breath. "Wait a sec, Lindz. I need to talk to *you* about something."

Lindsey stopped halfway out the door. "What's up?"

"Close the door."

"Why?"

"Just close it. Trust me."

"Ooookay." Lindsey closed the door and walked back into the room. "Is this something I need to sit down for?"

"Probably."

"Oh, God, what happened? You joined Brittany's cult?"

"She's not in a cult."

"So, you're "saved" now?" Lindsey said, making the quote marks in the air with her fingers. "You're a Born-Again?"

"Will you knock off the religion hating for just one minute please? This has nothing to do with that."

"Then what is it? Oh, my God, don't even tell me you are switching to *cheer* leading! Drill team is one thing. At least you're dancing, but…"

"Will you stop…?"

"I can't stand all that rah rah stuff. I mean, school spirit is one thing, if you're into that kind of thing, but..."

"I'm not switching to cheer leading. Will you shut up for a minute?"

"Okay, what?"

"I need to talk to you about something that has to stay absolutely between us and never be spoken of outside this room and even then only when it's just you and me present."

Lindsey frowned. "Okay. Now you're scaring me."

"Promise me you won't be upset with me or make fun of me."

Lindsey shook her head. "I can't promise you that."

"Why not?"

"Because I have no idea what you're going to tell me. What if what you tell me is so hilariously ridiculous that I burst out laughing uncontrollably? Then, through no fault of my own, I will have broken my promise to you."

"Okay fine. Just promise to keep it to yourself then."

"I promise."

"I slept with Matt Kildare."

Lindsey immediately grinned, and then burst out laughing. "Really? Good for you, Trace." She got up to leave.

"Sit down, Lindsey. I'm not kidding."

Lindsey looked at her closely, the grin still heavily on her face. She peered at Tracey's eyes, studying her face. She knew when Tracey was lying. Right now she saw no sign of deceit. Her grin vanished. "Oh, my God," she whispered, sitting down. "Oh, my God!" she repeated, this time much louder.

"Shhh!" Tracey pointed to the door, not wanting their mother to hear.

Lindsey nodded urgently, her eyes big as saucers. She took several moments to let the truth sink in, her hand still covering her mouth.

"Okay," she said. "Wow! That was a bit of a bombshell, Tracey. Try to warn a girl before you drop that kind of news."

"Sorry. I thought telling you to close the door and promise not to mention it to anyone sort of was a tip off."

"So anyway," Lindsey said. "You actually did it? You really had s-e-x with Matt Kildare?"

"Actually, you don't need to spell s-e-x, Lindz. If mom hears, I'm guessing she'll figure out that particular code."

"Actually," Lindsey replied. "I wasn't doing that for mom."

Tracey smiled slightly. "So s-e-x is a dirty word?"

"It just seems less real when you spell it."

"Well in this case it's real whether you spell it or not."

Lindsey put her hand over her mouth again. "I can't believe it, Tracey. You really did it with Matt Kildare?"

Tracey nodded sheepishly.

"Well?" Lindsey prodded. "I don't know how to react. What do I say? Are you happy about it? What was it like? Tell me everything."

Tracey shrugged. "Actually, I can't figure out whether I'm happy about it or not. I'm pretty confused about my feelings right now. That's kind of why I wanted to talk to you about it. Maybe you can help me figure things out."

"Just like real sisters," Lindsey answered ruefully. "Not exactly our style."

Tracey shrugged. "Well, let's get a new style. I need a sister right now."

Be careful what you wish for...

Lindsey, for some reason, didn't find a reason to inject her patented sarcasm. Rather she got serious and sat up straight, ready to listen. She actually seemed interested in being sisters. Tracey told her the whole story, beginning with the magical chance meeting with Matt Kildare at the party. She told Lindsey how Matt had talked to her, how nervous she had been, and how sweet Matt had been toward her. She told her about that first kiss out on the dock by the lake with the full moon glimmering off the water; how she had been so nervous she could barely keep from shaking, but how Matt had been so gentle and caring. He had instinctively known it had been her first kiss and had made sure it was perfect for her. Even as she told the story, she couldn't keep from smiling as she thought back to that magical moment.

Lindsey actually felt a little choked up. She knew that Tracey had always had a thing for Matt Kildare. He was pretty much the only boy she had ever looked at since the sixth grade. Lindsey was pretty sure that Tracey had been in love with Matt even before she knew why those feelings existed or what they even were. Usually, Lindsey would use this knowledge to mock her older sister, but as Tracey told her story, Lindsey couldn't help but feel amazed. How many girls actually got a shot at their dream guy? Sure, Tracey wasn't in love with some celebrity, but so what? Just three days before, Matt Kildare had been as out of Tracey's league as Justin Timberlake. Well…maybe not quite, but Tracey never would have thought that Matt could ever be interested in her. Then, in the blink of an eye, everything changed. Tracey's dream to be Matt Kildare's girl had come true, if only for a night. Lindsey imagined the real question today was whether or not it had been worth it.

This question caused Lindsey to wonder about true love. Was it possible to love someone from afar? Could you actually love someone you had never even spoken to? Tracey had certainly spent a great deal of time pining for Matt Kildare, but now they had been together. They had not only spoken and spent time, but they had *been* together. For *real*.

Tracey continued, describing in detail the drive to the shore, where they had walked on the boardwalk, talking about their lives. She had told him how this was the closest thing to a date she had ever been on and how she had never really had much of a life. He had told her how his life felt like it was crumbling around him. He was losing his elite status on the football team. He and Emily were always fighting and getting back together. He had no idea what he was going to do with his life. College was a year away and he had no clue what he wanted to do. Tracey told Lindsey that it had actually made her feel a little more confident to know that this super popular guy who had all the confidence in the world on the surface was just as scared and uncertain as anyone else.

She told Lindsey how they had kissed on the boardwalk. Matt had been a perfect gentleman and though they had kissed her for a long time, he hadn't tried to push it any farther. Finally, he invited her back to his home. His parents were away for the weekend and he had the place all to himself. He had been clear that he would not pressure her in any way, and she could do or not do whatever she wanted. To Tracey, the invitation was enough. As she recounted her emotions from Friday night, Tracey began to realize that the entire time she had *wanted* to sleep with him. When he invited her over, there had been no question in her mind that if he wanted her, she would be with him. This realization was something of a breakthrough for her. It certainly cleared up a little bit of her confusion. There was no real question as to how it all had happened. She had *wanted* it to happen.

Lindsey sat through the entire story in rapt silence, her mind alternately floating between Tracey's narrative and her own thoughts about love and sex. As she listened to her sister recount her story, she thought of how she and Kevin had discussed sex one night before he had left for Japan. It had not been quite so romantic sounding back then. Kevin had not responded with an eagerness to get her clothes off. He had not expressed any urgency at all about getting her into bed. She remembered that her thoughts about sex had not been the result of a physical desire to do it. It had been more mental than that. She had been almost clinical in her thoughts and how she had expressed them to her boyfriend. As she listened to Tracey, she actually felt something change. Her mind began to see things differently. She did not immediately have the urge to go out and have sex, but all of a sudden, it didn't seem quite so scary, quite so intimidating.

Tracey finally came to the part where she woke up and felt the urgent need to get out of there. She went through the entire story about how she had to go back in and find her purse because her phone was still in there and how she had called Brittany to come get her. That was when Lindsey finally broke in.

"I'll bet that was a fun call to make."

Ahhh! There she is! Lindsey's back.

"Actually," Tracey said. "It wasn't so bad. She was surprisingly understanding."

Lindsey raised her eyebrows. "Brittany Morgan was understanding about you having sex outside of marriage on your *first date*? Or whatever it was?"

"Believe it or not, yes."

Lindsey pursed her lips. "Interesting."

"Why is that interesting?"

"Because Brittany is a Born-Again. They have very specific opinions on things like this, don't they? I'm wondering why she didn't take the opportunity to beat you over the head with her Bible."

Tracey laughed. "You need to stop watching so much T.V. Brittany is actually a very down to earth person. She does have opinions about sex, but she also doesn't try to make everyone around her live the way she chooses to."

Lindsey shook her head. "I'll believe that when I see it."

Tracey chose to let this part of the conversation go. There was no point in trying to get Lindsey to change her mind about Brittany.

"So what do you think I should do now?" she asked. "That's the real question I need to answer."

Lindsey shrugged. "Honestly, you're asking someone who now has even less experience than you do."

"But you are great at analyzing stuff. Your mind works that way. You see all the options. Help me out."

Lindsey blew out a deep breath. "Okay, let's step back. You had sex with the guy of your dreams and he did nothing that you can really call him out on, right? He didn't trick you or seduce you or anything like that?"

Tracey didn't like how this was starting out. "Yes, but…"

Lindsey held up a finger. "It's not about fairness right now. You wanted an analysis. I'm trying to give you one. Leave the emotion aside for a minute."

Tracey rolled her eyes and sat back. "Fine. I can't pin any blame on Matt for anything."

"Good. So the sex was consensual. There was no significant drinking involved, and you admit you wanted him at least as much as he wanted you."

"Yes." She was starting to feel slutty again.

"But when morning came, you had buyer's remorse?"

"What?" Tracey exclaimed. "No! I didn't have buyer's remorse. I just panicked."

"But since he was Mr. Perfect, and you can't place any blame on him, you're going to have to explain why you left the way you did."

"Why do you want to place blame on Matt so badly?"

Lindsey's face was incredulous. "Because he clearly took advantage of a girl who obviously worships him, and used that to get her into bed."

"It wasn't like that."

"Well, tell me how it was then. Because when I dream of what my first time will be like, it always ends with me waking up in the arms of the guy, not sneaking out at daybreak, hoping to God he doesn't wake up and catch me sneaking out."

"That's not fair."

"Well, I don't think it's fair for a guy who has slept with half the girls in the county to do it with my sister, who wasn't ready for it."

"Now you're just being mean."

Lindsey looked at her sister seriously. "Tracey, I'm not trying to be mean, but if you had been really ready to have sex with Matt Kildare, or anyone else for that matter, we would not be having this conversation right now. We would be talking about what a great time you had and how you always imagined it would be, and how in love the two of you are, and all that crap."

"It *was* a great time," Tracey mumbled halfheartedly, feeling about one inch tall.

"I don't doubt that in the moment you felt like it couldn't be any better. But the next morning something obviously changed.

You *still* can't decide whether or not you did something wrong. Maybe that's Brittany's influence. Maybe not, but you can't deny that when you woke up, you felt wrong. Now, if everything was so great, if you were really ready for all that, why would you feel that way?"

Tracey's eyes were beginning to tear up. "I don't know," she mumbled softly, all of the fight drained out of her.

Lindsey had a great deal of compassion for Tracey at that moment. She backed off.

"Look," she said, as Tracey began to break down. "It doesn't even matter right now. Let's just figure out what we're going to do.

Tracey couldn't even speak anymore. She just came closer to Lindsey and lay her head on her sister's shoulder. Lindsey, wrapped her arms around her and held her tightly. Neither of them could remember a time when they embraced in such a way. Even Lindsey couldn't keep the tears from flowing.

Chapter 14

Kevin got out of the car and walked to the Grace Gospel high school building, which was a world all its own. The building had been constructed with the intention of being a self-sufficient enterprise, where the high school class could not only hold their Sunday and Wednesday meetings, but also their parties, sleepover events, movie nights, and game nights. They had their own gym, their own bathrooms, their own kitchen, their own vending machines (which raised money for various charitable enterprises the group got involved in), even a game room with arcades, ping pong, pool, and darts. The main meeting room had a high tech atmosphere with a kind of "Saturday Night Live" feel to it. Generally the group would congregate in the game room for twenty minutes or so of munching on bagels and Danish while playing games and chatting amongst themselves. When the meeting was about to start, the lights would be dimmed and everyone would make their way to the main room, where the morning would begin with music, skits, announcements, videos, and whatever else the leaders had prepared. One piece flowed into the next as the technical team worked to produce seamless transitions, everything ultimately culminating in the final thirty minutes, where a leader would present the lesson for the day.

Gavin Dalyrimple ran it all, but he was especially grateful for the expertise of Kyle Hester. Kyle was a twenty-8 year old technical guru who had put together the entire room's audio, video, lighting, and IT. He also assembled a fantastic tech team to operate the equipment each Sunday and Wednesday. The tech team was comprised of a couple leaders and also students who wanted to learn a/v. Kyle was always looking for new kids to train and was so passionate about his craft, that he never failed to make it look and sound awesome on Sunday. It was such a consistently cool production in the eyes of the kids that Kyle never had a shortage of kids interested in being a part of his team.

As Kevin made his way to the game room, he passed by several high school kids who tried not to stare at him. Not all of them went to Kendall High School, but every single one of them had heard about what had happened on Friday night and most of them had seen it online by now. There were lots of whispers and stares as he strode through the building. As he entered the game room, he saw that there was already about thirty kids present. Generally, they had close to one hundred on Sunday mornings. This particular youth group had become quite a social hub amongst much of the local community's Christian children. Many parents switched churches because the youth program at Grace Gospel was so successful and they wanted their kids to be as involved as possible.

The music was up-tempo and the lights were just dim enough to give the room a club-like feel to it. As he walked in, Kevin saw eyes turning in his direction and tried not to pay any attention to it. Having grown up in this church he knew most of the regular attendees and felt pretty much at home. Today was a bit unusual because of the circumstances. Gavin Dalyrimple saw him from across the room and quickly came over to greet him.

"Hey, dude," he said, shaking Kevin's hand. "How are you? I saw the game on Friday but took off before the scene afterwards. Are you hanging in there?"

Kevin nodded. "Yeah, it's no big deal, really."

Gavin nodded. "Yeah, well that game was a big deal. You were awesome out there."

"Thanks. I think we took Trinity by surprise. This week will be different."

"Yeah? Who ya got this Friday?"

"Veritas."

Gavin pursed his lips and let out a whistle. "Whew! Trinity and Veritas back to back to open the season? At least you get Veritas at home, right?"

Kevin nodded. "Home opener. Hopefully we stay focused. All this crap going on is going to distract everyone."

A few students came over and joined the conversation. They told Kevin how great a game he'd had and how they admired what he did, sticking up for his mother. He nodded and smiled, thanking them, but not saying much more than that.

Brittany Morgan saw him and came over. "Hi, Kevin."

"Hi, Brittany. How are you?"

"I'm okay." She smiled. "Hey, we have something in common."

"What's that?"

"Your girlfriend's sister happens to be a good friend of mine."

Kevin nodded. "Oh yeah. Lindsey mentioned that to me last week. She thinks you're gonna make Tracey a Christian."

Brittany made a face. "Well, did you set her straight?"

Kevin grinned. "Of course not. In fact, Yavs and I ordered some literature from a cult online and I was thinking of spreading it all over Tracey's room for Lindsey to find."

Brittany's mouth opened in horror. "You better not do that! That's not funny Kevin." But she began to laugh as she saw the teasing look on Kevin's face. "Lindsey really does think I'm in a cult though."

Kevin shook his head. "No, she doesn't. She's just a major league smart-alec. Half the time she's just pushing buttons, and the other half she's…actually, she's usually pushing buttons the other half of the time too. You can't let her bother you or she'll never stop."

Brittany looked at him a little closer and smiled. "You *really* like her, don't you?"

"Why do you say that?"

Brittany shrugged, still looking at his eyes. "I don't know. Your eyes changed when you started talking about her. They got softer somehow."

He laughed. "Okay. I guess I *do* like her. She's really cool to hang out with and doesn't bother me with a lot of nonsense. Lots of times we just sit around, talking about stuff, but also not talking at all."

Brittany smiled. "Plus she's really pretty, right."

Kevin's smile grew wider. "Well, there's that. She's more than "really pretty", Brittany."

"I know she is."

They walked together over to the breakfast counter where they each got a danish. They sat down on bar stools and continued to chat. Brittany and Kevin had known one another for virtually their entire lives. Karen Timmons had a not-so-secret wish for her son to come to Christ and one day marry Brittany.

"She's so sweet and so pretty," Karen Timmons would say. "...and so smart, and so helpful, and she's a strong Christian. She'd make a wonderful girlfriend for you, Kevin. I pray that God calls you to Himself soon, before someone else grabs her."

Kevin never denied that Brittany Morgan was all of those things. The truth was he really liked Brittany. They had always talked and gotten along. He could see himself dating a girl like Brittany, but eventually they would come to the inevitable impasse of religious differences. He simply wasn't in the same place she was. They could never work out because she could never separate that one part of her life from her relationships. It would be counter-intuitive to her. It would drive her insane. She would know the entire time they were together that she was in a relationship that God would disapprove of. They would be "unequally yoked", to put it in scriptural terms. A Christian dating/marrying a non Christian was specifically mentioned in scripture as being an ill-advised pursuit because the two participants are essentially heading in opposite directions. Non believers are heading away from God. There is no other direction for them to head in. Christians are being drawn to God. Even when they sin, their lives are still heading toward God because He is using all of the good and all of the bad to bring His people closer to Himself. So two people heading in opposite directions begin their relationship in bad shape, no matter how in love they might be.

Brittany always knew this and had taken great pains to tamp down the attraction to Kevin she had always felt. Pretty much every girl wanted him, and she was no different, but she leaned on her faith and did her best to think of him as a friend who really needed her prayers, not her admiration. As with Tracey, she saw

Kevin as a soul who was searching for something. He might not even realize it, but his pursuit of knowledge, his pursuit of athletic excellence, or whatever else he strives after, it was all to fill a void that could not be filled by our human pursuits. She knew it. She even knew that Kevin himself knew it. He had been in this church long enough.

The teaching at Grace Gospel pulled no punches when it came to man's sinful nature. There had been many a disagreement between the pastors and some of the members of the congregation regarding the attention given to the subject of sin. One member even went into the office of the senior pastor and told him very directly to "Knock it off. All this stuff about sin all the time…people don't want to hear it." Soon after that, he preached on the doctrine of election and predestination and all hell broke loose within the congregation. Meetings were held, plans designed to have the pastor removed, threats made to organize a mass withdrawal from the church. Through it all, the pastors held firm, pointing to the Bible, and stating very clearly that "if it is mentioned in that book", they would preach it.

Within a month of that statement being made, the weekly attendance of Grace Gospel had dropped from over six hundred per week to just about two hundred. Many came back within the first six months, bringing attendance up to about three-fifty. But the leadership remained steadfast in their commitment to preach what the Bible taught, and Grace Gospel survived. Now, ten years later that three hundred fifty had quadrupled. The weekly attendance swelled to almost fifteen hundred between the two services. The new building, which was now nearly three years old, was designed to hold two thousand at a time when filled to capacity, but with seven hundred or so per service on a Sunday morning, it was a perfect size. The leadership attributed all of the growth to God having blessed this congregation for standing firm in its commitment to His Word.

Brittany had witnessed all of this, as had Kevin, so she knew he was well aware of what the truth was. She didn't know what was keeping him from turning his life over to God though. It puzzled her. How can you be around it for so long and not be affected by it? Tracey was far easier to explain. She had never been exposed to the gospel. Not really. T.V. doesn't count, especially when Christians on T.V. are either homicidal maniacs running around killing people, or else they're portrayed as judgmental hypocrites. No, Tracey's unbelief was a product of her upbringing. Brittany hoped to pierce through that one day by being a good friend to her and showing her that Christians were loving and caring people who really do want the very best for everyone.

    Kevin was a different story. How do you break through to someone who already knows it all just as well as you do? He could probably quote the Bible better than anyone in the church, but he still didn't seem to believe it or care enough to apply it to his life. Brittany wondered how she might be used in Kevin's life. It might be a frustrating thing, but she vowed to pray for the opportunity to be an influence in Kevin's life for God.

    Kevin left the Youth Center between services and headed over to the main church building. At this point he had almost forgotten about Friday night and was pretty relaxed as he entered the building and found his mother already seated in the sanctuary. She was laughing and talking with a group of women. Kevin looked around and out of the corner of his eye he caught sight of Arthur Rifkin heading his way. He was about sixty-five years old and had been in this church since its inception over forty years ago. He considered himself to be a founding member. Kevin considered him to be a pompous busybody.

    For the most part, Grace Gospel was a pretty down to earth church. The doctrine was rock solid and no holds barred. They did not pull punches and did not apologize for preaching what they saw as the truth of God's word. But, as in any church, there were those who thought of themselves as particularly gifted, insightful, godly, etc. There were those who made it a point to now all the gossip and felt like they had a right to comment on the lives of everyone else. It was actually just like any other group of people really. Church people are just people. Kevin remembered a brief conversation he had witnessed after one Sunday morning service. A newcomer was speaking to the pastor and told him that he had always hated church because it was full of hypocrites.

    After a brief pause, the pastor responded, "Yes, you're right. But there's always room for one more."

    And that really did sum it up. Church is just a collection of people. The people are no better than those who didn't come that morning. Most of them don't really claim to be either. But there are always going to be those that do. Arthur Rifkin was one of those. He was one who had made Karen feel bad about her divorce and then about her subsequent marriage to Jeff. He stuck his nose into the business of many people. Now, he was making a beeline for Kevin, a stern look on his face. Kevin remembered his promise to his mother. He sat down and waited.

"Young man," Arthur Rifkin said to him. "I'd like to speak with you."

"Certainly, sir," Kevin replied.

"Concerning your actions Friday night, I was deeply disturbed when I heard what had happened."

Kevin decided to have a little fun. "Well, sir. Please don't worry. I'm fine, and my mom's fine. Everything is okay, but I appreciate your support."

"Whoa there, son. I didn't say I supported your actions. I think they were atrocious."

"I agree. That guy should never have touched my mother."

"But you should not have gotten involved."

Kevin nodded thoughtfully. "I can see how some people might agree with that."

"But you think you were right?"

Kevin shrugged. "Right and wrong is subjective, isn't it, Mr. Rifkin? We all do what we think is right at the time."

He shook his head. "No, son, the Bible is very clear about how we handle situations like that. We do not get into fights. We do not attack others, do we?"

"We?"

"Yes, we," replied Mr. Rifkin. "Christians don't get to respond like that."

Kevin nodded knowingly. "Ahhh. I see the problem. Well, Mr. Rifkin, the truth is, I'm not a Christian."

"Excuse me?" The older man looked as though someone had just slapped him in the face.

"I'm sorry," Kevin replied. "But I'm not a professing Christian. I have never claimed that I was."

"Well then you have even bigger problems."

"Perhaps," Kevin agreed. "But you can see now why our opinions differ so greatly."

"Son, you should open up a Bible some day."

"I've read it cover to cover many times."

"Well then, maybe you ought to think about it some."

"Actually, I do," Kevin pointed out. "Quite often, believe it or not. Right now I'm thinking about Proverbs 26:17."

"What?" He began opening his Bible and flipping through the pages while Kevin looked on. He probably shouldn't have said that, but it was too late. As Mr. Rifkin read the passage, his face turned bright red. "Oh, you're a funny one, aren't you?"

Karen Timmons had seen the two talking and thought it best not to let it go on too long. She quickly excused herself from the group and hurried over to Kevin's side.

"Hi, Art! How are you today?"

Arthur Rifkin turned to her and said, "Hello Karen. Your son and I were just discussing his actions on Friday night and he has just told me some very disturbing news."

"Has he?"

"Yes. He told me that he is not a Christian. Now you tell me, what kind of household are you and that Timmons guy running?"

Kevin immediately jumped up, looking Arthur Rifkin squarely in the eye, the playful grin and soft green eyes replaced by a steady, laser-like gaze. "Mr. Rifkin," he said in his patented steady monotone. "This is one of those times in life where you need to be very careful about what comes out of your mouth next."

Arthur Rifkin gulped slightly and kept his mouth clamped shut. He took a step back.

Karen pointed at Kevin. "Kevin, go sit down."

Kevin held his eyes steady on Mr. Rifkin's. "Kevin!" she repeated in a harsh whisper. "Go!"

Brittany Morgan had come in just at the end of the exchange. She quickly assessed the situation, came over, and took hold of Kevin's arm, guiding him away. Kevin slowly took his eyes off the petrified Arthur Rifkin and let Brittany pull him along to where his mother had been sitting. Brittany stayed with him, making sure he didn't turn back and make things worse.

"Don't worry about that guy," she said. "What? Was he giving you a hard time about Friday?"

Kevin sat down. "It's no big deal. He'll probably never talk to me again, so at least I got rid of him."

"Can I sit with you?"

He looked up at her. "You know I have a girlfriend, right?"

She turned red. "That's not why...you don't really think...Oh that's real funny," she said as Kevin's serious face cracked and he began laughing. "I would never do something like that, you know that, right? Especially to Lindsey. She's Tracey's sister."

Kevin nodded. "I know. You're just easy to pick on."

"Gee, thanks." She sat down.

Kevin had to hear from several more members of the Grace Gospel congregation, but most were actually supportive. Some secretly admired what Kevin had done, but they would never admit to that in church. There were some who suggested he might have handled it differently, but most were understanding of the reactions of a young man defending his mother. Many of them mentioned the game as well. Kevin had been so impressive that even several people he had never even met previously came up and introduced themselves, telling him what a great game he played. Much to Karen's delight, Brittany stayed close the whole time. Kevin knew what she was thinking but quickly dispelled any notions she might be getting from the scene.

"We're just friends, Mother. There is nothing going on and nothing *about* to go on. Brittany is best friends with Tracey, Lindsey's sister."

Eventually, the service ended and Kevin and Brittany parted ways. Karen and Jeff spent several minutes talking with friends and drinking one last cup of coffee before going home. Kevin suffered through a couple more comments about Friday night, but he managed to avoid getting into any more arguments. In just a few minutes he would be out of the danger zone.

Chapter 15

Monday morning hit Kevin like a ton of bricks. Having spent virtually his entire weekend in the shop working on his Christmas ornaments, he had managed to forget that there was a city around him that was reacting to his Friday evening exploits. Kendall Township was brimming with hope for their varsity football team and they were also rallying around their budding super star, Kevin Sinclaire.

Kevin knew full well that there was going to be an issue throughout the week. Jerry Hoffinger had made it clear that Kevin was to keep as low a profile as possible and not to make any inflammatory statements, even to other students. This wouldn't be a problem for Kevin. He wasn't much of a braggart anyhow. He figured that he would walk into Kendall High to the typical back-slaps and high-fives he'd always gotten from other students. He assumed that there would be girls who would be interested in him because of the status of being around the player who had been named the MVP of the game. He had no idea what was in store for him.

When Karen Timmons pulled up to the curb at the school, there were several reporters talking to students, their cameramen dutifully recording everything that was said. The Kendall High student body was having their day in the sun. Their Cobras had dismantled the defending state champs and spirits were still flying high. The reporters were getting their fill of "VENOM!" chants and black and silver towels being waived for the cameras. It seemed like everybody was getting in on the act. The faculty didn't know exactly how they ought to handle the reporters' presence, so they nervously followed them around to make sure nothing inappropriate was being said or done.

When Kevin got out of the car, the throng swarmed to him. He was mobbed by the student body and likely would have been hoisted onto their shoulders for the cameras, but the teachers had finally had enough of the mayhem, and began disbursing the students. Kevin was surrounded by the reporters, thrusting their microphones into his face and asking a million questions at once.

"Kevin Sinclaire, how do you feel about being called a "psycho case" by some Holy Trinity fans?"

"Mr. Sinclaire, what do you think of the efforts being made to keep you from playing in this Friday's game?"

"Mr. Sinclaire, do you care about the safety of the other players?"

"Do you like to hurt people?"

Kevin didn't give them any answers at all. He didn't even say "No Comment" like Mr. Hoffinger had instructed him to. He just strolled along as though they weren't even there. He made his way over to where Tony and Scott were standing, near the veterans' monument over by the flag pole. The reporters continued their tirade, seemingly unaware that he was ignoring them. Tony and Scott had amused expressions on their faces as Kevin bumped fists with them.

Scott nodded at the reporters crowding around them. "You gonna talk to them, or what?"

Kevin frowned. "Talk to who?"

Scott gestured to all of the reporters. "Uh, you're fan club.

Kevin glanced around as though he had just been made aware of the presence of so many reporters. He nodded. "I guess I should make a statement, huh?"

Tony shook his head. "Bad idea." He addressed the crowd. "Hey! He has NO COMMENT, so beat it!"

Kevin patted him on the back. "No worries, Yavs. I got this."

He stood up on one of the benches and motioned with his hands for silence. When everyone quieted down, he pulled a piece of paper from his book bag and began to unfold it. Just about every local TV reporter quickly got their cell phones out and signaled for their stations to go live. Kevin Sinclaire was about to break his silence.

"I have a statement I'd like to read, and then I have to get to class so please hold your questions until later." He cleared his throat. "I'd like to begin by discussing the many emerging markets in a global economy."

The reporters all immediately frowned, and began wondering what the heck this kid was talking about.

Kevin continued. "As you all know, the key to survival for any of us is to create a synergistic relationship between the consumer market and…"

He went on for at least a full minute before the TV stations figured out that he was having them on. Some reporters tried to cut him off, but Kevin was absolutely in a zone, reading his "speech" from the obviously blank piece of paper he was holding. He went from topic to topic in an increasingly ridiculous monotone. The frustrated reporters didn't know if they were wasting their time or if they were recording pure gold from the fourteen year old. But they knew that this young man was having a great deal of fun at their expense. One by one, they drifted away until Kevin was left alone with his friends. The students milling about the campus were getting a huge kick out of the confused and embarrassed journalists.

Kevin was sitting on the back of the bench, Tony and Scott standing in front of him, laughing and giggling over his antics.

Scott slapped him on the knee. "Dude, I am in awe. Did you plan that?"

Kevin shook his head and shrugged. "Nope. I just made it all up as I was standing there. I can't believe they stuck around so long. What a bunch of goons."

Tony was still shaking his head when he glanced over his shoulder. He quickly snapped his head back around to Kevin. "Whoa, Dude. Check it out. One o'clock. Emily Vasquez is heading this way."

Kevin flicked his eyes over Tony's shoulder. Sure enough, Emily was heading toward them. She was wearing faded jeans with black heels and a "Kendall Cobras" T-shirt, but every single boy in the area followed her with their eyes like she was in a pageant gown, each one of them wishing that she'd talk to them even for one minute. She purposefully strode over to the group of freshmen ball players, her striking blue eyes riveted on Kevin. She had those Columbian blue eyes, which seemed to have been bred in that one country specifically for the purposes of drawing men to Columbian women. Her grandmother had once told her that blue-eyed Columbian girls needed to be very careful how they used their eyes because the boys were powerless against them. She stopped just in front of Kevin, ignoring the other guys standing there, with their slack-jawed looks frozen on their faces, her flowery smelling perfume seeming to hold them in a state of hypnosis. She looked at Kevin, a slightly seductive semi-smile on her face.

"Hey, Kevin. Do you remember me?"

Like anyone could possibly forget Emily Vasquez. "I remember you. How are you, Emily?"

"I'm good." She glanced from Tony to Scott, slightly amused, and continued. "You guys were great on Friday night. I just wanted to say congratulations, and I was sorry you weren't at the party. I wanted to dance with you."

Kevin nodded. "I was with my girlfriend," he said pointedly.

Emily nodded at that. "That's cool," she replied, a knowing look on her face. "Well, I guess I'll see you guys around." She looked pointedly at Kevin, who returned her stare with an unamused one of his own. She turned and strode away, making sure she stayed in his line of sight the whole time. Tony and Scott finally got their tongues back.

"Geez!" said Scott, leaning heavily on Tony. "She is *so* hot. She totally wants you, Kev."

"I really don't care to be honest."

Scott shook his head in disbelief. "How can you not care? Did you see her? Couldn't you smell her perfume? What was that anyway?"

Tony looked up thoughtfully. "I don't know…lavender?"

Scott shook his head. "No. It was more flowery than that. Plumeria?"

"Or maybe Jasmine…"

"Will you guys shut up?"

Tony leaned on Kevin's shoulder. "Dude, you're in serious trouble, you know that, right?"

Kevin shook his head firmly. "No trouble at all, Yavs. I'm with Lindsey and that's all there is to it. I don't want Emily. Emily has no chance."

Tony looked at him. "No chance? *Emily Vasquez* has no chance? Look, buddy, I love Lindsey and all that, but Emily is perfection. You just don't get hotter than that. She's supermodel hot, and then some." His eyes drifted to something behind Kevin. "Oh…my…God…" he whispered, nudging Kevin to get him to turn around. Scott's eyes were wide open and his mouth was once again slack-jawed.

Kevin turned in his seat, and his eyes widened to match the other guys, though he managed to get control back almost immediately. He was staring at something he had never seen before. Lindsey had just gotten out of her mother's car with her sister, Tracey. Neither of those two girls had ever set the world on fire with their apparel choices, Tracey being too conservative and Lindsey doing everything she could to be as plain as possible. Tracey had obviously made some changes over the summer to at least loosen up and look good. Lindsey had begun the school year just like she had ended that previous year. But right now, what Kevin was staring at was something extraordinary. Lindsey was wearing a black dress, sort of form-fitting, but not too tight. She had never worn a single dress since she and Kevin had begun to date. She had on sandal type shoes with thin straps around her ankles. Most of the time Lindsey wore flip-flops or sneakers. She generally kept her hair pulled back in a pony tail or a braid, but today, her gleaming black hair was down, falling past the middle of her back, which really completed the overall look.

Lindsey didn't look angry, but she also wasn't smiling, which somehow added to the sexy look rather than take away from it. She walked right up to Kevin who had gotten down off his perch on the bench and waited for her. As soon as she got to him, Lindsey wrapped her arms around Kevin's neck and pulled him close for a kiss that took just a second or two too long. There was an audible murmuring among the onlookers. So, Kevin Sinclaire apparently had a girlfriend.

When she finally released Kevin from her embrace, he held her by the shoulders and said, "Wow. What was that for?"

Lindsey smiled, her eyes never leaving his. "For you," she said simply. She looped her arm through Kevin's. "Shall we?"

Kevin smiled. "Let's."

She glanced at Tony and Scott. "Hi Scott…Antonin, how are you? Do me a favor and stop gawking at me, Antonin."

As Lindsey and Kevin walked away from them, Tony leaned on Scott's shoulder. "Tell you what, Six, I hate it when she calls me Antonin, but just then, I didn't care."

Scott nodded, still a little glassy-eyed. "Yeah."

When they entered through the front doors of the school, all eyes were on them. Kevin and Lindsey made their way through the crowd of students, nearly every one of whom turned an watched them. Kevin Sinclaire was a Kendall celebrity now and the guys watched his every move while the girls stared contemptuously at Lindsey, who stood tall, her eyes silently telling every female around that Kevin was already taken. *So keep your hands off!* Her heart was beating a thousand times faster than normal, but she managed to play the part of Kevin Sinclaire's girlfriend to perfection.

Emily Vasquez was leaning against her locker, talking to another girl as Kevin and Lindsey passed by. Her eyes widened slightly as she took in the newly attired Lindsey, who seemed to be walking alongside Kevin with a different attitude to go along with her new clothing style. She had to admit, Lindsey was beyond stunning. In Kendall High School, the girls thought nothing of stealing a football player away from another girl. Sex was a powerful weapon, but one thing that no one wanted was to face rejection. Lindsey had taken a huge step in the game of intimidation today. Any girl who wanted Sinclaire would have to possess not only the looks, but also the swagger that Lindsey was showing today. Emily respected Lindsey's bold efforts.

"Good for you, girl," she said softly, throwing Lindsey a quick thumbs-up. Lindsey looked right through her, drawing a serious grin from Emily. "I think I like this girl."

At Lindsey's locker, Kevin stood there, looking amused as she quickly opened the door and pulled out the books for her first two classes. She knew he was staring at her.

"What?"

"Nothing," he replied. "You just look really nice today."

She closed her locker door and looked at him with her eyebrows raised. "Nice? I look nice today?"

"Well, yeah."

She softly touched her hand to Kevin's face. "Sweetheart, I don't look nice."

"You don't?"

"Are you kidding me? Tell me I just didn't walk through this school looking like the girl next door."

Kevin nodded. "I see. No. You don't look like the girl next door. You look like the girl everyone *wished* lived next door."

"Aww! Thank you, handsome. And you look great too in your shorts and flip-flops."

"Seriously? How was I supposed to know we were dressing for the prom?"

"Real funny, jerk."

*****

Tracey was in a state bordering on panic. She had been so grateful for the spectacle that Lindsey created because of the cover it afforded her to enter the school unnoticed. If Matt Kildare was lurking anywhere near the entrance, he would have been distracted long enough for Tracey to slip in and hurry away to her upstairs locker. The problem right now was that she hadn't seen Matt at all when she snuck in behind the glamorous entrance of Kevin and Lindsey. She was counting on him being visible so that she could avoid going in his direction, but he was nowhere to be seen. Tracey had to quickly duck into the nearest stairwell before she could be discovered.

While she and Lindsey had come up with a plan of attack on how to deal with the inevitable conversation with Matt, Tracey knew that she could not handle it right now. It was one of those plans that sounded great when you were talking about it in your bedroom with your sister, but when it comes to actually going through with it…well, it isn't the same.

Ya know, the good news is that you haven't hit rock bottom. Things can get way worse. What if he comes into this stairwell?

Now she was stuck in the stairwell, practically hyperventilating. Brittany had already texted her three times, and the fourth was coming in now. Tracey responded and within thirty seconds Brittany peeked in to see Tracey sitting alone on the steps.

She quickly hid the grin that was beginning to creep onto her face and got serious.

"Come on," Brittany said. "Get up. Matt is right around the corner. Let's get you to your locker and then to homeroom."

"You saw him?"

Brittany nodded urgently. "Just now. Upstairs is clear."

They hurried up the steps. Tracey hesitated at the door, turning to Brittany. "Do I look okay? Not panicked or anything?"

Brittany smiled. "You look awesome. Get out there."

Tracey took a deep breath and looked apprehensively through the window in the door before pushing it open and tentatively stepping across the threshold. Once in the hall, she and Brittany quickly headed off to where their lockers were situated in the sophomore wing. Both freshmen and sophomore lockers and homerooms were on the second floor, while the upperclassmen were downstairs. Tracey felt safer now that she was out of Matt's territory, but she also knew that he had spent a lot of time up here last year when he and Emily were dating. He could show up at any moment and see her. She quickly got her locker open.

Thank God you remembered the stupid combination! Things are looking up.

"Oh, my God!" Brittany turned white as a ghost.

Tracey looked up. "What?" She saw the look on Brittany's face. "He's here?"

Brittany nodded, trying not to look at him. He hadn't spotted Tracey yet, or at least, he hadn't indicated he had. He was talking to a couple of cheerleaders, grinning and flirting just like always.

Tracey took a quick peek, and then closed her locker and grabbed Brittany's arm, heading away from Matt and around the corner. They hurried to homeroom, Tracey not breathing until they were safely inside and seated at desks that were out of sight of the hall. Tracey figured she'd be safe until lunch. That was going to be very tricky.

Unless...just hit the vending machines. Fill your stomach, get through the day, and bring lunch for the rest of the year. You don't ever have to see him again...

When the bell rang for period one, she hurried out of the room and made her way to her first class of the day, U.S. History I. As she approached the room, she was just beginning to settle down when Matt Kildare came around the corner. He was alone, and looked right at her. Before she could stop herself, she met his eyes with hers. He gave a nod, clearly indicating that he wanted to come see her. Tracey didn't know what to do, so she quickly smiled and ducked into her classroom. Fortunately, Matt didn't chase her in. She was safe for the moment.

Smooth move, Trace. Now you can try to explain that one too.

*****

If Lindsey thought that her little stroll through the school on the arm of Kevin Sinclaire had sent a message that he was already taken, she was absolutely right. Everyone in the school now knew that they were together. If she thought that it would make a single bit of difference to the girls who had set their sights on him, she was sorely mistaken. Sure, there were some freshman girls and even a few sophomores who took one look at the couple and knew they would never have a chance at him, but to the juniors and seniors, Lindsey might as well have been invisible.

The second she disappeared into her AP History classroom and Kevin turned to head toward the library, than they descended on him like vultures. Tony would later comment on the Hitchcockian scene he had witnessed as Kevin tried to walk through the halls that morning. These were literally the hottest girls in the entire school falling all over themselves and one another to introduce themselves to a freshman. It was bizarre, but Tony also found it very amusing at the same time. He stood back and aimed his phone at the scene, recording as much as he could until the warning bell rang and he had to run to class.

It didn't end with that one single moment for Kevin. Everywhere he went throughout the day, he was besieged with girls trying to talk to him. It was every young man's fantasy to be literally showered with propositions from girls. Most boys enter high school hoping that just one pretty girl will even *talk* to him, perhaps go to the dance with him, maybe even be his girlfriend. Every freshman boy fantasizes about the junior and senior girls, who look so much older and more glamorous than the girls their own age, but are so far out of reach. The younger boys would spend half their freshman year daydreaming about what it would be like to have one of those older girls as their girlfriend. Kevin

Sinclaire, on the fourth day of the school year could have any girl he chose. What no one understood, or perhaps more likely, they just didn't care, was that he had already chosen his girl.

The older girls in Kendall High School simply didn't see Lindsey as competition. After all, they were the top of the heap at this school. They had cars, jobs, and the kind of freedom that could only come with a few more birthdays. This would be the one period of their lives where the ladies would consider it more advantageous to be older. Being older meant that the freshmen boys worshiped you. They would never date a freshman. That would be just a little weird. But Kevin Sinclaire was different. He even *looked* different. Forget about how old he was, the guy looks like he just stepped off a movie set! He's already six feet tall with a body that looks like it belongs in the Olympics, or carved into the side of a mountain. He wasn't a *real* freshman. He was a mythical god who had destroyed the hated Holy Trinity Crusade. He was the defender of his mother. They especially liked the way Frank Higgins' wife put it: "He attacked my husband like a *mad dog*!" The term "Mad Dog" was already being bandied about in the Kendall High lexicon. It added an element of danger to his already larger-than-life image. It only served to further ignite the interest of many of the females in the student body.

Throughout the day, as Kevin tried to focus on his classes, which he could accomplish with little effort at all, he was approached often by girls seeking to introduce themselves. In every instance he tried to politely explain that he was already dating someone. He really was becoming overwhelmed by all of the attention. He was used to girls liking him. It was the kind of thing he'd always had to put up with, mostly because of his deep green eyes, which were so striking that the girls used to always ask him to look at them so they could inspect them. That was back in grade school. They still stared at his eyes, but now they did so from afar, the innocence of curiosity no longer the driving force behind their interest. Now, his eyes had a different affect on them. His gaze now caused the girls to feel butterflies circling in their stomachs, to make their skin tingle.

As he spent half his day explaining his relationship status, he became amused at how these girls stared at his eyes as he was talking. He began to loosen up. His demeanor became less off-putting and more social. It was actually kind of neat that girls so much older than he was would feel so compelled to talk to him. His initial desire to be left alone began to give way to a personality that had not shown itself since last school year. While he still had no intention of dropping Lindsey, he saw no reason to be rude or abrupt about it. Between periods, he spent the time roaming the halls, talking to friends and other football players, smiling and laughing at jokes. He smiled at the girls as they tried their best to be noticed by the next big Kendall High super star. This is how it had always been for Kevin. Somehow, over the course of his trip to Japan, he had pushed his personality down in favor of the more serious warrior mentality that was so prevalent in that culture. Now, he could feel the weight of that facade melting away. The most popular kid from Gentry Road Elementary was back. To most, Kevin simply appeared more relaxed and comfortable. To his friends, he was just back to normal.

*****

Lindsey's day was not going well. It had started off perfectly. She had accomplished exactly what she had set out to do, let everyone know that Kevin was taken and that she was just what the star of a football team needed on his arm. She had hoped that it would limit the amount of attention the girls would pay to her guy, but within minutes of the end of the third period of the day, roughly two hours after she and Kevin made their grand entrance, she knew it was hopeless. As she walked the halls toward her next class, she could see the crowd around Kevin. He was smiling and talking, both to guys and girls alike, most likely about the game or the fight afterward. She could see both the guys and girls hanging on his every word.

She didn't even bother to try to say hi. She just headed directly to her next class. But Kevin caught her out of the corner of his eye, and immediately broke away from the group. He hurried over to her, quickly scooping her up like a knight in shining armor. She almost screamed, throwing her arms around his neck, afraid that he would drop her.

"Hey, you clown! What do you think you're doing?"

He put her down, and grabbed her hands, bringing them up to his lips, kissing each one.

"I saw you passing by."

Lindsey leaned on the lockers behind her. "I guess you were able to escape the pile of girls, huh?"

He glanced back over at the crowd of Brettes and cheerleaders talking to the football players. "Don't worry about them. It's just one big social club. You're always invited wherever I am."

It actually helped a lot to hear that. "It just makes me nervous, all those girls around you."

"Like I said. You don't worry about me. We're together. I'm *all* yours."

She leaned in and lay her head on his chest. "Just don't break my heart, okay?"

He kissed her head, wrapping his arms around her tightly. "Never."

For about five minutes Lindsey felt on top of the world again. But as she sat at her desk, waiting for her AP Biology class to begin, she overheard two girls talking about Kevin. They were seniors, Christie Banner and Ariel Gordan, and they knew Lindsey was Kevin's girlfriend. It sounded like they wanted her to hear what they were saying.

"I promise you this, before homecoming, I'm going to get with him."

"His girlfriend is sitting right over there. Maybe we should let her know that her boyfriend is fair game."

"If she doesn't know already, she's gonna find out. He's gonna set records *on* the field and *off.* Know what I mean?"

They giggled, seeing Lindsey tense up. But she didn't turn around. She felt a hand on her arm, and looked over. It was Emily Vasquez, standing and facing the two senior girls.

"Why don't you two knock it off?"

"What do you care, Emily? You'll probably be the first one he gets, won't you?"

Emily didn't even blink. "Maybe you two should worry about getting your shots first. You think Kevin Sinclair wants to sleep with a couple of walking STDs?"

Lindsey almost burst out laughing.

"Oh, you're real funny, Em. Like you're not gonna go for him, right?"

"Don't worry about what I'm gonna do. Worry about competing with *this*." She gestured to Lindsey. "You two bimbos don't have a prayer."

"Whatever, Emily." The seniors turned away and took their seats.

Emily took the seat next to Lindsey, who was taking deep breaths. "Don't worry about those two idiots."

Lindsey nodded. "Thank you…for all that."

Emily nodded, a kind smile on her pretty face. "No problem," she said after a moment. Class was about to begin. "Listen, just play it cool, okay? You already have him. Don't let these people get under your skin."

Lindsey nodded.

"You have lunch sixth period, right?"

Lindsey nodded again.

"Let's sit together. I promise you no one will mess with you."

Chapter 16

When Lindsey left the lunch line at the start of sixth period, she immediately saw Emily Vasquez, gesturing to her from the back of the room. Emily was sitting alone in a booth by a window. While she was the sort who drew near constant stares from the boys wherever she went, the girls did their level best to ignore her. Lindsey made her way through the throng of students to the back of the room and joined Emily, who had a look of playful amusement on her face.

"What?" Lindsey asked apprehensively.

Emily's amused look grew into a bewildered smile. "Do you really not see this?"

Lindsey cocked her head, confused. "See what?"

"Look around you, girl. Everywhere you go, these boys can't take their eyes off of you."

"Yeah right. Whatever." The thought alone was troubling enough. Lindsey didn't dare look around for fear that it might actually be true. She still wasn't sure what Emily Vasquez wanted from her, but considering the brewing situation between Tracey and Matt Kildare, anything was possible. But she had stood up for Lindsey earlier and that counted for something.

Emily took a bite from her wrap. "What did you *think* was going to happen when you put that outfit on this morning?" she asked between mouthfuls.

Lindsey lost her appetite. She put her head in her hands. "I don't know. I was just trying to…"

"Oh, I know what you were trying to do," Emily gave her a knowing grin. "And guess what? You did it. The whole school knows Kevin Sinclaire has a girlfriend. They all know his girlfriend is seriously hot. So what's the problem?"

Lindsey just shook her head. "I guess I thought it would back some of them off, but I think it only made everything worse."

"It didn't make anything worse," Emily replied. "The truth is there was nothing you could have done. He's a football star and girls like football stars. The fact that he's absolutely gorgeous is what makes it worse. There isn't a girl in this school that doesn't want him. And guess what? By the end of the year, if he really *is* a star, there will be girls coming at him from *other* schools too!"

Lindsey pushed her tray aside. "Great. That sounds wonderful."

Emily pulled the tray back. "Eat, girl. All is not lost. I'm just telling you the lay of the land. Now you can strategize. Sun Tzu said all battles are won or lost before they are ever fought."

"Sun Tzu?"

"Yes, Sun Tzu. "The Art of War"? You're in AP History right?"

"Yes. I know who Sun Tzu was, but why are you quoting from "The Art of War?""

Emily pointed her finger at Lindsey. "Get it straight, sister. You are in the fight of your life if you hope to still be Kevin Sinclaire's girlfriend this time next year."

Lindsey shook her head pessimistically. "I'll be lucky to still be his girlfriend this time next *week.*"

"Naw," Emily replied. "You probably have at least a couple weeks or so. Maybe more since he's a pretty good guy. At least he seemed like a good guy when I talked to him earlier."

"You talked to Kevin?"

"Oh yeah. Right before you got there, I guess. He told me all about you. He was fine. Don't worry. He didn't seem interested in me at all, if it makes you feel better."

"Are you going to sleep with Kevin?"

Emily leaned back, surprised. "Whoa! Where did that come from?"

"Are you?"

"Are you being serious right now?"

"Yes. Just tell me if you are because I can't take games. I know I can't stop you, so just tell me if you are going to have sex with Kevin."

"You act like he doesn't have any say in it."

"I know all about you, okay."

"Oh you do?" Emily smirked. "Tell me, what do you *know* about me."

"I know that every guy in the school wants you. I know that you and Matt Kildare go out...sort of, but since you both like to have sex with other people, you guys aren't officially boyfriend and girlfriend. I know if you wanted Kevin, it would just be a matter of time before you got him."

Emily nodded thoughtfully. "In other words, I'm the school slut."

"I didn't say that."

"Well, what would *you* say you said?"

"I didn't call you a slut. I just know that if Emily Vasquez wants a guy, Emily Vasquez always gets him."

"Is that so?"

"Look, are you going to answer my question or not?"

Emily laughed and shook her head. "You really are a piece of work, Lindsey Overton, aren't you?"

"Whatever." Lindsey had enough. She began to get up.

"Wait a minute," Emily said, reaching out to grab her arm. "Don't go. Sit. Eat. Talk to me."

Lindsey sat back down, her face flushed and her eyes were beginning to redden. Emily looked at her thoughtfully. She felt pity for some reason that she could not explain. It really wasn't her style. Here was a girl who stood between Emily and a guy who was about to reach mythical status in this school, but she found herself feeling like there was something else at stake. She felt like maybe there was something more important to be gained here than just getting the guy. She found herself very connected to this girl. She found herself wanting to help her, to guide her through this confusion, to just be her friend.

Emily leaned close. "You asked me if I was going to have sex with your boyfriend. The answer is no."

Lindsey tried to believe her. "Is that a promise?"

"I swear, I'm not going after him."

Lindsey considered this for a moment.

Emily held up her little finger. "Want me to pinky swear?"

Lindsey finally cracked a smile. "Why not." They locked little fingers and shook on it.

Lindsey asked, "Why would you promise that to me?"

"I don't really know." Emily shook her head. "A gesture of friendship, I guess? You look like you could really use a friend right now. And believe it or not, I don't have a many girlfriends. Guy friends, yes. But very few girls really like me here."

Lindsey frowned. "And you want to be *my* friend?"

"Why not? You need a friend, don't you?"

"I guess."

"Do you have any friends?"

"Not really. Just Kevin."

Emily nodded in understanding. "Ahhh. So that's it. You're afraid of losing your best friend, not just your boyfriend."

Lindsey raised her eyebrows and nodded. "Yeah, I guess that's it. I never thought to put it like that, but…yeah. He's more like a best friend."

"But one that you kiss, right?"

Lindsey blushed a little. "Yes, one that I kiss."

Emily nodded slowly. "And other things…?"

Lindsey hesitated. Emily's eyes widened.

"Oh…I figured you two…" She looked closely at Lindsey. "You mean, you haven't?"

Lindsey shrugged, somewhat embarrassed, and shook her head.

Emily was stunned. "You mean not even once?"

"No."

"I can't believe it."

"Why is that so hard to believe? We're fourteen. It's not like we've been together for three years and we're seniors."

Emily shook her head. "No, it's not that. It's just that…I mean, the way you two were in each others' space earlier. It's so…comfortable. It's like…like you already know each other that way, you know? It's hard to explain, but if you look closely, you usually can tell the couples that are doing it. They begin lose that separation, that fear of getting too close in public. They kind of get comfortable with one another. It's actually kind of romantic. You two look like that to me. That's why…Are you serious? You two have never ever done it?"

Lindsey began to laugh. "I'm *pretty* sure. To be honest, we have never done more than kiss. He is actually very careful about that."

Emily got serious. "Okay. That changes everything. Do NOT let that information get out. Whatever you do, act like the two of you are in bed every night. Don't discuss it with *anyone*. Don't offer details if they ask you. Say nothing. Just smile, shake your head and act like they're pathetic for asking you to begin with."

"Okay. Why?"

"Because whatever this is all about to you, for everyone else, it is about nothing but sex. They all want to date a football player. They know that dating football players usually means that sex has to be on the table because football players can usually have sex if they want to. There are plenty of girls who are willing to do it just casually. So, you can't let them know that you guys aren't having sex because it will open the flood gates."

"But why would it matter? Aren't they going to go after him with sex anyway?"

"Good question, and the answer is yes, but right now, believe me, they all think he's doing it with you."

"They do?"

"Trust me. They already assumed it just because he is a football player. You all but confirmed it with your little entrance this morning. Now they know that it's not just about stealing someone's boyfriend. They will have to up their game because his girlfriend is probably hotter than they are."

"Okay." Lindsey was beginning to understand.

Emily continued, "But if they get wind that Kevin is not getting it from you, then all bets are off."

Lindsey frowned. "Why?"

Emily shrugged matter-of-factly. "Simple. It doesn't matter how pretty you are, how sexy you dress, how you act, whatever. High school guys want sex. If he's not getting it from *you*, they all know it's just a matter of time before someone offers their services."

Lindsey nodded. "So, you're telling me that I need to start having sex with Kevin?"

"I didn't say that. You have to do what you think is right; what *you* want to do. If he's ready for sex and you aren't, I don't think he should try to pressure you. But you need to know that *he* is going to be pressured on his end, by the guys *and* the girls. Sex is a big topic of discussion, believe me. He's going to hear plenty of stories and meet plenty of girls. It's going to get very hard to keep him faithful if the two of you are not doing it. You just need to think about it and figure out what you want and what you're willing to do. It's better to make a plan now than to have to come up with one on the spot. Remember? Sun Tzu.

*****

To the entire school Kevin Sinclaire was already more than just another freshman ball player. They were a dime a dozen. No, this freshman was different. By the end of the day he was walking the halls like a conquering hero, and many of the students were already calling him "Mad Dog". He was beginning to get used to his celebrity status. He caught up with Lindsey right before last period. She could see his relaxed demeanor right away and wondered if it was a good sign or bad.

As they were getting ready to part ways for the final period of the day, a very pretty brunette came up and introduced herself.

"Hi, Kevin? I'm Alli. Two ells, one i. I'm your Girl."

Kevin exchanged glances with Lindsey, who said. "I guess she's your Girl."

Alli smiled and raised her eyebrows. "You know that every varsity starter is assigned a Brette Girl, right?"

Lindsey leaned against the wall and looked at Kevin. "You knew that right, Kevin? Every varsity starter gets their *very own* Brette Girl."

Kevin nodded. "Yes, I heard her, Lindz. Nice to meet you, Alli."

Alli continued. "So, what do you like?"

Kevin hesitated, his mind quickly considering the potential for trouble a question like that could cause in front of a guy's girlfriend. Lindsey was quick to jump in.

"Yeah, Kevin. What do you *like*?"

"I, uh...I really don't know."

Lindsey smiled sweetly at Alli. "He's just being shy." To Kevin, "Go on, Sweetheart, tell the pretty Brette Girl what you like. Tell her *everything* you like."

"I, uh..."

Alli shook her head and said, "Look, it's not like that at all. What kind of *treats* do you like? Cookies, cakes...stuff like that. We prepare them each week before the game and do stuff like decorate the players lockers and stuff."

Lindsey nodded matter-of-factly. "See that, Hon? They bake you treats and decorate your locker every week. Isn't that *wonderful?*"

Kevin just did his best not to act interested in the whole deal. It really wasn't all that hard, but he felt like the ice was melting under his feet. "It sounds just fine."

Alli went on, "I'll tell you what, I make great chocolate chip cookies and brownies. Why don't we start there and you can think about it for next week?"

Tony walked up just in time. "No walnuts, kay? I *hate* walnuts." To Kevin he said, "They always ruin perfectly good brownies with stupid nuts." Back to Alli, "Hey, do you know how to make those chocolate cookies with the peanut butter chips in them? They are the best. But you hafta be careful you don't burn the stinkin' things. The chocolate cookies always like to burn on the bottoms if you're not careful."

Alli raised her eyebrows, smiled uncertainly, and turned back to Kevin. "If you think of anything let me know, okay?" She walked away with Tony staring at her every step.

"Yum." It was all he could think to say.

Kevin looked at him. "You know, you're not helping my situation by staring at my Brette Girl in front of my girlfriend."

Tony didn't even blink. "Have a little respect. They work hard. And Lindsey doesn't care about her, right Lindz?"

Lindsey shrugged. "Of course not. Not at all. Why would I care about little brunette seniors shaking their butts and boobs in front of my boyfriend, baking cookies and brownies and crap for them all the time? And don't think I'm not aware of what she really meant when she said "treats"."

Tony looked at her. "She wasn't talking about cookies and brownies?"

Lindsey shook her head. "You guys must think I'm a real idiot."

Tony asked again, "Wait a sec, Lindz, cause my Girl said something about treats too. Are you saying that she really meant…you know…like *treats?* Like *not* food?"

Lindsey stared at him. "Antonin, you're an imbecile, you know that?" To Kevin she said, "Why do you hang around this dope?"

Tony put his arm around Kevin. "He hangs around me because he loves me. Now I gotta get to class." He gave Kevin a big wet kiss on the cheek. "See ya at practice, lover!"

Kevin just stood there, nodding. "You know, I hate it when he does that."

Lindsey was still unhappy. "Well, you better enjoy that one, because *I'm* not kissing you anytime soon."

"Wait! Why? What did I do?"

"You are a filthy whore, that's what."

"I didn't even do anything!"

"But you wanted to."

"No I didn't. She wasn't even pretty!"

"You're a liar. I know you're lying because you can't look me in the eyes right now."

He looked her right in the eyes. "That girl is *not* pretty."

"You are such a liar, and her name is Alli, and that's with two ells and one i."

"I don't care what her name is," Kevin said grabbing Lindsey around the waist. He pulled her in and tried to kiss her.

"Don't even kiss me, you pig."

"Oh, now I'm a pig because they assigned a Brette Girl to me? You heard her, every starter gets one."

"Get off me. I can't stand you right now." She shrugged him off and walked away.

Geez, he thought. *And this when I didn't even do anything.*

*****

Over the next three days, her routine changed very little. Tracey found ways to sneak around Matt throughout the day. He seemed to want to talk to her, but never pushed too hard, so Tracey managed to avoid him by hiding in the bathrooms, and classrooms. She knew she was only prolonging her embarrassment, but she couldn't help herself. It was like trying to avoid a root canal by taking pain killers. Eventually, she knew she would have to face the situation, but every time the opportunity was in front of her, she chickened out.

Wednesday morning, right after homeroom, and following a particularly harrowing near-miss with Matt on the way in, Tracey was hurriedly walking from her locker to her homeroom with Brittany when Matt Kildare suddenly appeared, walking right between them, scaring the daylights out of both of them. Brittany actually would say later that she was reminded for just a split second of the story of how Jesus had appeared, walking with the women on the road to Emmaus.

Matt placed his arm around Tracey's shoulders lightly, asking Brittany, "Do you mind if I borrow her for a minute?"

Brittany nodded wordlessly and watched as Matt steered Tracey off to the side of the hall, out of the path of students going in all directions. She stood for a moment and watched, wanting to be there for her friend, but also realizing that some things you have to do alone. She slowly tore herself away from the scene and walked off to class, knowing that for the next forty minutes she would not be able to concentrate even a little bit. She would spend all of that time wondering what happened.

Tracey was a little shell-shocked. All of the minutes spent sneaking and hiding and worrying and anticipating just such an event all went away and she was now face to face with what she feared most. Matt gently led her to a spot along a bunch of lockers. He stopped, put both hands on her shoulders and stood in front of her.

"Now *stay*. No running away." He had an amused grin on his face, but Tracey's eyes were shut tight. "Open your eyes, Tracey."

She slowly opened them, a rueful smile coming over her face. A cloud of humiliation seemed to descend and envelope her.

This sucks. Now what?

It was hard to tell whether Matt was mad or amused. He just stood there, arms crossed, waiting for her to catch up. Tracey finally looked him in the eyes, her heart skipping about thousand beats and then literally melting in her chest as she once again got lost in the ocean of Matt Kildare's clear blue eyes. She had no words.

He touched her cheek lightly. "I get it, okay?"

Oh, my God, that feels good!

She nodded slightly, feeling even more embarrassed, but not really sure why. Matt continued, "Look, it's *my* fault. I should have thought about...or just talked to you...I don't know. I just don't want you to hide from me anymore, okay? It hurts my feelings."

She almost burst out laughing at the thought, but instead she felt an overwhelming sense of relief. She even felt her eyes welling up a bit, her throat hurt a little from choking up, but she felt as though a huge weight had been lifted from her shoulders. Matt opened his arms, and she timidly leaned forward, allowing him to hold her gently. The warning bell sounded, one minute to get to class. Tracey wanted to scream.

Of course that stupid bell would go off right now!

He let her out of his arms. She reluctantly backed up.

"Get to class," he said, pushing a wisp of her bright red hair out of her eyes. "Sit with me at lunch?"

Oh, my God! Speak up, for God's sake! The man is talking to you!

She nodded. "Sure," she managed to sputter out.

"Okay then. I'll see you at lunch. He smiled. "By the way," he said, leaning in close. "Just so you know, you're just about the only good thing that has happened to me in weeks. See you at lunch."

He smiled and winked at her, then turned and walked away, leaving her even more speechless than ever.

He's just gonna walk away? Who drops a bombshell like that and then walks off? Does that mean he might be thinking about you as more than just some one-night thing? Yeah right. Matt Kildare? Get real, Trace. But he did say it, didn't he? You are the only good thing...

As Matt headed off around the corner, his arm was grabbed from behind. He spun around to face a very angry Emily Vasquez. She was seething, having witnessed virtually the entire conversation he'd just had with Tracey.

"What was that exactly?" she demanded, her hand still gripping his arm, her nails digging into his skin just a bit.

He shrugged her hand off. "What difference does it make to you? You haven't called in five days."

"That's because you're a jerk and you treated me like some little slut on Friday night."

"So? You're not my girlfriend, Emily. So stop pretending you care about me."

"You seriously think I don't care about you?"

"It doesn't matter. I have to get to class. We have like ten seconds." He turned away and headed down the corridor. Emily followed.

"Well, we need to talk, Matt. What is going on between you and Tracey Overton?"

Matt smiled slightly, but didn't slow down. "What do *you* care, Em? We don't have to answer those questions. That's *your* rule, remember?"

"Well, it matters in this case."

"Really? Why?"

"Because I'm friends with her sister."

"Oh?" Matt asked. He shook his head. "No, you're not. You don't have friends, Em. That's why you're at my house just about every night…or I'm at yours."

She was about to respond, but he stopped at the door to his class just as the bell sounded again, signaling the start of class.

"We'll have to talk later. See ya." He went in.

Emily stood there for a moment, mouth open, still seething. She turned on her heel and went towards the Math wing and her AP Calculus class, still wondering what the connection was between Tracey and Matt.

Chapter 17

Tracey couldn't recall a single thing that had happened since her run-in with Matt Kildare. She felt as though she were floating on air and the only thing she could think about was getting to spend her lunch period with him. He actually *wanted* her to sit with him. She sat through three periods over the next two hours and all she could think about was Matt. Brittany finally caught up to her right before third period, wide-eyed and eager to know what had happened. As soon as she saw the bright smile and the twinkling of Tracey's eyes, she knew that all was well, but she wanted the details. Tracey told her that she'd tell her everything at lunch, but as they entered their College Prep Algebra classroom, Brittany grabbed her by the wrist, sat her down at a desk, and sat down at the desk next to her.

"Dish," she said. "I can't wait til lunch."

Tracey laughed, and then quickly and excitedly related the entire conversation. Brittany shook her head in amazement.

"Wow," she said slowly. "All that worrying and he wasn't upset or anything? He really just wanted to talk to you."

Tracey nodded. "Yeah, but I think the worrying made it even sweeter in the end."

Brittany grinned. "Do you think he'll want to date you? Like, make it official?"

Tracey shook her head. "No idea. I'm just planning to sit there, chew with my mouth closed, and try not to do anything humiliating."

"Well, I'll stay with you just in case."

"What do mean, stay with me?"

Brittany stopped and spread her hands. "You're not going to go in there looking for him, are you?"

"Well, I…"

"No! No, no, no. We're going in and getting lunch, and then sitting down just like we always do. If he wants you, he'll come find you."

"But I…"

"Will you trust me? Don't go in there all desperate, looking for him like he's something special. *You're* the one who's special. Start acting like it. He can come find *you*."

"Uhh, I don't know."

Brittany pulled her along a little. "Come on. Trust me. I won't be a third wheel. When he comes, I'll take off. Trust me. He'll come."

They went into the cafeteria and after paying for their meals, found an empty booth near the back corner. Matt came in several moments later with Anquan Griffin and Mike Doyer. Vivian Parker was with them, holding Mike's hand. They'd been together all through high school. She was captain of the cheerleaders and probably the most popular girl in Kendall High. The group moved through the cafeteria like royalty, the guys high-fiving the other players, Vivian quickly heading over to where the girls were congregating. Matt glanced over at Tracey and grinned. He got into line with his friends, but after purchasing his food, he broke off and came over to where Brittany and Tracey were sitting.

"Is this seat taken?" he asked, sliding into the booth next to Tracey.

Tracey was all of a sudden very glad Brittany was there with her. Her presence gave Tracey confidence.

"It is now," she said.

Ten seconds later, Anquan Griffin slid into the booth next to Brittany. "Wassup, y'all?"

Brittany smiled. "Hi, Anquan."

Little by little, the group seemed to ease its way in the general direction of their booth. It must have been the magnetism of these guys, who just seemed to draw everything to themselves. Tracey sat there in awe, a smile pasted on her face as she listened to the flurry of greetings, smack talk, and gossip. Matt was quick to make sure everyone knew who Tracey and Brittany were, though Brittany needed few introductions. It was far less painful than Tracey had ever imagined. She never would have thought that she could possibly ever be accepted so easily into the group of popular kids. She wondered fleetingly if it was because she was with Matt, though no one seemed to question what he was doing with her. They simply included her in the conversation and to Brittany's amusement, Tracey did her best to join in.

It wasn't the romantic lunch Tracey had been daydreaming about, but in many ways it was better. She was, for the first time, an insider in a world that she had only previously observed from a distance. It had always looked like so much fun to be around these people. It always looked like these people were so much happier than everybody else. Their crowd was noisy and enthusiastic, the boys rowdy and obnoxious, while the girls, who all seemed to be gorgeous to Tracey, knew just how to handle everything going on around them. For the first time in her life, she was on the inside of *that* world. She had to admit, it felt really good, especially since she was sitting right next to the veritable king of Kendall High.

As everyone cleared their trays and began to disperse, heading off to the Common Area or outside for some fresh air, Anquan bashed fists with Matt and took off after a group of Brette Girls, one of whom he had his sights set on. Brittany slid out as well, smiling at Tracey and saying goodbye to Matt before going off to sit with some other friends a couple of seats away.

Matt looked at Tracey. "Wanna take a walk?"

Tracey smiled and nodded. "Yes."

As they went outside together, Tracey could feel some stares. She suspected that anytime Matt Kildare was talking to a girl who wasn't Emily Vasquez, it was news, but since no one really knew who she was, it was particularly unusual. They strolled quietly for several minutes, walking side by side in the sunlight. There was a bench off to one side of the quad, just at the edge of the grass. Matt led Tracey in that direction and hopped up on the bench, sitting on the back rest. Tracey sat down on the bench, not wanting to make a fool of herself by falling off the back of a bench in front of Matt Kildare.

He began, "Sooo. I just wanted to tell you again that I'm sorry if you felt uncomfortable."

She replied, "No. Don't apologize. It was totally me. I woke up…and, I don't know. I just…didn't know what to do."

He nodded. "It's cool. I wish I would have woken up before you."

Tracey smiled. "I don't know how I would have handled *that* either."

"Well," he replied. "I would have kissed you a whole lot."

This is information that would have been useful SATURDAY MORNING!

Tracey smiled shyly. "Really? I guess I was afraid that you might wake up and realize that you had just spent the night with…"

He made a face. "Wiiiithhhh????"

Tracey shrugged. "Well, with *not* Emily."

Matt made an "ah-hah" face. "Oh." He shook his head as a slight smile crept onto his face. "Is that what your problem is? You think I cheated on Emily?"

"No, it's not that. I think I get your relationship with Emily, but…it's just…"

He waited expectantly.

"I mean, Emily's so pretty."

He nodded. "Uh huh?"

Tracey's eyebrows were raised. "I mean, really pretty. Emily is stunning, and sexy."

"Okay? And you're not. Is that what you're saying?"

"Exactly."

Matt grinned. "You're kidding me, right?"

"It's not funny, Matt."

"Actually, Tracey, you couldn't be farther from the truth."

Matt gestured out over the space in front of them where a hundred kids were hanging out, talking, and tossing a ball around.

"Let me ask you something. Have you ever walked through the halls of this school with your head up?"

Tracey frowned. "What?"

"Yeah. When you walk through the halls, do you look at the people around you or do you put your head down and stare at the floor when you walk?"

"I guess I…"

"Because if you looked around once in a while, you'd notice that the guys in this school can't take their eyes off you."

"Stop. That's not funny."

"The past three days, every time I tried to get to you and you ran away, I saw how all these guys watched every move you made. Trust me because I'm one of *them*. Let me tell you something else, Tracey. Friday night, I didn't feel like I was doing you any favors. I felt lucky to be with you."

"You did? Because I felt that way too." Tracey looked at him, hesitating just a little. *Just go for it already!* "Maybe we could get together Friday night after the game. I promise to stick around this time."

Matt shook his head. "You really need to take a good look at yourself. See yourself the way *guys* see you. You have it all. Trust me. You are perfect. Absolutely perfect. I wanted to make sure I told you that."

Tracey all of a sudden felt a sinking feeling. *Did he just brush that off?* "Something tells me there's a 'but' coming."

Matt shook his head. "No 'but'. I mean it. I hope you and I will be friends. I love talking to you."

Tracey swallowed hard, her throat starting to close. *This can't be happening before it even starts.* "But, that's it, though. You just want us to be friends."

Matt shrugged. "Tracey, believe me when I tell you this, okay? If I didn't care about you, I would tell you anything you wanted to hear to get you back into bed. I'd do that until you finally got sick of me or I got sick of you. Then we'd end like a horrible train wreck. I don't want that to happen. You couldn't find a worse boyfriend than me. I lie. I cheat. It's way easier to have no girlfriend than to have a girl pissed at me all the time. This way, everybody knows what's up. Emily is *always* pissed at me, but that's just Emily."

Tracey sat there glumly. Her eyes tearing up. Matt slid down to her on the bench and put an arm around her, pulling her to his chest.

"Don't cry, Trace. I swear to God, I would rip your heart apart. I am awful at relationships."

Tracey pushed him away. "Will you stop," she cried, tears just creeping out of her eyes. "You keep telling me to look at myself the way everybody else sees me, but why can't you look at yourself the way *I* see *you*."

Matt laughed. "Are you kidding? I could never come close to living up to the way you look at me. Listen, I *love* the way you look at me. You make me feel special. You really do. But you also don't know me. All I'm saying about you is that guys think you're hot. That's all. The rest is up to you. But every guy in this school wants to go out with you and you ought to act like it. But every girl in this school knows that I'm just a blond-haired, blue-eyed jock that likes to party and loves girls. They don't expect anything else and I don't offer it."

Tracey got control of herself, wiping away the tears. "Well, I don't get that from you when you talk to me."

Matt nodded. "I know. And that's what I want it to be like between us."

Tracey was finally getting her feet under her. "Oh, I get it. You go and act like a jerk all over school and screw every girl you see and then we'll hang out and you pretend you're not really like that? I don't think so."

He shook his head. "That's not what I meant."

Tracey shook her head. "Look Matt, I am new to all this, so I really don't know what to say here. I love the time I spent with you. I wouldn't trade it for anything. But I want a real relationship."

He nodded. "And you deserve one. I'm sorry, I just have nothing to offer a girl right now. My life really kind of sucks."

The warning bell sounded.

Tracey shook her head. "That's not it. Someone who feels that way would want a girlfriend. You want a girl, just not me. You want Emily."

Matt shook his head. "It's not like that."

"Of course it is. And it's okay." She stood up. "I have to go. I'll see you later."

"Tracey..."

She walked off. *That was awesome! Kick him to the curb, girl, just like in the movies. Now, do NOT turn around. Whatever you do, DO NOT look back over your shoulder. Pick a spot straight ahead and focus. Oh my God, what if he's following? We just barely got through that! If he starts acting all cute...*

Tracey walked quickly into the building through the glass front doors of the school. She continued through the hall to the stairs, alternately crying and then wiping the tears away. Fortunately the halls were nearly clear as there was only seconds remaining to get to class, which for Tracey meant gym. She quickly grabbed her gym bag from her locker and then hustled down stairs and into the girls locker room, where the class was already there and changing into their shorts and sneakers. Brittany saw that Tracey was red-faced and puffy, but before she could make a move, Emily Vasquez quickly approached tapped Tracey on the shoulder.

"Hey, what is going on with you and Matt Kildare?"

Tracey looked over her shoulder. "Nothing."

Emily shook her head. "It doesn't look like nothing to me. He's all touching your face this morning and then you guys are all alone talking at lunch. I saw that through the window last period. What is going on?"

"Nothing. Leave me alone, Emily."

"What? You try to get him to take you out and he hurt your feelings?"

Tracey ignored her. The whole class seemed to be watching. She could even see Lindsey across the room, trying to make her way over.

"What's the matter, Tracey? You have a little crush on the big football star? You think he'd ever go out with someone like you?"

Tracey said nothing.

"Huh, Tracey? You really think Matt Kildare would ever go out with a nobody like you? Why can't you even look at me?"

Tracey took a deep breath and stood up straight, turning to look Emily in the eye.

"Why you crying, Tracey? He break your little heart when he told you he didn't date little nothings like you?"

She stared straight ahead, nodding. "Yeah, Emily. That's it."

Emily started to say something else just as Lindsey got to her, grabbing her by the arm. Emily looked closely at Tracey, her jaw dropping slightly in surprise. She shook Lindsey off and came a little closer as Tracey stared straight into her eyes. It was like a stare down, but Emily was not trying to win a contest. She had seen something, but could not believe it.

"No way!" she exclaimed, her eyes wide with shock. "You slept with him, didn't you?"

Tracey's eyes widened. Then she blinked. "You're crazy, Emily. Leave me alone."

"Oh, my God, you did, didn't you?" Emily's mouth was

hanging open in disbelief.

Tracey said nothing and shut her locker, walking past Emily and heading for the gymnasium. Emily quickly caught her breath and hurried to catch up.

"You had sex with *my* boyfriend?"

Tracey kept walking. "He's not your boyfriend, Emily."

"Trust me, you little slut bag, you don't want to play games with me."

Lindsey was trying to get a hold of Emily, but the sophomore would not be held back. The entire class was witnessing the altercation. Tracey knew it was not going to end by ignoring Emily, so she made a snap decision to have it out right then and there and spun to face her.
"Fine, Emily, you want to do this here? Let's talk! He's *not* your boyfriend! You two just *screw* each other all the time. But you like to *screw* other people too, so you two aren't officially going out, are you? Now, what's the problem?"

Emily was taken aback, but she wasn't that easily thrown. "So you admit it? You had sex with Matt?"

"What difference does it make, Emily?" Tracey practically shouted through her tears. "He doesn't *want* me. He wants you. So go get him. He's all yours."

Emily didn't let it end. "All mine? I already knew that. You could *never* take a guy from me."

Tracey looked at her, for the first time feeling like she had the upper hand. She choked back her tears. Emily should have let it go. By continuing the way she did she revealed her own weakness. For a split second she was able to see through the façade of Emily Vasquez, right through to her darkest fear. She knew didn't need to continue the fight any longer. She just smiled putting as much compassion as she could muster into the look on her face.

"Well…there you go."

Chapter 18

The rest of the week found Matt Kildare and Tracey Overton is a reversal of roles of sorts. He spent the better part of the day avoiding her as much as possible. He wasn't hiding from her exactly. He just felt awful about how they had left things. She seemed really mad. She had a right to be too, but he actually really liked her and was doing his best not to damage her as he had to many girls before. Girls had always liked him and he had always taken full advantage. Most of the time it ended badly to one degree or another. He knew that the longer the two of them dated, the worse the breakup would be when she finally got tired of his cheating and lying.

He understood what had compelled her to leave his house Saturday morning. At the time he had been quite disappointed to wake up alone. He had actually fallen asleep thinking about how great she was and how he was looking forward to waking up to her the next morning. It had taken all his self control not to take her up on her offer to "try again" this coming Friday. He felt there was something special about her and for some reason he felt protective of that. He didn't want to be the one to ruin her and he knew that he would ultimately do just that because he was a "god-awful boyfriend". That was what Emily had told him last year after they had first started dating.

You really couldn't find a more attractive girl than Emily Vasquez no matter how many schools you searched through. But that didn't stop Matt from indulging himself at every opportunity. He had figured that his relationship with Emily would end just like all of his previous ones had, but he didn't know Emily. She hadn't cried or whined when she found out about his nonsense. That's what she called it, nonsense. She had certainly slapped him around a little, no doubt about that. And he realized right then that Columbian girls seemed to know how to slap a guy around. He had received his share of slaps from girls, no doubt about it. In fact, his friends considered him to be a connoisseur of sorts, of slaps. He would rather be slapped by just about anybody than a Columbian girl.

She hadn't ended their relationship. Rather, she simply created new rules. She decided that there was no reason to break it off. In fact, there was no reason he couldn't have all the fun he wanted with whomever he wanted. She wouldn't try to chain him to the porch. But the rules floated both ways. She could do whatever *she* wanted too. There would be no whining or complaining, no jealousy or outrage. When they were together they would not discuss their other exploits. When they were together, it would be about just them. On their own, they could do what they wanted. And all this from a *freshman*! Matt was always amazed when he thought about how a freshman could be so open to an arrangement like that. But Emily had even been the one to propose it. She was an interesting person and Matt had always loved to be around her. They still fought constantly, but he figured, what the heck? That was the whole point.

In truth, he believed that he and Emily had something very special. They might even be in love. He was pretty sure she loved *him*. She could act as tough as she wanted and pretend she didn't care about all the other girls, but he knew that she was hurt just a little bit more every time she found out about his latest conquest. He tried to care about that, but he could not keep from acting on his impulses. There were just so many girls always throwing themselves at him, offering their bodies just to be able to tell their friends that they'd been with the Kendall High star.

Emily had been the first girl he'd ever been with who'd understood that. She had realized that in order to be with certain guys, you would have to understand that the rules were different. Kendall High School football players, particularly the stars, generally played by their own rules when it came to relationships. Emily was willing to deal with that as long as Matt didn't shove it in her face. He respected her in his own way. He even cared about her a great deal, but he knew he wouldn't know love if it slapped him in the face. He did recognize that he felt differently about her than he had ever felt about anyone else.

That is, until Tracey Overton had appeared on the deck at the Penner party. Tracey didn't engender the same feelings he had for Emily. These feelings were quite different. He figured that the reason was because the two girls were such polar opposites. Emily was a super confident young girl, absolutely comfortable with her sexuality and eager to explore it. Tracey was a timid soul, completely vulnerable and almost afraid of her feelings. She was a caring person who would make a terrific girlfriend if he was the type who could remain faithful. He had actually considered giving that a shot, but knew that he could only last for so long. Eventually the temptation of other girls would overtake him. Emily alone would break him down in a matter of weeks just to prove that she could.

No, Tracey Overton was far better off without Matt Kildare. The realization of that depressed him even more than he had been before. His life had taken such a drastic turn for the worse ever since football camp had begun. He knew he was in a rut but could not figure a way out. Kevin Sinclaire was the real deal. It was likely that he would take over as the number one receiver and Matt really couldn't blame coach, Mike, or anyone else for that. The goal was to win games and Sinclaire could help this team do that. Matt was all of a sudden relegated to the number two receiver. His dropped passes wouldn't help his cause either. He couldn't believe how tight he had been on Friday night. Sinclaire had taken over the game and Matt couldn't hold onto a simple pass.

He was feeling the pressure on a few fronts. College would happen whether or not he received any athletic scholarships, though he entered his senior year expecting offers from numerous schools for both baseball *and* football scholarships. Now, he figured he would have to rely on the baseball to come through for him. If Sinclaire was going to take over like this, Matt would probably fade into obscurity on the football field. Even if he didn't get any offers for baseball, the Kildares had all the money they needed to send Matt to whichever school he wanted to attend. All he had to do was get accepted.

His mother constantly wondered about his relationships. She saw how he acted with the various girls he spent time with and she was generally appalled at the way he treated them. She was now beginning to make her feelings more clear as he was approaching the age where his relationships ought to be getting more serious, or at least, more respectful. She was beginning to voice her disappointment more often as he didn't seem to be demonstrating any change in his behavior. She seemed to like Emily, which was mildly amusing since Emily had been the one to create the current relationship situation.

Matt was pulled out of his thoughts one night by a knock at the door of his bedroom. He sat up on his bed. Before he could speak the door cracked open and a voice came through.

"Matt? It's me." He chuckled. *Emily. What a surprise.*

She came in and saw the smile on his face. "You knew I would come over, didn't you?"

He shrugged. "Not really. I'm glad you did though."

She came quickly to him and kissed him deeply. He tried to say something to her, but she stopped him.

"Not a word. I don't want to talk right now."

Later, they lay together quietly, each lost in thought. Emily was thoroughly convinced that they were made for one another. It chagrined her to no end that she could find a way to make Matt see it the way she did. To her it was so obvious, and she didn't need Brittany Morgan to tell her the way things *ought* to be. When things are right, they're right. And when Emily and Matt were together, things were usually right. But tonight, as they lay together, Emily had never felt farther away. Matt was closing himself off to everyone around him. She had seen it coming, at least they way he was shutting out his friends and even his family, but she would never have thought in a million years that he would push *her* away as well.

And then he had gone and slept with *Tracey Overton*! It shouldn't have been such a big deal to her. Tracey had never been a real threat in the past. She had certainly come a long way from that tall, lumbering mess she had been back in grade school. Now at least she was in some kind of shape and seemed to be fairly talented. She had zero confidence, but what could anyone expect from a girl who could never even muster the courage to answer when a teacher called her name during role call?

So what business did she have hooking up with Matt Kildare? How does something like that happen? Emily felt like she had a pretty good grip on how things went in high school and one thing she knew for a fact was that no matter how many shows or movies they made about the ugly duckling getting the prince, it never turned out that way, especially not in high school. Hollywood was Hollywood, but high school was the real world. There was simply no way a Tracey Overton would ever get a Matt Kildare. He had way too many options for him to bother with a girl like Tracey. Matt wasn't interested in the challenge of a difficult conquest. He liked girls who were ready and willing to party. There was no shortage of them surrounding the football program. Matt had just about all he could handle plus Emily.

So why Tracey Overton? The thought kept ringing in her head. She hated the idea of obsessing over another girl, but she couldn't shake the feeling that Matt had somehow achieved a milestone in his life and didn't seem to realize it. Over and over in her mind Matt's hand kept coming up and lightly stroking her cheek, brushing that little wisp of hair away from her eyes. It was such an innocent gesture, corny, or even cliché. But to Emily it had been more than that. There was something in his eyes, in the way he'd looked at her, that made it different. She couldn't count the number of times Matt had done something like that to her, gently touch her, stroke her hair, lightly brush the back of his fingers across her cheek. But she could never remember him looking at her the way he had looked at Tracey earlier.

Emily had known immediately that something was up, but had not been prepared to find out how far things had already progressed between Matt and Tracey. It had taken some piecing together, but she had finally figured out the "when" and the probable "why", but now she found herself wondering about the "what now?". Tracey had certainly dropped a pretty big hint that she knew something Emily didn't. Earlier, Tracey seemed to have already given up on having any sort of a relationship with Matt. Why? Something had happened, but Emily had no idea what it was and couldn't bring herself to ask Tracey. She had all of a sudden gotten so smug that Emily was not about to give her the satisfaction of begging for information. Since there had been nothing filtering through the Kendall High grapevine, it meant that whatever had happened had been strictly between Tracey Overton and Matt Kildare, perhaps when they were sitting together at lunch.

If Emily wanted information she would have to get it from Matt, but they had a strict rule about discussing other girls or guys when they were together. Emily would have to try a little finesse and not ask the direct question.

"Hey, not to break our little rule here, but you might want to give your friend, Tracey a call."

"Why?"

"Because it's all over the school."

"What's all over the school?"

Now he's just playing dumb. "You two, and your secret little fling. Everyone knows about it."

"Hmmm. I wonder why that is."

Emily looked up at him. "You heard?"

He sniffed. "Did I hear? Everybody heard about your little tantrum. You thought it wouldn't make the rounds?"

"I wasn't thinking about it really. Have you spoken to her?"

Matt sat up, and Emily's head fell onto the bed.

"Real nice," she said.

"Look, if you want to say something to me about Tracey then just say it."

Emily got up and sat with her legs under her. "Fine. What's going on between you two?"

"That's easy. Nothing."

"Nothing?"

"Nothing."

Emily was incredulous. "So after all that, there's nothing at all going on between you and Tracey Overton?"

"Correct."

"That makes no sense, you know that, right?"

Matt shrugged. "It doesn't have to make sense. It's just the way it is."

Emily stared at him, waiting for more. "Well?" she finally said. "Are you going to tell me what happened?"

"Nope."

"Why not?"

"Because it's against the rules."

"What rules?" Then she rolled her eyes. "Are you serious? You're really not going to tell me?"

Matt had a funny look on his face. "Why do you care so much about Tracey and me? Every other girl I've been with and you never say a word. Why this one?"

"Because this one is different and I think you know that."

Matt considered for a moment. Then he nodded slightly, almost absently. "Yeah, I guess she is."

*****

Kevin and Tony waited outside the school on Friday morning. They had begun carpooling since they lived so close together and neither wanted to take the bus. Tony's mother, Renatta, dropped them off on her way to work, and Karen always picked them up after football practice. Both boys, being early risers, liked to get to the school early to hang out outside and chat while Kevin waited for Lindsey. Tony especially liked to be there when Lindsey and Tracey arrived because it meant that maybe Brittany would be along at some point. He was determined to talk to her this year.

When the girls arrived, Lindsey immediately went to Kevin for her kiss and hug. She was still looking amazing, though today she was not wearing her new wardrobe, but rather simple black stretchy pants under a short black skirt, and Kevin's white "away" jersey, to the chagrin, she hoped, of Alli the Brette Girl. The jersey was huge on her, as it was on all the girls, and even the guys without their pads on, but she somehow made it look amazing. As the rest of the student body began to arrive by bus and car, the quad filled up with black and silver and white and black jerseys. Those who did not have a jersey generally wore all black on game day. If you showed up for school at Kendall High on game day without at least a black shirt on, there was a good chance you wouldn't make it home that evening. Even the chess and drama clubs wore black. Even the teachers wore black. Kendall High on Fridays during the fall was an ominous building to walk into if you were just visiting from another city.

Many of the students had the latest version of the all black Kendall High Football T-shirt that read "Kendall Cobras" in silver on the front left breast, and the simple mantra "VENOM" splashed across the back in black with silver outline. Every year there was a new version of this shirt and it sold very well in the school store and at games. This was an item created exclusively by the Brette Girls and was responsible for a large percentage of their annual budget. But this year, Kevin Sinclaire arrived, and after his monumental game on Friday and the subsequent moniker assigned to him inadvertently by Maggie Higgins, they scrambled over the weekend to design a second T-shirt.

This Friday morning, the Brette Girls unveiled their new product by having three large vans round up all of the Brettes before school and dropping them off at the same time. When the doors to the three vehicles opened, forty junior and senior girls poured out onto the Kendall High quad all wearing identical Kendall High "Mad Dog" T-Shirts, featuring a snarling beast which looked to be a rabid dog morphing into a cobra, the venomous teeth dripping blood and the green eyes glowing. The shirt was done in the standard black and silver, with the red blood and green eyes the only deviation from this traditional look. The back of the shirt still had the "Venom" logo. Since the Brette Girls were currently the only ones who had this particular item, the entire school wanted to know if they would be available before game time. They assured everyone that a special sale would be going on during the lunch periods at the school store and the shirts would be available at the Brette Girls' booth at the game.

Kevin, Tony, and the girls watched the scene unfold. It was an impressive way to debut their new product, Kevin had to admit, though he felt a little embarrassed by the individual attention he was sure to get as a result. Sure enough, Alli Sylvester made her way over to Kevin and presented him with a complimentary "Mad Dog" T-shirt since he was the inspiration for it in the first place. She even had one for Lindsey, who was standing there fuming at the way this girl kept batting her eyes at Kevin. She almost threw it back in Alli's face, but at the last moment, just took it and smiled at her. She needed Kevin to know she could handle herself in these situations, but every time she looked at him she felt him slipping farther and farther into the abyss of Kendall High celebrity. Alli headed off to continue displaying the new shirt for all to see. Lindsey watched the pretty brunette and wondered how long it would be before she moved on Kevin.

Lindsey really needed to talk to Emily, but the two hadn't

spoken much since Wednesday. Emily had been virtually silent on Thursday in their Biology class and Lindsey didn't want to push. She had said hi, and Emily had replied in a reasonably cordial tone, but that had been it. She could not gauge whether or not Tracey's relationship with Matt would ruin their budding friendship. It was kind of a scary thought considering that she had no real girlfriends and her life was in a state of flux, the uncertainties surrounding her relationship with Kevin creating so many questions and fears that she felt like she needed someone to talk to all the time. She and Tracey had begun to draw a little closer with their conversation over the weekend, but then they had both sort of gone their separate ways again.

Lindsey did her best to snap out of this funk. Today was not the day to dwell on these things. This was game day. One thing Emily had told her was that game day was all about the team. And the one thing that set the player's girlfriends apart from every other black-clad student, especially the Ladies, was the jerseys. The girlfriends always got to wear the jerseys of their boyfriends. On Fridays when the Cobras had a home game, they were the only ones in the entire school who had on white, the color of everyone's away jerseys. They stood out like glittering diamonds in the sea of black that swarmed the halls of Kendall High every Friday.

"And you are wearing number twenty-seven," Emily had said. "Right now, there's not a more popular number to have on. You get to walk these halls as royalty when you put that jersey on, so look good in it."

Lindsey took these words to heart and made sure that she walked with her head up, her arm loosely holding onto Kevin's, not so much that she appeared to be clinging to him, but enough to let everyone know that she was not just his good friend. The message had been sent throughout the week and Lindsey knew that everyone else knew who she was. And Emily had been right about the jersey. The girls couldn't stop looking at it. It was like some kind of holy grail that they all just wished they could touch. She could see their envious looks. She did her best not to look cocky or superior. What Lindsey didn't want was to be thought of as stuck up.

Tracey followed behind the spectacle that was Kevin Sinclaire. He and Lindsey were now always surrounded when they walked the halls. She usually just stayed in the background, in the shadows, but since the argument between her and Emily had gotten out along with her secret about her night with Matt Kildare, she had nothing left to hide, and all of it had given her a certain credibility. The girls looked at her like she was the real deal, or something like that. At least they weren't looking down their noses at her. After all, Matt Kildare was still the most popular guy in Kendall High School, and she had been with him. While that was not a particularly exclusive group, it was a pretty elite group. Matt generally only went with the hottest girls he could find.

As she watched the scene in front of her she imagined her and Matt walking together like Kevin and Lindsey, surrounded by the entire student body like a couple of Hollywood celebrities.

"Pretty crazy, huh?" Tony was walking next to her, watching along with her.

She nodded. "Yeah, pretty crazy."

He looked at her, a slight frown on his face. "You seem sad."

She took a breath. "Not really sad. I just feel a little blah today, you know?"

"Yeah, but you're making me sad, and I can't have that, so I need to cheer you up."

She smiled. "Is that right? And how are you going to do that?"

He put his arm around her neck and pulled her in close to him. "By being your escort all day."

Oh, Good God!

"No, you don't need to do that…"

He put his hand up. "It's already done."

"What I mean is I'm feeling much happier now."

He kept holding her tightly. "Nope, I don't believe it. I'm going to cheer you up all day. It's my mission."

"But…you're…suffocating me."

"What? Oh, sorry." He loosened his grip. "I'm not as gentle and delicate as Kev."

"I can see that." Tracey couldn't help but smile. He was so funny and goofy, but in a really nice way. Since there was probably no way to get rid of him, she let Tony lead her through the throng of students, him arm still around her shoulders. She had to admit that even though this was just a joking around thing, it really felt good to have a guy walk with her like this. She stole several glances at Tony as they walked. He seemed to have an easy grin always on his face. Even when he was serious, his dark brown eyes seemed to always have a sparkle of humor in them. He was greeting just about every person who walked by, so their progress was slow.

How does he know everybody? It's the first week of school and he's a freshman!

Tony had the sort of personality that precluded him from feeling any sense of embarrassment in most situations. He wasn't always trying to be the center of attention, but he had the "gift of gab" that allowed him to simply walk up to someone and start talking. He was also sure to include Tracey in all of his conversations. He introduced her to everyone. By the end of the day she felt there would be very few students she hadn't talked to.

You're going to be late for homeroom.

Tracey didn't care. She just stood by her "escort" and allowed him to take her wherever. She really wanted him to lower his arm so she could hold it the way Lindsey held Kevin's, but she quickly rejected that thought as it might seem weird to Tony if she started clinging to him like his girlfriend.

Although...

By the time they got to her homeroom, the bell was sounding.

"Right on time!" Tony exclaimed. "I am good."

Tracey nodded. "Yeah, but now *you're* late."

He brushed that off. "Football players are never late on game day. I'll come get you in a few minutes."

"Are you seriously going to escort me everywhere today?"

"Absolutely, unless you really don't want me to."

Are you kidding me?

She tilted her head. "Actually, I would like that very much." She stood on her toes and gave him a peck on the cheek. It took all her courage to do that and she hoped desperately that he wouldn't hate her for it. "See, you're cheering me up already."

He beamed, winked at her, then turned and headed off to his classroom.

Chapter 19

After third period, Tracey hurried out to the hall to see if Tony would be there to walk her to the cafeteria for lunch, but before she could find him Matt Kildare appeared from around the corner. At this point, Tracey had no reason to avoid him though they had not spoken since their conversation in the quad. They pretty much stayed on opposite sides of the room during lunch, neither wanting to create any further complications or argue in any way, especially publicly. But today, Matt had decided that he needed to talk to her. He grinned at her as he approached. Tracey had to bite her lip to keep from smiling. She still thought he was absolutely gorgeous, and with his black and silver football jersey on, he looked even more so.

"Hey," he said, sidling up to her. "Can I walk you to lunch?"

"Actually, I'm waiting for someone," Tracey replied.

"Who? The freshman, what's his name? Yavo, or something?"

"It's Tony," she replied. "Only his friends call him Yavo."

"Yeah, that's right. Well, I asked him if I could cut in for this period. He said okay, as long as I'm nice to you."

She nodded. "I'll kill him."

Matt grinned. "Come on. I thought we could at least be friends."

"Let's get to lunch."

As they began walking, Matt asked, "So, this Yavo character…you two a thing?"

"It's Tony, and no. He was just trying to cheer me up."

"Are you sad? Not because of me?"

She shook her head. "I'm not sad. He just thinks I am and so he's going to cheer me up for the rest of the day."

"How about tonight after the game. Will he be cheering you up then too?"

She looked at him and wrinkled her forehead. "You're disgusting!"

Matt looked confused, then his eyes widened. "No, no, no. That's not what I meant. I was just wondering if the two of you were going to be hanging out after the game."

"I have no idea what I'm doing after the game *or* what he's doing. Why?"

"Nothing. I just think you can do better, that's all."

She smirked. "Is that right? I can do better than Tony? And what would be better than Tony? Better looking? Better what?"

Matt put his hands up. "Hey, I'm just saying that there are better options for you than a freshman."

"Like a senior? Give me a break. You don't even know Tony. What difference does it make to you anyway?"

"Look, forget I said that, okay. Let's get together after the game."

"Are you nuts? I'm not sleeping with you again, Matt."

"You seemed to be into it the other day."

"The other day it seemed possible for the two of us to be together in a relationship, a *real* relationship. What happened to Emily?"

"Nothing happened to her."

"So, you two are together."

"I wouldn't say that."

"Oh? Well, what would you say?"

"I don't know."

"You don't know? Matt, you're not making any sense at all. If I go ask Emily in gym class if it's cool if I go out with you tonight, what kind of reaction will I get?"

"Excuse me?" The shout came from right behind them. It was Emily. Who knew how long she'd been there. She looked at Matt. "Want to tell me what you two *lovebirds* are discussing?"

Tracey looked at Matt. "Yes, Matt. What was it that you were asking me?"

Emily looked a little confused. Matt simply shrugged and walked off.

"Whatever. I'm outta here."

Emily's eyes were focused like a laser on Tracey. "What's going on, Tracey? I thought there was nothing going on with you two."

"There is nothing going on, Emily."

Emily shrugged and gave Tracey doubtful look. "It sure looks a whole lot like *something* is going on, Tracey. You're walking the halls together. Weren't you walking with that Tony guy before? What is going on?"

Tracey tried to remain calm. "Listen, Emily, there is nothing going on between Matt and I. You're my sister's best friend so let's try to keep things civil, okay? That's the best I can do for you right now. I have to get to lunch."

She left Emily standing there even more confused than before.

*****

Kelly Presidian found Tracey right before lunch. "Hey, Tracey. Got a sec?"

Tracey smiled. "Of course, Miss Kelly. Sorry I haven't been around this week. It's just been super busy."

"That's no problem." Kelly looked concerned. "Listen, I heard some things this morning and I just wanted to make sure you're okay."

Tracey, turned a little red. "I was hoping you'd missed that."

She took Tracey back to her office. "Are you okay, sweetie?"

Tracey shrugged. "I'm working on it. I can't really figure out how I feel right now."

"I'm guessing this was your first time?"

Tracey nodded.

Kelly took a deep breath and smiled. "Well, I've got to hand it to you. When you take the plunge, you do it in style. Matt Kildare? You didn't exactly start at the bottom, did you?"

Tracey smiled. "I've kind of been in love with him for years."

Kelly nodded, seeing the hint of pain behind the smile. "Want to talk about it?"

Tracey didn't know what to say. "It's just...You think you want something, you know? Then you get it, or sort of get it, and it doesn't feel like you thought it would."

Kelly nodded. "Honey, it never does. I think that's just the way life is. When we want something, it always starts out as something small, a fantasy that can never happen, but sometimes it grows into a wish, then a *real* desire, and sometimes even a need. But at some point we have elevated it so much that it can never measure up to our imagination."

"I guess that's what I did with Matt."

"So it wasn't all that great?"

Tracey shook her head. "Oh, no. Matt was amazing. He was perfect. It's just the way I feel now. I thought I'd be happier."

Kelly nodded in understanding. "Listen, sweetie. It was your first time. Of course it was confusing. You're fifteen years old."

Tracey frowned. "So you think I should have waited?"

Kelly shrugged. "I didn't say that. Everyone's different. You're not the first girl to have sex at fifteen and you won't be the last. But you're at the age where everything's confusing. Sex only complicates it even more."

"It just seems like sex is such a huge part of relationships."

"It often is. At your age, the boys are eager to get started. And football players, especially in *this* school, move even faster because they can. You have to decide for yourself what the right path is."

Tracey sat quietly, lost in thought. Just talking through it all really helped her.

"Do you love him?" Kelly asked.

Tracey shrugged. "How would I know? I think I do. I can't stop thinking about him. But it doesn't matter because he's still with Emily."

*****

4th period lunch on Fridays was always a louder and noisier affair than usual. As it was the earliest of the four lunch periods, it was generally the one assigned to those participating in football and its related programs. This enabled the players to attend the afternoon meetings and prepare for things like Friday pep rallies. Kevin liked it because he was up so early in the morning that he was usually starving by 4th period anyway. On Fridays, the players and cheerleaders were always in a upbeat mood, creating a party atmosphere in the lunch room.

Kevin and Tony always sat together with Scott Webber and whoever else felt like joining them. After they ate, Kevin and Tony strolled through what was known as the common area and made their way outside to get some air for what was left of the period. Scott remained behind talking to a cute sophomore cheer leader named Kami who had made it quite clear that she *really* liked the young quarterback.

"Kevin! Wait up!" The shout came over the din of the students shouting and psyching themselves up for the game. It was Brittany Morgan, hurrying through the crowded room after them. Tony took a deep breath.

"Brittany," he muttered.

They waited for her to catch up. She walked outside with them.

"What's up?" Kevin asked when they were clear of the noise.

Brittany put both her hands flat together like she was going to start praying. Kevin recognized this as the way she acted when she had something very serious to say. He frowned.

"Listen," she began. "You have to talk to Lindsey."

"Okay. Why?"

Brittany leaned in close. "Look, I don't usually pry into other people's business, you know that, right?"

"Sure, what's the matter, Brittany?"

"It's just that Lindsey has been talking a lot to Emily."

Kevin stared at her blankly. Brittany's eyes were locked on his. "And?"

Now she looked confused. "What do you mean "and"? She's been talking all week to Emily *Vasquez*."

"So? What does it matter? They're friends. They met on Monday."

Brittany threw her hands up slightly. "I guess it doesn't if you don't mind your girlfriend becoming besties with the school…" She looked around furtively. "…with the school…slut."

Kevin shook his head. "I don't know. Lindsey…"

"Look," Brittany said. "I sit right behind both of them in AP Biology and they spend the whole period talking about sex *every day*. Lindsey is asking a lot of questions and Emily is answering them.

Do I need to spell it out for you?"

Tony was nodding. "Yeah, Kev. Maybe this is bad."

Kevin shook his head again. "Well, Tracey is hanging around the school…" He looked around furtively, mimicking Brittany. "…you know…the school…*Christian*. Maybe it's no different."

Tony looked at Brittany. "He has a point."

Brittany shrugged and replied, "Fine, except for one thing. I would love to get Tracey to come to salvation. I don't try to hide that. What do you think Emily's intentions are?"

Tony turned back to Kevin and leaned on his shoulder. "Yeah, dude, your point was kind of stupid."

Kevin pushed Tony away. "Will you shut up?" To Brittany, he said, "All right, but it doesn't really matter. I don't know what I'm supposed to do about it. Lindsey can talk to whoever she wants to. It's not really my business, especially considering the fact that pretty Brette Girls are baking me cookies and stuff."

Brittany shrugged. "Look, I don't know what you should do either I just thought you should know." She turned on her heels and headed back inside. Tony walked alongside her.

She stopped and looked at him, her big blue eyes waiting expectantly. He said, "Listen, I want you to know that you and I are on the same page here, all right? And I don't want you to worry anymore about it because *I* am on the case. I'm on it like white on rice, okay? Like cold on ice; like dots on dice."

"Dots on dice?"

"Yeah, you know how there are dots all over…it doesn't matter. The point is that you and I are like this here." He held up his hand, showing her his right middle finger crossed over his index finger. She nodded, her forehead wrinkling in the process.

"Uh huh."

"And between the two of us, we're gonna straighten this whole mess out."

Brittany didn't know whether to laugh or what. She held in her laughter, but couldn't keep the smile from creeping onto her face. She held up a hand and nodded, then walked away before Tony could go on. He came back to Kevin and picked up his backpack.

As he dug through it, he said to Kevin, "I'm coming to church with you on Sunday."

"Oh yeah?"

"Yeah. Ask your mom if I can sleep over Saturday night."

"I don't think so."

"Come on, man!" he pleaded. "I need an in."

"An "in"? You'll never get her, dude. Find someone else. I'm serious. It *ain't* gonna happen."

Tony shook his head. "I'm not talking about having sex with her. This is serious."

"Well, in that case..." Kevin rolled his eyes

"Can I sleep over or not?"

"I'll ask. It's probably fine."

"Cool. Ah, here it is." He pulled out a notebook and opened it up. "Check this out. I've been working on it for Brittany. I'm gonna recite it to her on Sunday."

"Recite wha...? Oh God."

"Ahem!" Tony stood up straight and began, "I am an eagle. You are a dove. Even though we are different, we are meant to fall in love."

Kevin stared at him.

"Well? What do you think?"

Kevin didn't smile. He took the notebook gently from Tony's hand and read the poem to himself. "I want you to listen very carefully to me," he said, holding up the notebook. "Do NOT read this to Brittany."

"Well, I was gonna memorize it..."

"NO! DON'T memorize it! Forget about this idea."

"You didn't like it?"

"Dude, are you really gonna call Brittany Morgan a dove?"

"Well, it rhymes with love."

"Yeah, I get that it rhymes with love. Don't say that to her."

"But other than that, it's a good idea, right?"

Kevin looked at his friend. "You are a hopeless nitwit, you know that?"

"More like a hopeless romantic."

"Hopeless clown, maybe."

"Brittany's gonna fall for me, I promise you."

Kevin shook his head. "Brittany doesn't even know your name. And she doesn't want to either. She only dates *Christian* guys, if she dates at all, which she probably doesn't."

"That's fine. I'll do whatever it takes."

"Whatever it takes," Kevin repeated. "It doesn't work that

way, dude."

"So how does it work?"

"You don't get to say you're a Christian and then Brittany Morgan falls for you."

"So what do I have to do?"

Kevin looked at his friend closely. "Are you seriously asking me?"

Tony eagerly nodded. "Yes. I am seriously, straight-faced, asking your advice."

Kevin shook his head. "Leaving aside the religious part which you can't overcome and you can't fake with her, not for very long at least, you really just need to be a great guy. Brittany Morgan is kind of old fashioned. She likes good looking guys who can be gentlemen. Now, I happen to think she likes guys like *us* deep down inside; you know, a little dangerous, maybe a little crazy? I think all girls do. She and I have always gotten along well. So I think you would have a shot just by being a really thoughtful, good guy. But that *still* won't be enough. Brittany Morgan *will not* date a non Christian. That much you can bet on."

Tony nodded slowly. "So, for now, I just show her what a great guy I am. I start going to church and see what happens."

"You're seriously going to start going to church? For a *girl?*"

"Not for a girl. For Brittany. She's *the* girl."

Kevin had known Tony for over three years and in that time there were only two girls that ever had a significant impact on him. Emily Vasquez was the first. Of course Emily had an impact on every guy. Tony could barely put two sentences together when she was around. Emily approached boys with an intimidating air about her that stripped away any phony confidence a kid might be putting up. Even guys who were very secure had trouble keeping it together around her. For Tony, she was the essence of sexy.

But if Tony had a hard time talking around Emily, he had a hard time *breathing* around Brittany. The words he had just spoken to her were more than all the words he had previously spoken to her combined. He had simply never been able to muster up the courage to talk to her. He couldn't stand the thought of those big blue eyes rejecting him. But at the same time, he couldn't stand the idea of never going for it. He had encouraged Kevin when Lindsey spent weeks trying to ignore his advances last year. Was he really going to be a coward when it came to taking his own advice? Was he really going to chicken out? The answer to that question was a decisive no. He would at least take a legitimate run at Brittany Morgan this year. If that meant going to church and singing some songs and all that, then that is what he'd do.

*****

Lindsey sat in Biology class after a day filled with even more attention than she had received on day one when she walked the halls with Kevin, he as the new star of the football team and she as his girl. That walk seemed like a million years ago. Today, she's still Kevin's girl, but now she's a presence even when he's not around. It felt strangely good, almost empowering to be looked at by so many people at once. She had been so sure she would hate the attention, but for reasons she could not explain, it was becoming intoxicating. She had gone from the bottom of the totem pole to somewhere near the top. She still had mixed emotions about it, but she figured that had more to do with the uncertainty of her relationship with Kevin. For now, though, she was Kendall High School royalty.

Emily Vasquez walked in and headed straight to her desk next to Lindsey. She immediately fixed her eyes on Lindsey.

"Tell me about Matt and Tracey."

Lindsey raised her eyes. "Really? You don't talk to me for two days and the first thing you say to me is not even hi."

Emily rolled her eyes. "I'm sorry, okay? I shouldn't have ignored you. I just needed to think about things. I wasn't sure if I should be mad at you or not."

"Why? What did I do?"

"You knew about Matt and Tracey and you didn't tell me."

"And I should have told you all about my sister and your "not boyfriend"?"

Emily shrugged. "That's what I was trying to figure out, okay? I'm not used to having girlfriends. Cut me a little slack on this one."

Lindsey smiled. "Apology accepted. You could at least tell me I don't look ridiculous in this jersey."

Emily frowned, looking Lindsey over. "You look all right, I guess."

"All right? I was going for a little hotter than that."

Emily laughed. It was really great how Lindsey could make her laugh. Emily rarely had moments where another girl had that effect on her. Lindsey had a natural dry humor and a quick-witted cynicism that made some very funny things come out of her mouth.

"I'm just messing with you. Trust me, girl, you look *extremely* hot. Those jerseys are like instant hotness around here."

They bantered for a few more seconds, but Emily brought the conversation around to Matt and Tracey again with a little more tact this time.

"So, can I ask you what you know about your sister and Matt?"

Lindsey shrugged. "There really isn't all that much to tell. As far as I know they got together Friday night and didn't talk again until the other day. It looks like they aren't really together. I thought that was because of *you*. Tracey said that he didn't want her."

Emily nodded. "Yeah, she said that, but I don't know what that means. He didn't say anything to *me*. And then I see them talking earlier today. It feels like something's up, but I don't know what."

Lindsey shook her head and shrugged again. "I can ask her, but I don't know how much she'll tell me. Plus she knows we're friends. And she knows you hate her. That really sucks for me, by the way."

"Sorry. But if she goes after Matt, I might have to kill her."

"Maybe you two could just sit down and talk."

"Maybe. But if she has her eye on getting Matt, then there's nothing to talk about."

Beginnings

Chapter 20

Lindsey and Emily arrived at the "Nest" about twenty minutes before game time. Lindsey had experienced a taste of the Kendall Township fan base the previous week sitting in the stands while Kevin had carved up the Holy Trinity Crusaders, but nothing prepared her for what she was about to witness at the Cobra's home opener. First of all, she had never been to a Kendall High home football game. The facility itself was second to none. Fifteen years ago, right after the Cobras won the state championship, the booster committee began a massive fund raising campaign for a new state of the art football field and facility. The campaign lasted three years and was such a success that the resulting facility rivaled any high school facility in the region.

When you arrive at the Cobra's Nest, you park your car in the lot and make the trek along the main concourse past all the practice fields, one of which had previously been the game field. The main gate had four main entrances designed to keep the traffic flowing. You could purchase tickets, if there were any available, at two stations on either side of the concourse. Once you enter the facility the whole concourse opens up into a large circular court where several permanent structures housed the official Kendall High vendors including the Lady Cobras with their T-shirts and other wares, the Kendall school store, which carried the official

Kendall High School gear. On one side of the court was the refreshment stand which included a full kitchen facility as well as a massive smoker for bar-b-cue and rotisserie.

But the real sight was the stadium itself. Most people would snicker if you told them you were going to the "stadium" for a high school football game, but in the case of the Cobra's Nest, it was an accurate description. The playing field was sunk nearly thirty feet below the level of the court. From the court you could watch the entire game if you wanted to and could get there in time to stake out a spot near the railing underneath the massive jumbotron. The court was situated behind one of the end zones and directly above the home team locker room, which was at field level and accessed from the field as well as from a long gradual ramp at the rear behind the court. The other three sides of the stadium were enclosed with seats stretching up into the heavens. Seating nearly twenty thousand, the Cobra's Nest was a magnificent sight, especially considering that fact that it was for high school football. It was a masterpiece orchestrated by Leo Forsythe and the rest of the program committee.

But if the facility was impressive, it paled in comparison to the fans that occupied it. To Lindsey it looked as though the whole world had turned black. No one from Kendall Township would even think to show up in anything other than black. But they didn't stop at just black shirts. They wore *all* black. The women even carried black purses, often specifically purchased for these football games, some of which sported the silver Cobra logo or had the VENOM mantra emblazoned across the side. Some had on black Kendall Cobra hats, while others wore black and silver headbands or bandanas. If a Kendall fan could get it in black, they usually wore it or brought it to the game.

The only people who could acceptably wear any other color were once again the girls who had on players' jerseys. Just like in school, these ladies were shown the utmost respect because they were seen as taking care of the Cobra boys, and if you were close to a Cobra, you were respected by the Kendall crowd. Lindsey, with her number 27 jersey was received like a visiting princess. Even Emily was a little blown away by the reception. At the snack line, Lindsey once again never had to pull out her money. A stranger smiled at her and picked up the tab for both girls' snacks. He gave Lindsey a quick thumbs-up, smiled again, and headed off to the stands.

As they made their way to their seats, the Kendall crowd seemed ready to explode. Lindsey saw that nearly everyone had the same small black towel that Emily had insisted they each bring. They were called "Venom Towels", aptly named for the silver VENOM insignia on one side. When this crowd started twirling those towels above their heads, it was an awesome sight. If there was a "twelfth man" in high school football in these parts, it could be found at the Cobra's nest at Kendall High.

*****

Throughout a week filled with relationship turmoil, the celebration of a promising start to the Kendall High Cobras' season, and everything that goes along with the start of a new year of high school, a huge question mark lingered in the background. Kevin's actions after the game the previous Friday night had set in motion a chain of events that culminated in a series of meetings, telephone conversations, and finally the potential for legal action. The Kendall High Program Committee, led by Leo Forsythe, was on full alert because one of their players was under fire. Kevin Sinclaire was in danger of being suspended from further participation in New Jersey High School athletic activities.

There were two issues that became hurdles for Kevin to have to clear. The first, and most obvious was whether or not the prosecutor's office intended to file charges against Kevin for assault. Certainly there were opinions on either side of the issue, but the overwhelming sentiment outside the Holy Trinity fan base was that Kevin was more admired than anything else. The support he was receiving from the citizens was overwhelming the prosecutor's phone lines and by Wednesday morning a press release was put out confirming that Kevin Sinclaire would not be arrested and no charges would be pursued. The investigation was considered closed.

Maggie Higgins placed a strongly worded call to the prosecutor's office after being informed of the decision and was politely reminded that her husband, having clearly been the one who instigated the scene after the game, had not been cleared of any wrongdoing and could easily be charged with multiple counts of assault himself. In fact, Jerry Hoffinger, who was representing

Kevin, had made it clear that if Kevin were to be negatively impacted in any way as a result of this incident, they would publicly call for charges to be brought against Frank Higgins and apply all the pressure he could muster to force the prosecutor to take action. In the end, Maggie Higgins bit her tongue and came out in a spirit of forgiveness and apologized publicly to Kevin and his family for the unfortunate incident. She asked that the NJSHSAA would not penalize the "young man for attempting to defend his family".

There was still some outcry from citizens of several cities. The loudest complaints came from the people of Veritas, who just happened to be the team that would come to Kendall this Friday to play in the Kendall High School home opener. The Athletic Association chalked this up to a transparent attempt to cripple a team before a game and ignored it.

Kevin, with his legal troubles behind him, would be able to play Friday night. But then the Veritas people came up with a more creative angle. There was a meeting on Wednesday evening and a plan was hatched to appeal to the State Athletic Association to suspend Kevin Sinclaire on the grounds that he was mentally unstable and should be examined prior to being cleared to play football. The insidious part of the plan was that they were going to wait until the last moment on Friday evening and get a judge to order Kevin's suspension pending a mental health evaluation. He would miss the game and then he would be some other team's problem.

Jerry Hoffinger had the scoop on this even before the meeting had begun. The legal community is populated with a larger percentage of gossips than any other group of people. Jerry's finely tuned legal sense had picked up on some of the signals early on in the day, and he had already begun to suspect that something was up. He made sure that he was made aware of who was attending the late night meeting and that filled in some of the blanks. He knew an effort was under way to bring some sort of legal action. It would be an end run around the Athletic Association, but if done right, the mess wouldn't be cleared up until after the game. He knew that the way to accomplish this would be to wait until the last moment. That gave Kendall High all day Thursday and Friday until game time to prepare their counter.

It was more than enough time for Jerry and, unlike the rest of the legal community, he knew how to keep a tight lid on his actions. He made all the calls himself and finally set up a lunch with Judge Henry Gilbert, from the appellate court in Trenton. He explained the situation to the Kendall High School graduate, who immediately called his aide and told him to clear his schedule for Friday afternoon, from three o'clock on. He promised to be at Kendall High School by 5:00 pm. That was all Jerry needed to hear. Henry Gilbert was an honest man and a fair judge who hated these kind of legal maneuverings. It appealed to his sense of justice to be sitting there waiting to drop the hammer the instant the unjust order came in. Kevin Sinclaire would be allowed to play.

Jerry kept all of this to himself. As he suspected, there was nothing done on Thursday. The Veritas group had put all their eggs in the basket of keeping Kevin *legally* sidelined for this game. They never even submitted an appeal to the Athletic Association, a fact that did not escape the notice of Justice Henry Gilbert, who was monitoring the situation himself from Trenton. A properly submitted complaint to the Association would have at least lent credibility to their legal maneuver. They could have said that the Association was not moving quickly enough and their kids were in potential danger so they asked a judge to step in. Without that piece, there was no real foundation for their complaint in Judge Gilbert's eyes. By Thursday evening, he had cleared his entire afternoon for Friday, intending to get to Kendall early and see how this all played out. He didn't want to get stuck in a traffic jam and be late. He and Jerry would grab a late lunch, wait at the Kendall High field house, and then enjoy a high school football game. He had been sorry to miss last week's game.

Right on cue, at five-thirty, word came down from state officials that a judge from the courthouse in Veritas had signed an order forbidding Kevin Sinclaire from playing in any further games until he could be examined by an approved physician to determine whether he was mentally fit to play interscholastic sports. Kevin was officially suspended from league play. One half hour and a single fax later, the order was overturned pending an appeal to be scheduled later, if the plaintiffs so desired, and Kevin Sinclaire was officially cleared to play. There was very little fanfare over the whole issue, except for the fact that the Veritas coaching staff had obviously been informed that Kevin would be sidelined. Jerry Hoffinger and Judge Gilbert had a little fun training their binoculars over at the visiting team's sidelines, picking out those who were most likely a part of the conspiracy to have Kevin suspended. There was an awful lot of cell phone activity going on amongst the Veritas faithful, but nonetheless, they would have to face the Kendall High Cobras at full strength. They didn't appear to be all that pleased about it.

*****

    Tracey stood ready to explode into her routine which would accompany the players entrance onto the field, which was due to take place in mere moments. She was dressed like the rest of her drill team and the cheerleaders in all black with silver trim. Her red hair was pulled back in a tight bun with a black and silver hair band around it. All the girls had little black and silver cobras painted on one of their cheeks by two of the Brette Girls. Many had dyed their hair jet black and inserted silver extensions or glitter or ribbons for effect. The cheerleaders took their places in two rows, one across from the other creating a gauntlet of black and silver standing in front of the huge paper banner the Girls had painstakingly crafted for the expressed purpose of having the football team burst through it and tearing it to shreds as they were announced.

    Tracey got set just in front of the banner with her three teammates. When the music started, they would charge forward, one at a time and execute their handsprings and flips in perfect sequence, increasing in difficulty and complexity as they progressed, culminating with Tracey's Triple Full, a fully extended flip while twirling 360 degrees three times before landing. If timed perfectly, she would hit the ground just as the singing started and the players tore through the banner. The fireworks and other pyrotechnics would go off and the players would charge across the field and gather around their captains. As she checked her outfit and made sure her ankle support was in place, she could hear the players gathering behind the banner. She glanced up at the massive countdown clock on the jumbotron behind her. It was nearly show time.

    The Veritas crowd had tried to come out in force for the game, but they were no match for the Kendall faithful, who were shouting "VE-NOM!" over and over again at the tops of their lungs. Though the Veritas Vikings represented a city that was a very tough, low income, high crime area, and their fans were not easily intimidated, they were on Cobra ground today and the crowd let them know it. As their players came out onto the field in their white away jerseys and purple pants, the VE-NOM chant grew louder and more forceful as the black and silver towels began to twirl.

Finally, the clock hit zero, and the opening chords to the Kendall Cobra's team song, ACDC's "Back in Black" came crisply over the PA system. Tracey and the other girls immediately charged into their routine as the crowd went absolutely crazy. As she began her complicated sequence, Tracey could not believe how loud it was on the field. She could barely think at all. Her heart was beating furiously in her chest and it was all she could do to maintain focus. She soared, twirling through the air in her final technique, the Triple Full, perfectly executed, and as her feet hit the turf below in a perfect finishing pose, the words to Back in Black began. Instantly, all eyes turned to the banner, which was immediately ripped to shreds as the Kendall High Cobras came charging out to the announcer's words: "And now introducing YOUR Kendall High Cobras! They are led by their team captains: Starting Quarterback, Mike Doyer! Wide Receiver and Defensive Back, Matt Kildare! Starting Tailback, Anquan Griffin! And Starting Middle Linebacker, Ozzie Winfred! Please welcome back, in his fourth season, Head Coach Larry Shultz!"

The crowd, having waited for this moment since last season's disappointing finish, and following the exciting start last week, went absolutely out of their minds as the team charged out onto the field. The roar was deafening on the field as Kevin rushed forward with his teammates. He had little time to enjoy the rush of his first home game because as quickly as they had gathered for a quick huddle, the captains were called to the center of the field for the coin toss, which was won by the Veritas Vikings, who promptly chose to get the ball first. Their goal was to keep the ball out of the hands of the explosive Kendall High offense.

Kevin trotted out to the roar of the crowd, who clearly were chanting "Mad Dog" as he entered the game. Right from the opening snap, he knew this game would be different. It was one thing to surprise a really good team, but quite another to go into a game where they were expecting you. The Veritas defense came out with a vengeance. They attacked the Kendall offense relentlessly and the Kendall players seemed to be intimidated right from the opening whistle. It was a different story for the Kendall defense. Kevin and the Cobras were just as aggressive as Veritas on defense. The game was settling into a hard hitting match with very little ground given up by either defense.

Late in the first half, Mike Doyer got into trouble. As he faked an handoff to Anquan, his foot got caught up and he stumbled backward, catching himself before he fell, but the timing of the play was off. He scrambled to his right with three Veritas defenders making clean runs at him. He fired the ball just as the three defenders converged on him at the same time. The pass was incomplete, landing well in front of Kevin. Doyer was left in a twisted heap on the turf, clutching his left foot, which was now shoeless. The shoe had come off as he was being dragged down. He looked to be in extreme pain. The trainers came rushing out to tend to him as the Veritas players went to their sidelines and the Kendal offense took a knee, watching as their quarterback lay grimacing on the ground in obvious pain.

After several moments of trying to ascertain the damage, the trainers called for the cart, which came promptly from the end zone and pulled alongside the injured player. With assistance from the training staff, Mike Doyer got himself onto the back of the cart and was quickly taken to the locker room for further examination. He was still apparently in extreme pain and his foot looked almost entirely purple from swelling which had come on quickly and furiously. Scott Webber immediately began warming up his arm with Kevin catching passes for him.

Scott came into the game having not taken a single snap in practice with the starters all week. He knew the offense, but it was not an offense designed to make use of *his* skills. It was really Mike Doyer's offense. He tried to be efficient and take some kind of control, but it was fairly apparent that the guys were on the verge of giving up. They were giving a halfhearted effort and he was getting buried on every play. At this rate, the Kendall Cobras wouldn't have any quarterbacks left for the second half. For his part, Kevin wondered at the play calling and why they were not trying something else rather than the same old thing.

With less than three minutes to play in quarter two, and the score still tied at zero, Scott called the play in the huddle, a running play to Anquan. He also made a decision and called a second play and told the guys that they were running a hurry-up style for these plays and they should rush to the line and get set as soon as the first play was over. He looked at Kevin and the two exchanged knowing looks. This was a risky shot because they were going off script. Who knew how Coach would react to this kind of mutiny? But they wanted to win, so they figured it was time to go for it.

After Anquan ran for little gain, the team stunned not only the Veritas defense, but also the Kendall coaching staff by quickly getting back to the line under the urgent shouting of Scott Webber, who never looked to the sidelines for a play. As the coaches stood with their eyes wide and arms spread, Scott took a very fast snap and rolled immediately to his right as Kevin streaked down the field, running inside, then breaking up field in a fly pattern. Scott didn't wait for Kevin to make his break before letting fly a deep pass. The Veritas defense was caught totally by surprise and never got properly set. Their secondary could only watch, stunned, as Kevin streaked by them and caught Scott's perfectly timed pass in stride near the sidelines and raced ahead of everyone for the first score of the game. It was an eighty-eight yard catch and run.

The Kendall crowd, having been stunned into a dull roar with the way the game had gone thus far, finally had something to cheer about and they didn't hold back. On the sidelines, Scott had to face a stern looking Coach Shultz, who just put his hand on top of Scott's helmet, nodded, and said, "Great pass. We'll talk about it later." Who knew what that meant, but at least he and Kevin had made the most of it if he was going to be punished. He had no regrets on this one.

The first half ended with the Cobras leading by one score. Matt went to the training room and found Mike Doyer sitting on a couch, his foot immersed in a bucket of ice water. He was still obviously hurting, but would not leave the Nest until the game was over. His parents were there with anxiety one their faces. Matt looked at Mike.

"How bad?"

Mike looked at the floor. "Doc thinks it's broken."

Matt frowned. Mike Doyer was his best friend and a fine quarterback, but his real passion was baseball. He was a pitcher that was probably going to have a multitude of scholarships as well as the likelihood of being drafted by a major league baseball team right out of high school. There was a demand for pitchers who could throw a ninety plus mile-per-hour fastball. Mike's fastball was over ninety-five mph and had wicked movement. He had a real potential for a pro career. As Matt looked down at him, he knew they were both thinking the same thing. It had been a broken toe that had ruined Dizzy Dean's brilliant pitching career. Matt could see the anxiety and fear on his best friend's face.

*****

As the halftime celebration went on, there was real excitement on the Kendall side of the stadium. All anyone could talk about was that "Sinclaire kid" and how he was the difference maker. There was alarm as to the quarterback situation though. Everyone knew that Scott Webber was the next in line, but he was still a freshman. Could a freshman come in and lead a team to states? Lindsey and Emily sat eating nachos and pulled pork, once again paid for by an admiring Kendall fan. The girlfriend of Kevin Sinclaire was becoming royalty both inside and outside of the school. Emily was amused by Lindsey's shocked amazement over all the attention.

"Just accept it girl! Your boyfriend is becoming *the* Kendall Cobra! You are *his* girl. Just hang on tight and enjoy the ride."

Lindsey nodded, wondering just how tightly she would have to "hang on". The bigger Kevin got, the more attention he would receive from females, which meant that the temptations would be continually mounting and the pressure for him to act on them would also be increasing. She turned to Emily, a concerned look on her face.

"I think I have to have sex with Kevin," she said.

Emily almost choked on her soda. "Keep it down, will you?" she said, looking around. "Good thing no one's listening."

"I think I have to," Lindsey repeated.

Emily shrugged. "You don't *have* to do anything."

Lindsey rolled her eyes. "You know what I mean. If I don't get with the program, he'll find someone who will."

"The program? You really think he'd break up with you for that?"

"I don't know, but how much can a guy take? How much can I *expect* him to take?"

"Let me ask you this," Emily said. "Do you want Kevin Sinclaire to be the first guy you have sex with?"

"Definitely."

"So what's the problem?"

Lindsey was confused. "Wait a minute. You keep telling me that I shouldn't do something I don't want to do and I should wait if I'm not comfortable with it."

Emily nodded. "I know, and all of that is true. But you are convinced that you *must* sleep with Kevin in order to keep him. That's pretty cut and dry. So I would say that if you love him and want to stay with him and you really *want* him to be your first, then what's the problem?"

"The timing," Lindsey sighed. "I wish I could wait a little longer."

"You can," Emily said. "You don't *have* to do it."

"But you just said…"

"What I said was that if you're convinced that this is the only way to keep your boyfriend, and you *want* to keep him, then think about whether it's more important than getting the timing right. If it's worth it, then go for it."

"This sucks."

"Or you could just talk to him."

Lindsey shook her head. "He'd just tell me that he doesn't care about that stuff and we can wait until I'm ready."

Emily raised her eyebrows. "Well there you go. Do you think he'd break up with you after saying all that?"

"I honestly don't know what he'd do, but these girls are literally all over him."

*****

After the halftime routines were done and the game was moments away from resuming, Tracey made her way to the court and purchased one of the wraps sold at the concession along with a bottle of water. She was greeted by dozens of fellow students, all with something complimentary to say about her performances. Several young men chatted with her as well, and all of a sudden she realized that her life was changing radically. She went up into the stands and saw Lindsey and Emily in deep conversation. She found her seat with the rest of the drill team and prepared to cheer for the

Cobras along with the rest of the insane Kendall fans. She was curious to know how loud it would be in the stands because on the field it was pretty deafening. She knew she wouldn't care though. She couldn't wipe the smile from her face.

The Cobras came out to the roar of the crowd and from the very first snap it was clear that things were going to be very different than the first half. Scott Webber took the Cobras down the field on an efficient but very up-tempo drive lasting four minutes and consisting of thirteen plays, culminating on a perfectly thrown fade pass to Kevin in the corner of the end zone. The Veritas offense never had a prayer. As in the first half, they simply couldn't move the ball. They had gained less than fifty yards on offense in the first half and the second half was even worse. The Veritas quarterback, Shawn Mitchell was skittish after one of Kevin's hits earlier in the game. The Cobra pass rush was all over him and they caused him to make a series of errant passes. By the end of the game, Kevin had snatched a school record 4 interceptions, including one he ran back for a touchdown. On offense, the Cobras were suddenly unstoppable as Scott Webber engineered three more consecutive touchdown drives and then another two in a row, passing the ball to six different receivers for a second half total of over four hundred yards passing to go along with his hundred plus ion the first half. He now held the Kendall High record for passing yards in a game and had done it in little more than a half of football and against a very good defense. Kevin Sinclaire had been spectacular, catching sixteen passes for a total of two hundred sixty-seven yards and three touchdowns plus his interception return. The freshmen had taken over the team and the Kendall crowd was thrilled at the performance.

Chapter 21

Throughout each Kendall High School football season, there are certain events that are held annually and everyone always shows up to them. The first is the Penner party, always held right after the first game of the season. But during the bye week, when the team has a week off, and no Friday night game, the head coach traditionally hosts a party. This is simply and aptly referred to as the "Coach's Party. Following the homecoming game, the Friday after Thanksgiving, Leo Forsythe always throws his annual gala event, where he goes all out and puts pretty much every other event throughout the year to shame. For the past three years, the Kildare's have let Matt throw a party following whichever game he chose. This year, he had committed to week four, though he now wished he could cancel it. In election years, the mayor sometimes hosted an additional party, though this year, he was such a shoe-in his campaign had decided it wasn't necessary and why waste the money?

On weeks where no particular party was scheduled, the postgame festivities generally wound up at the home of Lester Fontaine. These parties had a decidedly more relaxed feel to them because virtually no adults ever came out to them. These parties were all about letting the kids have their fun in a place where they could be monitored, sort of. To Les, that meant not letting anyone drive home drunk. He always had a canvas sack with him, in which he held everyone's keys. If you wanted to drive, you had to pass the Les Test before you could get your keys back. If you couldn't do it, then you could always crash for a while and go home in the morning after Les shoveled huge amounts of pancakes and eggs down your throat. He had a walk-in refrigerator packed with food for each week's party. He always had a five gallon bucket filled three quarters of the way with his special blended pancake batter. He had stacks of eggs, as well as plenty of bacon and breakfast sausage. Many of the partiers just crashed at Les's every Friday night because he fed them so well on Saturday.

Les didn't mind, especially when the athletes came. He was the biggest sports fan in the whole world. When it came to the Kendall High School Cobras, there was no one who was more passionate that Lester Fontaine, except maybe Jasper Parney, the lunatic who before each home game painted his whole body black and silver and dressed in a very fierce looking skull mask and nothing more, other than a pair of black cycling shorts that were at least a size too tight. Less was passionate in a different way. He knew every single detail of every single player on the team, really in the whole southern region. He could quote statistics from around the league and knew just what matchups were the most interesting from week to week.

Lester took all of that information and his passion and put it to use on his web page, which was dedicated to Kendall High School sports. Football was his true passion, but Lester Fontaine knew everything about all of the other sports as well, right down to the girls swim team and field hockey. On his site you could find stats and scores from all over the region for every sport that Kendall High took part in and even some they didn't. His site had grown from a simple hobby to a full blown business complete with advertising revenue as well as memberships which granted access to Lester's weekly Kendall High School football webcasts as well as his live daily sports talk show, which was a Kendall High favorite because he often took the time to interview the student body about the various sporting events. In Kendall Township, Lester Fontaine was generally considered to be the authority on the Kendall Cobras. He had overcome a lot of adversity to achieve this distinction, the most obvious and certainly the biggest was the fact that he was in a wheelchair. Lester Fontaine had no legs.

To be more specific, he had lost both legs just above the knees. It had happened one week before his twelfth birthday. He had gone to a job site with his father, Lester Sr., to visit his uncle and check out the massive building project that would ultimately become the new mall, located just outside Kendall Township. When they arrived, a crane operator was moving 16" x 20' I-beams one at a time from a ten foot tall stack to wherever they were needed. As luck would have it, one of the beams, got hung up, and rather than set it down and try again, the crane operator managed to shake it loose. It would have been fine except that in jarring it loose, it caused the beam to swing and spin, slamming into the beams on the top of the stack, causing a chain reaction that sent virtually the entire stack tumbling to the ground in an avalanche of iron and steel.

What nobody knew as the stack fell was that little Les Jr. had gone behind the stack to peer into the ten foot deep concrete pit that would ultimately become the mall's main boiler room and utilities control room. As the stack fell, Les Jr. was knocked half into the pit, his legs trapped under the pile of beams, while the rest of him dangled upside down, unconscious in the pit. Had the pit not been there, Lester Jr. would have been killed under the weight of many tons of steel. As it was, his lower legs were crushed beyond any hope of repair. The doctors did all they could, but they were unable to repair all the damage and before long, infections began to set in, endangering his life. They were forced to amputate both his legs above the knees.

*****

When Lindsey and Emily arrived, the party was already in full swing. The music was loud. Many football players were there, dancing and hanging out with cheerleaders and Brette Girls. There were stacks of pizzas on the center island in the kitchen and bottles of soda and water lining the counters. The rules for the Fontaine party were simple. Eat all you want. Drink all the soda, juice and water you want. If you want to drink beer or alcohol, bring it yourself. Don't ask Les to provide booze because you will be sent home. Don't even think about bringing drugs of any kind. Everybody who drove to the party must drop their keys off with Les. The idea of an adult throwing this kind of party all the time for high school kids is bothersome for many citizens. Les never really thought about it. He had been throwing parties for the football team ever since he was in high school. While he was still in school, his parents had allowed him to tap his enormous settlement each year for a one time sum that he had to make last for the entire year. He generally used that cash to fund his web projects in the spring and summer, and then he used it to fund his "fall fiestas". After he graduated, he was still so close to the program and its members that he just continued the parties. The kids loved them, and he felt like he was providing a safe environment for them to blow off steam. The police would never bother them because his brother, Jeff Fontaine, was a detective in the Kendall Township Police Department and Les had a bunch of cops over often for a regular card game. On top of that, this was Kendall Township, where the rules were just a little bit different for the football players. As long as they stayed out of public trouble, no one really bothered them.

Lindsey spotted Kevin entering amongst a crowd of newcomers, mostly football players and Brette Girls, including Alli Sylvester. She rolled her eyes and glanced at Emily, who had an amused little smirk on her face. She looked at Kevin, who seemed to be enjoying himself and all the attention, though he wasn't particularly focused on Alli. When he saw Lindsey, he broke away and came over.

"Hey," he said.

"Hey, yourself. I guess you came over with Alli?"

Kevin glanced back at the group. "We all came over in a few different cars. I was not in Alli's. Stop worrying about her, okay?" He took her hand and led her away.

Emily, watched them for a moment, then found Matt in the crowd. She went and grabbed him, kissed him, and then dragged him to the living room, which was basically the dance floor.

"Wait," he protested. "I need a drink first."

"First we dance, and then we drink," she replied. "And *theeeen*...well...you know." She smiled seductively.

Sometimes Matt could get himself into a mood where he could insulate himself from Emily's seduction, but most of the time, she just had to smile or stare into his eyes, and he was a goner. He could not often bring himself to say no to her. Even though in his heart he knew they were going nowhere, he could not bring himself to push her away. He wondered if Emily really wanted to be with him or if he was just a bigger challenge than other guys because he didn't just want her. He wanted his freedom as well. She clearly wanted more. He wondered why Emily wasn't enough for him. He wondered even more why she was wasting her time with him, especially this year, when things were going backwards for him. It kind of bothered him that he had the chance to be with a girl who was clearly the cream of the crop in terms of beauty and even brains, but he was unable to commit to her. Emily was an A student. He knew it, though her wild reputation often covered up that fact. What more could he want? Sure, they fought all the time, but that was mostly because she was becoming resentful of the other girls. He knew he could clear up most of their problems simply by committing to a monogamous relationship with Emily Vasquez. But something always got in the way.

As they danced, Emily's heart was racing. She loved being with this guy, but she was getting restless. She thought about all the time they had spent together. She knew that there was no one who knew Matt Kildare better than she did, and yet she couldn't shake the feeling that he had let Tracey Overton in on something Emily had been unable to get from him. Emily knew that Matt loved her in his way, which was really sometimes hard to feel, especially when he was in one of his moods. But the way he held her and kissed her had to be different. When things were going well between them, she couldn't imagine ever being with another guy. But he was two years older. He was going to be at some college next year. Was it really worth it to try to stay together until he left? Would it be simpler to just move on and try to forget him?

The school year was just getting under way. She didn't think she could handle going to school at Kendall High right alongside him and never getting together again. She thought of Lindsey, faced with a similar fear, though Emily thought Lindsey was getting way ahead of herself. Would they both lose their guys together? What a pathetic pair they would be if that happened. What if she lost Matt to Tracey? That thought was almost too much to bear. It was one thing to lose to an older girl, maybe one who might even be able to go to college with him the following year. Emily could understand that, even if it did make her sick to think about. But to lose him to a girl who had no clue about guys, who had no real social skills at all. Sure she could dance, but she shouldn't be competition for Emily Vasquez.

    And yet she was. When Emily thought of Tracey, she remembered a shy, slightly heavy, unusually tall redhead from the fifth grade who usually had some sort of redness all over her face and who never spoke. As the years passed, Emily saw Tracey change in every way but her demeanor, like she had no idea that she was changing physically. Now, Tracey had come into her own. She was beginning to realize the effect her appearance was having on boys. She was starting to explore the social network at Kendall High. It wouldn't take long for the guys to start going for her.

    Emily actually considered befriending Tracey. Lindsey was great. Maybe Tracey would make a cool friend. Emily imagined she and Tracey walking the halls together as the hottest duo in the school. Lindsey had Kevin and they were fast becoming the "it couple". With Emily's help, Tracey could join her at the top of the coveted "Hottness List". That is actually a real list, by the way. And yes, it is spelled with two Ts. The Hottness List is an online list managed by a completely stereotypical computer nerd named Ryan Tibbitt, who one day decided to go around and ask every person in the school who they thought was the hottest male and the hottest female. No one thought much of it until he started the rankings. Most people did these things digitally. But to maintain the "One Vote Per Student" rule, Ryan actually created a spreadsheet, which he then printed out, and went around and with pen and paper, collected his data, inputting it all manually into his webpage, where you could go and see who was the hottest in the school. That was back in the late nineties. To this day, Ryan still maintains the site, though he employs a couple of students each year to go around and collect the information. During the month of December, three or four students would go around surveying the student body. On January first, last years' page will be archived and the new page will go up.

    Emily was currently at the top of the list. She had the distinction of being the only freshman who had ever made the Hottness List. Matt had been on it since his sophomore year. He and Emily were also on the list as last year's Hottest Couple, though she was pretty sure Kevin and Lindsey would take that honor this coming winter. She wondered if Lindsey would unseat her in the Hottest Female category. Probably not. There was a personality issue with Lindsey. She had the looks, but didn't want the attention. Kevin could indeed unseat Matt though, which would do wonders for Matt's self esteem.

But could she really be friends with Tracey? It would help solve the problem of Tracey and Matt. She and Lindsey became friends and Emily promised to lay off Kevin. Friends don't go after friends' guys. Tracey would be forced to find another guy. It was a kind of cheap way to win, and Emily didn't want to be a desperate clinger. If Matt wanted out, she would have to deal with it, but first she would have to find a way to get at his true feelings. She felt like he owed her that much. She leaned back a little and looked up at him. He was holding her so close that she had trouble getting her arms up over his so that she could wrap them around his neck. She pulled him down slightly and then jumped up softly, bringing her legs up around his waist so that he was carrying her as they kissed and danced. It was her signature move, though she only ever tried it with Matt. He held her up so easily it was like a demonstration of his strength and her trust in him.

*****

They were sitting on a couch in a relatively quiet room. They had walked in silence for several moments, each lost in thought. Neither felt like breaking the silence. Lindsey's mind was waging a war with her heart. She was convinced that Kevin was beginning to change his mind about sex, though he had made no mention of this to her. She felt like because he had drawn a line in the sand of sorts with her earlier in their relationship, he would not cross it now that things had changed. But he had drawn no such line with the other girls who were fawning over him and basically throwing themselves at him.

So what did that mean for them? Were they stuck? Was there hope for a meaningful relationship or were they doomed to a silent struggle where they circled one another until everything disintegrated between them? Lindsey was grateful for the late nights when everyone was asleep and she could finally let the tears flow without anyone asking her about it. She could not imagine a worse feeling than the burning sensation she felt across her heart as she imagined what life would be like without Kevin Sinclaire in it.

As she now stared into his gorgeous green eyes, she was too petrified to give voice to her fears. His gaze seemed so loving, so compassionate. He made her feel like she was the only girl in the world without ever saying a word. Actually, in moments such as these, she wondered where her fears came from. Could he ever look at another girl the way he was looking at her right now? Can guys do that? Can they go from girl to girl creating the same magical feeling in each one?

Kevin just stared. He knew she loved to look into his eyes, but she had no idea the spell her bright blue eyes put *him* under. He couldn't figure out why she seemed so worried about their relationship. She was clinging to something she could never lose. She seemed to believe that another girl could take him away from her. He couldn't figure out a way to make her understand that it could never happen. He told her straight out right from the beginning, but all she seemed to see was a crowd of half-naked girls leading him off to bed. On one hand he thought it was up to him to make her feel more secure, but on the other hand, he couldn't be sure that her fears weren't a symptom of perhaps a deeper desire to end things so she didn't have to live such a public life. Kendall High School football players were like celebrities within the Township. Lindsey preferred a quieter existence. Kevin wasn't sure it was right to drag her along as he garnered such attention. Ultimately, he figured it would all work out, but his heart was torn between his desire to be with this amazing girl and his desire to excel on the field. He hated that he might someday soon have to choose.

"What are you thinking right now?" she asked.

He smiled wryly. "I'm trying *not* to think. It's been a crazy week. I just want to sit here with you."

She nodded. *So much for that.*

"How about you?" he countered.

She took a deep breath, about to unload her burden, but just couldn't do it. She slid in closer to him, curling up in his arms as he lay back in the corner of the couch. Having failed to take the opportunity to talk through her concerns, she closed her eyes, not wanting him to read the uncertainty on her face. She just couldn't bring herself to start the conversation she wanted so desperately to have. Why couldn't he see it?

*****

Tracey timidly approached the door to the Fontaine house. Really, it was an estate, located in somewhat familiar territory. Lester Fontaine's home was about a mile from Matt Kildare's house. The neighborhood that Matt lived in ended just across the street from Lester's property. Les had built his house about a hundred yards back from the street and had left all the trees in front. A long driveway took visitors back to a large parking area. Tracey had come with a couple of girls from the drill squad. They seemed to know their way around and just walked in ahead of her.

Tracey froze for a second in the doorway.

What are you doing here?

The truth was that she had no idea what to do at a party. The Penner party had been intimidating enough, but at least there had been some structure to it and adults around. Here, there was no supervision, save Les, and he was nowhere to be seen. Brittany had warned her about this place. Tracey had begged her to come with her, but Brittany had refused. For one thing, she wasn't even allowed to come. The truth was that she didn't want to.

"The real purpose for going to those parties is either to get drunk, stoned, or have sex, or a combination of those three things," she had said. "It's not a place where I want to be."

She had suggested for Tracey to come over her house, but Tracey wanted to spread her wings a little bit and be a part of the whole Kendall High experience now that she was becoming known. Who knows? Maybe she would meet someone.

Now she was beginning to regret that decision. As she surveyed the scene, she noticed that everyone appeared to be having a good time. They were dancing, drinking, and in many cases, making out. It seemed like a happy, fun, and relaxed atmosphere, but Tracey couldn't help but feel a little dirty. Maybe it was the fact the she had no one to talk to. She moved through the house until she came across the kitchen, where she found the food and drinks. The wheelchair bound Les Fontaine was in there, just tossing some freshly fried up hot wings in sauce. He gestured to her.

"Hey, come over here and try one of these."

Tracey reluctantly went over and picked one of the wings from the bowl and tried it. It was delicious. She couldn't hide the expression on her face. Les had gotten it just right, with the perfect blend of flavor and heat. He grinned when he saw that she was impressed.

"Yep, you can always count on ole Les to have the perfect party food. That hot sauce recipe is my own special blend." Everything Les made was "his own special blend".

Tracey nodded appreciatively. "They're very good."

"Great." He pushed the bowl over to her. "They're all yours."

"Oh, that's okay. I can't eat them all."

He waved her off. "It's no problem, I've got plenty more coming. Hey, did you drive here?"

"No, I came with a couple of other girls. One of them drove."

"Okay," he said. "Make sure I get their keys if you see them."

He turned back to the fryers and began preparing for another round of hot wings. Tracey took her bowl of wings and ate in silence for a couple of minutes.

"You gonna eat all of them?"

She spun around and saw Tony standing there, looking hopefully at her wings. She playfully guarded them with her arms.

"Get your own." She smiled.

Tony looked hurt. He made his best sad face, sticking out his bottom lip. Then he brought both hands together as though he were praying.

"Please?"

"Oh, all right." She slid the bowl over to him and watched him gobble several down.

He wiped his face and fingers with a napkin. "Brittany here with you?"

She shook her head. "No. She won't come here. She thinks all anyone ever does here is get drunk and have sex."

Tony nodded, stripping another wing clean in one bite. "She's probably right. Man, these are good! Hey, Wheels! I hope you got more of these comin."

Les, with his back to them, shot him a thumbs up. He absolutely loved it when the kids liked his cooking.

Tracey looked at Tony harshly. "*Wheels?*" she whispered. "Seriously? You have to call him that?"

Tony frowned. "What's wrong with Wheels? I think it's an awesome name."

"It's rude...and insensitive."

Beginnings

"Really?" He turned to look at Les. "Hey Les. Is it rude and insensitive to call you Wheels?"

Tracey rolled her eyes.

Les laughed, never turning to face them. He was focused on cooking his wings. "Dude, if you win games at Kendall High, you can call me anything you want to."

"Tell you what, Wheels. I'll never call you late to dinner. That's a promise."

"Right on, One-Niner."

Tony turned to Tracey. "See that? Lester Fontaine knows my number. I didn't even have to tell him that."

Tracey shook her head. "Well, aren't you just famous?"

"Hey, who peed in *your* Cheerios?"

She giggled slightly and shook her head. "I'm sorry. I just feel really out of place."

"No problem." He started dancing toward her as a new song came one. It was an up tempo number, and Tony started shaking and gyrating to the beat. Tracey couldn't help but laugh. He was ridiculous. Tony held out his hand.

"Shall we dance, my lady?"

"What is this, sixteenth century England?" she replied.

"Huh?"

"You just said...never mind. Sure let's dance." Tracey had never been to a dance. She had never danced with a boy before. Well, not like this. On stage didn't count. This was a social function. She was glad for her contemporary dance classes. Dancing was the one thing she actually felt confident doing.

As they entered the dance room, though, she froze. Tony felt the tug on his hand as he was leading Tracey through the crowd. He turned and saw the frozen look on her face. She stood transfixed, staring at something past him. He turned to survey the scene. Matt Kildare and Emily were locked in a not-so-subtly sexual embrace, her legs around his waist, kissing deeply, still moving together to the sound of the music. It was about as passionate as he imagined two people could be in public with their clothes still on. He turned back to Tracey and moved in behind her, his hands on both of her shoulders. He leaned in close to her so he could talk into her ear.

"Okay, we have two choices. One, we can go in there and dance like those two are not even in the room almost having sex in

219

front of everyone. We can dance and have a great time and ignore them, proving to them both that you don't care and are over that goon. How's that sound?"

She didn't move. Tony could feel her about to lose it.

"Okay. That's why we have *two* choices. Here's what we're going to do. I'm going to get you out of here, okay?"

She nodded slightly, still frozen in place. She felt like any movement would cause the tears to burst out. Tony came around in front of her, blocking her view of the couple. He got her attention.

"Look at me." Tracey's pained eyes lifted to meet his. "We're going to turn and walk out, okay?"

She nodded. He turned her shoulders, and she slowly made her way out of the room, always guided by Tony, who never let go of her. He steered her through the house, his arm around her like any other couple taking a walk. Outside, he let her go, but she could no longer hold the emotions in. She collapsed into his arms, sobbing. He held her, not sure what he should do. Tony wasn't really prepared to console a heartbroken girl. It wasn't really his area. Kevin was the one who always had all the great advice. Tony was a joker. He liked to laugh and make others laugh. He didn't really know how to handle grief, so he just stood there, his arms around the still sobbing, shaking girl.

Chapter 22

They kissed deeply and for long periods of time. Lindsey loved this. She wanted it to always be like this. At some point she knew that she would want things to progress. But right now, she loved being in the arms of this guy, their lips touching, his hands in her hair, or on her back or arms. She loved that he wasn't trying to grope her, or peel off her clothes. She could be completely vulnerable with him without any worries that he would bring pressure to bear on her to go any farther than she wanted.

But her mind would not let her enjoy the feeling for long. Even as his full and complete attention was focused on her and her alone, Lindsey could not shake the nagging sensation that she would have to make a decision soon about going further. Why did this have to be so hard, so confusing? Their relationship had always been so easy. It had always been so comfortable. They talked about everything. She always knew that she could count on Kevin to be her very best friend no matter what. It had been like that from the moment she had let him into her world.

These thoughts led her to one conclusion. She had to rely on what was real. She had to focus on the one thing she knew to be true in this whole messy affair. It was so simple she had not given it any attention at all. She had known it all along, and yet in her mind she had rendered it insignificant. But it was everything. Lindsey was in love with Kevin Sinclaire.

She stopped kissing him and pulled away, bringing her legs under her, facing him. She looked into his eyes as deeply as she had ever done, drinking in the beautiful deep green.

He frowned slightly. "Are you okay?"

"I love you." She couldn't believe she actually said it. She waited for him to respond, but he was obviously surprised and unsure of what to say.

"Kevin, I love you. I'm *in* love with you. I just needed to tell you that."

He nodded, getting his wits back slowly. It wasn't often that Lindsey could catch him by surprise like this. For a brief second, she was quite pleased with herself.

He finally responded. "I love you too."

She breathed a sigh of relief. "Are you sure? I said it because I needed you to know. You don't have to say it back if you don't mean it."

"Is this about sex?"

She straightened up. "Sex? Why would you ask that?"

"I don't know. It just seems like things are weird. Now you tell me you love me. I don't know what brought it on."

"Brought it on? Why did something have to bring it on?" She stood up, beginning to feel the pangs of humiliation.

"I didn't mean it like that. Sit down. I'm sorry."

Lindsey no felt completely stupid. She backed away. "I need to…I'll be right back."

"Lindsey…"

"I'll be back. I just need to go for a minute."

*****

She ran out of the room, trying her best to hold it together. After making sure Kevin hadn't jumped up to follow her, she took a moment to compose herself. Then she headed for the main room. Emily was no longer in there dancing, so Lindsey quickly walked through the house, finally finding her, seated on Matt's lap, laughing and partying with a group of Cobras, Brettes, and cheerleaders. Lindsey walked over and tapped her shoulder. Emily looked up at her.

"I need you."

Emily could see the redness in Lindsey's eyes. "What's the matter?"

"I need you, *now*." Lindsey turned before anyone could see her tears. She headed for the door. Emily jumped up and followed.

Outside, Emily's eyes were wide with concern. "What happened?" she asked. Lindsey kept walking quickly away from the house. She went part way down the driveway. Emily caught up and grabbed her.

"Stop," she said. Lindsey spun around, her eyes filled with tears. She was trying to control her sobbing, but it wasn't working. "Tell me what happened."

Lindsey could barely get words out. "I...I...made a huge...mistake."She managed.

"What mistake?" Emily prodded. Then her eyes widened even more. "No!" She shook her head. "You didn't...Did you?"

Lindsey was trying to get it together. Emily was still shaking her head. "I mean...Kevin actually...you guys really...?"

Lindsey looked at her, frowning. "Did we really what? What are you talking about?"

Emily shrugged. "Nothing. What were *you* talking about?"

Lindsey's mouth dropped open. "Were you talking about sex? Did Kevin and I have *sex*? That's what you thought we were doing?"

"Well...I don't..."

"Is that all you ever think about?"

Emily pointed to herself. "Me? Really? Girl, *you're* the one who can't stop thinking about sex. Oh, I have to have sex with my boyfriend or else he'll have sex with someone else. Oh, I don't really want to have sex right now because I'm not ready, but my boyfriend is going to want me to do it, so I guess I *have* to do it. Oh, but if I have sex with him, he'll get tired of me quicker and find someone else."

"I don't sound like that."

"Lindsey, all you do is talk about sex and mope around because you think Kevin is going to have sex one way or the other and you'll lose him if it's not with you."

"Well, we didn't just have sex, to answer your question."

Emily nodded. "I guess not. So, what happened?"

Lindsey closed her eyes. "I told him I love him."

Emily rolled her eyes. "No!...No, no, no, NO! Tell me you did

NOT just say that!"

Lindsey just stood there wordlessly.

"Are you being serious right now? You went in there and told Kevin Sinclaire that you love him?"

Lindsey nodded.

"I can't believe this!" Emily was stomping all over the driveway. "Of all the stupid…How could you go and do that? That is the last thing you do! You never, under any circumstances tell the *guy* that you love him! Never, never, NEVER!"

She stomped back toward Lindsey. "Listen to me. There is a series of steps in a relationship. One step leads to the next, understand. You have to go in order. Telling someone you love them is definitely the last step. How could you…? Arrrggghhh! Why would you go and do something like that?"

Lindsey shrugged and shook her head. "I don't know. It just came out."

"It just came out? That's all? What are you, some kind of Turrets victim? You can't think before you speak? You just blurt out everything that pops into your little pea brain?" she poked Lindsey in the forehead as she said the word "brain".

"It felt right at the time."

Emily rolled her eyes. "Oh, well, that's just great! It felt right at the time? And then what? Six seconds later you come running out crying?"

"Will you stop being mean and tell me what to do? He's waiting for me."

Emily paced back and forth staring up into the night sky, shaking her head. "Okay, fine. So, you tell the guy you love him. Then what?"

"Huh?"

"What…Did…He…Say?

"Oh, uh, well, eventually he said that he loves me too."

Emily looked at her intently. "*Eventually*? What exactly does that mean…eventually?"

Lindsey shrugged. "Well…at first he kind of just sat there, sort of surprised I guess."

"Oh…Ya think?"

"And then I said it again."

"You WHAT?"

Lindsey slumped and her chin sunk to her chest. "I told him I loved him again," she mumbled.

Emily put her fingers to her temples. "Of course you did." She shook her head. "Because once wasn't enough, was it? I love you, sweet heart! What? No response? Let me REPEAT MYSELF like some kind of DESPERATE FRESHMAN!"

Lindsey was devastated. "But he said it back to me."

"Yeah, he did…eventually."

"You don't think he meant it?"

"Good God, girl! I don't know. He probably *did* mean it. So what? There's no way for you to tell, is there? And so what if he loves you? What difference does it make?"

"Well, if he loves me, he's probably not looking to hook up with other girls, right?"

"And you think that getting a guy to say the words to you is some kind of force field against all these other girls that are after him?"

Lindsey shrugged. "No, but…"

Emily held up a hand. "Stop. There is no "but". You need to understand that there is a way to play the game and a way not to. And you are not playing the game like a winner."

"Emily, please. This is not a game to me."

Emily nodded. "Finally! You've pinpointed the problem! Lindsey, no one cares whether or not *you* think it's a game. These girls are not interested in you or how you feel. They are interested in one thing, and one thing only. That is getting the guys. They want to party with the Cobras. It's *all* a big game to them. Who can get him first? Who can get him the most? And the biggest quest going on right now? Who can get him from *you*? Because that is the real challenge, to get a guy from his girlfriend. And they don't care what it takes."

Lindsey just stood there, her mouth slightly open as the reality of the situation began to sink in. Emily saw the understanding begin to creep into her eyes and nodded.

"Get it? It is all one big game to everyone but you…and probably Kevin for now. But you need to get it through your skull that you need to *play* the game in order to win it."

"But I don't want to play head games with Kevin."

Emily shook her head. "It's not like that. First of all, the game isn't *against* Kevin at all. Think of him as the prize for winning. That's what they all think of him. You win this round, you get to sleep with him. Someone else might win the next round, and on and on. *Your* goal is to keep him from becoming anyone else's prize. And that is a whole lot harder than you might think."

Lindsey sat on the ground. "So, I really blew it tonight?"

Emily took a breath and shrugged. "Impossible to tell until you get back in there and talk to him."

"Okay." Lindsey got back up and headed back toward the house.

"Hey!" Emily shouted. "Where do you think you're going?"

Lindsey turned. "You just said to go back in there and…"

"Noooooo! Not right now, you're not."

"But you just said…"

"I was speaking figuratively."

"It sounded pretty literal to me."

"Well, it was figurative."

""Get back in there" were your exact words."

"Yes, "get back in there" in the *figurative* sense. You're in no shape to go in there and face him after this debacle."

"But I told him I'd be back."

"Well, you're not going back in there, *chica*. The way you're going, you might propose to him."

"That's not funny."

"No," Emily said. "It's not. But you are staying out here while I go back in and talk to your guy for you, then I'll get *my* guy and have him take us home."

"You're going to talk to Kevin for me?"

"Yes."

"You're not talking to Kevin."

"Why not?"

"Because he'll think things are weird between us."

"Sweetheart, thing *are* weird between you right now. That's why I need to go in there and get the lay of the land. You and I are going to get together tomorrow and make a plan."

"I thought we were going home to your place tonight."

"*You're* going home. I'm going to go to Matt's house and finish the night in style."

"Is that what you call it?"

"Don't start with me, Lindsey."

Beginnings

*****

After several moments, she stopped crying, but stayed where she was, her head on his shoulder, her arms wrapped tightly around his waist like she was afraid to let go.

"I'm such an idiot," she finally mumbled, still standing there with her head on his shoulder.

Tony responded, "No, you're not. Not to me."

She finally realized that he was still holding her, and pulled back slightly. "I'm so sorry I just did that to you. I feel so stupid."

Tony brought his hands up to her shoulders and stood her up straight, looking into her eyes. "Listen to me. You are not stupid at all. And you didn't do anything to me. You needed a friend. Here I am."

She smiled ruefully. "It seems like you're always there when I need a friend."

He smiled. "See that? What are friends for?"

They stood there for several moments in silence.

Tony finally broke the silence. "Listen. Do you want me to walk you home?"

She really wanted to get out of there. "It's kind of a long walk from here."

He shrugged. "That's cool. If you feel like walking, I'll walk with you."

He held out his arm. She nodded and looped her arm through his. They headed down the long driveway together, her head on his shoulder.

As they walked, Tracey began to relate her unfolding saga with Matt. To this point, she had only told Brittany and Lindsey the story. Had she thought about it, she would probably not have told it to Tony, but he was such a good listener. For someone who spent so much time loudly making his presence known, joking, or chattering on about irrelevant nonsense, he seemed to have a softer side that really made him compassionate and understanding. He didn't seem to be judging her. He didn't seem to be mocking her. He just listened, asked a question or two here and there, held her closer when she started to get emotional, but never in a way that made her feel uncomfortable. In fact, Tracey felt especially comfortable with Tony.

"So," she finally said. "Do you regret walking with me yet?"

"Nope," Tony replied.

"Well, you must have an opinion of some sort."

"Not really."

"I just told you my deepest, darkest feelings, how sad and scared I am, how I don't know what to do, and you have nothing to say about any of it?"

He smiled. "I wish I had an answer for you, but I can barely keep from puking when I get near Brittany, so I wouldn't know how to handle what you're going through. I mean, in a way, I envy you."

"You envy me?"

"In a way. You got the guy you wanted, even if it was only for a minute. You still *know*. Right? You didn't *know* what it would be like before, but now you do. The not knowing might be the worst part."

"Maybe, but at least before, I had an intact fantasy. Now it's all ruined."

"No. That's where you're wrong. It's not ruined. It's just real. Real is not always clean and neat and pleasant. But at least you *got* your fantasy. I think most people would take their chances with *getting* the fantasy versus not getting it if they had the choice."

Tracey shrugged. They walked in silence for a moment, then a thought struck Tracey. "Wait a minute. Did you just say Brittany? As in Brittany *Morgan*?"

"I did. Why?"

"You know she's my best friend, right."

"Sure."

A smile crept onto Tracey's face. "Are you telling me you have a thing for Brittany?"

"A 'thing'?" Tony's face wrinkled as though he were smelling a filthy rag. "A 'thing' is when you think someone's cute or hot and you like them and want to meet them, okay? You know how you felt about Matt Kildare before? Times it by a million. That's what I feel about Brittany Morgan. And you can't tell her all this."

Tracey "zipped" her lips and threw away the key. "Mum's the word...Wow, though! I never would have guessed. You and Brittany?"

"Why? Is it too weird? Kevin thinks I'm crazy."

They continued to talk as they slowly made their way to Tracey's house. Tracey had no idea how Tony felt about it, but she was grateful for the long distance. She felt so much better talking to Tony. While she had reacted well to Tony's revelation that he had such strong feelings for Brittany, she was secretly jealous that Brittany unwittingly had garnered the devotion of such a great guy. One the other hand, Brittany was highly unlikely to start a relationship with Tony strictly because he was not a Christian. She had made that quite clear to Tracey on several occasions. So maybe there was something to wait for, to be prepared for down the road. At least she could foster a great friendship with Tony that could lead somewhere. The worst that could happen was…

Uggh! The FRIEND ZONE!

Tracey's inner voice had been relatively silent during the entire walk, but as so often happened when her nerves tightened, it came back. It was always there, hovering under the surface, ready to pounce when she gave it the slightest opportunity. She grimaced at the idea that she might wind up caught in a relationship with Tony that neither would want to risk, thereby ruining their chance for a more romantic one. She resolved not to let that happen.

Good luck with that.

Chapter 23

He looked like he was ready to go golfing. Tony was standing in front of the long mirror on the back of Kevin's door, carefully combing his hair, determined to look his very best for this occasion. Kevin, wearing a pair of shorts and a Kendall Cobras football T-shirt, was shaking his head grimly. This was going to be ugly. He had never seen Tony act this way over a girl. Sure, there had been those girls who left him tongue-tied; with whom he had trouble getting the words out right. But Brittany Morgan, for some reason, had altered his mind. His whole personality changed when her name came up. Most of the time he was a world class joker. He got away with some of the most outrageous things when speaking to girls. He never did that when it came to Brittany. He got very serious. He never joked about her. She was *the* girl, he had once told Kevin. He was prepared not only to go to church, but to also "dress the part", as he told Kevin. As Kevin looked at his best friend, he couldn't help but feel sorry for him.

"Dude, this is a bad idea."

Tony shook his head. "Negative. This is the best idea I've ever had."

"You have a zero percent chance of getting together with Brittany Morgan."

"See, now you're just being a pessimist. Trust me on this one

Kevo. It's in the bag."

"In the bag?" Kevin shook his head. "You're delusional. She will only date Christians. Why is that so difficult to grasp?"

Tony looked at him. "So you're saying I can't become a Christian."

"Seriously? You want to be a Christian?"

"Why not?"

Kevin put his head in his hands. "You can't be this dense. You don't just join up, okay? You're not going to walk in there and fill in a membership form with an email and a password. Christianity is not a club. It's life. It's how people choose to *live*. It's more than that even, but you don't know anything about it."

"I know that *Brittany's* a Christian."

"Yeah?"

He shrugged. "What more do I need to know? Brittany's great. You told me that yourself."

"Yes," Kevin replied. "She *is* great. I love the girl. This isn't about her. It's about you."

Tony looked at him. "Listen, I'm not an idiot. I get it, okay? I don't know anything about Christianity."

"Finally, we're getting somewhere."

Tony continued. "But I do know that I can't stop thinking about Brittany Morgan. She's special. I have to at least see what it's all about. If I don't go to church and check it out, I'll never know. And then I'll never have a chance with her."

"Even if you do become a Christian, you'll still never get her."

"Yeah? Why's that?"

"Cause you're an idiot."

Tony turned back to the mirror and smoothed out his shirt. "Yeah, but I look good. Better than *you* do, at least."

"I'm not trying to pick up girls at Sunday School?"

"I hope not. You're dressed like a scrub. You should really think more about your appearance."

"Are you serious right now? This is the first time you've put on a shirt with buttons since I've known you!"

"Really?" He didn't mention the fact that his mother had taken him out the day before to purchase this outfit.

"Well, you forgot to cut the tags off."

"What?" He quickly looked all over his clothing as Kevin burst out laughing. "Very funny, punk." He dove at Kevin, crashing into him and sending them both tumbling over the opposite side of the bed. He landed on top of Kevin and pelted him with jabs to his lower back and then punches to the back of his legs, trying to give Kevin a Charlie-horse. Kevin just covered up as best he could and took it all, laughing hysterically.

"Your…hair…It's getting…messed…up!"

*****

As they got out of the car and headed to the High School building, Kevin could see the nervous anticipation on his friend's face. He knew that as excited as Tony was to see her, he would be on unfamiliar ground. This is Brittany Morgan's turf.

"Look," Kevin said. "This is an away game."

"Huh?"

"You're walking into a hostile environment."

"What?" He stopped walking. "I thought you said anyone could…"

"Not that," Kevin interrupted. "This is Brittany Morgan's church. These are Brittany Morgan's friends. She grew up here. She knows everybody. You are all alone."

"I have *you*. You have my back, right?"

Kevin shook his head. "No one's going to try to fight you, idiot. Your *problem* is that you can't speak when she's around and you've now chosen to go where *she* is most comfortable to try to pursue her. It's a stupid plan."

Tony stared at him for a moment. "Well…that's nitpicking, isn't it."

"Look. Here's what we're going to do. We go in there and just play it cool. We grab a bagel…"

"They have bagels in there?"

Kevin looked seriously at his friend. "Can you focus for a minute? I feel like I'm talking to a stooge."

Tony put his hand on Kevin's shoulder. "Will you relax? You're making me nervous. I got this. Everything's under control."

"It's all under control? Tell me, do you have another poem prepared?"

Tony hesitated. "Well…"

Kevin shook his head. "Do NOT recite a poem to her, least of all in front of everyone. It's not going to work and you're going to embarrass her, not to mention yourself."

"But it's really good..."

"I don't care if it's great."

"It *is* great."

"I don't care."

"Do you want to hear it, at least?"

"No."

"I think you'll change your mind once you hear it."

"If you start reciting a poem to Brittany Morgan, I'm going to beat you in front of everyone."

Tony considered for a moment. "You think she'd feel sorry for me then?"

Kevin shook his head helplessly. Tony slapped him on the back. "Relax, my friend. You are in good hands. I am all over this. Everything is going to be okay."

As they entered the building, Kevin tried one more time. "Listen. Can we just see what happens if we play it cool?"

Tony shook his head, looking around. "Will you knock it off?"

"You're plan will not work. I am trying to save you from humiliation in front of a bunch of strangers, *and* Brittany Morgan."

Tony laughed.

"What's so funny?"

"You always say Brittany *Morgan*; never Brittany; just Brittany Morgan."

"No I don't. Besides, who cares?"

"Not me. I love hearing you say her name."

Kevin stopped. "Okay, that's weird."

"Yeah, it kind of came out wrong. See, now you're making me nervous."

"Oh, sure, it's all my fault. I'm the reason you can't talk to Brittany *Morgan*."

They approached the entrance to the main room, the music playing and they could hear the activity going on behind the closed door.

"Here we are," said Kevin. "There's still time to make a good plan."

"Shut up and get your game face on." Tony stretched his shoulders and neck, bouncing on his toes as he did before every play in football games. "It's go time."

Kevin rolled his eyes and pushed the door open. The boys were greeted quickly by some of the regular kids who Kevin knew, and then by several leaders. Kevin introduced to Tony to everyone and they chatted for a few minutes about football and school. Brittany saw them and came over to say hi. He felt Tony begin to freeze up. It was like a magic spell that Tony couldn't avoid. He nudged Tony to try to snap him out of it. Tony nudged back, his jaw clenched.

"Hey guys," Brittany said cheerfully, a bright smile on her face.

Kevin glanced over at Tony, who was trying to smile pleasantly and keep cool. "Hey, Brit. You know Tony, right?"

"Sure," she replied, still smiling. "Nice to see you, Tony. Is this your first time here?"

"Uh, yeah. Actually, it's my first time in any church."

"Really? You've never been to church at all?"

Tony shrugged. "My parents aren't real religious, I guess."

"And Kevin never invited you?"

Tony looked at Kevin. "Not really, no."

Kevin just shrugged.

Brittany smiled. "Well, Kevin only comes because he has to anyway. But I'm glad you came. Did you get a bagel?"

She led him over to the breakfast counter. Kevin saw his opportunity to slip away, just like he'd promised Tony he would. He figured Brittany would talk to Tony for ten or twelve minutes, and Tony would be so tongue tied and incoherent that afterwards, he would give up on this whole insane idea.

He was wrong about most of that. Brittany stormed over to him in less than five minutes with Tony trailing sheepishly behind her.

"Are you serious?" she asked Kevin, who sat there, his mouth full of a blueberry bagel and cream cheese.

"Hmm?" was all he could manage without spitting all over her. He had to close his eyes to control his laughter.

She leaned in close so that no one else could hear. "You brought him here to ask me out?"

"What? That's ridiculous." It was all he could do to keep his face straight. She shook her head and started to walk away. Kevin hopped down off his stool, glaring at Tony, who was grinning ruefully. "Hey, don't go. What'd this idiot tell you?"

She stood there for a second, not sure whether to prolong the conversation or walk away.

"We were talking and I asked him what he really hoped to get out of coming to church, you know, spiritually? I was trying to see where he was with God and maybe he was really searching, but he told me that he knew I only dated Christians, so he figured he should start coming out."

Kevin looked at Tony. "You couldn't leave that part out? You had to dump the whole thing on her on the first day?"

Tony shrugged. "I didn't feel like lying to her. I really...never mind. It doesn't matter." To Brittany, he said, "Look. I'm sorry, okay? I didn't mean to be weird."

She looked from one to the other for several seconds. Finally she said, "Fine. Whatever. You guys need to behave."

As she walked away, Tony shook his head and shoved Kevin slightly and said, "Dude, I *told* you this wasn't gonna work!"

Kevin said, "I swear I'm strangling you later. I won't do it on holy ground, but I'm definitely going to cut off your air supply for at least three minutes."

"I probably deserve that."

They were seated near the back of the room as the lesson began. Both were settling into their thoughts; Kevin and his Lindsey troubles and worries; Tony and his epic failure with Brittany. He sat there contemplating his defeat when Gavin Dalyrimple's voice cut through his thoughts. His head snapped up, and he began to pay attention to what was being said at the front of the room. Tony couldn't follow all of the religious sounding words and phrases, but as those words and phrases were hashed out and explained, he found himself captivated. The lesson dealt with God's original design for the lives of people. He had never been to church before, so Tony had no idea how to compare what was being said to other religious teaching, but as he sat there, considering the points being put forward, he found himself comparing his own thoughts on life to them. They really didn't match up at all. This confusion made him pay even more attention.

He pulled his phone out of his pocket and pulled up a note taking app. He began typing in some questions as they came to his mind. Within the first fifteen minutes of the lesson, Tony had ten questions listed. Now he wished he had waited to talk to Brittany, not because he wanted to use these questions to try to hit on her, but she was probably the only one he knew who might answer them for him. He decided to continue writing out the questions and figure out who to ask later. By the end of the lesson, he had stopped bothering to number them because it was taking up too much time and he was forgetting important questions. Gavin Dalyrimple closed the lesson with a prayer and then dismissed the group, most of who began to file out to head to the big church or find their parents and go home. Tony lingered in his chair as Kevin began to rise. Brittany came over. She grabbed Kevin's arm and led him away. He turned back to Tony, still sitting there wordlessly.

"See what you did? Now *I'm* in trouble."

She took Kevin to the outer room.

Tony sat in his chair, still scanning over his list of questions, barely noticing that Kevin had left the room with Brittany. He was glad for a moment to think about some of what he'd heard. Gavin Dalyrimple came over and spun a chair around, sitting in front of him.

"You know, I saw you typing away during the lesson." He grinned. "I assumed you were playing a game or texting a girl, but it looks now like you were actually taking notes."

Tony stared at the screen. He nodded slightly. "Yeah. I didn't bring paper and I wanted to write down some questions about the lesson."

"Well, that's always encouraging to hear. Anything I can help you with?"

Tony shrugged. "I don't know. These are all probably really stupid, but I've never been to church, so I guess I'm really far behind."

Gavin shook his head, smiling in understanding. "It may seem like that, but it doesn't exactly work that way. Some of these kids have been coming to church for years, but that doesn't make them advanced Christians. My guess is that your questions are probably not stupid at all. Try one on me."

Tony took a breath and began his question. Gavin Dalyrimple did his best to walk Tony through everything the Bible had to say about each question. Tony's fascination grew with every word, every verse. He couldn't explain it, but what he was being told just felt right. It wasn't a magical feeling, like all of a sudden he was changed, but he just felt like something was beginning to click in his mind.

*****

"I can't believe you would do that, Kevin. It's not funny."

"It's a little funny."

"Kevin, this is serious to me, being here, worshipping with other Christians."

"I know."

"So, why would you let him do this? Couldn't you take a minute to explain things to him? *You* know I can't date him. He's not a Christian."

"Trust me, Brit, I have been trying to talk him out of this for days. Believe me, it's well covered territory. But he felt like he had to try. So he tried. You shot him down. Now it's over. No big deal."

She shook her head. "You guys are unreal."

Kevin tilted his head. "Look. The guy likes you, okay? He wanted to ask you out. He can barely think straight when you're in the room."

She frowned. "Are you serious?"

"I'm serious. I've never seen him like this with other girls, so cut him a little slack and be nice."

She was blushing a little. Kevin hid a smile. "I can't go out with him," she said. "I don't want to hurt his feelings. Can't you tell him for me?"

"Nope. This is your fault. You have to fix it."

"How is this my fault?"

Kevin laughed. "You don't get to be pretty, smart, sweet, and perfect and then have *me* crush the hopes and dreams of all your admirers. This is the burden of being beautiful."

"Geez."

"You've let guys down before, right?"

"Yes, but I've never had a guy come to church just to try to date me. It's actually kind of sweet. I shouldn't have gotten mad. I'll talk to him."

Brittany began to open the door to the main room, but stopped short when she saw Tony in deep discussion with Gavin.

She turned to Kevin.

"He's talking to Gavin."

"Really? About what?" He went over and looked through the window.

"I don't know. I don't want to interrupt."

Kevin sat down. "Oh well, I'll wait for him. Can you tell my mom what's going on and that we'll be in soon?"

She looked back at the door. "How about I wait? That way I can talk to him and explain things. We'll come find you in church. Save us seats."

*****

Tony and Gavin talked for the better part of a half hour while Brittany waited in the outer room. Kevin had texted her once a few minutes ago, asking what was up. She told him that Tony was still in there with Gavin. Finally, the two stood up, shook hands and Gavin pointed Tony in the direction of the church, presumably where he thought Kevin would be. Seconds later, Tony came through the door. Brittany stood up, smiling. Tony hesitated, looking uncertain.

"Is Kevin around?"

Brittany shook her head. "He went up to the church. I told him I'd take you to him."

"Am I in trouble?"

She smiled again. "No. And I'm sorry if I hurt your feelings earlier."

"Ahh, don't worry about it. It was my fault. I'm an idiot. Oh, and Kevin didn't have anything to do with it, by the way. He told me the whole time that it was stupid."

"It's not stupid," she replied. "Maybe misguided, but actually, it's kind of sweet."

Tony raised his eyebrows. "I can live with that."

"Can I ask you a question?"

He nodded. "Shoot."

"Are you going to keep coming?"

"I think so."

"But you know I can't go out with you, right?"

Tony nodded sadly. "Yeah, but I think I still need to come."

She looked at him. "*Need?*"

He shrugged. "Yeah, I think so. I just had a conversation with Gavin and I think I want to keep coming. At least for now, you know?"

Brittany could barely contain her excitement. "Are you saying that you came today and didn't believe at all, but now you think you do?"

He shrugged. "I don't know. Something feels different. We'll see, I guess."

"This is amazing. You can't even understand. I pray about things like this all the time, and now I get to see it happen." She smiled. "I know, I'm a dork. I'm just very happy for you right now."

Tony nodded. "Thanks." Kevin was right about her. Brittany Morgan was great. For whatever reason he all of a sudden felt like he *could* talk to her. He wasn't nervous. He was still pretty much in love with her, but it was different now.

*****

"So, you're a Christian now?" Kevin was unconvinced. Tony was a master prankster and joker. You could never be sure with him.

"Why is that so hard to believe?"

"It's not that it's hard to believe. I just know how this day started and how it went, at least the Brittany stuff. Now, all of a sudden, you are a changed man."

"*And?*"

"And nothing. You better not be playing games with her, that's all. I go back a long way with that girl. She's like a sister. If you're trying some phony religious conversion on her, just forget it right now."

"It's not a phony conversion. It's not even a conversion. I don't even know what that means. I just have a lot of questions. Some things seemed real to me in there today. Even in church, I felt different. Something spoke to me. Maybe it was because I've never been in church. I don't know. I'm just gonna go again and see what's what."

"And it's not about Brittany Morgan."

He held up two fingers. "Scout's honor."

Kevin shook his head.

"What?" asked Tony. "It's two fingers, right? How many fingers for Scout's honor?"

"Who cares?" Kevin said. "You were never a boy scout. Anyway it's three fingers. But I *know* you had your fingers crossed with the other hand anyway."

"No I didn't."

"You're lying to me, aren't you?"

Tony laughed. "Boy, you are one paranoid fellow."

He held out his left hand and raised three fingers of his right hand. "I promise not to try to trick Brittany Morgan into going out with me."

"Good enough."

"But if she falls in love with me on her own…"

"I think I might just kill you now and save myself the aggravation."

Chapter 24

Tracey had dance classes Saturday afternoon and evening and Brittany had church on Sunday morning and met with a church group Sunday evening, so the two only exchanged texts over the weekend. It wasn't until Monday on the way to lunch that they were able to talk and discuss Tracey's depressing Friday evening party experience. Brittany was sympathetic, but she had warned Tracey about what those parties were like. It wasn't really a surprise to her that Matt and Emily would have been together.

"I don't care what they tell everybody," she told Tracey. "Those two are an item. They have been for a year now."

Tracey shrugged. "I don't understand how it works between them."

Brittany shook her head. "Me neither, but since neither one seems to care about anything but sex, I guess it works for them."

Tracey shook her head. "It can't be all about sex. Matt's really not like that."

Brittany smirked. "Trust me. Ask anyone. Matt Kildare is *all* about sex. He goes after anyone that looks good to him, but he never has a girlfriend. Emily is the closest thing. Maybe she's so pretty he wants her around all the time. Maybe she's just really good at it. Or maybe it's because she's willing to be there when he can't find anyone else. Maybe it's the same for her."

Tracey didn't respond. She just walked in silence as they entered the cafeteria. Brittany could see that she had struck a nerve with her friend. She stopped, grabbing Tracey's arm.

"Wait a minute. I know that you are still getting over all this and your feelings are still a little raw, but you don't still have a thing for him do you?"

"What?" Tracey said, a little too quickly. "Of course not. Matt and I are done. We never even began. But either way, I'm not going there. I just think I know a different side of him than you. He was really sweet, and not pushy with me. You make him seem like a sex-crazed stalker. He's not like that."

As they ate their lunch, Tracey kept feeling like Matt was glancing over at her. She was too afraid to look herself, but also too afraid to get Brittany to check for her because she would think that Tracey was hoping for something to happen between her and Matt. The truth was that Tracey didn't know what she was hoping for. The one thing she was finding out was precisely how quickly life moved in Kendall High School. Her entire life had changed in a matter of weeks and the past ten days had seen the most drastic of all.

She finally took a breath and shot a quick glance over at where Matt was sitting, among a loudly bantering group of guys and girls. He didn't seem to be looking at her. She focused on her food. She and Brittany continued their conversation and Tracey began to feel a little better as she always did after talking to Brittany. She appreciated that Brittany didn't spend all their time preaching to her about God and what the Bible said about everything. Brittany's comments and advice always made sense, even if Tracey didn't always agree. And Brittany never seemed to go through the roller coaster ride of emotions that Tracey somehow found herself on. She wondered why that was. Brittany would point to God if Tracey ever asked, but could it all be that simple?

As they parted ways after lunch, Tracey walked toward her next class, lost in thought. She absently stopped at her locker and exchanged her morning books for some afternoon ones and made sure her homework was in her backpack before she closed her locker. She almost jumped out of her skin when Matt Kildare was standing there behind her locker door. She quickly regained her composure.

"Very cliché, Matt," she said, turning and walking away, trying to conceal the fact that her heart was pounding in her chest. She actually slightly adjusted her shirt just in case he could see the *thump thump* through the material.

This is where you need to play it very cool.

He walked with her. She couldn't breathe.

My God, he smells good!...That's probably not helping is it? Sorry.

"I wasn't trying to scare you," he said. "I saw you looking at me in the cafeteria and figured you wanted to talk to me about something."

"You saw me looking at you?"

"Yeah."

What, the one time? Don't think so.

She shook her head. "No, you didn't."

"Why? Cause you weren't looking?" He was smiling at her.

Don't even think of telling him you looked. Wipe that smug grin off his stupid face.

"What can I do for you, Matt?"

I love it! Don't even acknowledge it. You are on today!

"What can I do for you, Matt?" he imitated, his voice ultra-serious. "Come on. You're not mad at me still, are you?"

Oooh! He thinks you're mad at him. How to handle...?

"I was never mad at you, Matt." She kept walking.

"Well then why won't you slow down and talk to me?" He gently held her arm to slow her down. "You know, like a couple of grown-ups?"

Really? This coming from the guy who is such a jerk that even though he knows he's a jerk, won't stop being a jerk long enough to have a real relationship?

"I have to get to class." She turned away again.

He stayed with her. "Fine, but can we at least walk slow so I can talk to you?"

She slowed down a little.

"Guess what," he said.

"I'm not guessing." Lindsey played this game all the time and instead of getting to the story, spent the whole time ridiculing her guesses and then demanding that Tracey guess again.

"I know where you live," he said ominously.

Tracey stopped and looked at him strangely.

"Hey! Relax!" he laughed. "I'm not stalking you." Tracey nodded slightly. "For real. I gave your sister a ride home the other night."

Tracey nodded. Lindsey didn't mention that one, though Lindsey seldom talked to her at all. They had not talked much since their little "breakthrough" the week before. They both had been lost in their own little worlds. Matt though, had somehow entered both.

Yippee!

"Soooo," he continued. Tracey rolled her eyes.

Oh, here we go? Hey, what if I came over late at night? Do you think we could have sex in your room? Or why not sneak out? I'll pull up with my lights off and we can go back to my house and have sex?

"…I was thinking…"

"I bet you were."

He laughed. "What I was *thinking* was that since I already know where you live, and that piece of information shouldn't go to waste…maybe I could pick you up later and we could go for ice cream or something."

Yeah, it's the "or something" that I'm mostly concerned with.

"Or something?" she asked.

"No "or something". Just ice cream," he said, grinning. "I promise I won't work any Kildare magic on you tonight."

Gimme a break.

"Well in that case…" she said sarcastically.

He jumped on it. "Great. I'll see you at eight. Gotta get to class," he said as the one minute warning bell sounded. He turned and hustled off down the hall, leaving her standing there wondering what had just happened.

"Wait," she called helplessly after him, as he disappeared around the corner. "I was being sarcastic," she said to herself, rolling her eyes and wondering what she had just gotten herself into. Sure, it was only ice cream, but what then? Matt was up to something. He and Emily had sure looked like they were together on Friday night.

There, there. And you were handling him so well. Let's leave the sarcastic irony to Lindsey from now on. She's better at it than you. Next thing you know…awww, never mind.

"Lindsey! Wait up!" Tracey hurried to catch up to her sister, who was waiting with a puzzled look on her face. It was between

periods.
"What's wrong?" she asked as Tracey came up.
"Nothing exactly," Tracey replied. "But I need to ask you a quick question and I need a straightforward answer."
"I have no idea where your pink and green skirt is."
"No, it's not about...wait, did you take my pink and green skirt? I was looking for it this morning."
"I just said..."
"Nevermind. That's not the question anyway."
"Okay." Lindsey waited. "Are you going to ask me something, or not?"
"I need a straightforward answer. No fooling around, okay?"
Lindsey frowned. "Uhhh. Okay?"
"Are Matt and Emily still together?"
"Why? Are you still hung up on him?"
"No, I just..."
"Because you told Emily..."
"Shhhh!" Tracey put a finger to Lindsey's lips.
Lindsey's eyes widened. "Okay. What?"
"Are Matt and Emily...still...to...ge...ther?" Tracey asked slowly and pointedly.
Lindsey nodded. "As far as I know. Why? What's going on?"
Tracey let out a sigh. "Nothing yet. I'll talk to you later on. Will you be home tonight?"
"Late. I'm eating dinner at Kevin's. Mom'll probably pick me up at eight-thirty or nine."
"Okay. I'll talk to you then."
"Tracey," Lindsey said seriously. "Don't mess with Matt, okay? It won't go well, and Emily's my friend. There's a code about that or something."
"There's a code about your sister's friend's boyfriend?"
"There *should* be."
"Don't worry. I'll see you later."

*****

He picked her up at eight o'clock. She had just enough time after drill practice to shower, eat a quick piece of chicken and some rice, and get ready. She spent several minutes deciding what to wear. Not wanting to let him think she was trying to look particularly good, she decided on a simple ensemble of jeans and a black Kendall Cobras T-shirt. She did spend several moments on her hair. Pony tail or just leave it down? She pulled it back and put a black hair band in. Wouldn't want the hair to get into the ice cream.

Thankfully, when Matt pulled in, her mother was gone, so no need to worry about introductions or any awkward explanations. She also didn't want him coming to her door and inviting himself in. She doubted she could resist if he did, so she quickly grabbed her phone and went out to meet him. He was getting out of his car as she came out and he quickly moved to her side to open the door for her. He had done the same thing the night they met.

Oh, good Lord, he smells so good!

Matt had obviously gone home and gotten ready himself, putting on just a little bit of that cologne that Tracey couldn't get enough of. It was very subtle and fresh smelling. It wasn't really perfumy. She could imagine cuddling on a couch with him watching an old movie and her just basking in that scent.

You are in trouuuubllllllle!

At the ice cream parlor, they sat across from one another in an outdoor table. He ordered his usual vanilla and chocolate swirl with chocolate jimmies. She got a sundae with vanilla ice cream and strawberry topping. For several moments they just sat there, eating their desserts. Tracey couldn't help but notice that his eyes rarely left her. Rather than make her feel uncomfortable, she felt strangely good about it. She had given him no reason to pursue her. In fact, you could argue, since they'd already been together, there was little reason for him to pay such attention to her. Historically, after Matt Kildare had been with a girl, he found others to occupy his time.

"So," he said, a more serious look on his face.

"So," Tracey replied, meeting his eyes.

Geez, he's gorgeous! Let's try not to stare.

"So," he repeated. "I didn't like the way we left things between us. That's why I wanted to see you."

She nodded. "I didn't like that either, though I don't know what we could have done differently."

"We could have *not* had sex." He said it, then sat there and waited.

Whoa! Hello! No warning?

Tracey caught herself before choking on her ice cream.

"Wow!" she said. "I wasn't ready for that. Matt Kildare regrets having sex?"

He shook his head. "I don't *regret* it at all, except that now everything is weird between us."

"And you don't think that has anything to do with the fact that all this happened between us while you were still with your girlfriend?"

"She's not my girlfriend, Tracey. It's not like that between us."

"Are you sure? Because she hates me right now. And the only reason for her to hate me is because I was with *you*."

He sat back.

"Why do you need things to be okay between us, Matt?"

He looked confused. "What do you mean?"

She looked at him seriously. "Did you use Kildare magic on me last week, Matt?"

He frowned. "What?"

"You said something about "Kildare magic" earlier today."

He laughed. "Ohhh! What? Do you think I put some sort of sex spell on you?"

She shook her head seriously. "No. But this whole time, I've been thinking that everything that happened that night was because I wanted to make it happen. You let me make all the decisions and you were extra careful not to push me in any direction, but I wonder if that was just a technique used by a very experienced guy to get a naïve girl into bed."

His eyebrows raised. He nodded. "Wow. And you think I'm that good?"

"I think you've been with a lot of girls, Matt, yes."

He shook his head. "Tracey, you have the complete wrong impression of me. Have I been with a lot of girls? Yes. Is it always because I have some sort of expertise? Definitely not. I have my game just like everyone else. It might work for me better than most, but I am not that subtle. I don't generally go after all night projects. The girls I hook up with are usually looking to party with me. It's because I am a Kendall High Cobra. They think I look good. Whatever. But I don't put a lot of time in trying to make it happen. If I get shot down, which does happen, I move on to the next one. I never chase a girl. So, this is not normal behavior for me."

She was looking down thoughtfully. "So, what do you want

with me? You *are* still with Emily."

He leaned back in his chair. "I don't know. I really don't. I guess I just want to be friends with you."

"And you don't think Emily would object to that friendship?"

"Why should she?"

"She *hates* me! What more reason does she need? Listen, for me, it doesn't matter what Emily thinks. But she *is* my sister's best friend. That matters to me. The fact that she hates me is hard enough, so I keep my distance and try not to make it worse. But you and I can't be friends because she'll go crazy. And I can't say that I blame her."

"So," he said. "That leaves us as friends who can't really be friends? That sucks."

Tracey nodded. "It does suck. But you slept with me while at the same time sleeping with Emily."

"God, I wish."

She threw her napkin at him. "You're disgusting." She laughed, shaking her head. "That's not funny, Matt. You know what I meant."

He opened the door to his car for her again. Before she could get in, he took her hand. She turned to him. He kissed her softly on the lips. She started to hesitate, but she was through fighting her feelings. She brought her hands up to his neck and pulled him closer. They kissed for several moments right next to his car with the door open.

This has got to be what Heaven feels like.

At first, Tracey's mind wouldn't let it happen, but there was just no denying her feelings for him. Every time she looked at him, her mind went here. She had kissed Matt Kildare a million times in her dreams. She knew she could never kiss him enough to satisfy her. And he kept it right on that level. While she was pulling them close together, Matt had his hands lightly on her waist. They never moved from there. He wasn't trying to go any farther. He was perfect.

As their lips parted, he brought his hands up to hers, pulled them around his waist, and held her tightly. She could remember very little detail about their first night together. She remembered what happened, but very little about how she had felt and what it felt like to hold him. Tonight, she was keenly aware, trying to lock every single memory into her mind; how soft and wonderful the kiss had been; how his strong arms held her, making her fell like nothing could touch her; how gently his hands touched her face.

But she felt guilty. Riding home with him in silence, Tracey knew that this was all a mirage. Tomorrow they would reenter their little Kendall High world and Matt would have Emily Vasquez on his arm, her lithe body wrapped around him between every period, kissing him and God knows what else. Tracey knew that whatever happened tonight, Matt Kildare was not hers. For whatever reason, he belonged to Emily. Tracey was a distraction. She knew that she was a distraction that, at least for the moment, occupied a sizable bit of his mind, but she also knew that she was not Emily. And she had made the decision that she would not have sex with Matt again. At least, not like this.

Not a word was said as they pulled up in front of Tracey's house. Her mom's car was in the driveway, but Tracey knew that she would be in her study, grading papers or reading. Matt shut the car off and turned to her.

"Do we need to talk?" he asked.

She shrugged. "I don't know. What is there to say?"

"I guess not much." He reached across and took her hand. She let him.

"What do you want from me, Matt?"

"I don't know." He studied her hand, running his fingers lightly across her palm. "I wish I could tell you that we could be together."

"Do you even want that? Not just with me, but with any girl?"

He frowned, still lightly touching her hand, still staring at it absently. "I wish I had an answer to that." He straightened up in his seat, still holding her hand, but no longer stroking it. "You want to know something? I don't think I would even know how to be someone's boyfriend."

She looked down at her lap. "What's so hard about it?" she asked softly.

He chuckled. "It seems stupid to you, I can tell."

"It's not stupid." She looked up, and then at him. "Okay, well, maybe it does sound stupid, but so what? My real question is why not change if that's what you want?"

He shrugged. "Do you really think a person can change? I

mean really change, like from one lifestyle to the complete opposite?"

Tracey didn't really know the answer to that. She shrugged. "I guess it doesn't matter if the person is unwilling to change. I believe that change takes determination and effort."

"I don't think I could do it."

"Then there's your answer. But what are you missing out on?"

He looked at her. "I guess I'm missing out on you."

And there you have it. Life totally sucks.

She couldn't help but choke up a little bit. She knew her eyes were getting watery and her face was probably getting flushed. Matt held her hand in both of his.

"Hey, don't cry," he said softly. "We don't have to talk about this right now."

They sat in silence while Tracey composed herself. She took her hand back to wipe her eyes and settle herself. Matt took it back as soon as he could.

"We could kiss," he said. They both giggled at that. It was a tension breaker, releasing the pent-up emotion that had been hanging over them. It brought them both back down to earth. He pulled her closer. She let him, but hesitated just slightly.

"I can't have sex with you," she said.

He smiled. "That's fine."

She looked him in the eyes. "Please don't seduce me, okay? I'm serious. I'm trusting you to stop me because I can't stop myself with you."

She could see the impact that her words had on him. He nodded slowly, his eyes a little glassy. He didn't usually have the trust of a girl. In his world it was everyone for themselves. Tracey was vulnerable around him and she was trusting him not to take things too far. She slid close to him and for the second time that night, completely lost herself in a deep, passionate kiss.

*****

"You promised."

Lindsey was standing in her doorway.

"Wha?" Tracey was half asleep. She had finally made it inside after things had gotten very steamy in Matt's car. Nothing particularly extraordinary had happened, but she had felt like they were bordering on going too far. He had not broken his promise to keep things safe, but she had felt herself losing all control. Matt Kildare just had that effect on her. She managed to end the kiss and get out of his car. He followed, apologizing the entire time, though in his mind, nothing had really happened. He had caught up to her halfway across the lawn, and she had spun around unexpectedly and launched right back into him, kissing him almost uncontrollably, practically dragging him to the ground. He held her up. Then she regained her senses and pulled away.

"I'm sorry," she said. "I can't do this."

"It's okay," Matt was still holding her. "Let me walk you to the door."

When they got to the door, he let her go, but she still was clutching his shirt. She looked up into his eyes.

"I don't want you to leave."

He smiled at her. "We're not having sex tonight, Tracey. I made a promise."

She smiled and nodded. "Yes you did." She put her hands around his waist. "But we can still kiss."

And they did, for a long time.

"You told me you wouldn't mess around with Matt Kildare." Lindsey was not going to let her sleep, so Tracey sat up in bed.

"I don't remember promising you anything."

"Yeah? Well you said that there was nothing going on between you and Matt."

Tracey considered that for a moment. "At the time there wasn't."

"And now?"

Tracey sighed. "And now..." She thought back to the amazing passionate evening she had just experienced. "Now...I really don't know."

"You don't know? Seriously? How do you not *know*? You were kissing him all over the front lawn."

"You saw that?"

"Saw it? It's kind of right outside my window. A little hard to miss."

Tracey smiled. She didn't really care if Lindsey saw it, or anyone else for that matter. She would kiss Matt Kildare in front of the entire school.

"What's so funny?" Lindsey demanded. "Am I supposed to keep this from Emily?"

Tracey shrugged. "I don't really care if you tell Emily or not."

"You don't care? Emily will destroy you. She's only leaving you alone because you're my sister, but if she finds out that you are messing with him, she'll go berserk."

"Whatever," Tracey waved her off. "She either needs to get Matt to commit to her or deal with the fact that he likes other girls...me included."

Chapter 25

"I'm gonna kill him."

Emily's blue eyes were on fire with rage.

"You're saying you had no idea?"

Emily was doing her best to control herself. She shook her head. "I am *literally* going to kill him," she repeated. She turned to Lindsey. "Do you know he's been over my house pretty much every night since those two had their little "talk" in the quad?" She actually made the quote marks in the air with her fingers, which Lindsey hated, but resisted the urge to mention it.

"Not including Monday night though."

"*Yes*! Monday night too! He came over like nothing had just happened! Like he wasn't just playing tonsil hockey with that little…" She looked up at Lindsey. "I'm sorry, but I might just have to kill *her* too."

Lindsey grimaced. Emily had really put her on the spot. She had heard through the Kendall Township grapevine that Matt had been seen at the Ice Cream Place Monday night with a pretty redhead, and not just eating ice cream. She had grabbed Lindsey first thing in the morning as she entered the school and sat her down on a bench in the cafeteria and asked her straight out if she knew anything about it. Lindsey was not about to lie to her and Tracey herself had said that she didn't care if Emily found out, so she admitted that she knew. Fortunately, Emily was way too furious with Matt to notice that her new best friend had failed to mention any of this to her for two days.

"You can't blame Tracey," she said weakly, not wanting to fan the flames of rage, but desiring to keep her sister from humiliation if at all possible.

"Oh, really? Is that how you feel about all those girls after Kevin? Hmm? It's not their fault?"

Lindsey shrugged. "I hate that they do that, but I know I can't stop them. And anyway, aren't you the one always telling me that this is how the game is played?"

"Don't even start with me."

Lindsey smiled, all of a sudden amused by the turn of events. "Wait a minute." She pointed at Emily. "You have all this advice about how to handle the situation with *my* boyfriend and the crowd of girls that want to get with him, but when *your* guy, who you *let* have sex with anyone he wants to…by the way, I never understood the thinking on that one. But when *your* guy takes my sister out for ice cream and then makes out with her or whatever, it's all of a sudden a murder spree? Explain this to me."

Emily sat there, shaking her head. "This isn't a group of sluts chasing him around, looking for a quick good time and a night of partying with a Kendall Cobra. This is one specific girl who probably couldn't care less about all that. That's the type of girl that can get in the way of a relationship like ours."

"But Tracey isn't actively pursuing Matt. I know for a fact that she does her best to stay away from him. But he came to her and somehow got her to let him take her out."

"*Somehow?* See? That's what I'm talking about. What does that mean, *somehow?* He asked. She said okay. That's what happened. He didn't *somehow* get her to go. She *wanted* to go!"

Lindsey shrugged, standing up. "Okay, so she wanted to go. So what? *He* still pursued *her*, not the other way around."

"But *she* said okay! She could have said no."

Lindsey leaned against the wall, looking down at Emily, who was now seated on the bench, seething. "Do you really think Tracey is able to say no to Matt?"

Emily looked up at her in disbelief. "Oh, don't give me that. All that crap about Matt Kildare and the Kildare magic…"

"I'm not talking about that."

"...and how Matt Kildare can get any girl he wants whenever he wants..."

"That's not it."

"...and how girls are powerless when Matt Kildare turns on his famous charm and smiles just right with his bright blue eyes..."

"Emily!" Lindsey almost thought she would have to slap her, just like in the movies.

"What? He's not some kind of god. He's just a guy."

Lindsey nodded. "Yeah, I know. All of that is true. But Tracey is in love with him. She has been for years. So he's not just a guy to her. She is just in love with him."

Emily's face was filled with emotion. "Yeah," she said, her voice cracking as her throat tightened from the cry she was holding back. Her tears were just starting to spill over her cheeks. "Well, so am I."

Tracey had seen Emily take Lindsey aside and watched just long enough to know that something bad was up. Emily must have heard about Matt and her kissing at the Ice Cream Place. Now she was likely dragging it out of Lindsey and describing all the ways she was going to ruin Tracey's life. Hopefully Lindsey would be able to do something to soften that punishment.

This is going to be bad.

The conversation didn't last long, and Lindsey came towards the corner where Tracey was hiding. Emily had gone the other way, presumably to inflict bodily harm on her "boyfriend". Lindsey walked by her and kept walking. Tracey hurried alongside her.

"She knows, doesn't she?"

Lindsey raised her eyebrows. "You could say that."

"Well? What'd she say?"

"Not much. Let me ask you something. Do you want to be cremated or would you prefer a regular burial?"

"Very funny."

Lindsey shook her head. "You think this is fun for me? She wants to set both of you on fire."

"On fire?"

"Yes. She's Columbian, you know. They have very creative ways of killing people in Columbia."

"Like setting them on fire?"

Lindsey nodded. "And they also do this one thing where they tie you up and hang you by your feet…"

"Okay. I think I get the picture. So Emily is going to kill me. What do I do?"

Lindsey shrugged. "I'd stay away from her. Maybe she'll kill Matt first and go to jail and then you won't have to worry about it."

"But then her family would probably hunt me down, right?"

Lindsey turned to her. "You don't get to joke about this, Tracey."

"What do you want me to say, Lindsey? Emily is mad. She'll probably make my life miserable for awhile. I'll deal with it."

"We'll see how you deal with it."

******

She had calmed down somewhat while talking to Lindsey. The initial anger had been dialed back to a simmer, but by the time Emily got to the top of the stairs, it had reignited to raging flames once again, and as she approached Matt from behind, hearing him laugh turned it to white heat. One of the guys saw her coming and his eyes widened when he saw the look on her face. He gestured to Matt, who turned around just in time to take the full force of Emily's shove right in the gut.

"Ooomfff!" The air sucked right out of him as she slammed him backward against the lockers. The crowd around him spread out, giving her plenty of space, but they didn't disperse. They stood there watching as she lit into him like a windmill in a tornado, raining punches and slaps down on him like a maniac, all the while shouting names and insults at him. All he could do was try to cover up and catch his breath. She wasn't hurting him anyway, and eventually she'd get tired. He'd been through it before, only maybe not quite *this* intense, and a touch less public.

Emily finally tired of swinging at him after about thirty seconds of all out war.

"What in the world is your problem?" Matt asked when she backed away a little.

"Shut up!" she said, swinging at him again. This time he easily caught her hands and held them.

"Get off me!" she shouted.

"Calm down."

"Get off me, you scum bag pig!" she wriggled furiously until he lost his grip.

"Do not hit me again, Emily. I'm serious."

"Or what?" she asked. "What are you gonna do? Sleep with Tracey Overton again?"

"What?"

"Don't even act like you don't know what this is about, you jerk."

A teacher finally showed up. He was one of the many on the faculty who were very sympathetic toward the football players. He scribbled a quick pass. "Take it somewhere quiet, please, Mr. Kildare."

Matt and Emily headed down the hall toward a stairwell where they continued their conversation. She was fuming, barely holding it all together.

"You know what I'm talking about, Matt. Don't even make me explain it to you."

He shrugged, his eyes wide, his head shaking. "I have no idea what you could be this mad about."

"No idea? Are you that dense? You really don't know?"

"What are you talking about, Emily?"

"Where were you Monday night, Matt?"

"With you!" he replied, a bewildered look on his face, his arms spread out.

"With me? Really?"

"Yes," he said. "I'm pretty sure I've been with you every night this week."

"Yes," she said. "You have. Where were you before you came over Monday night?"

"What difference does it make?" he shrugged, a cocky grin coming over his face. He realized now what it was all about.

The slap came out of nowhere. Emily hit him so perfectly that the clap echoed throughout the stairwell for what seemed like a full minute. Matt was almost spun around as he recoiled from the blow. Emily didn't even take time to enjoy the results of her surprise attack.

"Ooowww! You friggin psycho!" he shouted. "Whacked out Columbian nut case!"

"You think it's funny that you disrespect me by coming over my house and climbing into my bed after being with another girl, one you know I can't stand?" she demanded.

Matt held his hand to the side of his face. It still stung like crazy and his ear was ringing. He could taste the blood leaking into his mouth from the inside of his cheek. He didn't let her know about that though.

"This is about Tracey again? You don't get to go there. We have a rule about things like that. I don't answer to you, Emily. That's the way you wanted it."

"Yeah," she replied. "Well right now, we're going to make some new rules."

He raised his eyebrows. "New rules? What new rules?"

Emily nodded. "We're going to start over right now, okay?"

"Start over?"

"We are going to sweep this all away right now and forget about everything that has happened and figure out what to do from here."

Matt shook his head. "I don't want to hear about any new rules, Emily. You're a lunatic. It's a lot of fun when you're in a good mood, but right now? Not so much."

"Do you love me?"

"What? Are you joking with me right now?"

She leaned against the railing, looking down at the floor below. "It's a pretty straightforward question, Matt." She turned back to him, smiling, and shrugged slightly. "It's either a yes or a no."

"It's not that simple."

"It sounds pretty simple to me, Matt. You either love me or you don't. It's been about a year. We've been together what? A hundred times? More? How many hundreds of hours have we spent talking about things. Don't pretend you don't have enough information. Yes or no?"

He didn't answer right away, still thinking it was some sort of set-up. His mind was racing. "Are you pregnant?" he asked.

She spun around from the railing. "What? Are you crazy? Why would you ask me that?"

"I don't know!" he replied. "You're acting all loony and now you want to know if I love you and stuff. What is going on?"

"Matt, we've been seeing each other pretty regularly for about a year..."

"We've been having *sex*! We haven't been boyfriend,

girlfriend."

She tilted her head. "I'm the closest thing you've ever had to a real relationship, and you know it. But that doesn't even matter. You should be able to answer the question."

"Why don't *you* answer the question?"

"Me?"

"Yeah," he said. "Do *you* love *me*?"

"You really want to know?" Emily raised her eyebrows, and stepped toward him.

"Sure. Does Emily Vasquez love Matt Kildare?"

She stopped right in front of him and looked him in the eyes. "With all my heart," she said, then softly let out a long slow breath. She couldn't believe she actually said that to him. She had never once given voice to her feelings, but after saying it to Lindsey she all of a sudden wanted to tell Matt himself, almost as much as she wanted to kill him.

Matt just stood there, trying to process something he never expected to have to deal with. Emily Vasquez rarely, if ever mentioned love other than to mock its adherents. She had a scornful disdain for anyone who believed in such a cliché and traditional notion. Having declared her love for Matt represented a one hundred eighty degree shift in her thinking. He didn't get it.

"Are you joking with me?"

She dropped her smile and looked at him with a deadpan gaze. "Seriously? I tell you something pretty earth shattering for me and you think it's a big friggin joke?"

"No," he said quickly. "It's not a joke, but you have to admit, this is pretty out there for you."

"Well, now it's your turn." She leaned back against the railing and waited.

"I don't know what to say to you. I have never thought about this."

"Well, what is your gut telling you?"

"To run."

"Very funny. Look, Matt, if you don't feel the same way about me then fine, but I can't do this anymore." She reached for the door handle.

"Emily, wait." He rolled his eyes and shook his head. "What is it you want?"

"I want to know how you feel about me, Matt."

"And it's either love or nothing?"

"No," she considered. "It doesn't have to be love or *nothing*." She thought for a second. "I think it has to be respect at the very least."

"You don't think I respect you?"

"I *know* you don't respect me, Matt. How else do you explain what you did to me Monday night?"

"What I *did* to you? I didn't *do* anything to you."

She shook her head. "You really think it's okay to go from one girl to the next without so much as a day in between?"

"That's our life, Emily. It's the one you said you wanted."

"Fine," she said. "Well, I don't want that anymore."

"You're going sex-free now?" he said with a doubtful smirk on his face.

She shook her head sadly. "Maybe I just want to have sex with a guy who only wants to have sex with me. Maybe it's better like that."

He shrugged. "I can't decide that right now."

She nodded. "Well…take all the time you need. Only don't come over until you figure it out." She opened the door and headed through, but she stopped, holding it open and turned back to him. "You know something? I never thought I'd ever let a guy hurt me like this. Congratulations, Matt. You managed to surprise me after all this time."

That actually stung. He never wanted to hurt Emily. He looked at the ground for a second.

"Em…" But he was talking to a closing door.

Chapter 26

Lindsey was feeling her sanity slip away. Following a second game where her boyfriend had been magical on the football field, she marveled over how he had once again managed captivate the already explosive Kendall Cobra fan base. The reaction of the student body was even more impressive. They were in awe of the freshman player. If the first game produced a sense of excitement among the Kendall High students, the second one produced awe. There was no other way for Lindsey to describe it. And the effect it was all having on Kevin was beginning to take shape. He was starting to accept the role the students and even the entire Township were thrusting upon him. She could not accuse him of being cocky or arrogant. He really wasn't. They were looking for a leader, someone to take their beloved Cobras to the promised land. Kevin had come along and captured their imaginations.

She needed to talk to him, but they were never alone. At dinner the other night, the night when her sister had decided to go all PDA with Matt Kildare, she had been unable to get Kevin alone for any length of time. Mrs. Timmons kept talking to her. She was a great lady and Lindsey really liked talking to her. She treated Lindsey like her own daughter and Lindsey wasn't used to the attention from an adult but kind of liked the attention from Kevin's mother. She secretly wondered if her approval would help keep

Kevin faithful. It was a desperate wish, but guys were goofy like that. They'd cheat on their girlfriends all day long, but don't let mom find out! Kevin probably wouldn't cheat, but maybe his mom's approval about his girlfriend would make a little bit of difference. Every little bit helped at this point, Lindsey figured.

She had started to talk to him in the morning, but Emily had grabbed her before she could get into it and now she was worried about Tracey and whether or not Emily had satisfied her bloodlust with Matt. The story was all over the school within two periods. Lindsey hadn't seen or heard from Emily since their little pre Matt conversation where Emily had expressed her feelings in a way Lindsey hadn't expected. She needed to talk to Tracey and Kevin both, but even though Tracey was the more pressing issue, Lindsey chose to seek out Kevin before his lunch period. She grabbed him as he approached his locker to deposit his books.

"Hey, you," he said, giving her a kiss on the cheek. "How's your sister? Did Emily get her yet?"

"I don't know. I haven't seen either one of them all morning."

They walked toward the lunch room together. Lindsey finally just asked the question straight out.

"Are things weird between us, Kevin?"

"Are they weird?"

"Yeah," she said. "You know, because of what I said the other night. I feel like we never really talked."

"Well, we didn't. Emily came in and told me to forget what you said and that we'd talk later."

"Oh…so, did you forget?" she asked hopefully.

He grinned. "Until just now, when you reminded me." He put his arm around her shoulders, pulled her close, and spoke into her ear. "Lindsey, you are *my* girl, and I am crazy about you. I don't know if it's love right now. I won't say it until I can be absolutely sure. But I can't imagine being with anyone else."

She nodded, putting her head on his shoulder. She noticed Alli Sylvester looking at them and shot her a quick smile and a wink. Alli turned away. Lindsey wrapped her arms around Kevin and walked with him. She came to a decision right then and there.

"Guess what I think?" she asked.

"What?"

"Hey, Lovebirds," a voice broke in. "Break it up." Emily grabbed Lindsey's arm. "I need you." She practically dragged her away.

"What are you doing?" she protested. "I was walking contentedly with my boyfriend."

Emily made a face. "Did you tell him you love him again?"

"Ha, ha. For your information I was about to tell him I want to have sex when you interrupted."

"WHAT!" Emily shouted. Heads turned toward them. She lowered her voice. "Tell me you didn't say that to him."

"Well, not yet. I was about to."

Emily shook her head. "What is the matter with you?"

"What? I've been thinking about it all this time and now I've made a decision."

"You have?"

"Yes."

"And you have decided you want to have sex."

"Exactly."

Emily shook her head. "No."

"No, what?"

"You're not having sex with him."

"Excuse me?"

"You heard me."

"Well," Lindsey said. "I'm going to have sex with my boyfriend."

"No."

"What do you mean, no?"

"Do I have to shake you?" Emily asked. "Because I'll shake you. You want to ask Matt if it's a good idea to mess with me?"

"This is a good idea," Lindsey said.

"Oh really?" Emily folded her arms in front of her. "Exactly why?"

"Because I'm ready. I've thought about it and this is what I want."

"You do."

"Yes."

"You're saying you want to have sex."

"Yes."

"How do you know you're ready?"

"How do I know?" Lindsey asked, thinking about it for a minute. She smiled. "Because my body is telling me."

Emily raised her eyebrows. "Oh? What's it telling you?"

"It's screaming out for Kevin Sinclaire! It wants to feel the warm embrace of love and passion!"

Emily didn't smile. "How can you say that crap with a straight face?"

Lindsey laughed. "I really can't. It just happened."

"You're in an awfully good mood for someone who's about to make a stupid mistake."

"What is your problem?"

Emily sat down on a bench. "Uggh! You don't want to know."

Lindsey nodded. "But you're going to tell me because you just dragged me away from my boyfriend for the second time today."

"You're lucky I grabbed you this time before you screwed up again."

"Are you going to tell me or should I go tell Kevin what I was going to tell him?"

Emily shook her head. "Matt and I are at a crossroads."

"I'll say," Lindsey laughed. "I heard you knocked the wind out of him and then went all Sean Young on him."

Emily frowned. "Sean Penn?"

"Whoever. By the way, is Tracey still alive?"

Emily raised her eyebrows. "Oh, that's right. I still have to get her. She's fine…for now."

"So what's up with you and Matt?"

"I told him I loved him."

Lindsey shook her head. "I don't have time for this."

"I'm serious."

"No, you're not. You just making fun of me. You went nuts the other night when I…"

Emily shrugged. "Sorry?"

Lindsey looked at her. "You're serious." Emily nodded. "You're *serious*?" Emily nodded. "You're telling me that after all that crap the other night about not playing the game right and all that crap…you went and told Matt Kildare that you are in love with him."

Emily nodded, her head in her hands.

Lindsey shook her head. "I don't even know what to say."

Emily still had her head in her hands. "Well, figure it out, sister. Because I gave him an ultimatum."

"What?"

"I gave him an ultimatum."

"You gave Matt an ultimatum?"

Emily nodded ruefully.

"I'm almost afraid to ask."

"Ask what?"

Lindsey shook her head. "What was the ultimatum?"

"Oh," Emily said. "I told him that we either see each other exclusively or we don't see each other at all."

Lindsey nodded, keeping the grin from forming. "And you think he'll go for that?"

"I don't know. I *did* tell the guy I love him."

"Yeah," Lindsey replied. "That was kind of my argument the other night and you crapped all over it."

"I know."

"Did I sound as stupid then as you do right now?"

"Yes."

*****

The circus surrounding Kevin Sinclaire was gaining momentum. He was not only surrounded all the time in the school corridors, but after the Cobras demolished the Veritas Vikings in the second half of game 2, most of the starters were under siege by the student body, the Kendall fans all throughout the Township, and now the local media, who saw the Kendall Cobras as the team to beat in the region, a far cry from where they had left things the previous season, having finished with three straight losses. This year, the "Freshmen Surge" (that's what the press was calling it) was giving a fresh jolt of Cobra "venom" (that's what they were saying) to the Kendall High team. It was corny and cliché, but at least they were all being interviewed for the evening news telecasts.

They were leery of Kevin after his stunt following the Holy Trinity game, but he was still the big star. He was already setting records for single games both on offense and on defense. He was being hailed as the "best high school freshman to ever put on cleats". His "Mad Dog" image was also gaining steam. He was routinely referred to as crazy or psychotic by "man on the street" interviews, especially by fans of the other teams in the league. The attention had gotten so bad at home that Karen Timmons had shut off the ringer on her home phone and prayed every day that no one would get a hold of her cell phone number.

Lindsey was having trouble getting any time alone with him all week. Between classes there was always something going on, plus there wasn't much time to have a real conversation anyway. After school he had football and then was in his shop until all hours getting his Christmas products ready for sale. She wasn't upset about it. His words had comforted her greatly but she really wanted some time alone to tell him what she had decided. She thought it might take some convincing to get him on board, but in the end, Lindsey was confident that they were heading in the same direction.

Friday, after the final bell sounded, Lindsey headed down to where the players entered the locker room to see if they could talk for a few minutes before the team gathered to board the bus leaving for tonight's game at Seaside. She got there just as Kevin appeared. He was always among the first to get there. On practice days, he and Scott Webber, along with whoever wanted to show up with them, spent the early minutes working on their timing, getting in sync for the upcoming game. Today, he was just early out of pure habit. He smiled as he saw her and came over, hugging and kissing her.

"What a wonderful surprise, my lady," he said in a pretty passable British accent.

"Might I trouble the good mister for a word?" she replied in an even better one.

"Absolument," he switched to French, which he couldn't really do very well.

"Okay, knock it off," she said. "I have something important to talk to you about."

"Now?" he asked. "I have to get to practice pretty soon. Can it wait?"

"I just want to tell you what I'm thinking and then you can get back to me later when you have time to think about it, okay?"

"Okay…shoot."

"Okay," she began. "First, I've been thinking about this a lot and it's not a whim or some crazy notion that just occurred to me, okay?"

"Okay." Kevin frowned, a slight grin on his face. He wasn't used to this kind of preamble with Lindsey.

"So here's what I think…"

"Yeah? What do you think?" Tony came up and bear hugged

Lindsey from behind, lifting her up into the air. She didn't even react.

"Antonin," she said calmly. "Please put me down."

"What's my name, little lady?"

"If I have to ask you again…"

"Okay, okay." He put her down. "What's up, girlfriend of my friend?"

"Huh?" she said, looking at Kevin, who shrugged.

"He's been reading a lot of poetry, trying to come up with something to recite to Brittany Morgan."

Lindsey turned to Tony. "Brittany Morgan? Seriously? What's wrong with you?"

"What?" Tony said, looking from Kevin to Lindsey and then back again, like Kevin was going to offer some support. "Hey, I go to church now too."

Lindsey nodded. "Is that right?"

"Yep. Tell her Kevo."

"Tony goes to church now too," Kevin said absently high fiving Scott Webber, who had just shown up. "Hey, Lindz. Gotta go. Hold that thought. We'll have to talk after the game, kay?" He kissed her on the cheek and headed into the locker room with the guys.

Tony hung back. "Hey, Lindsey. If you have any advice about Brittany, let me know."

He barely got into the locker room before she could kick him in the butt.

Chapter 27

Friday night was like a pressure relief valve in Kendall Township. From Monday morning to Friday afternoon, the build up to game time got increasingly more intense. It had always been like this in Kendall Township. This is big time sports. These teams are playing for the big prize, the state football championship. Sure, there are state championships in the other sports, and Kendall had competed for several in its storied history. They had even won their share. The boys and girls soccer teams had both won state championships twice. In baseball, Kendall had won three state titles in the past ten years. The girls basketball team had been a dynasty in the nineties, having won five in ten years including three in a row from '95 to '97. But their football team has been in a bit of a slump. The closest they had come recently was losing in the semi final round six years ago.

To some extent, the Township's fanatical enthusiasm for the Cobras football team extended to all of the other Kendall sports teams. Show up at any Kendall Township sports event and you'd see it. The fans still all wore black. The "Venom" logo was still prominent throughout the stands where the Kendall fans sat. There was an intensity about the Kendal fans, no matter the sport. They expected to win. They demanded it. And the athletes often responded.

Game 3 was at Seaside High. The Seaside Sharks played on a very well-kept field less than one block from the beach. The Sharks were one of those teams who were always competitive. They were generally among the teams vying for the division and every now and then they would win it. Their luck usually ran out shortly thereafter in the state playoffs, and they never seriously contended for a state title. Their fans were an easygoing bunch. The city of Seaside was an island town, and as anyone on the mainland will tell you, island people are a little bit different. They rarely left the island, except if they were unfortunate enough to have a job that took them over the bridge to the real world. They generally lived their whole life on the island, raised their family on the island, and then as their kids grew up, they would repeat the cycle. They loved their high school sports too and cheered wildly when their teams scored and won. They took losses in a good natured manner, never making their kids feel like they had disappointed the city for losing. In short, they had very little in common with the Kendall fans.

When Kendall High came to town, it was like a blanket of ominous clouds descending on the city. You knew it was coming even before the first fan crossed the bridge. You could feel it. It was eerie how the entire feel of a town could change just by the presence of a single group of people. As the black-clad Kendall supporters gathered several blocks away, it was like a swarm of angry, vengeful, black and silver hornets buzzing around looking for someone to sting. They had gotten their social media up and running and managed to get a huge contingent to come all at the same time so that they could walk in together as one giant group, all dressed in black. Their team was intimidating after their performance in the first two games of the season, but they were nothing compared to the almost sinister presence of their fans. When Kendall High comes to town, there is no such thing as a "home field advantage." The Kendall supporters take care of that.

Lindsey and Emily joined the crowd, walking to the field, both wearing black home jerseys. Despite all of their troubles of late, Emily still wore Matt's jersey, the big eighty-eight barely discernible because of its size which was about ten million sizes too big for her. Lindsey, of course, wore Kevin's number twenty-seven, drawing constant stares from those around her. She wore it well, tucked neatly into her black skirt, which fell to just a couple of inches above her knees. She was constantly asked if she was Kevin Sinclaire's girlfriend and the reaction when she confirmed it was always over the top. They all wanted to know what he was like. Was he really crazy like he was on the field? What was it like to be his girlfriend? Were his eyes really that green, or was he just wearing contacts for effect? She smiled and answered most of the questions as Emily looked on. She had dealt with a similar thing the year before when she had first donned Matt Kildare's number eighty-eight, though Lindsey had it far worse. Matt Kildare was popular, probably the most popular kid in Kendall High. Kevin Sinclaire's star was rapidly approaching supernova status. His public demeanor, not really talking all that much to the press, not really looking for the attention, not dancing or carrying on when he scored or made a play on the field, all served to create this mystique about him. All he had to do now was win a championship and he would be a legend in Kendall Township forever.

As Emily walked beside Lindsey, she couldn't help but feel a little proud. She had coached Lindsey on how to handle herself as the girlfriend of a Kendall Cobra. Lindsey was stunning when she dressed up, but hated all the attention and had lived her life trying to avoid it at all costs. But she was in love with Kevin Sinclaire. She knew she could not have him and maintain the same quiet and peaceful existence. With Emily's help she crafted a public persona. Emily had explained that things would be easier for her if she didn't run from the attention, but rose above it. Play the part they were thrusting on her. The key to it all was *playing* the part. Be an actor. If they want a royal princess, be their royal princess. Lindsey struggled with it at first, but was now coming around to it.

The people wanted to know her because they wanted to know Kevin. They had created this mythical couple in their minds. Lindsey gave them what they wanted. She couldn't act like a stuck up princess, she had told Emily, so she decided to be the "people's princess". Emily had gotten a kick out of that, but Lindsey was getting the idea. You have to go with it. Lindsey couldn't imagine having to do this on a large scale the way celebrities and real royalty had to. Emily told her that the pressure on celebrities was nothing compared to what the Kendall Cobras faced in this Town.

*****

The action on the field almost immediately took a turn for the worse for the Seaside Sharks. Kendall High won the coin toss and deferred, allowing the Sharks to have the ball first. Coach Shultz wanted his defense on the field first to set the tone for the game. Kevin and the defense took the field against a Seaside offense who clearly didn't want to be there. They had spent the week watching film from the Veritas game and knew that they were in trouble. It's hard to coach fear out of a group of young men. Kendall had come into camp with a really good defense. They played hard and competed in every game. What had been injected into them with the insertion of Kevin Sinclair and Tony Yavastrenko into the lineup was something altogether different. This defense was not the same group although the players were mostly the same from last year. This group of players was mean. They were relentless. They were out there to destroy. It's bad enough to have to deal with a true hitter like Kevin Sinclaire, who apparently bordered on the psychotic, but when the entire team took on that persona, it was all about overcoming fear. The Kendall Cobras didn't give them the opportunity to do that.

Kevin and Tony blitzed the quarterback from opposite sides of the line on the first play. The quarterback didn't even try to avoid them. He just dropped to the ground before they could hit him. That was pretty much it for the Seaside offense. They tried to move the ball with their speedy running back, but he was a speed guy, flashy and tricky, not big enough to dish out any punishment to opposing tacklers. The Cobra defense teed off on him on every play. By the end of the first quarter, he had rushed the ball for negative twenty-seven yards.

The Kendall offense was the big question mark coming into the game. Mike Doyer was out for who knew how long? Could a freshman back up come in and succeed? They knew that Scott Webber ran a different offense than Coach Mayfair had in place. But over the previous weekend, with Scott's input, they made some changes that they expected to help the team begin the transition to Scott's spread attack. Having witnessed Scott's abilities under tremendous pressure in the previous week's game, Coaches Mayfair and Shultz struggled with how to have Scott play quarterback in their scheme. He was used to calling his own plays and creating a game tempo that kept the opposing defense off balance. This coaching staff was used to having control over every play. How could they get Scott on the same page with them and not risk losing games? Coach Garrett Somers stepped in when they became exasperated, shaking their heads.

"Guys," he had said. "I have the same issue with Sinclaire on defense. I let him roam and trust his instinct because he's the best football player on the field, bar none. Imagine being Scott Webber, with all those weapons, with a mind that sees and feels the game at lightning speed, with the ability to sense what the defense is going to do, and then being told not to follow your instincts."

And with that comment, the decision was made. Scott Webber would run his offense within the scheme the coaches came up with. They created a plan for plays and tempo and practiced it all week. Kendall High scored touchdowns on all three of their first quarter drives. Scott found Kevin for two early scores, including a 70 yard bomb that Kevin caught in stride in the middle of the field with no one anywhere near him. He coasted to the end zone. Scott Webber, determined to spread the ball around to all of his weapons, tried to get Matt Kildare involved as well. Matt made several catches, and even had a very nice thirty yard run where he dragged half the defense along with him for ten of those yards. He would finish the game with decent numbers, but he had dropped several passes and for some reason was not running great routes. He just was not getting open.

It really didn't matter, because the offense was clicking on every other cylinder. The second half was dominated by Anquan Griffin and the Kendall High running game. Scott only threw six passes in the entire second half. For the Sharks, the only moment of any note at all in the game came at the end of the third quarter, on a spectacular run by Anquan Griffin, who plowed through the middle of the Seaside defense, spun off one tackler, and broke to the outside with two men to beat. Matt Kildare held one off with a running block down the sidelines. The other never saw Kevin coming. He hit the kid at a full sprint, right on his shoulder, and both boys went flying into the Sharks bench. Anquan soared across the goal line as the quarter ended. It was the longest run of his career.

As Kevin picked himself up from the ground, a couple of Seaside Sharks got in his face. He pushed them away. This set off the entire team, which surrounded him and jostled him around. After several seconds of trying to push through the gang of red and white, Kevin had enough. He lit into the kid in front of him, driving a fist into his gut and doubling him over. As the kid bent over, Kevin grabbed his shoulder pads and hurled him to the ground at the feet of his teammates. Several stumbled over their teammate and fell to the ground. Fists were now flying as the Sharks saw what had happened. Kevin was at the center of a mob of angry boys. He kept his cool. With all the padding on, he really was in no danger, but they were pissing him off. He focused on one or two in front of him and started pelting shots on their arms, their guts, and then he used his legs to kick their legs out from under them. Before long, he had thrown eight of them to the ground.

By now, the refs were blowing their whistles and running over to break things up. The Kendall offense, which had rushed to the end zone to celebrate the touchdown now hurried back to defend their teammate. At the same time, the Kendall bench cleared. By now the fight had spilled out onto the field. As the two teams came together, the Kendall crowd was going ballistic. They had seen the cheap actions on the part of the Sharks and were booing them, but they loved Kevin's heart. He was fully into it with three Sharks, who were trying to surround him and get him together. Tony saw it and plowed into one of them, sending him to the ground. When the kid tried to get up, Tony drilled him again. Kevin, who's helmet had been pulled off earlier, took on the other two himself. As the first guy stepped to him, Kevin swept with his right leg, connecting just below the knee of his opponent's left leg, knocking him off balance. At the same time, his fist struck just under the helmet of the kid. It would leave a pretty nasty bruise. The kid went down. The second kid tried another approach. He rushed in with his head down and tried to bull rush Kevin to the ground. It didn't work and Kevin sent him sprawling to the ground as well.

The refs and coaches slowly, but surely got the boys under control. Most of the Sharks were only too happy to have the fight end. The Cobras were itching for more. As the teams split up, Kevin searched around for his helmet. It was over by the Seaside bench. He brazenly walked over to get it. He was confronted by a wise guy Shark, who stepped in front of him. Kevin didn't even hesitate, but launched a series of blows to the kid's midsection. In the space of three or four seconds, Kevin landed more than ten shots, and the kid went down like a rock. Coaches and refs scrambled to get between the kids. Coach Garret Sommers got hold of Kevin.

"Son, you need to calm down out here before you kill one of these kids." He said quietly.

The Seaside Sharks lost the fight, and then they went on to lose the game by a final score of seventy to nothing. Three late touchdowns were completely unnecessary, but the Cobras were so furious on the sidelines about the cheap shots directed at their star, that they stepped on the gas just to make a point and put the rest of the league on notice. Kevin finished the game with four touchdowns and over 250 yards, but the big star of the game was Anquan Griffin and the running attack. He posted nearly three hundred yards rushing and had five touchdowns. It was the most dominant and one-sided football game anyone had ever seen and the Kendall Cobras were 3-0.

Chapter 28

As they walked into Lester Fontaine's living room, Lindsey and Kevin were greeted like never before. The entire team and then some had come out to be a part of the 3-0 celebration. Kevin had cemented his place in Kendall history not only as a great player, but as the guy who took on the entire Seaside Shark bench. It was the kind of reputation building moment that people look back on later in life and say, "that's the moment when it all changed". Kendall Township was alive this night. The cell towers were lit up with texts and conversations going on about how the Sinclaire kid kicked the crap out of the whole Seaside team. They were talking about how crazy he must really be, and how they were so glad that *their* boys didn't have to play against a kid like that.

Kevin walked in to a chorus of cheers, pats on the back, high fives, chest bumps, hugs from the girls, which annoyed Lindsey, but she figured let them have their silly fun. *He's all mine.* She was feeling particularly confident tonight. The entire Township knew who she was now. Sitting in the stands in horrified disbelief as she watched her boyfriend attacked by a mob of Seaside Sharks, Lindsey could do nothing but sit there and hope he made it out okay. As the scene unfolded, she heard the Kendall crowd cheering him on, the ominous "VE-NOM" chant growing ever more intense as the rest of the Cobras waded into the fray. That was when she realized that Kendall Township saw these games not as some simple high school sporting event to go watch on a Friday night. They saw it as war. And now they had a player who apparently saw things the very same way and would not back down no matter what. As he walked back across the field with his teammates slapping him on the back, he let out a blood curdling "VenoooooM! scream to the Kendall fans, spreading his arms wide, holding his black helmet up. It nearly caused a riot. The stands on the Kendall side of the field sounded like a jet engine.

Lindsey could barely think with the noise so loud. She had never seen Kevin in such a state. As the team gathered on their respective sides of the field, Kevin stalked the sideline in a barely controlled rage. No one talked to him, touched him, or even went near him. They left him alone in his own world. When the defense went back out, the Kendall fans were then treated to a demonstration of all out war. Kevin played the entire quarter at full speed, slamming into an opposing player on every single play, inflicting punishment unlike anything the Kendall fans had ever seen. He was completely out of control. The Seaside Sharks had been dominated up to this point anyway, but Kevin took their defeat to another level of humiliation. By the end of the quarter they were barely running plays. The quarterback was laying down to avoid any contact, the receivers were not even trying to catch the ball, even blockers avoided Kevin, giving him free runs at the ball carriers, who also didn't bother to take him on. It wasn't even football in the fourth quarter.

The Kendall fans surrounding Lindsey looked at her then with even more awe than before. It was surreal the way they seemed to project Kevin's performance onto her, like she was somehow able to harness the wild beast on the field. She did her best not to let it embarrass her. Emily even seemed different, though *her* thoughts were likely on Matt and what would happen to their relationship. Emily hadn't said much, so Lindsey gave her some space to think. She would be there if Emily needed to talk.

Kevin had not escaped the earlier fight unscathed. His appearance tonight was a testament to at least two blows he received. He was just a little puffy around the outside of his right eye and there was a small cut as well that had bled throughout the fourth quarter. It had looked far worse than the injury actually was, but the blood running down his cheek had given him an even more fearsome appearance. Now, it was just a little scratch in the middle of a very red and ever darkening puffy area on the side of his head and face. It would probably hurt like crazy in the morning and he would probably have a wicked headache, but for tonight it was a battle wound, to be worn with the honor of a conquering hero.

Lindsey, the girlfriend of the hero was at once dragged away by a crowd of girls, all of them wanting to get to know her. This was a startling change from the past few weeks where they had all but ignored her and even outright disrespected her by trying to get her boyfriend away from her. Emily came over when she saw the helpless looks Lindsey was shooting her way. The grin on Emily's face for some reason settled Lindsey's nerves. Lindsey had no idea what to do and couldn't shake the feeling that these girls had just succeeded in separating her from Kevin. She could see that Emily had read her thoughts and was having a good laugh at her expense. It was comforting because the one thing she had come to believe over the past couple of weeks is that Emily absolutely had her back.

She came and sat with her as the group of girls settled into their conversations, mostly about the guys. Lindsey was asked question after question about everything from her clothes to Kevin. She answered them, all the while rolling her eyes on the inside. This was exactly how she had always imagined popularity would be. She hated that she felt this way about it. She hated the thought of being a little snot. She even felt like a snotty brat just thinking about it. But it was a part, a role that she simply had to play. It was going to be harder playing that role in front of the people she saw every day. Some things you just can't fake. So she would have to find a happy balance between the real Lindsey, who didn't want the attention, and the role she would have to play for everyone else. She was thankful to have Emily around. At least Emily knew the real Lindsey.

At a moment of quiet, she leaned over to Emily. "What is going on right now? I feel like Alice in Wonderland. I'm freaking out. Where's Kevin?"

Emily chuckled. "Don't worry. You're fine. Everything's good. Kevin's with the guys reliving their little brawl. I think they might reenact it later on for us all to relive with them." She laughed, trying to hold it in, but failing miserably.

"Oh God. I can't stand it. Are you serious?"

Emily was near hysterics. "I'm serious. They are a bunch of idiots."

"They better not reenact that, Emily, I'm serious. And stop laughing. It's not funny." Lindsey had a comedian's ability to withhold laughter no matter how funny the joke or situation. Kevin could crack her and sometimes Tony even got to her. But Emily was a lightweight in this area. She had very little practice making people laugh, but her laugh was infectious and Lindsey's stoic façade soon cracked and she smiled.

"Now listen," she said. "Knock it off. Stop laughing. Why are these people being nice to me all of a sudden?"

Emily straightened up and shrugged. "Would you rather they all hate you?"

"It would make it easier to hate *them*, I think."

"True," Emily replied. "But have you ever heard the saying, "Keep your friends close…"?"

"Is that why you're so nice to *me*?"

"Oh, you're funny. How about I slap you around for a while?"

The party was going strong. The "dance room" was packed. Lindsey and Emily had moved from the girls section to the kitchen where Les had gone all out, barbecuing huge amounts of chicken, steak, shrimp, and other assorted goodies. He had gotten all the food prepared quickly so he would be free to talk all night as much as possible. He wanted this year's season to be properly documented. It looked like there was a real story emerging and he wanted to be at the heart of the story, telling it from the inside. That was the sole reason for continuing these parties so long after high school. A guy in a wheelchair had a lot of trouble getting around out in the woods where the typical high school parties were held. In order to get involved with the team outside of school he had begun having parties to get the team to come to him. He was able to use that mechanism to get the inside scoop and he had become known for getting the Kendall Cobra story from season to season.

High School was long since over for Les, but he still wanted the Kendall Cobra story. He was going from player to player, to the cheerleaders, to the Brette Girls, and anyone else he could get to offer their take on the Cobras' 3-0 start. He had already gotten plenty of input from the fans earlier. His story was shaping up to be as explosive as the game. As he wheeled through the house looking for the star of the game, he thought for the thousandth time that night what a brilliant idea these parties were. He had virtually unfettered access to everyone. The local press would kill for this kind of access. He didn't see Kevin straight away, but he hadn't spoken to Matt Kildare yet, and Matt just happened to be sitting alone in a small room off the living room where the girls were hanging out. Les rolled in.

"What's happenin', Matt?" he asked.

Matt shook his head. "Not much," he replied without much enthusiasm.

Les knew that something had been up with Kildare from the very beginning. When he saw the film from game one he realized that this Matt Kildare was different from the previous three seasons when he had been one of the few really consistent bright spots on the Kendall Cobra offense. Usually sure-handed, he was now dropping passes every week. If Scott Webber hadn't been determined to get him the ball, Matt might have had half the production he had achieved in tonight's game. For a guy who studies the players and not just the plays, Les easily knew that Matt Kildare was not right mentally.

"Feel like talking a little?" Les asked.

Matt shook his head. "I can't do an interview right now, man."

Les tossed his recorder and notepad into the carrier on the backpack strung across the back of his wheelchair.

"Forget the interview." He said. "I know you're not right. What's up?"

One thing about Les...he was really easy to talk to. Matt shook his head and began to tell Les the story of the past two months.

*****

Lindsey finally caught up with her boyfriend after two hours of talking and bantering and everything else that came with a high school party in Kendall. He seemed all talked out too, so they went to the dance floor and even though she wasn't really a dancer, she moved around with him to the music, her arms loosely draped around his neck. When a slow song came on, she moved in close to him and put her head on his shoulder and closed her eyes. She really wanted to talk to Kevin, but she was kind of talked out and this was a nice break from the emotional roller coaster of tonight's events.

Her serene moment was broken by Kevin tapping her on the shoulder. She opened her eyes and he gestured toward the kitchen. She turned to see Tracey, suspiciously dressed just a little too nicely. It wasn't a conspicuously nice outfit, but Lindsey was pretty sure that Tracey would have worn something less…*sexy*?…if she was not there specifically to see one particular Kendall Cobra. She stepped away from Kevin.

"Don't go away," she said. He nodded, leaning against the wall.

Lindsey made her way through the crowded room and caught up to Tracey, who now had her back to her.

"What are you doing?" she demanded.

Tracey turned to her and smiled. "Hey. What's up, Lindz? How's Kevin? His face looked pretty bloody. Is he okay?"

"He's fine. What are you up to?"

"Up to?"

"Yeah. Why are you dressed a little too cute?"

"You think this looks cute? Thanks."

"Don't aggravate me, Tracey." Lindsey pointed to the room off to the right. Emily is right in there. Why are you looking for Matt?"

"Who says I'm looking for Matt?"

"Oh, I'm sorry. You must be looking for that *other* guy you were making out with the other night."

Tracey rolled her eyes. "Why do you care so much about me and Matt? I mean I know Emily's your friend and all, but she doesn't own him. He's not her boyfriend. And he came to *me*."

"Yeah, yeah, yeah. Keep telling yourself that when he's mashing your heart into little pieces. You should see what he's done to Emily."

"Whatever Emily's going through is her own fault. She made her own mess."

Lindsey nodded and shrugged. "Right, and so now you want to go ahead and make *your* own mess."

"Look, I just want to see him and talk for a minute, okay?"

"Yeah, sure. Cause that's what you and Matt do is talk," Lindsey's sarcastic grin was humorless. "Listen, Tracey, you're really playing with fire here. Emily is trying to work things out with him. If she finds out that you're going for him, the situation will not be pretty."

Tracey shook her head. "I have to talk to him, Lindz. If there's any chance that he wants me, it's worth the risk to me. If I'm with Matt, I think I can live with Emily's temper tantrums."

Lindsey shrugged and stepped aside to let her pass. Tracey quickly decided to avoid the room where Emily was hanging out.

No sense in drawing attention to yourself at this point...

Les Fontaine leaned back in his wheelchair. "Man, dude. You are one twisted up nightmare, aren't you?"

Matt shrugged, sitting back and taking a sip of his water. Many of the kids at Les's party had come with their own alcohol, which Les ignored. Matt drank every now and then but he really wasn't in a partying mood tonight. He had only come because the guys had insisted, and it was pretty cool that the Cobras had started the season with a three game undefeated streak. There was cause for celebration. But his mood was affected by his girl situation as well as his performance on the field.

"I think it's all related," Les commented.

"What is?"

"Well, this Sinclaire kid comes along and takes the spotlight away. That's gotta hurt some, right?"

Matt shrugged. "I guess."

Les raised his eyebrows. "Come on, dude. He's a freshman. He took your spot."

Matt shrugged again. "He's the real deal though. It is what it is."

Les nodded. "He is that."

"It just sucks that I have to play second fiddle to him in my senior year, that's all."

"I get that. I really don't know what to say about it other than you guys could go all the way to states and it would be pretty cool to get a ring for your swan song."

Matt nodded silently.

"But then," Les continued. "You have these two girls.

Emily Vasquez, who by the way..."

"Is insanely hot," Matt finished. "I know."

Les frowned. "I was going to say she is very cool. I don't comment on how high school chicks look. That's a little creepy. But I have talked to her many times and she is insanely *cool*. That's what I think you risk losing by going after this...Tracey was it?"

"Yeah, but Tracey's pretty cool too," Matt said. "Not in the same way Emily is, though. They are pretty much opposites in every way."

"And I'm guessing that she's not really into the "*arrangement*" you and Emily have?"

Matt grinned finally. "Arrangement? No, Tracey wouldn't be into that at all."

"So, it's Tracey...or it's Emily and whoever else you can hook up with?"

Matt shook his head. "Not anymore. Guess what Emily told me the other day?"

"She's pregnant?"

"Very funny. No, she told me that she's in love with me and wants us to start over as boyfriend and girlfriend."

Les shook his head then shrugged. "Dude, that's insane. So she still loves you even though you hooked up with Tracey and then slept with her right after without telling her about Tracey?"

"Something like that."

"And this Tracey chick is in love with you too?"

"Yeah."

"You're sure about that? I mean she said it?"

"Well, no, she didn't say it. She just..." He shrugged. "It's hard to explain. Listen, assume they both feel the same way about me. What do I do?"

Les shrugged. "Shoot. I don't know. Which one do you like the most?"

Matt shrugged. "That's the problem. I like them both. They're both so different it's hard to compare them."

Les nodded. "Don't tell me you're trying to concoct a way to have them both. That will end in you losing both of them, I promise you that."

Just then Matt caught a flash of red hair passing by the door.

"Tracey!" he yelled, jumping up and opening the door all

the way.

Tracey turned and her face immediately lit up into a bright but nervous smile. "Hey!" she said. "I've been looking all over for you."

"I've been here talking to Les."

Les rolled out the door. "I'll leave you two alone. Nice seeing you, Tracey."

"See you, Les."

Chapter 29

She timidly hugged Matt around his neck. He kissed her and pushed the door closed. They didn't say much as they more or less picked up right where they had left off Monday night. After more than fifteen minutes of kissing the scene began to heat up. Tracey had not intended for the evening to progress much beyond kissing, but as she and Matt moved steadily down the path she found herself less and less willing to resist the tug of passion. It was as though all her wits were dulled and her desires were all that mattered. She wasn't thinking, only reacting to the call of physical pleasure.

Maybe it was something in the way he was acting, all passionate and romantic, that got her attention, or perhaps it was the reality of what was about to happen that snapped her out of her passion hypnosis, but something switched off in Tracey. She pulled away, surprising Matt, but even more so herself. She couldn't explain it, but this all of a sudden felt completely wrong to her. She straightened her blouse and skirt. She hadn't even realized how many buttons had come undone in the heat of the moment.

"Are you okay?" Matt asked, not sure if he had pushed too hard. He didn't think he was pushing, but Tracey was impossible to read. She didn't seem to have middle gears when it came to these kinds of situations. She was either totally shut off, like right now, or she was all out, like ten seconds ago. That she could flip that switch on and off so quickly made it hard for Matt to read her.

She was sitting, shoulders somewhat slumped, feeling quite dejected over this confusion and the fact that it came at such a very inopportune time. Why was this all so hard? Why couldn't she just be like everyone else? These kids did things like this all the time. It was no big deal to them.

They know how to have fun...

She shook her head. "I'm fine...I think...I don't know." She shook her head.

Matt slid closer so he could put his hand on her back. He was so gentle about how he touched her. Tracey closed her eyes, feeling his touch and wanting so desperately to lay back in his arms. Matt must have sensed it because he gently pulled her toward him. She resisted.

"I can't," she said. "If I come to you now, I don't think I could stop myself again."

"Is that a bad thing?" he asked.

Tracey shook her head. "I don't know anymore." She looked him in the eye. "Every time we've been together up til now, it always felt so right, like...I don't know...magical, or something. I've always felt that way about you. But tonight, I don't feel right. I can't do it. I *want* to in the worst way. I wish I could explain it better."

"You don't have to..."

There was a commotion outside the door, and then the door burst open. Emily Vasquez stood in the doorway, her eyes blazing as she glared first at Matt, then at Tracey, and then back to Matt. She entered the room slowly, the barely contained rage literally seeping out of her pores. Tracey could swear that it was visible, like steam. She vaguely wondered how something so beautiful could possibly contain that kind of hatred and wrath that was in Emily's eyes right now. She looked like a girl possessed.

Matt never moved from the couch. "Don't even start, Emily," he said.

Tracey grimaced. Here he was, caught red-handed, not actually in the act, but really, what difference did that make? Considering what had happened the last time he and Tracey had been found out, Tracey thought he might be a bit more apologetic, but he really wasn't. It was almost like he wanted the confrontation.

    Emily came close and pointed her slender finger at Matt's face. "You shut up," she said in a low voice, flicking him across the face with her finger as she said it. It didn't hurt him. She hadn't even thought about it as she did it. It was the reflex of someone on the *verge* of violence but not quite prepared to unleash it. She turned to Tracey, who was frozen in place.

    "You scared, little girl?" she asked. "Well, you should be. You and me are going to settle our little problem *right now*."

    Tracey's eyes widened. She shook her head. "I'm not fighting with you, Emily."

    Emily laughed. "Is that right? Well understand this, *princess*. I don't care if you fight back or not."

    Matt stood up. "Emily, knock it off. Leave her alone. This is between you and me."

    Emily turned from Tracey and shoved him as hard as she could, sending him slamming back down onto the couch.

    "You shut up!" she said, kicking him repeatedly at his legs. "First I'm going to smash your little slut's face in," she said, pointing at Tracey who cowered in fear. "Then I'll come back for you, you dirty little scumbag!"

    Lindsey, seeing and hearing everything that was going on, turned helplessly to Kevin and Tony. "Are you guys going to do something about this? That's my sister. She's scared."

    Kevin and Tony began pushing and pulling their way through the crowd in front of the door. Matt was trying to keep Emily from going after Tracey. He grabbed her wrist as she turned from him. That set her off into a furious rage and she literally jumped on him, clawing at his face, punching, slapping, and kicking. Tracey sat and stared for a brief second and then snapped out of it. She stood up and pulled at Emily's arm to try to get her off Matt. When Emily realized that Tracey had gotten involved, it nearly sent her into orbit. She turned violently away from Matt at the same time Tracey shoved her hard. She slammed into the wall and for what seemed like a full minute, but was actually about a second and a half, everything seemed to freeze in place. Emily's eyes flashed and she launched herself at Tracey just as Tony and Kevin got to the scene. As the girls clashed, the two boys got hold of them, Tony doing his best to get in between them shielding Tracey by wrapping his arms around her, Kevin pretty much catching Emily in mid air as she flew at Tracey. He wrapped her up from behind, locking her arm to her sides and picking her up. He dragged her to the other side of the room and held her tightly because she was struggling furiously and out of control.

He looked at the door and shouted to those standing there. "Everybody, get out and get away from here!"

No one chose to see what would happen if they disobeyed the freshman who was nicknamed Mad Dog and who howled and screamed during games and fought entire teams. They dispersed and soon the room was cleared. Emily was still glaring at Tracey. Kevin felt her tense body ready to lunge as soon as he let her go, so he decided to get her out of the room. He picked her up and carried her to the door. She didn't protest. When they got outside the room, Kevin put her down, but kept his arm tightly around her shoulders in case she decided to pull away. He guided her through the halls and out the front door where they walked together some distance down the driveway.

Emily was no longer resisting. By the time they got down the driveway, she was leaning on his shoulder, crying softly. Kevin stopped and held her. She didn't put her arms around him, though. Rather, she clutched the front of his shirt with both hands as she sobbed away on his shoulder. Kevin closed his eyes. He hated this. He could handle the violence, the yelling and screaming, and the fighting. He could deal with almost anything that came up in his life, but a girl crying always broke his heart. And a girl crying over her lost love was all the more heart wrenching now that he understood the emotions involved. Emily Vasquez was a unique girl. Her stunning beauty was always balanced by a cool confidence, and an all too often ignored intelligence. What very few individuals had ever seen from her was the sensitivity that was being revealed to Kevin in this moment.

He didn't know Emily. He knew *of* her. They had gone to school together when he was in seventh grade and she was in eighth, but they had rarely crossed paths. Rumors had always floated around about her and older guys. Kevin had never bothered to get to know her. He seldom searched out new friends, preferring to let them happen if and when they happened. That was how he and Tony had met. They went to school together and played football one year and they just became friends.

"I'm sorry for soaking your shirt," Emily said, looking up

at him. She was a mess. Her makeup was smeared all over her face, the tears had made little paths through the smears. "And wrinkling it." She smoothed it with her hand.

"No problem," he replied. "Are you going to be okay?"

She nodded. "I'm always okay. I'm Emily Vasquez, remember?"

Kevin nodded, a slight smile on his face. "You're my girlfriend's *best* friend. That girl loves you like a sister. You're family, so I'm asking you if you are okay."

Emily looked him in the eye. She quickly looked away.

"What's wrong?" Kevin asked.

Emily chuckled. "It's really stupid." She bit her lip. "I just…I can't look at you right now."

"Okaaay. Any particular reason?"

"I'm just really emotional right now," she smiled and managed to bring her eyes to meet his. "I'm really emotional and you are…just…so completely hot. I don't think I can handle being around you right now. I really need Lindsey."

Kevin laughed. "Well, Emily Vasquez is back, at least. You really have no problem talking to guys, do you?"

"Please don't think…I wasn't coming on to you. I was just trying to explain."

"It's totally okay," Kevin said. "You should hear some of the things these girls have been saying to me lately."

"I can imagine." Emily nodded knowingly. "But what you said about Lindsey? I feel that way about her too. She means the world to me. I would never try to come after you. Please believe that."

Kevin nodded. "I appreciate that. I know she trusts you. And I'm glad that she has a real friend. You're the only one she has."

"I wish she would come out here."

"Well, she in a tough spot. Tracey is her sister."

"I know," Emily said. "But I need to know if she's still my friend." She looked pleadingly at Kevin. "Could you…?"

"Sure. Wait here." He headed back into the house.

After the room had cleared, Tony released Tracey and she collapsed onto the couch, shaking from head to toe. She had never been in a fight before. Even though very little fighting had happened on her end, she felt completely spent, physically and emotionally. Lindsey came over to her and held her hand. She looked up at Tony.

"Can you find us a ride home? I don't want to call my mom with her looking like she was just in a fight."

"No problem." He went and found a teammate who volunteered to give them a ride.

Matt was sitting on the floor in the corner of the room, his head in his hands. He was more or less unhurt by the whole event. Emily had beaten him up pretty good, but he really only had a throbbing headache. She had scratched him nicely on his left cheek and his shins were bruised all over from her kicks. He looked up at Tracey, no clue what to say to her about it all.

"Hey," he said. "Look, I'm really sorry you're caught in the middle of me and Emily. I didn't mean for that to happen."

Lindsey immediately responded. "Yeah, well maybe you need to pick a girl and stick with her. That would solve some of these *unintended* consequences."

Tracey put her hand up. "Lay off him, Lindsey. It's not his fault."

"I didn't say it was just his fault. You're *all* idiots. *He's* an idiot for trying to have relationships with two girls at once, *Emily's* an idiot for having this "open" relationship thing with him where he doesn't have any responsibility to her at all, and *you're* an idiot for thinking it would be different with *you*. It's a love triangle of stupidity."

"You're a big help, you know that?" Tracey replied.

"You don't want help. You want approval for being an idiot. I guarantee you Brittany would have a cow over this. I don't really like that girl, but I bet we would agree on this. Tonight was totally self-inflicted."

Matt shook his head and sat there in silence. Tony had no idea what to do. Mercifully, Kevin appeared in the doorway.

"How's our girl?" he asked Tony.

"Not sure. From the way this conversation is going I think Emily was good cop and Lindsey is bad cop."

Kevin looked at Lindsey. "You're being the bad cop?"

"I'm not the bad cop. I'm the reality cop."

Tracey shook her head. "No, you're the jerk cop."

"And *you're* the stupid cop."

Tony was looking at Kevin. "See what I'm dealing with?"

"...and you're the holier-than-thou, self-righteous, I'm-better-than-you cop."

"Yeah? Well you're..."

Kevin held both hands up. "Shut up. You're both annoying cops." He pointed to the door. "Go talk to Emily," he said to Lindsey. "She's out in the driveway."

"I don't want to talk to her," Lindsey said. "I'm pissed at her right now."

Kevin looked her in the eye. "Get out there and talk to your *best friend*. We don't abandon our friends, Lindsey, ever; no matter what they do."

She saw it in his eyes. Kevin wasn't one to give orders. In fact, she had never heard him order anyone to do anything. Not like this. But something in his eyes told her that this was a non negotiable character moment for him. He was not simply telling her to do something. He was telling her something about himself, something deeply important to him, so much so that it was a part of his core. As she turned to leave the room it occurred to her that this might be a defining moment. He was revealing something to her about the depth of his relationships. His words rang in her ears.

"We don't abandon our friends, Lindsey, ever; no matter what they do."

It was such an absolute statement that it was almost ridiculous. But the look in his eyes made her think that he was not exaggerating. Tony had once told her that Kevin's friendship was so unconditional that he believed there was no way to lose him once he decided you were your friend. She remembered thinking that it was a nice sentiment, but didn't really think about it much after that. Now, she realized how seriously Kevin took friendship. He didn't just live his own life that way. He demanded it from *his* friends.

As she approached Emily, she wondered how she could face her. It was one thing to talk about hating Tracey, about how she was going to get her and all that, but it was another thing to act on those feelings with such hatred. Lindsey didn't know how to react to it. She didn't want to betray her sister. Kevin had to understand that, but he didn't seem to differentiate between blood relatives and friends. Maybe that was the point.

Beginnings

"Do you hate me?" Emily said when Lindsey got to her.

"Yes."

Emily slumped her shoulders. "Really? Please don't. I really need you right now."

"You tried to hurt my *sister*, Emily. What am I supposed to do?"

"I know. I'm so sorry."

"You're sorry?"

"What can I say?" Emily shrugged. "Tracey put herself in the middle of Matt and me. She's as much to blame as I am."

"I know," Lindsey said. "But Tracey would never try to hurt you, not on purpose."

Emily shook her head. "You don't move in on someone's guy and then pretend you care about hurting the other girl."

"So, what would you do if you were me?"

Emily shook her head and shrugged helplessly. "I'd take care of my sister," she admitted. She nodded her head toward the house. "Go ahead. Go get her out of here. I'll disappear so you guys can get her home without any more drama."

Lindsey nodded, tears unexpectedly starting to well up in her eyes. She blinked to try to stop them. Emily came over and hugged her tightly.

"Just know," she whispered in Lindsey's ear. "When I imagined taking care of my sister, it was *you* I was taking care of. You *are* my sister. I love you so much. Please call me."

Chapter 30

Anquan Griffin got behind the wheel of his car with Kevin up front with him. Lindsey and Tracey got in the back. As he pulled away, Tracey asked him if he would mind picking up someone else on the way home. It was no problem. She called Brittany.

"Who are you calling?" Lindsey asked. "Like I need to ask. Brittany?"

Tracey ignored her. "Brit? Hey, listen. I need you. Can you sleep over?....Just ask. I need you face to face…..It's serious…" After a short pause. "Awesome. You're the best. We're on our way to get you."

Lindsey was shaking her head. "You know what's funny?"

Tracey was looking out the window. "The way you can't mind your own business?"

"No, the way you run from the church girl to the bad boy like a yo-yo. She makes you feel good about yourself and then he makes you feel dirty and slutty…"

"Matt doesn't make me feel dirty *or* slutty."

"He makes you feel *something*. Why else were you crying even before Emily got to you? I saw the look on your face when the door opened. What happened?"

Tracey was glad the guys were up there talking, listening to music and discussing the game. They weren't paying the girls any attention at all.

"What happened," she said softly. "Was that I started to hook up with him and then I couldn't do it."

"Why?"

"I don't know. I felt so stupid."

"You *are* so stupid, you know that? You're a nincompoop."

"A what?"

"Nincompoop. That's your new name, Tracey the nincompoop."

"Nincompoop?"

"Yeah. That's you, a nincompoop."

"You know what? You're a lousy person to have around when a person needs some encouragement."

"Oh yeah? Well, you're a nincompoop."

"Are you going to keep saying that word until I throw up?"

"That's my current plan, yes."

*****

The buzzing of the phone mercifully broke through Matt's sleepless depression. He was sitting in the Kildare living room, watching whatever late-night sports show he could have on and ignore as he wallowed in self pity. What an embarrassing nightmare he was living! He couldn't get his mind to work on the problems though. All his mind would do was relive all of his depressing scenes from the past few weeks.

Glancing at his phone, he could see that it was from Mike Doyer. This late at night? The message was quite simple. "*Outside. 3 mins.*" Mike was coming over? Normally, Matt would never think twice about his best friend showing up unannounced. In fact, he and Mike had been best friends so long that Mike could come and go as he pleased. He even called Matt's parents "mom and dad." They had been texting back and forth since Mike's injury, but Mike hadn't been in school, trying to stay off his foot as much as possible. Matt hadn't mentioned the craziness of the past week. Mike must have gotten word about Emily and the party.

Matt pulled himself up and headed for the door. He waited for a minute or two on the front porch until he saw the headlights of Mike's car coming up the driveway. He went down the steps to meet him. Mike slowly and gingerly got himself out of his car. Matt grabbed his arm and helped steady him until he could get his crutches under his arms.

"Are you dumb or something?" Matt demanded. "What are you doing driving around with a busted up foot?"

Mike didn't look happy. "Do you think I wanted to drive over here? My best friend has been leaving me in the dark for weeks while he falls apart, and now he wants me to explain my actions?."

Matt shook his head. "You couldn't call?"

"We've been texting for a week and you're not telling me what's going on with you. I have to hear it from Viv. That sucks. I hear all this stuff from her or Quan, and then we text or talk and you don't even mention it."

Matt looked away. "Look, I know you're dealing with a lot. I didn't want to put all this on you."

"I'm your best friend, Matt. And this isn't just about right now. You've been spiraling for a while now. I didn't really see it before, probably because we all had so much going on, but now, since I'm pretty much on the outside right now, it's so obvious."

"What are you talking about?"

"I was at the game tonight, Matt. You look like crap. Are you hurt?"

"Hurt?" Matt responded. "No, why?"

"Dropping passes? Really weak route running? Your head's not in it."

"I'm doing okay."

"You look like crap out there, Matt." Mike was through beating around the bush. He wasn't on the team right now, but he was a leader. He was still the captain. "You've been in a funk since camp. Back then I got it. I let it go mostly, but now you're ruining your chances for the future."

Matt sighed. "There's really not much I can do about it. Sinclaire…"

"Sinclaire's a great player," Mike said. "He really is, Matt. Everything about him. He's fast. He's quick. He can catch anything that gets near him. He hits. He…"

"THANKS, Mike. Like I didn't know how much better he is than me."

Doyer grinned. "What I'm saying is, as great a player as he is, this is still our team. That offense is *our* offense."

"Not anymore," Matt said, picking up a few rocks and tossing them across the lawn. "Sinclaire and Webber. It's theirs now. You know what that makes us?"

"I'm afraid to ask."

"That makes us senior citizens." He tossed another rock.

Mike shook his head. "Okay, so what else is up? Viv said that you and Em are at each other's throats."

"Like that's so unusual?"

"Viv thinks so. What happened tonight?"

Matt took a deep breath and let it out slowly. "It's not even worth it, dude. I don't want to talk about it."

"Well start talking anyway. Emily caught you with some other chick…"

"It's not "some other chick", okay? Her name is Tracey."

Mike nodded slowly. "And you two have been…?"

Matt nodded. "Not really. Once, a couple weeks ago. We've only really talked since, kissed a little. Nothing much, really."

"But you like her."

"Yeah, sure. She's different."

"Oh," Mike looked out over the large field.

"What does that mean…"oh"?"

"Nothing," Mike said.

"It meant something, all right. What are you thinking?"

Mike shrugged. "Tell me everything."

Matt knew he was trapped. Mike was not going to let him off the hook tonight so he just let it all go. He told Mike all about how Emily had been on him to get more serious while at the same time he was getting more and more interested in Tracey. Throughout the whole story, Mike could see the anguish in his friend's eyes. He really was struggling with all of this. It was a little shocking for Mike to see. Matt Kildare never struggled with girls.

"Are you in love with this girl?"

"Who, Tracey?"

"Yes, are you in love with her?"

"No."

"Are you sure about that?"

"Yes."

"And Emily?" Mike asked. "Are you in love with her?"

"No."

"You're full of crap, you know that?"

"Why?" Matt replied. "Because I'm not in love?"

"No, because you won't admit it."
"I like them both. Why does it have to be love?"
"It doesn't...but it is."
"Whatever."
Mike started laughing.
"What's so funny?" Matt asked. It only made Mike laugh harder. It irritated Matt even more. "It's not funny, Mike." Doyer was laughing so hard he began to cough. "Yeah, go ahead and choke."
"This is awesome!" Mike said between bouts of laughter.
"Shut up, Mike," Matt warned.
"Matt Kildare is in love! Ha ha ha!"
"Don't piss me off, Mike."
"And the best part," continued Mike. "Is that he's in love with two different girls...at the same time! Ha ha ha!"
"I swear I will break your other leg for you."
"You can't make this stuff up, Matt!"
Matt rolled his eyes as Mike stood there chuckling and looking at him.
"Fine," Matt finally conceded. "I'm really into both of them. That's the best you're gonna get."
Mike waved a hand and nodded.
"So, what do I do?"
Mike shrugged. "That's simple enough. You have to choose."

Chapter 31

Tracey and Brittany were lounging in Tracey's room. Tracey was laying on her back on the bed, staring at the ceiling. Brittany was sitting at Tracey's desk, the chair turned to face the bed. Fortunately for Tracey, Lindsey had no interest in being around for the "sermon", though she *was* interested in seeing Brittany get mad and yell at Tracey. Since Tracey had pretty much ignored every piece of advice Brittany had given her, and now her life was crumbling, Lindsey figured there might be fireworks from the loveable Brittany Morgan. But in the end, she really wanted to go and think about Emily and decide whether or not to call her.

Tracey was relating the story of the week's events to Brittany, who, by the look on her face, was clearly frustrated at what she was hearing. Tracey tried to make her understand just how strong her feelings toward Matt had become, how he made her feel, and how she had so desperately wanted to be with him tonight. But in the end she couldn't go through with it, and now can't figure out exactly why.

"You know that little angel girl that sits on your shoulder and tells you what to do in every situation?" she asked Brittany.

Brittany frowned, then smiled uncertainly. She didn't know whether Tracey was being serious or not, but the look on her face told Brittany not to make too much of a joke out of it. She shrugged, wrinkling her forehead. "Yeah, I guess."

"Well, I didn't hear a peep out of *her*! She must have wanted him just as badly as I did."

Brittany nodded, still uncertain what to make of it all. "Okay…"

"What I mean is that every fiber of my body and mind and whatever else wanted him right then and there. I wanted him I pursued him. I had him right there in my arms. It was going to happen. Then I couldn't do it."

Brittany's eyes widened. "Well, that's a good thing, Tracey. You say it like something bad happened."

Tracey looked at her. "Are you trying to be funny? You sound like Lindsey."

Brittany shook her head. "I don't think this is funny at all. I think it's tragic. Did you call me up to console you because your plan to have sex fell through?"

"Of course not. I called you because you're my best friend. You usually have good advice for me."

"Yeah!" Brittany exclaimed. "Which you never ever take!"

"Why are you so mad at me?"

Brittany shook her head and chuckled humorlessly. "You know what? I'm not even mad at you. I'm mad at *me*!"

"You're mad at yourself? Why?"

"Because all the advice I've been giving you is bogus!"

"What?" Tracey frowned. "Your advice made all the sense in the world. I'm an idiot for ignoring it. That's why I feel so crappy. But it wasn't bogus."

"I don't mean it was bad advice. I think it was all great advice, but coming from a Christian, it was bogus."

Tracey shook her head. "I don't get that."

Brittany leaned forward. "I've been giving you sound, logical advice, right? It was advice designed to help you see the potential damage that you risk in pursuing certain paths. It made sense and might even have persuaded some people."

Tracey nodded and shrugged. "So, what's wrong with that?"

"What's wrong with it is that you could have gotten that advice from anyone."

"So? I got it from you. Isn't the point that I got the advice more important than where it came from?"

"Not to me. As a Christian, my advice shouldn't be the same as a non Christian. Sometimes the advice might be similar, but God is never going to be at the center of secular advice."

Tracey shook her head. "If it makes any difference, I don't think I would have followed any advice, with or without God in it."

Brittany was nodding her head up and down. "Exactly. That does make a difference. See, this whole time, I could have been giving you godly advice instead of trying to find a logical secular reason to do what's right. At least you would have been hearing the gospel all this time. That's actually how a Christian ought to advise their friends. I've been leaving out the most important information you could hear. I'm not going to do that anymore, Tracey. If you want to talk, I'd love to listen and be there for you, but I can't keep God out of the conversation. I am going to do my best from now on to give you scriptural advice from here on out. You're going to have to take that or leave it."

Tracey sat up and laid back down on her stomach, facing Brittany. "I never asked you to stop being you, Brit. I'm sorry I ignore your advice all the time."

Brittany smiled. "Are you ready to listen to some *real* advice right now?"

Tracey smiled back. "Please. Whatever you got."

Brittany nodded, opening up her Bible.

"You're going to read the Bible to me?" Tracey asked. "I thought you were going to give me Christian advice."

"Are you listening?" Brittany responded. "This is serious. I'm not going to tell you anything. From now on, we're going to go directly to the source."

"The source?"

"God," Brittany said. "God's Word. No more listening to my opinion about your problems. Let's see what the Creator of the Universe says about life and how it ought to be lived. Then if you want to ignore it, at least I've done everything I can do for you."

For the next hour and a half, Brittany took Tracey through the gospel message from start to finish. She pointed out how the world was created and what God's original design was for His creation.

"People were created to know God and depend on Him for everything in their lives. God wanted, and even still wants His people to be totally dependent on Him. And it doesn't mean that we sit around and wait for Him to do everything for us. It means that we rely on His interpretation of life, the world, and right and wrong."

Tracey had some questions, which Brittany did her best to answer. If she didn't know the answer, she didn't try to make it up or fake it. She just promised to take the question to people she relied on for advice. She wasn't trying to convince Tracey of anything. She had given up that pursuit. Instead she spent the entire time silently pleading with God to help her keep her own opinions out of it and let God's Word speak to Tracey's heart.

She showed Tracey in scripture that God's perfect Creation was corrupted when sin entered the hearts of His people. She explained that this caused an unbridgeable gap between God and humankind forever. Man had sinned and that sin spread like a cancer to every corner, nook, and crevice of creation, changing everything, especially the relationship between man and God. She showed Tracey how man was powerless to repair the broken relationship; how man, because his heart was so corrupted by sin, would never turn to God on his own; how left to our own devices, we would reject God outright. She showed her the results of such a world as written in chapter one of the book of Romans.

Tracey sat through most of this with her hand over her mouth, trying not to cry. The shame of it all was really weighing on her, pulling at her somewhere deep inside. The fact that Brittany was reading the words and really letting Tracey think about them, coming to her own conclusions, was a powerful thing. Tracey desperately wanted Brittany to offer her opinion on certain things. How could Brittany have such joy with such a bleak outlook? The Bible was depressing so far. But Brittany kept telling her to wait, that there was hope, but we have to first understand our reality..

Brittany did her best to stay on track. She intended for this night to be a full gospel presentation. She intended to lay it out all at once for Tracey to ponder. As she moved from the problem of man's sin and God's holiness to the salvation plan that God had ordained, she saw the light begin to flicker in Tracey's eyes. Now they were getting to something she had heard before. It was beginning to sound vaguely familiar and Tracey was now connecting some dots.

"And really," Brittany said. "What it comes down to at this point is whether or not you believe that what the Bible says is true.

If you do believe it is God's perfect Word, then you have to respond to what it says about life. You have to respond to what Jesus did."

Tracey had no words. "I don't know what to say, " was all she could come up with.

Brittany came over and put her hand on her friend's shoulder.

"How about I just pray and we'll see what God does?"

Tracey nodded and Brittany closed her eyes. "God, we've just looked at a lot of information from Your Word. We need you to help us understand it and we need You to make it real in our hearts. Amen."

*****

Several hours later, Tracey was fast asleep, emotionally spent by the events at the party as well as the conversation that she and Brittany had. Her emotional limit had been far exceeded and it made her physically exhausted. Meanwhile, Brittany was so energized by the evening that she was beyond any hope of falling asleep. Around two in the morning, she got thirsty so she slid out of the bed and quietly opened the door. She went downstairs to the kitchen, moving carefully through the dark house. She saw the kitchen light on. Some people kept a light or two on at night so she didn't think much of it until she entered the room to find Lindsey sitting there, staring absently out the window and spinning her cell phone round and round on the table. She looked over at Brittany but said nothing.

"Sorry," Brittany said. "I couldn't sleep. Do you mind if I get something to drink?"

Lindsey shrugged slightly and silently looked back out the window. Brittany shrugged herself, and went to the refrigerator. She found some milk, and then found a glass and filled it half way. Putting the milk back in the refrigerator, she glanced once more at the silent Lindsey. She looked so lost and despondent that Brittany decided to take one more stab at it.

"Are you okay?" she asked. "I mean…I know you don't like me and all, but…I'm a good listener."

Lindsey didn't move or respond. Brittany nodded.

"Okay then." She turned away, her drink in hand. "The

offer's always open."

"What do you know about forgiveness?"

Brittany stopped in her tracks. Turning back to Lindsey, she wrinkled her forehead. "Forgiveness?"

"Yeah," Lindsey said. "You're a Christian, right? Aren't Christian's all about forgiveness?"

Brittany smiled. "Well, I've never thought about it quite like that, but…yeah, you could say that Christians are "all about forgiveness". At least they oughta be. Why?"

"Well, how do you do it?"

"Do what? Forgive?"

"Yeah, I mean how do you start *doing* it."

Brittany thought for a moment. "Hmmm. That's a hard question. Forgiveness is a tricky thing. Why don't you tell me what happened. Then maybe I can give you a good answer."

Lindsey shook her head. "I really don't want to talk about it. I just thought you might have a quick thing you could tell me."

"A quick thing?" Brittany opened the refrigerator and poured a second glass of milk. She set it down in front of Lindsey and took a seat across the table from her. "I don't think there are any "quick things" when it comes to repairing a relationship. Are we talking about you and Tracey or you and Kevin?"

"Actually, it's me and Emily."

"Oh," she nodded. "Okay…Emily. You guys got pretty close then, huh?"

"Yeah, real close. Look, I know you don't like her, so it's no big deal if you want to pass on this."

Brittany shook her head, smiling. "Lindsey, I'm happy to help, if I can. And I don't have anything against Emily. She actually pretty much despises *me* though, I think."

Lindsey nodded. "You're probably right about that."

"So, what happened between you two?"

"She tried to hurt Tracey."

Brittany opened her mouth in surprise. "Really? Like, *tonight*? All this stuff with Tracey and Matt…*Emily* was there?"

Lindsey nodded. "She found out that those two went into a room together and went crazy. I tried to stop her, but she pushed past me and barged into the room and started beating up Matt, which normally I would think was pretty funny, but she was threatening Tracey and when Tracey tried to get her off Matt, she was ready to kill her. I'm not even joking. If Kevin and Tony hadn't gotten them apart, she would have hurt her. I know it."

Brittany was sitting forward in her chair, shaking her head in disbelief. "I can't even get my head wrapped around what that whole scene must have looked like."

"Ugly, is what it looked like."

"And now you and Emily are fighting?"

"Well, she's not fighting with me."

Brittany nodded. "I see. But *you're* having trouble letting it go?"

"Something like that."

"That's hard. Other than tonight, has she been a good friend?"

Lindsey nodded. Brittany could see the emotion in her eyes. Lindsey didn't like showing it. She was trying to act detached, but she looked like she was about to burst. Brittany got up and came around the table.

"Don't," Lindsey said, shaking her head. Her eyes were swollen and red.

"Don't what?" asked Brittany softly, pulling her chair closer to Lindsey. She sat and put her arm around Lindsey's shoulders, pulling her close so that their heads touched. Lindsey resisted slightly, but Brittany wouldn't let her pull away. She held her like that for several moments, letting Lindsey work through the tears. She stopped pulling away, but wouldn't cry.

Brittany said softly, "Lindsey, you don't have to hide it from me. Trust me when I say that crying works."

Even as the words came out of her mouth, Brittany could feel Lindsey shaking. She pulled her even closer and wrapped both of her arms around her, Lindsey's head now pressed across her chest as she sobbed softly. She stroked her hair gently and held her tightly, all the while praying in her heart that God would use this situation to give Brittany an opportunity to share her faith. The reality, she quickly realized, was that the opportunity was right in front of her. However, unlike Tracey, Lindsey was a hostile audience. She had been very clear about her disdain for religion in general. It unnerved Brittany. It wasn't the rejection necessarily, but she just had no idea how to put herself out there to a girl who had declared so clearly her disinterest.

As she held Lindsey in her arms, Brittany couldn't shake

the feeling that this kind of an opportunity may never come again. She felt horrible for feeling this way, but she was kind of grateful for the prolonged pain Lindsey was feeling as it gave her time to gather herself. But eventually Lindsey got control and straightened up. She got up and found a box of tissues, using one to dab her eyes. Brittany had an idea, but she never got the chance.

"My real problem," Lindsey blurted, "if you want to know the truth, is sex?"

Brittany sat, slightly stunned. Looking up at Lindsey, she wrinkled her forehead. "Sex?" she asked. "You and Kevin? You're already...?"

"No," Lindsey said. "We're not. Not yet."

"Not *yet*? Are you planning to?"

Lindsey shrugged. "I don't know. I don't even know why I'm talking to you about this."

Brittany raised her eyebrows. "Because this is *huge*. That's why you're talking about it."

"But you've never had sex," Lindsey said. "So you don't really know anything about it."

Brittany smiled. "Well, I guess if you're looking for pointers then no, I can't help you. If you're looking for advice, then I would say even without knowing anything about what your problem is that it couldn't possibly be solved by having sex."

"Of course you're going to say that."

"Lindsey, Christians have a view of sex that everyone else in the world may reject, but teen sex isn't something that *any* responsible person would encourage." She looked closely at Lindsey, then nodded knowingly. "Emily agrees with me, doesn't she?"

Lindsey's face was a mixture of frustration and confusion. "When I first met Emily, she had all the answers. She had great advice. She watched out for me. And yes, she thinks I should wait. I looked up to her for advice and she was always so confident."

Brittany frowned. "And now?"

Lindsey shrugged, leaning against the center island in the middle of the kitchen. "Now she's turning out to be just as screwed up as everybody else."

"And what? You thought that Emily had life all figured out? She's a year older than you."

"Yeah, but..."

"No," Brittany continued. "There's no but. You have it just as much together as she does. At least you have a *real* relationship with a guy. What does Emily have?"

"I guess not much, but she knows things. She was helping me a lot with my Kevin problems."

"Kevin problems? You and Kevin are having problems? I'm guessing that's what all this is really about."

"All this is about *everything*. My best friend is crazy, and my sister is screwing around with my best friend's guy, making her even crazier. *And* my boyfriend is constantly surrounded by half naked girls, seniors and juniors, I mean, who are literally telling him everything they want to do with him."

"That's a lot of stuff going on." Brittany was nodding in understanding. "I can't imagine having to deal with all those girls hanging on your boyfriend."

Lindsey nodded. "It's no fun. At some point he's going to want to…" She raised her eyebrows.

Brittany leaned forward. "Have sex with you?"

Lindsey shrugged. "*Or* someone else if I don't want to."

"I think I understand what you're getting at."

"Do you?" Lindsey asked. "Because what I'm getting at is this: In order to live this life with *him*, I have to have sex."

"And Kevin said this to you?"

"No, he didn't say it. But look at the reality."

"The reality?"

"Yeah," Lindsey said. "The reality is that these guys are able to have all the sex they want. Kendall Cobras don't have to wait for their virgin girlfriends to come around. They can have it any time they want it."

Brittany nodded, sticking out her bottom lip. "Yeah, you're probably right. But do you see the stereotype you're putting *Kevin* in? I mean, is Kevin Sinclaire just another Kendall Cobra?"

The look on Lindsey's face told Brittany that she had struck a nerve. It took her a moment to consider. "Actually, that's a really good point."

"Yeah," Brittany said, nodding. "I've known that guy my whole life, and I feel pretty safe saying this. You don't have to worry about him cheating on you or even leaving you just for sex with some other girl."

Lindsey had a skeptical look on her face. "I think we can

agree that neither one of us knows how a fourteen year old boy will react to all this. He's a rock star right now. At some point…" She shook her head.

Brittany tilted her head. "Yeah, maybe you're right. He *is* human. I forget that about him sometimes."

Lindsey smiled. "Sometimes I wonder…"

"But is it worth it?"

Lindsey thought about it for a second. "Worth having sex? Seems like a small price to pay."

"A small price? You think losing your virginity is a small thing?"

"It's going to happen anyway. Even you Christians eventually get married and do it. Really all we're talking about is the timing, right?"

Brittany shook her head. "The timing? You say it like timing means nothing. There's a huge difference between a fourteen year old having sex and a twenty-four year old having sex. That's one reason why twenty-four year olds aren't *allowed* to be with fourteen year olds. The timing."

"Well," Lindsey said. "I don't see any way to avoid it if I want to be with Kevin."

"That's insane, Lindsey."

"Maybe to you, to someone who plans to wait until she's thirty years old and married. The rest of us don't all intend to wait that long. For some people, sex is just another part of their relationships and not all that big a deal."

Brittany shrugged. Lindsey's mind was made up. "Okay. It's your life." She walked toward the stairs, but then stopped. "By the way, Lindsey. Call Emily. She doesn't have a lot of friends. I bet she really misses you right now."

Beginnings

Chapter 32

Brittany was excited. She knew that prayers got answered all the time, and that those answers were always perfectly timed and perfectly correct. She knew that the One who answers prayers was far wiser and had a far better view of life than those who were doing the praying. She knew that prayers were sometimes answered without anyone even realizing it. One of her biggest struggles was that she seldom noticed the little answers to prayers. She didn't always recognize the fact that there was someone holding and sustaining every single living thing simply by willing it to be so. She was painfully aware that she often failed to see the Creator among the creation. She was often bothered and frustrated when her prayers for the salvation of friends and relatives seemed to go unanswered. *Aren't these good prayers? Doesn't God want us to pray for these things? Then why doesn't He answer?*

She knew the answer to these questions. She knew that God was fully and completely in control. But she wanted so badly to bring her loved ones to faith. She wanted so badly to be used by God. She knew that what she *really* wanted was to be used in a way that she not only fulfilled God's desires, but also so that she could see it all unfold and understand her role in the plan. Call it pride. Call it ego. For Brittany, the worst part was the not knowing.

But today, she was seeing it in a different way. Over the past several weeks she had spent hours praying for Tracey. She prayed to be used as a godly influence in Tracey's life; that Tracey would see where true joy and contentment could be found, but most of all that Tracey would realize that she needed Christ. She had begun simply, just asking God to use her however he saw fit. As she and Tracey became closer, Brittany saw areas where she could get specific and ask God to work in those areas. She believed her prayers were being answered because Tracey seemed to be caught in flux between her life as a teenager on the verge of popularity and something else. Tracey was just now becoming aware of this. She had mentioned feeling as though she were being pulled in two directions at once. Brittany hoped that she wasn't the one doing the pulling, but God.

And now opportunity had fallen into her lap. She had once told Tracey that she was welcome anytime she wanted to come to church with Brittany and her family. She could sleep over any Saturday night and just come with the Morgan family. Brittany had left it at that, not wanting to push too hard, especially with Lindsey on the other side warning of all the brainwashing "the Christians" like to do. Tracey had always responded well to Brittany's religious points. She even asked a lot of questions, which was also an answer to specific prayers Brittany had made regarding God giving her ample opportunity to inject her faith into conversation.

She and Tracey had met at a tender time in Tracey's life. She was coming out of a shell that had protected her from a life of perceived ridicule, but had also served to leave her with a naiveté that made her dangerously unprepared for a dramatic evening with a very experienced guy who thought very little of sex and its impact on those who engage in it, particularly those who have never done it. Tracey's story of the fairytale evening that ended with the nightmarish morning had struck Brittany in a big way. What a shame it was to have such a momentous occasion ruined by fear and shame. She was convinced that God had never intended people to feel such shame, but now, just as the ground had been cursed by God, all of creation was also cursed so that life was hard, decisions were important and often painful when the wrong path is taken. Sometimes, a decision is made that cannot be corrected in a person's lifetime. Brittany believed that Tracey had made just such a decision.

But even after a life changing decision, one that went directly against God's ordained order, Brittany believed that God was still working. Tracey had slipped and stumbled over the past few weeks. She could not figure out what she wanted, or more importantly, what she needed. Matt Kildare was on and off towards her, hot one moment, and cold the next. He was with Emily Vasquez, and yet not. He obviously had feelings for Tracey, and yet couldn't bring himself to commit to them. Tracey found herself caught between her desire for the guy she wanted more than anyone else in the world, and her self-respect and dignity.

Brittany had done her best to advise her friend in a godly manner, but really, she had thought, what would a non Christian do with advice from scripture? Brittany had tried to give Tracey advice as a friend ought to but found it difficult to maintain her faithfulness to God's Word. She was treading a fine line between secular advice and godly advice. Finally, she could no longer continue doing it. She could no longer try to cloak God's Word in secular advice, and why should she? Her last conversation with Tracey had been one filled with what God's Word says about life, sex, and relationships. Stunningly, Tracey had sat through it all, paying attention, asking questions, seemingly very interested in what Brittany was telling her.

But the real shocker had come the following morning when Tracey announced that she wanted to come to church with the Morgans. Brittany had been so happy that she jumped into Tracey's arms, hugging he so tightly around her neck that Tracey couldn't breathe. Brittany had tears in her eyes all day and couldn't stop thanking God for what seemed to be an immediate and decisive answer to her prayers. She couldn't wait to see what God had in store for Tracey Overton.

As they approached the High School building, Brittany said to Tracey, "I forgot to tell you, Kevin's friend, Tony, might be here."

Tracey nodded, catching herself at the last moment. She almost blurted out what Tony had told her. She was having the hardest time keeping her face blank. "Oh, I love Tony," she said. "He's the sweetest guy ever."

"How well do you know him?" Brittany asked.

"Not real well. He walked me home from Fontaine's last week, and when I was feeling bad one day he walked with me between classes."

"That's right. I remember that. That was kind of sweet of

him."

"Yeah."

"He came to church last week to try to go out with me. Do you believe that?"

"Wow," Tracey said. "He must be really into you. Do you like him?"

"He's okay. He's definitely cute," Brittany answered. "But he's not a Christian, sooo…" she shrugged.

Tracey smiled inwardly. Just as she had suspected. "Well…"

"Although," Brittany went on. "He did seem to be impacted by the lesson last week. You never know, he could come to Christ. That would certainly make things interesting."

Tracey nodded. *Wonderful.*

Kevin and Tony got to the High School Building a little earlier than usual, but still after Brittany and Tracey. Tony had talked a little less about getting Brittany and a whole lot more about what he was reading about in the Bible he had borrowed from Gavin Dalyrimple the previous week. From the way he was talking, the two had been communicating through email and text all week, going over Tony's questions and thoughts. Kevin didn't have any problem at all with Tony's newfound interest in the Christian faith. In fact, he was happy for Tony. But Kevin wasn't the guy to talk about it with. Tony would have to make some friends in the youth group.

The four youths sat together. Tony had made it clear to Kevin that he didn't want to pursue Brittany too hard, so when they all sat down, he made sure that Kevin was sitting between them. For Tony, this kept a barrier between them that would serve to let her know that he wasn't trying to pressure her. It also would keep him from being able to look at her, which would completely distract him. What he didn't realize was that having Kevin next to her was a major distraction for Brittany. When they had sat together in church recently, she could barely keep her eyes on the pastor. She kept stealing glances at him. Her heart pounded mercilessly the entire time, seeming to echo throughout her whole body.

Brittany knew that it was all just temptation. It was a distraction that was designed to rob her attention from what was really most important, her relationship with God. These things popped up often enough that she was now able to recognize then rather quickly and usually dealt with them easily enough. This thing about Kevin was new. Sure, she had always had a bit of a crush on him. Every girl in the church did. Kevin was *that* guy. It was about his looks and even that little bit of danger that he seemed to express without ever saying a word. Brittany knew it was a superficial attraction and she could mentally work herself through the problem...when he wasn't around...when he wasn't sitting *right next* to her.

She suffered through the lesson, trying to focus on her friend, sitting on her right. Tracey had come in nervously and wondered immediately what she had been thinking. It scared her to imagine changing her life in a way that would make her so different from the rest of her family. Her mother and sister didn't believe in God. Would they reject her for her beliefs? Brittany was often criticized or made fun of in school. What if she'd had to deal with it at home too? How hard would *that* be?

But even as all of the possible ridicule, as all of the reasons to run out of the room right then and there flooded her mind, Tracey couldn't shake the feeling that she needed to be there. She felt that even though her life might be made more difficult as she stepped into faith, she had to do it. Not exploring faith was far more terrifying than anything else. Living an empty life, as Brittany and the Bible described, was something she could not bear to consider. As far as that went, she felt like she could relate to Brittany's willingness to suffer a little ridicule for her faith. Brittany's contentment and joy seemed to more than make up for it.

Tracey wasn't sure she followed everything correctly. She felt like she had walked into something that had already begun and everyone else knew what was going on, like watching a television series for the first time, and starting on episode six instead of starting at the beginning. But even with all that clouding her mind, she felt strangely at home. That was a little confusing. She was never at home with strangers. Lester Fontaine's parties were like walking into a different world for her. Those kids were all friends. They all knew one another. Though they welcomed newcomers, it was always uncomfortable because Tracey just did not *feel* like one of them. Here, she only knew Brittany, Kevin, and Tony. Kevin was not really a part of all this and Tony was only here for the second time. But she didn't feel uncomfortable at all. She felt a little stupid for not knowing what everyone else seemed to know, but she knew that she belonged here.

After the lesson, Brittany and Tracey walked together along the pathway leading from the Youth building to the church. Brittany didn't want to push Tracey for her thoughts too hard, but she didn't have to. Tracey was eager to talk.

"I can't explain it, but I really felt good being in there. I felt like an idiot, not knowing anything they were talking about."

"Don't worry about that," Brittany said. "You'll pick up on that really quick, trust me."

"Isn't there a beginner's class I could take?"

"Actually, there *are* classes to help you learn the basics. If you want to go, I'll go with you."

"You would do that? You wouldn't be bored?"

"Bored?" Brittany laughed. "Are you kidding? It would be the most exciting thing that's happened to me in a long time?"

"Really?" Tracey wrinkled her forehead, smiling at the same time. "It means that much to you?"

Brittany threw her arm around Tracey's shoulders. "*You* mean that much to me," she laughed. "If this is the direction you're going, I want to support you all the way. It helps to have a friend, especially if you're new to it all."

They sat through the sermon, Tracey doing her best to pay attention and try to put things together and Brittany feeling much better now that she wasn't sitting right next to Kevin Sinclaire. Tracey was worried that she wouldn't understand anything at all since she hadn't understood much in the high school classroom, but the pastor had such a great ability to make things understandable that she was actually grasping most of it.

She had been expecting something different than what she was experiencing. Her entire previous experience at church was playing checkers with Brittany several years ago when she had been way too shy to participate in the activities the other kids were doing. She had never gone into the main church. She had never heard a real sermon. Now she was experiencing it, surrounded by hundreds of other people, and it felt truly amazing.

The pastor was focused on something that Tracey had never really understood. He was focused on the heart. She had some experience with heartache. When he mentioned the emptiness human beings all felt deep within, she understood. When he spoke of the inherent need of all people to worship *something*, and how we all *will* worship something even if we don't realize it. She thought of her feelings for Matt. Everything was becoming clear. She had been *worshipping* him. If not *him* specifically, then certainly the idea of being with him. The relationship had totally consumed her. The reality of what a colossal waste it all was hit her hard. She even felt the pangs of shame as the pastor noted that all of the "worship" we offer to the things of the world really belongs to its Creator. She winced a little as she considered all of the things she had longed for in her life. How sad that she had spent so much time sitting in her room, just wishing for things.

Brittany felt and saw Tracey's anguish. On the outside, Tracey was sitting in rapt attention. Her eyes barely blinked as they followed the pastor's movements from one side of the stage to the other. But it was in her demeanor. She was sitting with hands clenched, knuckles white, the fingernails of her right hand digging into the back of her left. Her forearms were even tensed from the exertion. It was obvious to Brittany that Tracey's mind was racing to process all of the emotions, but was failing to keep up. Tracey looked like she was on the verge of collapse. Brittany softly reached over and placed her hand over Tracey's. Immediately, Tracey relaxed her clenched fists.

After the service, Tracey sat alone for several minutes, thinking. Even though she was dying to talk about everything with her, Brittany gave her some time to herself. She mingled just a few feet away with some of the girls from the high school group. Kevin and Tony passed by and Tony slid into the seat next to Tracey. Brittany took the occasion to slip away for a moment.

"Hey," Tony said to Tracey. "What'd you think?"

She smiled at him. "A lot to think about."

"Tell me about it. Last week I went home and couldn't stop thinking about what a scumbag I am."

Tracey laughed, her emotional turmoil all of a sudden subsided. There was something about Tony's presence that comforted her. She was glad that he was going through a similar process as she was. She was glad to know that he was going to be there each week.

Chapter 33

As the team poured out of the bus following the 45 minute drive to Southern High, they were greeted by a huge contingent of Kendall Township fans, all dressed in black, all cheering and pumping their fists or waving their black and silver towels. It was like a scene out of a pro football script. As Scott Webber made his exit, the cheering went up a notch or two for the starting QB. Anquan Griffin and even Matt Kildare got loud cheers. When Kevin hopped to the pavement, the crowd went bonkers, and the "Venom!" chants began. He didn't really smile. It was game day and Kevin didn't care about fans on game day. He didn't care about anything other than the game on game day.

They were there to take on the Southern High Spiders, which boasted one of the best quarterback prospects in the state, Vincent Marczack. He had the kind of arm that made college scouts' mouths water. He was a prototypical quarterback, tall and strong with a very fast release. He was also a deceptively fast runner. Though the Southern High football program was not usually in contention for a spot in the state championship tournament, this particular Southern team was not to be taken lightly. They could score quickly because they had fast receivers and a quarterback who did not make many mistakes. On top of all that, they had a big offensive line, who gave Vincent plenty of time to throw.

The Cobras got a dose of that in the first series of the game, when Vincent Marczack accomplished something that had not been done yet all season. He scored on the Kendall Cobra defense. After three lightning quick short passes, which put the defense on their heels, the Spiders then added in a little bit of their power rushing attack, pushing the smaller Cobra defense around and gaining yards in large chunks. They focused their blocking on Kevin Sinclaire, not letting him have free runs at their ball carriers. They didn't try to take him on head to head, but rather hit him from one side or the other, hit him low to take out his legs, or just get in his way so he could not make the full speed hits he was becoming known for. It was a good plan that took him out of a lot of plays. Then from seven yards out, Vincent Marczack faked a pass and darted straight ahead through the middle of the line and dove into the end zone for the first score of the season against the Cobras. The Spiders celebrated wildly at the accomplishment while the Kendall fans watched stunned at how easy it had been to march down the field on their boys. For the first time all season, the Kendall High Cobras were behind.

It didn't last very long. The Cobras didn't get the score back right away. They managed to get two first downs before bogging down and following yet another dropped pass by Matt Kildare, they were forced to punt. The Spiders didn't fare any better as the Cobra defense made some quick adjustments and quickly forced the Spiders to punt as well. On the next play, Scott faked a handoff, dropped back three steps and faked a pass to his left, then quickly spun and tossed it to the right, finding Kevin on a little "bubble screen", where he caught the ball with several blockers already set in front of him. He made two moves on would-be tacklers and then followed his blockers until he could break free and take off down the sidelines for an 80 yard score.

Kendall scored on their next two possessions as well, both on runs by Anquan Griffin, and both set up by catch and runs by Kevin Sinclaire. But the Southern Spiders did not go away quietly, gathering themselves late in the second quarter and posting a field goal, then another field goal after Kendall fumbled the kickoff. At halftime, the score was 21-13. Kendall blew it wide open in the third quarter after Kevin smashed Vincent Marczack on a blitz and Ozzie Winfred recovered the fumble. Two plays later and Scott Webber dropped back looking at Kevin the whole time, but at the last instant turned and tossed a perfectly placed ball to the back corner of the end zone where Matt Kildare was standing all alone. He easily caught it for his first touchdown of the year. The fans roared and waved their black and silver towels, the "VE-NOM" chants beginning to grow louder as they sensed the Cobras were about to ice the game.

On the very next Kendall series, Kevin put the game away with another long touchdown, catching a long pass from Scott and just outrunning the defensive players. Anquan Griffin tacked on another score and the Kendall defense cemented the game with a second half shut out. The Cobras were now 4-0. In the stands, Lindsey seriously wondered if her hearing was being affected by sitting with these lunatics, though she was beginning to get into it. It was strange, but now, when she put on the Kendall Cobra jersey, with that big number 27 across the front and back, her normal withdrawn personality faded away, replaced by...well, not the *same* Kendall fever as the rest of the maniacs in the stands, but when the Venom chant was on, her voice was there too. She even had a brand new little black towel with the silver "Venom" logo that she waved right along with everyone else. Undefeated after four games, the Kendall stands were abuzz with the talk of winning the division, and even, possibly, a trip to the state championships.

*****

Emily walked through the Kildare house, looking for Matt, doing her best to ignore the looks she was getting from the kids, especially those who were present for her meltdown the previous week. She really didn't care what any of them thought. They were a bunch of wannabes, hanging around, hoping to catch a glimpse of high school greatness, hoping to be invited in. They all wished they had something to offer just one Kendall Cobra starter, something that would make them an insider to what was special in Kendall Township. She had gotten that as a freshman. She knew she was special, had known it since she was twelve years old, when high school football players used to try to talk to her at the mall. They had no idea she was only twelve, and she learned from the experience. Boys were blind if the girl was pretty enough. But pretty was never enough for Emily. She wanted to be hot. And by the time she walked into Kendall High School, a little over a year ago, she was blazing.

She had gone from just another freshman to the pinnacle of Kendall High popularity. Every head in school turned when she walked into a room. The guys watched her every move and wondered what it would take to get her to talk to them. The girls watched and wondered how a freshman could capture the attention of the entire school without ever saying a word. She caught Matt Kildare's eye right from day one. From that point on, she was with Matt Kildare, Kendall High royalty, the greatest of all the Cobras...that is, until Kevin Sinclaire showed up. Kevin's rise didn't really faze her. He was just the next big thing. Matt was pretty well established as the king of this school. He and Emily together were the "it" couple for an entire year. His spiral downward from those heights was really more in his mind than anything else. He wasn't the best player on the team anymore, but he didn't have to be to maintain his status. And he still had Emily.

She had thought that it was over after her ill-advised tantrum the previous week. She had stayed away from him for the rest of the weekend, giving him space, all the while hoping to God he'd call and talk to her. He never did. He pretty much ignored her all week in school as well and she didn't push it. Matt would come around if and when he wanted to. She had settled in for what might be a bit of a wait. But then a couple hours ago, the text had come. Matt wanted her to come to his party. It didn't say much more than that, but Emily took it as a good thing. After another Cobra victory, one in which Matt had finally scored a touchdown, he was probably in a good mood and probably wanted to get things back to normal. Emily texted back that she would be there.

She found him out on the enormous back patio, the kind that was made for hosting large parties. Matt was smiling and talking to his father and Leo Forsythe. He was obviously in a far better mood than he had been in previous weeks. He looked relaxed, like the weight had finally been lifted off his shoulders. She approached rather timidly, hoping to God that word of last week's events hadn't gotten to his dad. Both of Matt's parents had always treated her like a daughter and she now wished that last week had never happened. Brian Kildare saw her and smiled broadly.

"Emily!" he exclaimed, coming around and taking her hand. "I was wondering where you were hiding." He guided her over to their group. "Leo, do you know Emily Vasquez?"

Leo nodded. "Of course. How are you, Emily?"

"I'm fine how are you?" she replied politely, looking at Matt, trying to gauge his mood. He smiled back, though it was a little grimmer a smile than she'd hoped. She didn't know what to make of it.

They had some small talk for a few minutes with the two men about school and the game earlier. Matt was engaged in the conversation, standing opposite Emily as they talked, his father between them on one side, and Leo between them on the other side. He never made eye contact with Emily. Now, she was worried. This was really bad. In the past, Matt couldn't keep his eyes off her. He had never been able to keep his hands off her either. He had always wanted to be standing right with her, an arm around her shoulders, a hand on her back, her hand in his, anything to maintain physical contact with her. She had always loved the attention from the most popular guy in Kendall High. Now, she felt like a leper, like some disgraced Amish girl that her loved ones couldn't even bear to look at anymore.

After leaving the two older men to their conversation, Matt gestured to Emily to follow him. She went alongside him off the patio and into the large grass field beyond. She had always loved to walk in this field with him, kissing beneath the huge oak tree off to the right, but tonight he was distant. He still hadn't touched her. This was really bad. It was the physical aspect of the relationship where Emily was at her best. It was there that she exercised her control. She also loved the mental part, where her quick mind and street-wise perceptiveness had always kept her a step or two ahead of most guys her age. But she wasn't really good at the heart stuff. Most high schoolers jumped headlong into a relationship, claiming that they were in love and that they'd always be together and all that. Emily never fallen victim to that. She knew that everything in high school was short-lived and that you couldn't count on anything to stick at this age.

Now, as she walked with a guy she really and truly believed she loved with all her heart, she was lost. She didn't know what to do. Matt was absently staring at the sky, walking slowly.

"Are you okay?" she asked.

"Yeah," he said. "Today was a little better than yesterday."

"I saw you score earlier. That had to feel good."

"It wasn't much of a play. *You* could have thrown that pass."

She shrugged. "I'm pretty sure you don't get points for degree of difficulty in football."

"That's true. Yes, by the way, it felt great finally scoring."

She nodded absently. Small talk was useless. It was safe for him and torturous for her. She no longer wanted to be there. This, whatever it was, whatever they'd had, was over. She knew it now. If she was honest, she'd known it for weeks. It was coming to the end of a long road, where she couldn't really see what she had been so sure was ahead, so she had kept plodding along, only to find that the road just ended, with nothing beyond. She knew he was struggling for a way to do what he called her to do, so she figured she might as well get it over with. With her heart aching worse and worse with every passing second, she began the inevitable conversation, the one Matt couldn't bring himself to begin.

"Say it," she began.

"Say what?" Matt asked.

Emily rolled her eyes and stopped walking. "Tell me what you called me here to tell me."

He opened his mouth, but no words came out. She stood there, heart completely broken, watching the first boy she had ever loved frozen in place, unable to do what he came to do, unable to end it. She turned away, the tears beginning to emerge.

"Emily," Matt said. "We're just no good together…fighting all the time…"

"No!" she turned to him, eyes filled with tears, but still able to muster up the contempt she was beginning to feel. She shook her head and walked right up to him, looking him in the eye. "You don't get to lie to me anymore. You don't get to pretend that your reason for this has anything to do with our relationship. You tell me the truth."

He backed away, spreading his arms out and shaking his head. "What more do you want from me, Em? I'm going to college next year. You'll have two more years…"

"You are such a coward! You're telling me that we can't spend this school year together because you're thinking so far ahead? Why can't you just tell me the truth? It's already over, Matt. We're done. We're finished. Now just tell me why."

He stared at the ground. "Fine. It's just…I don't want to hurt you, Em. I really don't."

"Matt, it's a little late for that. Just tell me."

"I want to go out with Tracey. That can't happen if we're still together."

Emily nodded. It was silent for several moments. "There it is, then." She turned away.

"Em, don't…"

She turned back quickly. "Just tell me one thing, okay? Up til now, I thought you made a joke out of being in a relationship with me because you really wanted the freedom to do your thing whenever you wanted and with whoever you wanted. You didn't want to be tied down. But you've known I wanted a real relationship for months now. Why her and not me? Why is it a joke with me and not with Tracey Overton? Why am I such a joke to you?"

His mouth dropped open in surprise. "You think…? The last thing you are to me, Emily, is a joke."

"Then what? This is about something. The first girl you really want a relationship with is not me, and yet who have you spent the past year with? I really thought I was special to you."

"You are…"

"Stop. No, I'm not. I can deal with not being special to every guy, Matt. You know me better than that. What's hard to live with is when you really believe the person you're with thinks of you a certain way, and then you find out that you're wrong. How did I miss that, Matt?"

"You didn't miss anything, Em. This is new."

Emily chuckled sadly. "Oh. Well, that's a relief." She leaned against a tree and put her head in her hands. After a few seconds, she collected herself and straightened up. "Anyway," she said. "I'm going to get out of here."

"Let me drive you home."

Emily almost laughed at that. "Yeah, right. That would help a lot, Matt. Can we make this anymore painful? Yeah, we could spend another twenty minutes together in a car." She pulled out her phone and began sending a text. "My mom's off tonight. She'll come get me."

"Can I ask you something without you getting mad?" Matt asked tentatively.

"This ought to be interesting."

"Are you going to make Tracey miserable now?"

Emily considered this. "That's actually very sweet, Matt. You're concerned for your girlfriend."

"She's not my girlfriend, Emily."

"Okay, your girlfriend-to-be. Whatever. The answer to your question is, no. I have no intention of going after Tracey. She's my best friend's sister, for God's sake. I almost lost Lindsey last week because of you two. Tracey's not worth it. She'll have enough to worry about dating you. Having her heart stomped by you is punishment enough. And I get a front row seat to that show, so what I'm going to do is go home and make some popcorn."

Matt shook his head. "I guess I deserve that."

"Yes, you do. And one other thing, Matt." Emily came closer. Her crying was over and her eyes back to an icy blue stare. "You think you've changed because you managed to let me go and actually make a choice for this other girl. But you haven't. You're the same. And before this football season is over, you're going to destroy this girl. And the big difference between her and I is that I will recover just fine. I can pick myself back up. But she's nothing like me. She has no idea who or what you really are or what this life is really like. And after you're finished with Tracey Overton, there won't be much of her left to pick up."

*****

She barely made it off the Kildare property before losing it completely. Emily's mother, Camilla picked her up and by the time they were on the road, Emily's tears were flowing full force. Everything she had held back while talking to Matt poured out of her while her mother sat helplessly beside her, trying to reach over and hold her daughter's hand. She had only rarely seen her daughter cry, and never over a boy. She had known that Matt was special by the way Emily had always talked about him. But even when Matt had hurt her, Emily had never cried in front of Camilla. She had shown anger and frustration, but never tears.

"What can I do for you, baby?" she asked in her soft tone, her light Columbian accent still very prominent even though her English was perfect.

"I need Lindsey," Emily said, pulling out her phone and quickly texting her between bouts of crying. "Can we go get her, mom?"

Camilla smiled at her daughter. "Of course." She was pleased that her daughter had found a girlfriend. She was always so focused on boys. She was always in competition with girls. There was little worse for a young girl than to be alone when girl problems came up. Breaking up with a boy was never easy, but that's when you leaned on your girlfriends.

When they arrived at the Overton's home, Emily quickly ran up to the door, really needing her best friend. Mrs. Overton let her in and directed her up to Lindsey's room before going out to meet Camilla. Emily went upstairs, knocked urgently on Lindsey's door, and entered. Lindsey was putting some things into the onStage bag she used for gymnastics class. When she saw the distressed look on Emily's face, her eyes teared up and she came over and embraced her. Emily broke down completely and the two nearly collapsed to the ground together as Lindsey was barely able to hold her up. Emily was sobbing uncontrollably. Lindsey moved her towards the bed so she could sit down. She had never seen Emily so completely broken. She had been angry, frustrated, confused, and even sad, but never anything like this. She was a shattered shell of herself. Lindsey soon found herself crying right along with her.

"Lindsey, are you all righhhhh, oh…sorry." Tracey came running in and then stopped short when she saw Emily, her face buried in Lindsey's arms. Brittany was right behind her, eyes wide and speechless..

Lindsey waved them out. "Get out."

"What happened?"

"I said, get out of my room!" Lindsey shouted. "This is none of your business."

Emily pushed herself up, her eyes still puffy and tears still running down her face. "No. It's okay," she said. She straightened up and looked right at Tracey. "Get a good look, honey. Enjoy it, because you won't ever see it again."

Tracey's eyes were tearing up despite the fact that she knew how much Emily hated her. She could see and even feel the pain in Emily's eyes. It drew her in. Brittany put a hand on Tracey's shoulder and tried to get her to leave them alone. Tracey couldn't leave. She sat down on the floor in front of Emily and looked up at her.

"What are you doing?" Lindsey shouted. "Leave!"

Tracey looked at Emily. "What did he do?" she asked softly.

Emily wiped her tears away. It was so much easier when your enemy was in front of you. "Like you have no idea?"

Tracey was surprised. "Me? Why? I haven't spoken to him since the last party."

Emily laughed. "Yeah? Well, you'll be talking to him soon enough," she said. And throwing a quick glance up at Brittany, she leaned forward. "And the next thing you know, he'll have you back in his bed, where you've been dying to get back to ever since the first time."

Brittany's jaw dropped open and her hands went instinctively to her mouth.

Tracey closed her eyes and shook her head compassionately. "I'm sorry, Emily. I wish he would have chosen *you*. I *can't* be with him. I've decided this already. I'm not going out with him if he asks."

Emily shook her head. "You and Matt...You both live in the same dream world. He really thinks he can change who he is and have a real relationship with you, and you really think you are capable of saying no to him if he wants you."

In the silence that followed, Lindsey gestured for Tracey to leave. Brittany silently urged her as well. Tracey got up. She hesitated for a second and took one more long look at Emily.

"I'm really sorry, Emily."

After they left, Lindsey quickly got up and grabbed her bag.

"Well, that was fun," she said. "Let's get out of here before she comes back and tries to give you a hug."

"I swear I'll slap her if she does."

"So," Lindsey said. "What are we doing tonight? I mean, other than being pathetic and crying all night?"

"We're going to watch a movie and I'm going to bawl on your shoulder until I fall asleep."

Lindsey slumped. "Really? We're not getting a sappy romantic comedy are we?"

"We're getting something that will cheer me up."

"Like what? You're not gonna make me watch a love story that will make you cry the whole time, are you?"

"Well, what do *you* want to watch?

"There's a Hitchcock marathon on all weekend," Lindsey replied hopefully.

Emily looked at her. "Seriously? Hitchcock? You think I want to watch a bunch of black and white murder films?"

Lindsey raised her eyebrows. "Or…"she ran over to her book case and pulled out a big box. "I have every episode of the Twilight Zone. We could watch them all."

Emily shook her head. "No way. This is *my* depressing nightmare. In *my* depressing nightmare you have to watch love stories with vampires and werewolves in it while I cry and wish the really hot vampire guy would turn *me* into a vampire so we could spend the rest of eternity together and in love forever and ever and ever. When it's *your* depressing nightmare, I'll come over and watch the Twilight Zone with you."

"Are we getting ice cream at least?"

"And candy and popcorn, yes."

"You're not going to eat the ice cream directly out of the container, are you?"

"Of course I am, why?"

"Because that's what all the depressed, pathetic, sad girls do in the movies and it always makes me want to puke."

"Depressed, pathetic, sad girls?" Emily said pointedly.

Lindsey shrugged, ruefully. "Oh right…sorry."

"And they make you want to puke? Why?"

"Because it's disgusting, that's why! All those spit germs all over the good ice cream. Then they never finish the box, so the spit stays on it and it goes right back into the freezer. Then the next time they eat the ice cream, the frozen spit melts in their mouth and it's totally disgusting!"

Emily's looked like she was about to throw up. "That's nasty," she said.

"Just put the ice cream in a bowl, okay?"

Emily rolled her eyes. "Okay, okay. I'll eat it out of a bowl. Any more demands? And why is this all about *you*? *I'm* the one who got her heart ripped out. Shouldn't you be worrying about my fragile condition?"

Lindsey wasn't listening. She was about to put the box away, but reconsidered. "I think I'll bring the Twilight Zone, just in case."

Brittany and Tracey retreated to Tracey's room.

"What was that," Brittany asked Tracey.

"What was what?"

"You kneeling in front of Emily and all that? What were you doing?"

Tracey shrugged. "I felt bad. She was really hurting. Didn't you feel sorry for her?"

Brittany nodded. "Sure, I felt bad, but she really tried to hurt you last week. I would think you wouldn't really care all that much if she got her heart broken."

Tracey picked up a thin black Bible from the drawer of her nightstand. She held it up. "It says in here to love your enemies."

Brittany was so surprised that she burst out laughing. Tracey turned red. "Oh, my God! Am I an idiot?" she asked.

Brittany quickly recovered. "Oh no, no, no. I was totally not laughing at you. I was just really surprised when you quoted scripture." She took the Bible from Tracey's hand and flipped through it. Tracey had placed little notes in between many of the pages with thoughts, questions, and quotes on them. They were scattered throughout both the Old and New Testaments.

"You read all this just this past week?"

Tracey shrugged. "What can I say? I read really fast."

Brittany raised her eyebrows and nodded. "No kidding." She smiled. "I love that you're reading the Bible, Trace! So, all that with Emily back there was you trying to love your enemy?"

Tracey sat down, "Something like that."

"That's really great. I think God's drawing you to Him. Do you?"

Tracey's phone buzzed. It was a text. When she looked at it, her face froze. There were two missed calls and a text, all from the same person. She turned the phone for Brittany to read. Brittany grabbed it and her eyes widened with anxiety as she saw the text message displayed on the screen.

Need to talk ASAP. Call me, Matt.

Chapter 34

For years, going to church had been a simple chore for Kevin. He went and did his best, most of the time, to stay out of trouble. He listened to what they teachers or pastors said and didn't fall asleep during the services. He did it all without complaining because his mother really was not asking all that much of him. In truth, she wasn't asking him at all. Church was a part of living in the Timmons house. That he didn't complain kept it from being unpleasant. She knew he didn't care about any of it, but that wasn't the point, he had found out. She saw it as her job to ensure that she did everything in her power to instruct her son in the things of God.

But now he was beginning to hate it. It had nothing to do with religion or God or Jesus, or anything like that. What Kevin was beginning to hate was the constant yammering of his best friend about everything he was reading and learning from the Bible. Tony was the kind of guy who loved to talk even when there was nothing to talk about. But when he latched onto something that interested him, he was like an excited kid on Christmas morning. For Kevin, it was torture having to deal with all the questions and interesting points Tony had come across.

Brittany loved every second of it, he could tell. She was so excited to see two new kids, whom she knew and had relationships with, in church each week. She saw how Tony's faith was rather instantaneous compared to Tracey's, though she was coming to it. He had almost immediately believed, though she had no idea yet whether Tony had actually accepted Christ. He was certainly reading and studying even though Brittany had never seen him with a book in his hands at school. Tracey was different. She was reading, apparently a great deal, if the notes in her Bible were any indication. But though she had obviously been impacted, and she seemed to be searching, hers was a more roundabout route, and the whole Matt Kildare confusion was not helping.

How Brittany wished that text had never come. The turmoil it had caused in Tracey's head and heart was immediate and powerful. Having heard from Emily that the break-up had occurred, and what Matt's intentions were, there was no doubt as to the reason for his calls and text. Now what to do? Tracey was caught between something she had so desperately wanted, and something she so desperately needed. Brittany did not have all that much experience in these kinds of situations, but one thing her father had told her was that the things we *want* are exceedingly difficult to give up, even for something we need more than anything else. She feared that Tracey would fall prey to her desires. She was in such a tender state, her faith couldn't be strong enough to withstand this kind of temptation, could it? Of course it could, if God made it strong enough, if she was really saved.

But Brittany could see the difference in Tracey's demeanor even as she smiled and chatted with Tony. There was uncertainty where there was once excitement. There was confusion where she had for the briefest of moments seemed to be heading toward clarity. Brittany was having a very hard time not feeling anger, or worse, toward Matt Kildare. He just kept popping into Tracey's life at the worst moments for her.

She went over to Kevin, seated alone at the breakfast counter, drinking a cup filled with orange juice. She noticed that he had kept away from all the conversation. It was strange for her to see how a guy who captivates the attention and admiration of so many could be so alone in life. He had always been a paradox, withdrawn while at the same time the center of attention. He had tons of people who wanted to be around him, yet he preferred solitude. Tony was the only one she had seen consistently around him. Brittany figured it must have something to do with the fact that Tony didn't care if

Kevin was a sullen jerk a lot of the time.

She looked back at Tony, sitting with Tracey and talking. They looked cute together, she thought. She looked back at Kevin.

"Hey," she said.

Kevin turned in his seat. "Hey."

She nodded back to Tony and Tracey. "What do you think of those two?"

He looked over her shoulder and shrugged.

Brittany made a face. "You don't think they look cute together?"

Kevin looked again and shrugged again. "Guys don't call other guys "cute"?"

She giggled. "You know what I mean."

"Why are you asking?"

"I just think they're really cute together."

"Well, Tony likes *you*, remember? He hasn't given up on you just yet."

Brittany frowned. "Really? He hasn't said two words to me since we talked the first time he came."

Kevin nodded. "Yeah, well, he's been kind of distracted lately with God and all that."

"God and all that?" Brittany asked. "Who are you kidding, Kevin? You believe every word of it, so knock it off."

He turned back to his orange juice. "Anyway, why do you want to get those two together? Just to get rid of Tony?"

She shook her head. "No. He's not even bothering me. And..." she glanced over her shoulder and whispered, "I kind of like having really cute guys hit on me. Don't tell anyone, okay?"

Kevin smiled. "I knew it."

"Hey, it's okay to like guys, right?"

"Whatever you say, Good Girl." He only called Brittany that name once in a while so as not to waste the effect, because she hated it.

Brittany just stared at him. Why did she let this guy get to her so easily? With those stupid green eyes...

"Can I tell you something in confidence?"

He looked back at her. "Sure. What's up?"

"Matt Kildare dumped Emily Friday night."

"Yeah, I heard. Lindsey's been over there ever since, trying to keep her from slitting her wrists."

"Oh, wonderful," Brittany said, shaking her head. "Like Matt Kildare's worth all that." She shook her head. "But what you don't know is he's got his sights set on Tracey."

Kevin nodded. "Well, she likes him too. It's not that big a surprise. Matt and Emily fought because he was into Tracey. So, it sounds like he made a decision."

"Yeah, well, that decision is affecting her negatively."

"Why?"

Brittany looked at him like he had three heads. "Seriously, Kevin? You think she can handle that kind of temptation right now? She's just now coming to faith. Matt Kildare is her biggest weakness."

"And you think putting her together with another brand new believer is the better option?"

"Don't you? At least they're equally yoked."

Kevin laughed. "I can't believe you just said that."

"What? Two Christians together, even if they're brand new Christians has got to be better than a new Christian and a non Christian, especially if the non Christian is Matt Kildare."

Kevin stood up, took Brittany's arm, and led her out to the outer room. When they were alone, he let her arm go.

"First of all," he said. "Neither one of those two have accepted Christ to my knowledge. So you're getting a little bit ahead of yourself, don't you think?"

"You don't know what's going on in someone's heart, Kevin. You can only judge what you see. And I see two people seeking God. That's good enough for me."

"Good enough for what? For you to start tampering with their lives?"

"I'm not tampering with anything."

Kevin laughed. "What do you think pushing those two to start dating is? Just good old-fashioned matchmaking?"

"That's not fair, Kevin."

He nodded. "I'll tell you what's not fair. Putting two kids, who may or may not be new Christians, together in a relationship. One of them has already had sex and is probably very interested in doing it again. Any guy who gets close to her could probably open that door if he plays it right. The other has no real idea what he is into with all the religious stuff. He's in flux right now, so if you put a knockout like Tracey in his lap, he might go for it. And I don't know if you've seen the way she looks at him, but it's only her friendship with *you* that's probably holding her back. She must know how he feels about you."

Brittany said nothing. She looked through the window in the door at Tracey and Tony, laughing and talking.

"So," Kevin asked. "Which is worse, having one new Christian in danger of blowing it, or two?" Before he went back into the main room, he turned to Brittany and pointed a finger at her. "And don't ever try to get me to play games with my friends again. I may not care about God and all that, but if Tony does, I support him. I'd never let him jeopardize that. You should have known that about me, Brittany."

*****

It had been a long and confusing weekend, made almost unbearable by the persistent calls and texts that Tracey was simply unable to respond to. She spent as much time as she could out of her house for fear that Matt would show up and talk to her. After seeing the "ominous" text, that was how Brittany referred to it, they had discussed how to handle Matt Kildare. Brittany had been adamant that Tracey needed to refuse any attempt by Matt to get together. She told Tracey that what she needed right now was time to get her heart right. She was leaning toward God right now, but getting into a relationship with a guy like Matt would take her in the opposite direction.

Tracey, as much as she wanted to take a firm stand here, wasn't sure she could say no to a direct proposition by Matt. If he really wanted to have an honest to goodness boyfriend girlfriend relationship with her, she kind of wanted that herself. It would be easier if he would stay away. She thought she might be able to stay away from him, but if he pursued her, she had little faith in her ability to hold up. Plus, she wasn't really all that certain about the whole church thing anyway. It was easier when she was depressed and feeling dirty, but with Matt making a clean break with Emily, those feelings might clear up. After all, Tracey was pretty sure that her unease stemmed from the fact that she and Matt were messing around while he was still with Emily.

In any case, she had been in no shape to deal with him over the weekend, but to prevent him from showing up Sunday evening, she had sent Matt a text telling him that they would talk on Monday. He agreed and Tracey rested a little easier Sunday evening. The only problem was that now she had to come up with a plan of attack for talking to Matt the next day. She had no idea what she was going to say if he asked her out.

Follow your head, or follow your heart.

This was a pretty stupid saying as far as Tracey was concerned. In her heart *and* in her head, Tracey wanted Matt. It was an entirely different part of her, someplace deep within, that knew a relationship with Matt Kildare would doom Tracey to prolonged heartache and pain. Brittany would have said that this was God speaking to her. Tracey wasn't about to attribute her feelings to God just yet, but she could not push the thoughts aside. They were every bit as prominent in her thoughts as her desire to be with Matt. What really frightened her was how willing she seemed to be to risk all of the pain she felt certain she would experience in a relationship with Matt.

Monday morning arrived, and after a fairly restless night, Tracy had really only one option. Stall. She knew she would never be able to avoid him. They were always in the same place. He would eventually track her down. The teachers didn't even care if he went to class for God's sake. He could just stand outside her classes and wait for her if he wanted to. Her only option was to take control and tell him that she could not discuss their relationship right now. She would just leave it at that and he would have to be okay with it or risk making her mad. It actually seemed like a good plan, though she had come up with it after a night in which she got less than two hours of sleep.

I'm dead.

Sure enough, Matt was waiting for her in the entrance way to the school. Tracey saw him from a distance as she and Lindsey were walking from the parking lot. Lindsey headed off to see Kevin, and Tracey was all alone to face Matt. She wished Brittany were with her. She should of thought of that. Having Brittany there would have made it easier. He'd be less aggressive then. But she took a breath and headed right for him, a pleasant smile on her face.

Stop the stupid smiling! You look eager to see him!

She dropped the smile, in favor of a more serious look.

What are you going to do? Tell him his dog died? Just look normal!

Matt opened the door for her and leaned down to kiss her. She pulled away slightly. A few eyebrows were raised at that. Tracey continued walking into the school. Matt followed, a little confused and now off his game. Tracey caught his expression.

Yeeees! That was awesome! Oh, my God! He doesn't know what to do! Keep walking! Keep walking!

Matt stayed with her. "Are you mad at me for some reason?" he asked.

Tracey shook her head. "Not at all."

He nodded. "Okay, then why the blow off?"

"I wasn't blowing you off, Matt," Tracey replied as she reached her locker. She couldn't stop her hands from shaking as she reached to enter the combination. She did her best to keep it together. "I just don't want everyone thinking that you and I are together."

He leaned against the locker next to hers as she opened the door and exchanged some books for what she had in her backpack. "Well, that's kind of what I wanted to talk to you about. You probably heard from your sister that Emily and I broke up."

"Oh, yeah," she said. "I kind of walked in as she was telling Lindsey all about it."

Matt looked a little remorseful. "Is she okay? She wouldn't return my calls or texts all weekend...or was that you?" He thought for a moment. "Oh, now I remember...neither one of you returned my calls or texts all weekend."

Tracey closed her locker. "Very funny. You really hurt that girl, Matt."

"I didn't mean to. That stuff with me and her goes back a ways. It was a really bad relationship, the way we treated each other."

"Well, that really sucks, Matt."

He nodded. "Yes, it does, and I'll talk to her as soon as she lets me. But right now I want to talk to *you* about you and me."

"There is no you and me," Tracey said, and then quickly put up her hand as he tried to interrupt. "And before you get into it, I really can't talk about it right now. My brain is fried over everything. I need a little space."

Matt put his head back against the lockers. "So, this is a blow-off?"

Tracey tilted her head. "It's not a blow-off. Right now, I'm figuring things out for myself. You confuse everything. I can't be with you and think straight. I think you know how I feel about you, Matt."

"I was kind of hoping we could pick up from where we left off."

She laughed at that. "We left off with me feeling dirty and ashamed and unable to go through with what we had started. I don't want to pick up from there, Matt. If anything, I want to start over. But we can't do that unless I can make decisions without you influencing my every thought."

He wrinkled his forehead. "I influence your every thought? That's kind of cool."

"It was a figure of speech. Now leave me alone for a while, okay?"

*****

"I'm completely confused."

Tracey had spent half the week torn between her strong desire to explore a potential relationship with Matt and everything she and Brittany had been discussing. She couldn't help thinking that this chance with Matt was one of those once-in-a-lifetime things that a person would always regret passing up. She had dreamed of kissing him. It happened. She had dreamed of having an intimate night with him. That happened too. She had dreamed of being his girlfriend. That opportunity was right in front of her. But she was hesitating.

Miss Kelly leaned forward in her chair, her elbows resting on her desk. "I don't understand why you can't have a boyfriend and still go to church and all that."

Tracey tried to explain. "Because Matt's not a Christian."

"Are *you* even a Christian? This is all pretty new to you, isn't it?"

"Yes, it is, but I'm pretty sure I believe it."

"Okay," Kelly said. "So you're saying that even if you don't have sex with a boy, it still would be wrong?"

Tracey's looked up to the ceiling. "I never thought about that. Is that even possible with Matt Kildare? A non sexual relationship?"

Kelly smiled. "Anything's possible, sweetie. And it's a good idea for you to slow things down with him and see what he really wants. Sex shouldn't be a deal breaker, should it?"

Tracey's heart began to pound. "You're right. It shouldn't."

But it might...

Kelly nodded. "Look, sweetie. You just said that it was the sex part that felt all wrong the other night, right?"

Tracey nodded.

"So, take that out of the equation. How would you feel about just dating the guy?"

Tracey's eyes got a little glassy. "I would really love that. As long as there would be no pressure. I wonder if he'd still be interested."

"That's what you need to talk to him about."

Tracey nodded. This was pretty close to perfect...if Matt went for it. She could have Matt Kildare as her boyfriend without all the pressure and guilt of sitting in church knowing the whole time that she was living in a sinful relationship. God couldn't possibly have a problem with two people spending time together with their clothes on, could He? This was the best of both worlds as far as Tracey could figure.

Bottom line...If you're lucky enough to get everything you want, just shut up and take it.

Beginnings

Chapter 35

An entire school week had passed. Tracey Overton had walked the halls of Kendall High without even so much as a nod or a smile in Matt's direction. Matt had expected a little of this after the way things had gone with her on Monday, but now he felt like it had gone on long enough. He needed some answers. He could not remember the last time he had gone an entire week without having a girl around.

"So, you're telling me that this sophomore is basically ignoring you, even though she knows you want her?" Mike fired the ball at his friend, who caught it and flipped it around a few times before flinging it back. Mike had come back to school the previous week, but then he had been out again so that he could travel out of state for more testing on his foot. Other than a few texts and phone calls, he hadn't been in the loop lately.

"I'm really not sure what the deal is." He caught another throw from Mike, whose right foot was still immobilized. He was throwing off his left foot. "She wanted space. I backed off. But it's been a week."

"And you're really looking to be a one-woman guy?"

Matt tossed the ball in an arc to Mike. "Yeah, I think so. She's a pretty cool chick."

"Emily was cool too. What happened there?"

"Nothing really," Matt said. "We just grew apart."

Mike laughed. "You just grew apart? What exactly does that mean? You're exactly the same as when you met her."

"Well, then *she* changed."

"Matt, *you* broke up with *her*. Obviously it was to go after this Tracey chick. What I don't understand is if you wanted a girlfriend, why not make that happen with Emily? She's a little more your speed, isn't she?"

"I could have done that. She was pushing for that the whole time."

"So, what's the deal? You basically ditch the hottest, coolest girl in school, next to Viv, of course, for this Tracey, who doesn't exactly know her way around, from what I hear about her. What's your point in all this?"

"I just really like Tracey," Matt said. "She's the type you settle on for a real relationship."

"Settle *for* maybe…"

"No," Matt shook his head. "Not "settle *for*". Tracey is a great girl. She'd be a perfect girlfriend. She's steady. She's sane. Emily's too uncontrollable."

Mike nodded. "Sounds like loads of fun." He fired the ball. Even without the use of his back foot, his arm strength was enough to put plenty of zip on it.

Matt caught it. "Hey, it's easy for you. You got your girl. I'm still looking for mine."

Mike shook his head. "Emily *was* your girl, Matt. You guys blew it with that stupid arrangement you had, but that can be fixed. This isn't making any sense."

"Why? You don't even know Tracey."

"I know the type, Matt. That's enough to see how it will end."

Matt tucked the ball under his arm and walked to Mike. "The type? What type is that?"

"The type that doesn't know what she's getting into," Mike said. "She doesn't know you. She just knows who you are, not what you are. You're going to crush her."

Matt looked away. "That's messed up coming from my best friend."

"Coming from your best friend? Look at what happened to Emily. How'd she take your breakup? How's Tracey going to handle it after a couple months when you tell her you want to see other girls? Or when she catches you with one of the Brettes?"

"That's not gonna happen, dude."

Mike shrugged. "Okay, listen, I gotta get out of here. I'll be on the sidelines with you guys tonight."

*****

As game time approached, Matt and the rest of the Cobras gathered in their field house for their pre game routines. They still had over two hours to go before they took the field. Most of the guys just hung around and talked. Some played cards. Others listened to their music. Before now, they had mostly taken this time for granted, not really having real routines. Now, some were getting superstitious, trying to remember everything they had done before the previous week's game. Kevin had always used the time to focus his mind. The guys all thought he was meditating. They were close, but really, he was just breathing, getting his mind in control of every part of his body. If Japan had taught him one thing, it was control.

Matt put on his uniform pants. Like Kevin, he wore them without pads, to give him greater flexibility and maximize his speed. He left his jersey over the shoulder pads hanging in his locker and stepped outside the field house. Walking out towards the field, he passed by the cheerleaders, running through their routines. The drill squad was out on the field, preparing for their halftime show. Matt watched from the court as Tracey executed her dance routines with the other three dances flawlessly as the band moved in perfect synchronization. It had never really occurred to him to come out and watch the marching band or drill squad practice.

As he watched Tracey move to the music, his heart beat just a little bit faster, and he chuckled to himself. He could watch her all night. His eyes never left the pretty redhead. He thought about the girl he had given up for her. Mike was right about one thing; Emily *was* the perfect girl for him. And she wanted him, had for a long time. But Matt threw that away. He told Mike he knew what he was doing. The truth was he had no idea. He had spent a lot of time thinking about what he wanted, but the night he broke things off with Emily he had been flying blind. If she hadn't set it off, he probably would have been unable to go through with it.

The truth was he had been in love with Emily Vasquez for an entire year and he had know it the whole time, but had ignored those feelings because he thought that she just wanted fun with a Kendall Cobra, to be the queen bee ahead of all the other girls vying for his attention. By the time she had finally made her feelings known to him, he had long since numbed his own feelings for her. It was a twisted relationship now, with far too many girls and guys in between them.

But it was a far different story with Tracey. Love was a bit too strong a word at this point, but he felt potential with her that he hadn't felt with Emily. That was what was really motivating him. As he watched her, the thing that struck him was how different she was from Emily and all the other girls he usually spent his time with. He wondered how it could possibly work out. Maybe that was what Mike had been getting at. Tracey had no idea how to function in Matt's world. As he thought about that, he realized that her problem was probably just that simple. In addition to that, Matt realized, Tracey had to be thinking about the role she would be stepping into, a role vacated by Emily Vasquez. There were bound to be expectations that she would have no idea how to begin to fulfill. As the drill team wrapped up their rehearsal, it finally clicked in Matt's mind. He quickly rushed down to field level and found Tracey as she exited the field. The drill team would go inside and get ready for the game.

"Tracey!" Matt called to her from across the field.

She heard her name and turned to see who was calling her.

Oh, no! No, no, no! Not right now.

Her stomach was already twisted in knots over him. She thought that a few days might make that go away, but it was steadily getting worse. Every morning she woke up thinking about him and every morning her stomach did somersaults for two hours. Now he was coming to talk to her. She was actually surprised he had kept his distance this long. As he approached he had a strange look on his face.

"I just need a minute or two," he said.

"Is everything okay? You look…"

"Everything's fine," he said quickly. He looked around. "Come over here." He led her toward the tunnel where the team would come out onto the field later that night. It was deserted right now.

"Matt, what's going on? Is something wrong?"

"Nothing's wrong," he said. "Listen, I know you asked me to back off, and I'm not trying to put any pressure on you."

Ughhh!

Flip-Flop! Flip-Flop! Her stomach was definitely not cooperating.

"But I think you should hear this. Maybe it will make a difference."

"Okay," she said. Flip-Flop. Flip-Flop.

"I think I know what's bothering you about going out with me."

"You do?"

"Yes. I'm just gonna be straight up with you. I think you're worried about having a relationship with me because of sex."

Is this guy reading your mind, or what?

FLIP-FLOP! FLIP-FLOP! FLIP-FLOP!

Her stomach shifting into overdrive, Tracey just stood there and tried not to pass out. She was sweating a little now and felt feverish.

Matt continued. "I don't want that to bother you. I want you to be comfortable with me, okay. So, here's what I think we should do. We just don't have sex."

"Whaaa?" Tracey was pretty sure she was delusional. She thought that Matt Kildare had just suggested that they begin a non-sexual relationship. Wasn't that supposed to be *her* pitch? She didn't think that her stomach could have gotten any more upset, but it did.

Matt smiled. "No sex. No pressure. No problem. And I'm all yours. No Emily. No other girls. Just you. What do you think?"

She did her best to straighten up and not lose it. "It *sounds* good. Is that what you really want? It's a pretty big change."

"I want *you*." He took her hand. "Whatever that takes."

Oh, my God, just don't puke on his game clothes. Please don't puke on him.

"Think we can give this a try?" he asked.

She nodded. "Let me think about it, Matt. Okay? Can I answer you on Monday?"

"Sure," he said, hiding his utter disappointment. "I'll see you then."

"Good luck tonight, Matt."

He headed off down the tunnel. She hurried outside and ran around to the back of the field house where no one could see her, fell to her knees, and threw up. She would have said yes right then and there, but he would have tried to kiss her and she didn't want their first kiss as girlfriend and boyfriend to end with her puking all over his face.

*****

The Creekside Devils were possibly the worst team in the league. They were one of those hot and cold programs that were awful almost every year and then they'd win the division and go to the state tournament out of nowhere. That hadn't happened in more than ten years. The town was in such close proximity to Holy Trinity that it was hard for them to keep their players in the public school system. In addition to that, they were still a reasonable distance from Dilliard, home of the St. Augustine Knights. They picked a player or two from the Creekside area every year. No one expected them to come to Kendall High and beat the Cobras, and they performed about as well as anyone expected.

They fought hard, but the Kendall Cobras were just in another class altogether. By halftime, Kevin had knocked their quarterback out of the game on a blindside blitz that nearly snapped the tall lanky guy in half. He was playing in a zone that frightened even Tony. The "Mad Dog" chants were now in full force. There were "Mad Dog" signs and banners in the stands and even the "Mad Dog" T-shirts were starting to become more and more prominent.

In the end, it was no contest. The Kendall Cobras coasted to a 49-14 victory. Kevin had already set the Kendall High receiving record for yards in a season and they had only played five games. In a week where the Kendall fan base had been concerned about a possible let down because of the run they were on and the upcoming week six match-up against the also undefeated Cumberland Cowboys, the Cobras had demonstrated an uncommon degree of focus. They were clicking on all cylinders and racing toward a division win.

While it was true that the Kendall Cobras were clicking as a team on all cylinders, Matt Kildare had just played possibly the worst game of his Kendall High career. He could not get himself

Beginnings

open against the defenders he was facing, and when he did, he was still dropping passes left and right. He couldn't blame Scott Webber either because the young quarterback was sticking with him. Kevin was facing double and triple coverage, so Scott was spreading the ball around beautifully. Matt was seeing a lot of passes each week, but his head was just not in it. On defense, he had slipped on a easy tackle and let a receiver get away from him for a long touchdown.

The coaches had enough and lit into him at halftime. It didn't help his performance in the second half, and he was the recipient of a second tongue lashing from Coach Shultz after the game. Even following a pretty easy win, the coach was seeing everything that could prevent them from success against the competition he knew they'd face in the State Tournament.

After the team was dismissed and everyone cleared out, Matt was still there, sitting with his head down, trying to figure out if any of it was worth it. He wasn't even a contributor on a team that was dominating the league. He could be catching passes and making plays, but he was blowing it. He was distant from his teammates. Most of the guys didn't know what to say to him. They tried to encourage him and support him, but he had withdrawn from them. He wondered if he ought to just quit. On top of that, his great idea with Tracey had blown up in his face. She couldn't wait to get away from him earlier. He'd be lucky if she ever talked to him again.

Just then, Tony Yavastrenko walked back into the locker room. He had left his bag in his locker and came back in to grab it. As he was about to leave, he stopped, looked at Matt, sitting there looking completely defeated. Tony shook his head and put his bag down. He leaned with his back against the locker at the end of the row. He tilted his head back until it rested against the locker behind him. He closed his eyes and took a deep breath.

"Kildare," he said slowly. "It's not your game, you know that, right? You're a great football player. Your problem is your attitude." He looked at Matt, who never even moved, and nodded. "You may not like the guys playing with you. They may not like you. So what? You think Kevin Sinclaire cares how you feel about him?" he waited a few seconds for a reaction. Matt just sat there, staring at the floor. "Do you even *want* to play anymore?" Getting no reaction from Matt, Tony shrugged. He picked up his bag and strode toward the exit.

Almost as an afterthought, he stopped and turned back to Matt and said, "You know something? We're going to win the state championship this year? Why not get your head out of your butt and come get a piece of that?"

Chapter 36

Monday morning once again came way too fast for Tracey. She had had a miserable weekend. Though the Cobras had won the game and were still undefeated, the pressure in Kendall Township was only building for them. Expectations were only getting higher and higher. For Tracey, the pressure was mounting personally. She had kept the conversation with Matt to herself until Saturday night and it continued to make her sick. She woke up Saturday feeling awful. She just couldn't bring herself to make a decision. She cried in her room most of the day, her stomach settling and then growing restless over and over again throughout the day.

Brittany had come over after dinner, when Tracey was feeling a little better. Tracey couldn't keep her secret any longer and even though she knew what Brittany's reaction would be, she told her about what Matt had proposed.

"No!" Brittany said. "No way! Absolutely not. You *can't* go out with him, Tracey."

"Even without the pressure of sex?" she pleaded.

Brittany shook her head. "It's not all about sex, Tracey. What kind of life would that be? You'd constantly have to compromise your faith in order to be with him. That's why we don't date non Christians."

"But I don't know if I'm a Christian."

That statement had caught Brittany off guard a little. "You don't think you're a Christian?"

Tracey had no idea what to say. She was struggling, caught between two lives, the one she had just begun in church with Brittany and Tony and those new friends she was still getting to know, and the life she had so desired and thought was lost just weeks ago. Was she saying that she wasn't a Christian because she wanted to justify going back to her old life?

She could see the disappointment in her best friend's face. Tracey felt as though she had betrayed Brittany in some way. She hadn't even made a decision about Matt Kildare at this point, but she had known that Brittany would have a strong reaction. But Tracey had thought that there was a compromise to be had here.

"Why can't I still go to church and also see Matt?" she asked.

Brittany shook her head. "It's not that you *can't* do that. It's just not wise. Matt has no interest in the things that are important to a Christian. It's not because he's deliberately trying to be that way. But he isn't a Christian. In his world, when he's caught between two opposite choices, he'll either go with the option that best suits his desires at the moment, or he'll compromise. It's just a different morality than ours."

"That's a little arrogant."

"It's not arrogant," Brittany said. "It's just that Christians believe in an absolute right and wrong. The rest of the world doesn't want to hear about right and wrong. They don't want to be judged."

"Well, we *shouldn't* judge them, should we? Doesn't the Bible say *not* to judge them?"

"Yes, it does, but it's not *we* that judge them, Tracey. It's God. They take it out on *us*, but it's God that they hate. They'd never admit that, but they don't really hate Christians. They hate God."

"You think Matt Kildare hates God?"

Brittany shook her head. "Not like that. He just doesn't care about God. Try explaining to him that the reason you and he can't have sex until you're married is because the Bible says so, and see what his response is."

They had continued their discussion until Brittany had to leave, but bright and early the next morning, after the Morgans had picked her up and taken her to church with them, they picked up where they had left off. Tracey had slept, but was absurdly tired and her stomach was still tormenting her. She simply could not get Matt Kildare's proposition out of her mind. What if he *was* able to date her without having to pressure her about sex? Couldn't they then date without her having to compromise her new and fragile faith?

She suffered through the youth service and then the church service, her mind completely floating between what was being said and what she could not push out of her mind. She was out of it all day, even after going home and sleeping for a couple more hours. Fortunately she was able to eat a little something late in the afternoon. She spent most of the evening thinking about Matt and floated back and forth between turning his offer down and taking him up on it. She drifted off to sleep after midnight thinking about it.

In the morning, she felt good. She was a little tired, but her stomach felt a lot better than it had over the weekend. She ate a light breakfast just in case and jumped into the back seat of her mother's car. Lindsey was in the front already, the wires from her ear buds dangling on either side of her head. She looked at Tracey through the mirror on the visor.

"I guess you're feeling better," she said.

"Yeah, much better. It was a long weekend."

Lindsey nodded, biting her lip and staring at Tracey somewhat strangely. Tracey was in no mood for her mind games, so she ignored the look. She had more important things to deal with. Matt would probably be waiting for her at the entrance again and she still didn't know what to say to him. She wanted so desperately to be with him but there was a nagging feeling of uncertainty inside her that just wouldn't go away. Her stomach rumbled slightly.

As she suspected, Matt was waiting for her at the entrance. As before, he followed her to her locker, this time not attempting a good morning kiss. Other than saying hello, he remained fairly quiet, greeting teammates and others as they made their way up to the second floor lockers where Tracey, her stomach slightly unsettled again, opened her locker and got her books for the early classes. Matt just stood there and waited.

Yeah, like you're capable of walking away from this…
Just do it already…

"Okay," Tracey finally said, smiling at him, her mind finally made up. "I'm all yours."

He closed his eyes and smiled. "Really? You totally had me worried. No one ever turned me down before."

Tracey went on. "I just want us to be clear though. We agree not to have sex, right? That means we keep our clothes on at all times and we are very careful about where we put our hands, right?"

Why don't we wear little padlocks on our zippers?

He nodded, still smiling. "Right."

"Are you really sure about this, Matt? If you want to take the day and think about it, I'm okay with that, and you won't insult me if you want to change your mind. I'll still be your friend."

Yeah, Matt. Wouldn't it be more fun with someone else? Why would you want to go out with a fun-killing wet blanket like me?

"I don't need to think about it," he said, taking her hand and bring her closer to him. "I just want Tracey Overton to be my girlfriend."

I love it when he says our whole name...

Just then, Tracey's stomach contracted and she doubled over slightly in pain. She began feeling very lightheaded. Were it not for Matt holding onto her, she would have fallen over.

"Tracey!" he shouted, holding her up. "Are you okay? What's wrong?"

"My...stomach," she managed, barely able to keep her feet under her.

"Okay," he said. "Let's get you to the nurse."

"No," she said. "I'll be okay. I just need a minute."

"Tracey, you almost passed out just now. Go in there and lay down."

He wouldn't take no for an answer, so she let him guide her downstairs to the nurse's office where he explained what had just happened. The nurse shooed him away and examined Tracey, taking her temperature, blood pressure, listening to her heart, and looking into her eyes and ears.

"You don't have a fever, but your blood pressure's a little high." She handed Tracey a cup. "Here, drink some water."

"Well, wouldn't *yours* be high too," she joked, sipping from the cup. "If Matt Kildare had practically carried you through the school?"

The nurse thought about that for a moment. She pointed at Tracey and chuckled. "You have a point there." She looked at Tracey. "How do you feel now?"

"Better." She took another sip. "I've had a stomach bug all weekend. I thought it was gone this morning. I even had breakfast, but it's kind of still there."

The nurse nodded. "I don't want you going back out there if you're still fighting a stomach virus. Why don't you lay down for a little while and see how it goes? I'll let your teachers know that you're here."

After a couple of hours with no symptoms, the nurse let Tracey return to classes just in time for fourth period...lunch, as if she was really going to risk eating. Tracey couldn't wait to get to the cafeteria and find Matt, though at the same time, she was not looking forward to Brittany's reaction to her new relationship.

"Hey! Feeling better?" Matt was coming towards her. He leaned in to kiss her, but hesitated. "You're not gonna infect me, are you?"

She grabbed the front of his shirt and pulled him the rest of the way, kissing him gently on his lips. "We'll just have to wait and see now," she said, looping her arm through his. They walked to the cafeteria. It was their first walk together as a couple.

Yeah, if you don't count the earlier rush to the nurse's office when you almost died in his arms.

There was no question about it. Heads were turning as they entered the cafeteria. Matt Kildare had a new girlfriend and news was spreading like wildfire. The headline was that the Overton sisters were now together atop the Kendall High A-List. Tracey couldn't believe the response. The girls were all over her. She was thankfully feeling much better and able to enjoy some of the attention. She didn't know what Lindsey's problem was with all of this. Tracey was having the time of her life.

When things settled down, she was tapped on the shoulder. Brittany was standing there, a slight smile on her face. She came to Tracey and hugged her.

"I see you made your decision," she said grimly. "I suppose I should say congratulations, but I feel a little sad right now."

Tracey held her tightly. "I love you so much, Brittany. Please don't be sad. I'm happier than I've ever been and nothing has changed. You'll see. Everything will be fine. Maybe I can even get

Matt to come to church."

Brittany giggled. "Good luck on that one. Just make sure you come every week, okay?" She got serious. "Be careful, Trace. You're in the deep end now."

*****

Tracey and Matt's relationship was the hottest news is Kendall High School next to the Cobra's undefeated streak to open the season. Everyone was used to the fireworks between Matt and Emily, but the two had always managed put their relationship, such as it was, back together. Now, Matt had apparently made a clean break with her and was with someone else. On top of that, this Tracey girl, while very pretty and likeable, was a virtual nobody at Kendall High. What was Matt Kildare doing, dropping the number one girl in the school for an unknown one?

Emily herself wondered this as she walked the black and silver carpeted corridors of Kendall High, knowing instinctively that all eyes were on her to see what her reaction would be to her new circumstances. She knew what they all were thinking; most of them anyway...*How the mighty have fallen*...There was no way to hide from the humiliation. You couldn't pretend that getting dumped was okay with you. The fact that she could have any *other* guy in the school didn't matter. It was that word...*other*...that mattered. There was one that she *couldn't* have, and that made her human, at least to the girls. Emily knew that many of them were secretly enjoying her humiliation, basking in the "coming around" of karma. Emily had lorded her position over many of them, particularly the previous year, when she had been a slightly obnoxious and arrogant freshman after she had gotten asked out by Mr. Kendall High, Matt Kildare.

She had come into *this* school year far less vocal about her status and carried herself differently. A year of being at the top of the pyramid had given her the kind of confidence that could only come from status. She realized that she didn't have to prove herself to anyone. Her position was proof enough. That she was worshipped by every guy in the school was proof enough. An entire year with the king of Kendall High School was proof enough. But now all that was gone. Yes, she had the looks. Sure, she had the guys, if she wanted. But it was the loss of status that really hurt; that and seeing the guy see loved so deeply with another girl. Heartbreak had become a regular reality for Emily Vasquez.

She found Lindsey between periods at her locker and came up behind her, laying her head on Lindsey's shoulder. "I love you, Lindz," she said. "You're my only friend."

"I will stab your head with my number two pencil."

Emily wrapped both arms around her. "Why would you do that? *I'm* the one supposed to be in a bad mood here. You have the best guy in the world and you're going to stab me in my head?"

Lindsey stood there, cringing. "Will you get off me? We need a plan."

"Uh oh. A plan for what?"

"We need a plan for Kevin and me."

"Okay," Emily said suspiciously. "Something tells me I'm not going to like where this goes."

"You're not, but you're still going to help me."

Emily raised her eyebrows. "I am? How can you be so sure?"

"Because I spent the entire weekend watching stupid vampires making out with humans with you."

Emily shook her head. "It was one movie, Lindsey."

"It was *five* movies! And you rewound them every scene and cried the whole time."

"I didn't rewind *every* scene. And if you watch them all in a row, it only counts as one."

"It was *five* movies, and you cried so much my shoulder is still pruney."

Emily leaned her shoulder against the lockers and lowered her voice. "You realize that I never cry, right?"

Lindsey looked at her. "I know," she said. "Trust me, I understand."

Emily nodded. "You're a good friend, Lindz."

Just then, Matt and Tracey walked by, hand in hand. Emily ignored them, keeping her eyes on Lindsey, who glared at Tracey. Matt nodded and smiled slightly, trying not to appear too overly happy in front of Tracey.

Tracey returned Lindsey's look with a roll of her eyes and a shake of her head. "My sister hates me," she said to Matt.

"She's *Emily's* friend," he said. "She probably hates *me* more."

"Oh, I'm sure of that."

"Want me to talk to her; tell her that Emily and I were done whether or not you and I got together?"

Tracey shook her head. "No, no, no. That's the last thing you should do."

"It'll just be really quick."

"You think so, but she'll have you spinning in circles for a half hour defending yourself against ridiculous nonsense and you'll *never* get your point across. Just leave her alone. She'll get over it. Or not. I don't care."

Lindsey looked at Emily. You okay?"

Emily nodded sadly. "Yeah. I just need to get used to that."

"So you'll help me?"

Emily sighed and nodded. "Of course. What are we plotting?"

"Sex."

Emily nodded once. "Ah hah." She pursed her lips. "You do realize that you don't have to make a plan? You need a time, a place, and a partner…in that order of importance."

"Exactly."

"Okay, so what do you want me to help with?"

"How do I get Kevin to go for it?"

Emily's eyes widened. "Oh! I thought the problem was that *you* weren't interested and *he* was going to start demanding it at some point."

"It was." Lindsey closed her locker. "Now, the problem is that *I* want to do it and he might take months to demand it from me."

"And now you can't wait?"

"I probably can," Lindsey replied. "But now I don't want to."

At the end of the day, Emily and Lindsey were outside in the quad, discussing how best to approach Lindsey's problem, when Tracey came over. Lindsey looked up and shook her head.

"What do you want, Tracey?"

"Can I talk to Emily…alone?"

Emily opened her mouth to reply, but Lindsey got there first.

"Why, so you can tell her a bunch of your Christian guilt forgiveness stuff? And by the way, how does a Christian girl decide to go out with *Matt Kildare* of all people? Weren't there enough guys at Sunday School?"

"Cute, Lindsey." Tracey stood aside. "Can you just leave for a minute?"

"Why? She's just gonna tell me everything you say anyway."

"Because!" Tracey blew up. "I don't feel like trying to talk to someone with *you* sitting there ridiculing everything I say. I don't care if she tells you and I don't care if you both sit here and laugh at me. Just do it *after* I talk to Emily, please. Now will you disappear for five minutes?"

"Why do you look so pale? Are you gonna start puking again?"

"No...What are you talking about?"

"What's wrong with you, Tracey? You get a new boyfriend and you can't hold your food down anymore? Maybe you're allergic to him."

Tracey closed her eyes and tried counting to ten.

"It's okay, Lindz," Emily said. "Just give us a minute."

Lindsey shook her head and walked off.

Emily set her icey blue stare on Tracey. "What do you want?"

Tracey looked down. "I know you probably hate me right now, so it won't mean much..."

"Why do you think I hate you? I haven't said a word to you or about you."

Tracey shrugged. "I guess I just assumed."

Emily shrugged and nodded.

"Anyway," Tracey went on. "All I really want to say is that I'm sorry you got hurt. I know that's between you and Matt, but I feel so guilty."

"And you want me to forgive you?"

"I don't know what I want, Emily. I just want you to know that I didn't go after Matt."

"I already know that. I don't care one way or the other."

"You don't?"

Emily stared at her with her icy blue eyes. "It doesn't *matter* to me how it all happened. He made his choice. It's just life. But I am glad about one thing."

Tracey shook her head. "What's that?"

Emily raised her eyebrows and leaned back comfortably on the bench. "I have front row seats for your misery."

Tracey took a deep breath and nodded. She turned away silently and walked back into the school. Lindsey came back over to Emily.

"So?" she asked after a few moments of silence.

Emily shook her head, her eyes still staring coldly at Tracey as she opened the doors to the school. "Nothing. She just wanted to make nice with me."

"Did she succeed? You have my permission to bash her."

Emily shook her head. "Not necessary. Believe it or not, all of this will come full circle. You can bet on that, and I won't have to do a single thing."

Tracey came home Thursday night so tired that she wondered if she'd make it up the stairs to her room before passing out. Her mother was now beginning to get worried. Tracey had been feeling ill all weekend and though it was nothing all that horrifying, it was becoming obvious that she wasn't getting enough rest. Tracey had such an overloaded schedule with school and all the after school commitments, plus she was now dating the most popular guy in school, a fact that Abby had just found out and almost screamed in delight at the fact that her daughter was suddenly so happy. She wasn't sure how the whole church thing was fitting in, but it was just another stress piled onto a fifteen year old girl who was not used to all of these demands.

Tracey landed on her bed, and closed her eyes. She was still battling fits of nausea throughout the day and it was causing her stomach to feel like it had been punched over and over again.

"Are you pregnant?"

Tracey exploded up from the bed, her eyes wide. Lindsey was standing in her doorway. "What?"

"Are you?" Lindsey asked again.

"Am I *pregnant*? Are you crazy? Is mom upstairs? Shut the door!"

Lindsey closed the door, walked into the room, and leaned on the desk. "Well?"

"Well, what?" Tracey asked. "What are you talking about? Why would you think I'm pregnant?"

Lindsey sat down at the desk. "You're throwing up every day. You're tired all the time. You're pale and achy. Plus you're getting fat."

"What?" Tracey lifted her shirt and stood sideways, looking at herself in the mirror. "No, I'm not."

"I just threw that last one in there. But the rest are true."

"So what? Those symptoms are also the symptoms of a

stomach virus."

"Yeah," Lindsey said. "And a stomach virus lasts a day or two. You've been like this for a week now."

Tracey shook her head. "That's because I'm not resting enough and it keeps coming back."

"Or you could be pregnant."

"But I'm not. I just need to rest, and maybe take a day off from school to make sure I get better."

"Or you could be pregnant."

"Will you stop saying that? I'm not pregnant."

"Are you sure?"

"Yes, I'm sure."

"You are? When was you're last period?"

"I don't know!" Tracey was getting exasperated. This was what Lindsey did best. "Are you some kind of doctor now?"

"You don't know? How do you not know?"

"I can't remember, okay? I've been pretty busy the last month or so. My periods are never that bad anyway."

"I know, it's because you're athletic, same as me, but *I* still know when they happen. Think. When did you last get yours?"

"Lindsey, what do you care anyway? You can't stand me. What difference would it make to you?"

"Because I'm going to have sex with Kevin and this is scaring me."

Tracey's mouth dropped open. She didn't know what to say to that. "Wow. That's… that's…great, I guess. When did you decide this?"

"Earlier today."

"Oh. And I suppose Emily think it's a good idea?"

"Actually I'm pretty sure she thinks I'm a bi-polar nutcase, but since I was there when you and Matt ripped her heart out and shredded it, then stomped on it and all that, she's going to support me and help me."

"I see. Well, I'm not pregnant, so you can feel free to go ahead and do…whatever it is you want to do."

Lindsey got up. "Okay," she walked toward the door.

"Hey, Lindz," Tracey said. Lindsey turned. "Make sure you're really ready, okay? For sex, I mean. Don't rush yourself on this one. Maybe you should take some advice here."

Lindsey nodded thoughtfully. "Get a pregnancy test, okay?"

Chapter 37

Friday morning began the longest day of Tracey's life. She had spent a sleepless night alternately looking online and then reviewing the past several weeks for symptoms that could be related to pregnancy. Lindsey was great at creating panic and turmoil. She was a button pusher par excel lance, and Tracey had fallen victim to her pranks all too often. Lindsey was so good at it that sometimes the joke could go on for months. She had a particular talent for squeezing ninety-nine percent truth into every lie, but it was that *one* percent that could drive a person like Tracey to madness.

Ultimately, Tracey chalked it all up to Lindsey's sick sense of humor. Sure, the symptoms *could* add up to pregnancy, but they could also be a simple virus, or a number of other possible conditions. Of course, Lindsey comes up with the one that scares the heck out of a young girl the most, pregnancy. Tracey eventually drifted off to sleep, but awoke early with a renewed sense of dread. She knew that she could not go on like this. She needed answers.

She did her best to focus on school. Matt walked with her between classes, his arm around her, gently massaging her neck, which felt amazing. She tried not to think about the possible nightmare going on inside her, but it was always right in the back of her mind, waiting to come out and torment her. What she needed was someone with experience, but the only person she really knew with experience like that, passionately hated her. Tracey almost bit the bullet and approached Emily, but then reconsidered when she recalled the icy stare from the day before. This would just fuel her predictions of doom and gloom for Tracey and Matt.

In the end, what Tracey decided was that what she really needed was a friend she could trust. But how would she break this to her? Brittany knew the story, but had no idea that there might be a dramatic twist in the near future. By the end of the day, Tracey had concluded that Brittany was the only one she wanted to know about her fears. She texted Brittany to meet her after last period, before they went to the locker rooms to prepare for tonight's game against the Cumberland Cowboys.

After the final bell, Brittany waited for her best friend at her locker. She was seconds away. Tracey kissed Matt quickly and came over to where Brittany was waiting.

"What's the matter?" Brittany asked. "You look like you've seen a ghost?"

Tracey grabbed her arm. "Come on. I need to talk in private."

They went into the bathroom and Tracey quickly searched through the room to make sure they were alone. Brittany was watching her in puzzled silence.

"What's going on, Tracey? Are you in trouble?"

"Oh," Tracey replied, pacing back and forth. It was the first real release of energy she had gotten all day. The past six hours had been a lesson in restraint for her. She felt like she was about to burst. "You don't know the half of it."

Brittany was worried now. "Tell me. What's going on?"

Tracey stopped pacing and looked at her desperately. "You have to promise not to flip out."

"I promise."

"No. Say you promise not to flip out."

"I promise...not to flip out."

"Okay," Tracey took a deep breath and let it out slowly. "I need you to go somewhere with me."

"All right. Where?"

"I need to go get a pregnancy test."

Brittany's eyes widened in horror. Her hand went up to her heart and she leaned on the counter.

"You promised you wouldn't flip out," Tracey said.

"I know," she replied, staring straight ahead like a zombie. "This is called *freaking* out, which I made no promises about."

Tracey stood in the corner and tried not to lose it. Brittany shook her head.

"You're pregnant?"

Tracey shrugged helplessly. "I don't know. Things are starting to add up. Lindsey suspects it." She did her best not to cry, but it was going to be a losing battle.

Brittany's tears were already beginning to drip. "Oh God. Why does Lindsey suspect you're pregnant?"

"I've been nauseous all week. I've been tired even when I get plenty of sleep. Cramps...and I can't remember when I had my last..." she raised her eyebrows and nodded pointedly.

Brittany nodded in understanding and closed her eyes. "Oh no, Tracey, this can't be happening."

"I don't know if it is yet. I'm trying to hold it together."

Brittany took a deep breath. "Okay, you're right. Let's not panic until we know for sure."

Tracey took a breath and let it out slowly.

Brittany said, "So how do you want to do this?"

"Let's run over to the drug store and get a test. We'll wait until after the game tonight and we do it at your place or mine. I don't care which one."

Brittany hesitated. "I can't be the one to buy a pregnancy test. If my dad found out something like that, I'd have a heck of a time explaining it."

"That's okay. I'll buy it. No one knows me anyway. Will you walk with me though?"

"Of course. And let's do the test at your house. I'll get permission to sleep over. Unless you think Lindsey will be around."

"She'll be out late with Kevin probably. We'll be alone."

Brittany nodded. "Okay. We have a plan. Let's go get a test. I think this will be the longest game ever."

*****

One more win before the bye. That was the mantra all over town. Kendall was brimming with excitement for the upcoming match-up between their beloved Cobras and the Cumberland Cowboys. If they could just pull off one more win against a very tough opponent, they would have just four more to go following the upcoming bye, setting them up for a possible undefeated season and a run at the state championships. Kendall hadn't had an undefeated season in nearly two decades, and after laying waste to the two best teams in the division, the Kendall faithful saw no reason why the Cobras couldn't make history this year. The expectations, which began as cautious optimism after the week one dismantling of the state champion Holy Trinity squad had now given way to much higher set of standards. The expectations couldn't be higher.

This was a bitter rivalry, mainly because of the fans of both schools. Nearly an hour drive from Kendall High School, Cumberland County High was another universe from the shore towns that the Cobras usually faced. The Kendall fans were used to being the "twelfth man" because of their noise and black clothing, and all the organized cheers and chants they did throughout the game. The Cumberland fans were nowhere near as organized as the Cobra cheering section, but they were every bit as maniacal in their approach to cheering for their boys. The Kendall fans would not dominate them tonight, especially on their home field. As the only other undefeated team in the division, this match-up would likely determine the division winner.

The rain never really made it to Kendall Township. It had been cloudy all week, but only a nominal amount of rain actually fell. As the team loaded onto the busses they were informed that the weather in Cumberland was dismal. Not only was Cumberland currently in the midst of a deluge, but it had been raining like that for three days, the result of a weather system that was moving slowly Southeast through the Upper Midwest from Canada. Cumberland was only catching the outer bands of the system, but it was wreaking havoc in their area.

Those players who had been on the Kendall team long enough to have played at the Cumberland field knew that they were heading into a sloppy mess. At least at the Kendall home field, with the new pro-style turf, the field would be okay to play on even in heavy rain. The Cumberland field was natural grass, and it didn't take much for it to become saturated. After three days worth of heavy rain it would be a real mess. As they pulled into the Cumberland High parking lot, their worst fears were confirmed. The rain, which had been coming down in sheets just moments before had backed off somewhat but was still steady.

The game was an exercise in futility. Kendall's high-powered passing game was all but neutralized in the downpour. Scott Webber could barely keep the ball under control. The receivers were running in what could only be referred to as slop. Their feet were getting stuck in the mud on every step. Kevin had his shoe slip off in the mud twice and came away with a soaked and muddy sock both times. The rain and wind pushed the ball in all directions and try as he might, Scott just couldn't get anything going through the air. He relied on Anquan Griffin and the running game to move the ball, but Cumberland's big defensive line was able to keep him under control.

If the Kendall offense was being slowed down by the weather, the effect it had on the Cumberland offense was infinitely worse. First, the Kendall defense had come into the game with one goal in mind: stop Daunte Solomon, the lightning fast running back who everybody said was a young Barry Sanders. He was virtually unstoppable, averaging over two hundred yards per game. But the weather was keeping him upright, unable to make the cuts and moves that made him so difficult to catch. At barely one hundred sixty pounds, he didn't have the size or power to take on a defensive line for an entire game. With the Kendall defense blitzing on every play, keying on the shifty running back, the Cumberland offense went backward more than forward.

The game, which was being televised as the "Game of the Week" for New Jersey High School football, was dubbed "The Mud Bowl" by one commentator. There was really no other way to describe the miserable conditions down on the field. Ultimately, it came down to the Cobra's ability to avoid costly mistakes and move the ball enough to win the field position battle. Nearly the entire game was played on the Cumberland Cowboys' side of the field. When the Cobras couldn't move the ball any further, they simply punted it deep into the Cowboys' territory and played ruthless defense.

With all that, the play of the game actually came on a passing play and it was made by someone who most people had written off for this season. In a scoreless game, Scott Webber dropped back to pass and was immediately under pressure, so he scrambled to his left and finally threw the ball high to the back of the end zone where somehow, Matt Kildare made a leaping catch, fully extended, his feet dragging on the ground, and sliding several feet in the mud after the catch, but holding on to the ball for the Cobra's first score. It was the play of the year for Matt, maybe the play of his career at Kendall, because it came at a point where the team really needed a score. In the second half, Scott added a second score, scampering in from five yards out, and Anquan iced the game with two fourth quarter scores of his own. Kevin had not scored. In fact, he hadn't even touched the ball on offense. Cumberland had locked him down early on and would not let him have any open space at all. His main contribution came on the other side of the ball, where he continued to play savage defense and disrupt the opposing team's offense. The Kendall Cobras walked off the Cumberland field covered head to toe in mud, soaked to the bone, but still undefeated, and heading into a well-deserved off week.

As for the Kendall Cobra's fans, the game was all they could have hoped for. It had begun as a scream fest between the home fans and them, but as the game developed into a miserable slop-fest, with little scoring early on, everyone sat relatively silent, waiting for something to happen. They were cold and miserable in the weather, but these Kendall fans stuck it out, going bonkers when Matt Kildare came down with that catch and then, in the second half, they got back into their usual chanting and yelling mode. After the game, everyone was glad to be getting out of there, but more than anything else, they were happy that their boys had made the ride home a pleasant one.

*****

Les Fontaine raced home from Cumberland High to prepare a mega feast for the conquering heroes. He had been pulling out all the stops lately, but tonight, he had a special surprise for the team. He hired a caterer and invited everyone in town to surprise the team. He enlisted the help of the Brette Girls to ensure that the entire team would be present, as well as everyone involved in the supporting programs. People had been over setting up the house for this event all day long.

The Brette Girls pulled off a minor coup and even got Coach Shultz to have the bus with the team come straight to the Fontaine House. He got the necessary approval from the school officials, which was easy since they would all be there waiting for the team anyway. Now, the Cobra players would all be at the party dressed in their black team sports jackets and black and silver ties, which were mandatory for all away games. As the bus pulled into Les Fontaine's driveway, the team cheered, sensing that they were in for a special evening.

The party had a far more formal feel to it than Les' usual functions. He was not really one to bring attention to his house since his parties had become legendary around town. It was best to remain low-key when you were the party house for the town. Not that there was much cause for concern. The rules for the football team in Kendall Township were fairly flexible. They got away with their partying as long as they weren't causing trouble around town, driving drunk, or fighting. But Les had a rule, you don't make noise when your parties were being ignored. It wasn't really a rule. He had just thought of it today, but he intended to add it officially at some point because it was brilliant.

As the team swarmed off the bus, they were directed around back to the rear patio, where Les had a live band and a DJ set up along with a huge dance floor. It seemed like the entire community had turned out for this night even though it was after ten o'clock. People were gathered all over the yard, around the pool, which had been closed for the winter just a few days prior. As the team came through the gates all eyes turned to them and they received a huge round of cheers, clapping and chants of "VE-NOM!" Many of the players raised their hands, pumping their fists, and shouted right along with the crowd. The local media was even there, cameras rolling, to report on the local reaction to the first place Kendall Cobras. As soon as the noise died down, the music started, the lights began flashing, and the dance floor was soon full. The party had begun.

Lindsey and Emily were there, seated on bar stools at a tall round cocktail table. They had gone to the game, driven by Lindsey's mom, Abby, but left ten or fifteen minutes early, when they had gotten word about the party. Abby was elated to get out of the weather and took the girls home to shower and get ready before dropping them at the Fontaine home. There was no place in the world Emily wanted to be less than at Lester Fontaine's house that evening, and Lindsey even tried to let her off the hook, but Emily insisted on being there with her. They had a plan and

Lindsey was going to need her support, and possibly her shoulder depending upon how things went.

As Kevin came through the gates, Lindsey smiled nervously at Emily, who gave her a reassuring nod. As he made his way through the crowd, people stopped to congratulate him, slapping him on the back, and rehashing not only tonight's game, but every game they had played thus far. It took him the better part of a half hour to wade through it all. By the time he got to their table, he was quite frustrated.

He leaned down to kiss his girlfriend. Lindsey looked him over. "Hey," she said. "You clean up okay."

"Gee, thanks," he replied. "Hello, Emily. How are you?"

Emily smiled. "I'm okay. Get used to all this. It only gets worse if you keep winning."

Kevin rolled his eyes. "That's *not* an incentive."

"Great," Emily said, looking at the entrance. "Your sister's here with her little friend."

Lindsey and Kevin looked to see Tracey walk in with Brittany, both all smiles as they were greeted by friends and players. Lindsey looked at Emily.

"You knew she'd end up here."

"I was hoping they'd get in an accident," she said absently. Then as she saw the looks on Kevin and Lindsey's faces, she added, "Nothing serious. Just enough to keep them away for a few hours."

Kevin saw Matt hurrying through the crowd to get to Tracey. He turned to Emily.

"Are you gonna be okay?" he asked.

She nodded. "I'll be fine."

"Of course she's gonna be fine," said Tony's loud voice just behind Kevin. "She's going to be fine because she's going to dance with *me*!" he announced. He was dancing toward them, snapping his fingers in time with the music and just as he arrived at the table, he slapped Kevin on the back way too hard. "How are you, my good friend?"

"Ahhh!" Kevin grunted. "I'm going to hurt you."

"Hey," Tony said, still swaying to the music. He had obviously carefully planned this little thing he was doing. "I have not come for you. I have come for *her*." He was pointing to Emily."

"*Me?*" Emily replied. She spread her hands like the godfather.

"Well, here I am. What can *brown* do for you?"

Tony looked confused. He stopped dancing. Turning to Kevin he mouthed, *brown?*

Lindsey rolled her eyes. "Her skin color, you dummy."

"Oh riiiight!" he said, the light going off in his eyes. "Cause your skin's bro...I get it."

"Will you get on with it?" Lindsey pleaded.

"Absolutely," Tony replied, snapping back into character. "I merely came over to inquire if the lovely young lady would like to dance."

Despite herself, Emily's mouth dropped open in amusement. "I'd..."

"*Inquire?*" Lindsey said. "You came to *inquire?* Is that anything like *asking* her to dance? You know, like normal people do?"

Kevin put his arm around Tony's shoulders and pulled him aside. To the girls, he said, "Excuse us for a minute."

"What's up, pal?" Tony asked when they were a safe distance away. "I think she likes me."

"Really?" Kevin said. "Because I don't think she's even met you. What is this character you're playing tonight? Two days ago you couldn't even string two sentences together around her. Now you're Casanova."

"Ah, my good friend," Tony replied in his newly discovered alter ego. "What you fail to understand is that what women want...no...what women *need*, is to be pursued. They need to be courted, made to feel desired." He smiled at Kevin. "This is me pursuing."

Kevin shook his head. "And you decided to test this theory on Emily Vasquez?"

Tony grabbed Kevin by the head, a hand on each side, and looked him right in the face. "Dude, life's too short to be afraid of these creatures. And have you *looked* at her? Oh my *God!* She's perfection. I have to do this *right now*..." He glanced at Emily one more time. "Whew! Or never, so back me up, okay?"

"Uh, okay."

"Good." Tony kissed him on both cheeks before Kevin could pull away, and returned to the girls' table. He held out his hand to Emily. "I believe an invitation is on the table."

Lindsey started to huff, but Emily took Tony's hand and stood up. "Lead the way, Maestro."

Tony was stunned. "Really?" he said.

"Yeah," Lindsey chimed in. "Really?"

"Of course," Emily replied, smiling at them all. "He had the guts to come over here and ask me in front of you two. Do you know how hard that is for a guy to do?"

"Yeah, Lindsey," Tony said. "It's not easy, is it, Kevo?"

Kevin shook his head. "Hardest thing in the world."

Tony nodded. "It's *extremely* hard, Lindsey. It's *scary*. You don't even know."

Kevin and Lindsey watched them head to the dance floor together. Lindsey was shaking her head. "What *was* that?"

Kevin laughed. "I don't know, but he just got Emily Vasquez to dance with him. My hat's off."

Lindsey nodded. "Tony and Emily; Matt and Tracey. The whole world's upside down."

Kevin shrugged. "It's all good. Everyone seems happy."

As the two headed off to the dance floor, Emily saw Tracey, standing with Matt, a smile on her face as they were talking to one of the school guidance counselors. She glanced over as Emily and Tony got to the dance floor, and her smile vanished. It took Emily nearly two full songs, and several more glances over at Tracey before it all began to make sense to her. When Tony had been escorting her around the school, when he had protected her, and then taken her home that night after their altercation, those had been acts of friendship on his part. Emily remembered thinking that he was acting like a brother toward her. But now she realized that something more had been going on. Somewhere along the line, Tracey had gotten attached to this guy.

When Emily had decided to dance with Tony, it was partly because he had made her laugh with his ridiculous act, but also because Lindsey had made it so much more uncomfortable for him. He deserved to get the girl this time. Plus he was very cute, funny in an out-of-his-mind kind of way, and totally harmless. He was the kind of guy you wanted to hang out with, and she just wanted to hang out a little after all the serious relationship stuff from the past few weeks. But now, there was an additional incentive to be friendly with Tony. It was obvious that Tracey had something for him. But it was equally obvious that no one seemed to know it. She must have kept it to herself, what with the whole Matt Kildare thing going on. Interesting.

Tracey was aghast. She was horrified to see Tony leading Emily Vasquez to the dance floor. He had been her friend throughout all of the difficult moments over the past few weeks. She couldn't bear the thought of him with Emily. It would have been tough enough if he had managed to get Brittany to let him take her out, but at least Brittany would have taken good care of him. Emily was sure to crush her friend eventually, although everyone was saying that about she and Matt. Why was he dancing with Emily anyway?

Knight in shining armor syndrome. He's the guy who rides to the rescue whenever a girl's in distress.

Brittany saw it too. Tony and Emily really seemed to hit it off out there. He was a pretty good dancer, and Emily was smiling. She looked happy for the first time all week. Brittany's heart hurt a little for some reason. It wasn't like she had any intentions of seeing Tony at this point, but you never know. He seemed to be pursuing his faith diligently, but like Tracey, he was so new to it, he wasn't connecting the lifestyle changes with the faith. It would come in time, but meanwhile he was with Emily, not the best influence for a man of fragile new faith.

Throughout the evening, the players were pulled up onto the deck for introductions and speeches. Many, including Kevin were interviewed by the reporters. Lindsey, wanting to find the perfect moment to put her plan into action, was growing frustrated. When she and Kevin finally had a free moment, Tony and Emily pulled them onto the dance floor. Those two were really seeming to hit it off, which was neat for Lindsey. She loved Tony. He was probably the funniest person she had ever met. He was so fiercely loyal to Kevin that she honestly believed he would lie down in traffic for him. She knew he would do the same for her as well. She loved torturing him and Kevin never gave her grief for it because he knew she adored Tony. She was pretty sure Tony knew it too though she would never say it. It would ruin all her fun.

But she needed Kevin alone. It was getting very late in the evening. The adults had mostly gone home, and the party had taken on a decidedly different feel. It was more like the usual

Fontaine gatherings. Many of the young couples had gone into the house to make out or drink or both. There was still music playing and the dance floor was still pretty full, but Lindsey knew that the night was going to be over soon and she had something to say to Kevin. He was coming her way, looking tired after a fairly lengthy interview with Les, who had been trying for weeks to get him. Kevin plopped down in the chair next to Lindsey and put his arm around her. She cuddled against his chest. It was now or never.

"I think we should have sex," she said.

He seemed to tense slightly, but didn't respond. She straightened up and looked at him.

"Do you even think of me that way?" she asked.

"Of course."

"So, let's do it."

He looked around. "Right *now*?"

"Of course not. Not *here* either."

"And you really want to do this?"

"Well, yeah, I do," she said. "I think it's about time, don't you?"

"I...yeah, I guess so."

"Good. Me too. So let's start working on it, okay?"

Epilogue

Tracey had been chagrined to find out that they had to put in an appearance at the Fontaine party. She and Brittany had wanted to get home and answer the big question. But the Brette Girls had made it clear that everyone was expected, and on top of that, Matt had called to make sure she was on her way. They figured they'd go for a little while and cut out as soon as possible, which turns into hours later. In truth, Tracey had a good time at her first party as Matt Kildare's girlfriend, especially since he had bounced back from his rough season to make such a great play.

All that fun ended when she had spotted Tony dancing with Emily. It was like s dark cloud had descended over her evening. Brittany had also been effected, though Tracey couldn't tell whether she was more troubled by the potential loss of an admirer or the fact that Tony was putting himself at spiritual risk by pursuing a relationship with someone not interested in faith. It was probably a mixture of both.

Matt dropped them off at Tracey's after the party. The two girls walked slowly to the front door, both of their hearts beating wildly, as though a terrible monster awaited them on the other side. They were like children who knew they had a dentist appointment coming up. Until they were actually at the dentist's office, there was little fear. But when they set foot in that office, the dentist appointment becomes real, and all of their fears come rushing to the surface at once. They made their way upstairs and quietly entered Tracey's room. Tracey went to make sure that her mother was sleeping so that there was no danger of her interrupting them. They sat and prayed together for several minutes, both desperately pleading with God for His intervention.

Finally, Tracey stood up and dug the tests out of her bag. They had gotten three different ones just to be sure. They went over the instructions carefully, and then there was nothing left to do. Brittany hugged her tightly, not wanting to let her go.

"Good luck," was all she could think to say. Her tears said the rest.

Tracey went into the bathroom and closed the door. She pulled out her phone and set the stopwatch app for five minutes. The tests all said the results would be ready in less than that, but she didn't want any surprises. She placed the phone in front of her and pulled each test from the box. She hadn't gone to the bathroom all night in preparation for this moment. She laid each test on the window sill next to her. As she sat on the toilet, she used each test as directed on the instructions, placing each one on the seat behind her, keeping them out of her sight. She hit the stopwatch button and watched as the seconds counted down.

She nervously rubbed her hands together and fought the urge to turn around and look at the three tests. The seconds ticked down.

"Trace?" Brittany called softly. "Are you okay?"

"Three minutes."

"Still praying."

The seconds ticked all the way down to zero. Tracey stared at the screen. The moment of truth had arrived. She had fought the urge to look for five minutes, but now that the moment had come, she couldn't bring herself to turn around. Finally, after what seemed like an hour, she took a breath and without looking at the results, got the three tests into her hand. She sat back down and closed her eyes, holding them in her lap. After several deep breaths, she opened her eyes and stared down at the results.

They were all the same. Tracey stared at them, a half smile crept onto her face, shaking her head.

Well...That's that.

A single tear fell down her cheek.

Excerpt from Heat

Book 2 in the Quiver of Cobras Saga

A big black and silver van skidded to a halt right in front of them. Kevin and Tony immediately reacted by dropping their bags and spreading out in defensive positions. As they did so, Kevin felt like the van looked vaguely familiar. Before he could complete the thought, the door opened and several scantily clad Brette Girls jumped out with menacing looks on their faces. Those looks didn't quite match their outfits, and even with five of them surrounding the boys, Kevin relaxed, an amused look on his face.

"Get in." The command came from the driver, a very pretty brunette named Calista Fontineau. Everybody in Kendall High School knew who she was. Calista was the president of the Brette Girls and her participation was evidence of the serious nature of the sorority. She was among the top five GPAs in the senior class and had several scholarship offers throughout the ivy league. Girls like that brought a great deal of credibility to the Brette Girls. Their insistence upon things like good grades and good citizenship did as well. It was a somewhat ignored fact in Kendall Township that the Brette Girls boasted a higher combined GPA than any single Kendall High program of more than twenty members.

Kevin and Tony exchanged amused glances. "I don't think so," Kevin said, a smirk on his face.

"Yeah," Tony added, putting his fists up in a boxers pose. "Try and make us."

The girls all laughed somewhat humorlessly. "They think they have a choice," said one who standing behind them holding a pair of handcuffs. This one was a petite blonde weighing less than a hundred pounds who had on what could only be considered as *barely* a bathing suit or negligee under an open full length a silk robe. They all had similar outfits. Some were obviously just bathing suits, while others were clearly more suited to the bedroom. Every one of the girls oozed sexuality and they were not being shy about it, though they were obviously serious about getting the boys into that van.

Calista shook her head. "You guys don't understand. You're coming with us one way or the other."

Tony raised his eyebrows. "What's the other way?"

Another Brette Girl appeared in the doorway of the van, also clad in bedroom apparel. She stayed inside because she was carrying a strange looking rifle in her hands which she currently had pointed at the ground. Kevin looked at her and then back to Calista.

Calista gestured to the girl. "That's Lori."

"So, if we don't come with you, you're going to have Lori shoot us?"

Calista shook her head. "Of course not, dummy. It's a tranquilizer gun."

Lori smiled. "I work at the zoo. This baby is used for putting down elephants. These darts are filled with etorphine. It's about one or two thousand times the potency of morphine. I wasn't sure how much it would take to knock out a human, so I just filled it up all the way just in case."

"Sounds like a safe plan."

Calista shrugged. "So," she said. "Please allow the pretty ladies behind you to restrain you with the cuffs so we can get on with it." She then smiled, licking her lips very slowly. "Trust me. You guys have nothing to worry about."

Tony thought about it. "So…the two of us in handcuffs with six insanely hot, barely dressed girls, all together in a van…? What could go wrong?

"Where are we going?" asked Kevin.

Calista shook her head. "That's not your concern."

Kevin said, "So our choice is either we get in the van with a bunch of beautiful, half naked girls, or they shoot us with an unspecified amount of sedative that will probably kill us, and then take us anyway?"

Tony nodded. "Hmm. Give us a minute to talk this over."

As the boys' hands were secured behind them, the bags were placed over their heads and they were led into the van and seated on bench seats. Actually, they were each sprawled across three girls on the seats. They both knew what was happening. "Brette Rides" are mythical in Kendall Township. Stories about them are never told from first-hand accounts. No one would ever admit that they had ever gone on a Brette Ride because doing so would ostracize the storyteller from all contact with the Brette Girls. No one wanted that. The stories are always told vaguely, almost like urban legends; a friend of a friend of a friend.... As the van pulled away, Kevin couldn't help but wonder how many guys dream about this kind of thing happening to them.

*****

The ride lasted forty minutes. Once they had gotten into the van, there was no further threats, other than the one about keeping this entire experience a secret. When they arrived at their destination, they were helped out of the van, and quietly escorted a short distance away. They could hear car doors opening and closing as they walked. Eventually, they were halted and told to stand still.

Calista spoke. "Girls, remove the handcuffs! Do NOT remove the bags, guys. That's our job."

There were several clicks as handcuffs were removed.

Finally, Calista announced, "And now, presenting this years' twelve Kendall Cobra Calendar Studs!"

The bags were removed from their heads, and twelve Kendall Cobras stood, blinking, their eyes adjusting to the bright lights. Cameras were flashing as the entire Brette Girl sorority clapped and whistled and screamed at the boys. The Brette Girls' Calendar Party was another legend, only it was one that was undeniably real. Each year, twelve Cobras were selected to appear on the Brette Girls' Cobra Calendar. They were always "kidnapped" if it was their first calendar appearance, and taken to a secret location, where an exclusive party was held in their honor. They were the only males present in a sea of beautiful and barely dressed Brette Girls numbering nearly fifty. The girls always made sure the ratio was such because once this calendar came out, these twelve guys would be the kings of the school, and royalty had its privileges.

In reality, the whole thing was a photo shoot. The guys drew out of a hat for their months and were then led to the appropriate room where the scenes for that month were set. Each guy posed shirtless, either in shorts or a bathing suit, *if* he had been on the calendar previously. First-timers all had to wear their underwear, whatever they had on at the time. That was the rule, and since each guy had four Brette Girls posing with them, all dressed in supremely sexy attire, there were very few complaints. This event had become the kind of thing that motivated the boys in Kendall Township to excel on the football field. Maybe, one year, they would get to pose half-naked with the Brette Girls. And who knew what would happen when the cameras were off?

Though the atmosphere created by the decor, the music, and, of course, the attire, was one of debauchery and sensuality, the Brette Girls conducted themselves very professionally. They needed to get pictures for their calendar and it wouldn't do to have the centerpieces of those photos looking like deer in headlights. Four gorgeous girls in bathing suits and underwear usually got the guys attention away from the cameras. The pictures were always stunning and sexy. The calendar was always a huge hit throughout not only the school, but the community as well, raising several thousand dollars per year, which went to the Brette Girls' official charity, a local organization that worked to help find a cure for leukemia.

After the shoot, they guys were treated to a royal feast, courtesy of the Brette Girls. They were seated at a long table, their seats corresponding to the months they'd represent on the calendar. On the one hand, this was great for Kevin because as Mr. January, he was seated right across from Mr. December, who happened to be Tony. The unfortunate thing was that just to Kevin's right sat Mr. February, Matt Kildare, who was also clearly not pleased with the arrangement. They nodded coldly to one another and that was that. An unspoken truce was called out of respect for their hosts.

Later, the boys were all cuffed and bagged again for the ride home. The location for the photo shoot was a closely guarded secret known only to the Brette girls. The vans dispersed and took their captives home, the girls warning them not to discuss the event with anyone. The calendar was a secret until they released it on Monday. They were uncuffed, unbagged, and let out. The vans then disappeared into the twilight as though nothing had ever happened.

Kevin and Tony stood in Tony's driveway, still reeling from the lightning fast sequence of events.

"Dude," Tony said, shaking his head. "Did all that just happen?"

"All what?" asked Kevin. "We're not supposed to talk about it, remember?"

"I know, or we'll be cut off."

"Lindsey's gonna flip out. This is exactly the kind of thing that she's worried about. And I can't even warn her."

Tony stared at him. "Holy crap! Do you think Emily will get mad?"

Kevin shook his head. "Nah. Emily knows all about it. I doubt she'd give it a second thought. But Lindsey's definitely another story."

Go to **www.aquiverofcobras.com** to find out more about Heat, Book 2 in the Quiver of Cobras saga.

Contact the Kendall High Cobras

Brittany Morgan - brittany@aquiverofcobras.com
Emily Vasquez - emily@aquiverofcobras.com
Kevin Sinclaire - kevin@aquiverofcobras.com
Lindsey Overton - lindsey@aquiverofcobras.com
Matt Kildare - matt@aquiverofcobras.com
Tony "Yavo" Yavastrenko - yavo@aquiverofcobras.com
Tracey Overton - tracey@aquiverofcobras.com

Follow your favorite Kendall Cobra online at
www.aquiverofcobras.com

About the Author

Christopher Merlino is married to Charmine Merlino, and the father of three beautiful girls, Alexis, Cecilia, and Isabella. He was born and raised in the Atlantic City area of Southern New Jersey. He is a fan of most genres of books from non-fiction historical and theological to fiction drama, action, fantasy, and comedy. He enjoys music and golf...Well...who really *enjoys* golf? He *plays* golf from time to time and generally refers to the game as "The Refiner's Oven". He is actively involved in the youth program at his home church and uses his love of music to help lead praise and worship in the youth ministry. He currently makes his home in Egg Harbor Township, New Jersey.